P9-CTP-879

04/2021

AVID

READER

PRESS

ALSO BY MICHAELA CARTER

Further Out Than You Thought

LEONORA
IN THE
MORNING
LIGHT

~&

MICHAELA CARTER

AVID READER PRESS

NEW YORK   LONDON   TORONTO   SYDNEY   NEW DELHI

Avid Reader Press
An Imprint of Simon & Schuster, Inc.
1230 Avenue of the Americas
New York, NY 10020

First Avid Reader Press hardcover edition April 2021

AVID READER PRESS and colophon are trademarks of Simon & Schuster, Inc.

For information about special discounts for bulk purchases, please contact Simon & Schuster Special Sales at 1-866-506-1949 or business@simonandschuster.com.

The Simon & Schuster Speakers Bureau can bring authors to your live event. For more information or to book an event, contact the Simon & Schuster Speakers Bureau at 1-866-248-3049 or visit our website at www.simonspeakers.com.

Interior design by Carly Loman

Manufactured in the United States of America

10   9   8   7   6   5   4   3   2   1

Library of Congress Cataloging-in-Publication Data has been applied for.

ISBN 978-1-9821-2051-1
ISBN 978-1-9821-2053-5 (ebook)

for Ty

On the threshold of a house of imposing size, the only house in a town built of thunderbolt stone, two nightingales hold each other tightly entwined. The silence of the sun presides over their frolic. The sun strips off its black skirt and white bodice. And is gone. Night falls at a stroke, with a crash.

—MAX ERNST, PREFACE TO *THE HOUSE OF FEAR*
BY LEONORA CARRINGTON

The girl, who had taken the appearance of a horse, did not move, but her nostrils quivered.

—LEONORA CARRINGTON, "THE OVAL LADY"

November 1997, Brewster Arts Gallery, New York City

At the first break in the conversation the artist makes for the door. She hears someone call her name, but she'd like a cigarette, and she keeps walking as quickly as her eighty-year-old body will allow through the crowded gallery. She hides behind a post—to rest, to catch her breath—and moves on. Her hips and knees and feet ache from all this standing around. She's never liked opening nights, feeling the eyes of the spectators on her, as if *she* were part of the show. If only she could be invisible, perhaps she wouldn't mind. She does her best not to look at the people, as they scrutinize and hypothesize, or at her paintings—all the evidence lined up against her, so to speak. A retrospective, the entire gallery is filled with her art. Sixty years of her life. Of course, she knows every inch of every canvas, as though they were extensions of her own body. The hyena and the horse; the maze, the minotaur, the egg and the cabbage, the white, alchemical rose; ghosts, witches, a spiral dance. Her menagerie of hybrids, the beasts she's known and loved. So many of her visions on display—it's a bit like forgetting to wear one's skin. Sinew, bone, heart and veins, there for all to see.

As she pushes the door open, breathing the gust of outside air, she comes face to face with a young woman, pen and notebook in her hand. "Ms. Carrington!" she says, smiling brightly. That's right, she had promised an interview. And there's a man with her, a camera over his shoulder. Another photo. "Would you mind?" the reporter asks. Leonora follows her back inside. "How about here, in front of *Sidhe, the White People of Tuatha de Danaan*?" She pronounces it correctly. She's done her homework.

As Leonora approaches the golden kitchen from more than forty years ago, the bull with that knowing glint in his eyes looks through her, the way he always has. Standing before the open door at the painting's edge, beside the bald, glowing beings feasting on soup and yams, Leonora looks off, through the glass front of the gallery, where a couple has stopped on the sidewalk. She watches the woman in her dark coat rise up on tiptoe, watches the white-haired man bow his head to kiss her. A flash. The photographer snapping her photo. For a second, Leonora has the sense of being inside her painting, back in that other world. Another flash, and in the mirrorlike window she glimpses a ghostly figure vanishing through the gallery's far wall. Feeling a wave of dizziness, she straightens her spine as best she can and presses her feet to the floor. For most of her life now she has entered that strange land on her own terms, has claimed it through her paintings and made it her own, but even so it still sometimes takes her by surprise.

"Might we sit?" says the woman, leading her to a small leather sofa.

"I can't be long." Leonora says. She's always hated interviews, the way the questions attempt to pin her down, knowing she'll show up in print—not *her*, but the way the interviewer sees her. Although, she must admit, it feels wonderful to rest her feet.

"Your art is so palpable, and yet so mysterious. Where do you get your inspiration?"

"I don't discuss that." Leonora looks out the window, but the couple has moved on.

"Like this painting. The Sidhe were Irish, faerie folk, weren't they? I read it was your nanny and your mother who told you stories about them."

"Yes. My mother's mother had told her we were descended from them."

"What is that one juggling? Moons?" The woman points to the glowing orbs in the painting. "Why does one have a spider's web?" The question hovers. It isn't that Leonora doesn't want to answer; she can't. She never could explain the things she sees. She sighs, thinking of that cigarette. The woman continues. "In your first great work, your self-portrait, there's a blur on the floor. Had you painted something and then wiped it out?" Leonora is quiet. The reporter shifts on the cushion, flips a page in her notebook. "Or *The Giantess*? I love how her hair is a field of wheat. Is she based on Demeter? Or possibly the Norse goddess Sif?"

Leonora reaches into the pocket of her coat. She takes out the soft pack of Vantage, fingering the cigarettes gently, as though she were holding a raw egg. "I don't talk about my art. Paintings are for what is not sayable." The woman blushes. Bending toward her notebook, she writes quickly. Poor girl. This can't be easy. Leonora stands, using the armrest to push herself up. It seems to take forever. "Come," she says. "Let's have some air."

Outside there's a wind. Leonora cinches the belt of her long coat, fastens the button beneath her chin. She breathes the cold air, and smells the acrid fumes of a passing truck. She lights a cigarette, and exhales. That's better. She offers one to the reporter, which she accepts with a smile. A truce, Leonora thinks, wishing she could enjoy this more. She's worked her whole life to get here, but she's never gotten used to the attention, the idea that what comes out of her mouth is somehow of note. But the woman has her pen and pad, and her fingers are red from the cold. Leonora moves closer, so she can talk quietly and the woman will hear her. "Was there anything else you wanted to know?"

"Do you consider yourself a Surrealist?"

Leonora balks at the term that has followed her through her artistic career as devotedly as a dog, as if she could be summed up in one word. "Part of the old boys' club?" She laughs. "No women could join, you know. Not officially. But the truth is I don't consider myself anything." Leaning against the front window of the gallery, she does her best to explain. "Egos are dangerous, fragile, too big for their own good. Like Humpty Dumpty, you know?"

The reporter nods, writes, and asks the next question on her list.

"Do you feel that, as a woman artist, your work has achieved the recognition it deserves?"

She thinks of the men—Dali, Miró, Picasso—and the enormous sums their paintings garnered even before they had died. She thinks of the frugality with which she's lived her life, subsisting on beans and rice and the cheapest cuts of meat. She chuckles, coughs, and takes a deep breath. There just isn't any point in being bitter. "Women's art sells for a fraction of what the men's goes for, and it takes women twice as long to make any sort of name for themselves. I'm one of the lucky ones. I'm old. I've lived long enough to see the world at least begin to notice us—as artists, that is, and not as the inspiration, that infernal notion of the muse."

"And Paris? What was it like in the thirties? You were twenty?"

"Twenty, twenty-one." Leonora takes a drag on her cigarette. Floating on the wave of nicotine, she remembers their flat on Rue Jacob, the white rocking horse in the living room, her easel by the window. "Paris was freedom," she says, thinking of Café de Flore, and the artists—Leonor, Lee, Man and the Éluards, Duchamp, Breton, Picasso, and, more than all of them, Max.

"And Max Ernst was your lover?" The woman grins, as if she's read her face, some inexplicable change in her expression. She seems to think she is the first person to be brave enough to ask, but Leonora can't be interviewed without being asked about him—the great man—as if she were no more than another Galatea. "What was it like, being with him?"

Looking at the sliver of sky, where a single star persists through the city glow, Leonora finds she is thinking of the morning church bells of Paris, and how, when they woke her, she'd pull him closer, and the warmth of his body would tow her back to sleep. "It was perfect," she says, surprising herself.

"Passionate?"

Leonora can't help but smirk. "We won't get into that."

PART I

Two Children Are Threatened by a Nightingale

Leonora, June 1937, London, England

It was Leonora's first dinner party as a grown woman, and Ursula and she were the hosts. The garden was Ursula's, but the party had been *her* idea—a garden party lit by the full moon, with white foods and attire because the moonlight called for it, and because Max Ernst was visiting London and had decided to join them.

She'd seen his art a summer ago, at the International Surrealist Exhibition in London. Beside Hans Bellmer's disjointed, life-sized doll, which had made her sick to her stomach, Max had displayed an assemblage piece—a girl's head molded in plaster and attached to a cord like a yo-yo. This had made sense to her. Up and down, lolling about, she'd been that toy, manipulated by someone who held the string, held the money and the power. Time to sever that cord, she'd thought. Then, she saw his painting *Two Children Are Threatened by a Nightingale*. Speaking to her in a language she understood, had perhaps always understood, but had never managed to articulate, it depicted the climax of an eerie story, a girl unconscious on an emerald lawn and another with a knife in her hand, the vicious nightingale just out of her reach. The most striking feature was the frame itself, which she'd felt an irresistible desire to touch. She ran her fingertips over the knob he'd attached, which made the painting's frame into a door. There was a man in the scene, and he was running on the roof of a house and reaching for the knob—as if he could open the door and leave the painting. The man held a girl in his arms. *But would he be able to save her?* she'd wondered, and felt her skin burn from the inside out.

And now, through the kitchen window, she watched Max and Lee Miller and Roland Penrose, sitting at the table on her friend's brick patio beneath a trellis of jasmine, a few white flowers open in the shape of stars. They were impossibly interesting, these Surrealists— not studying, but living their art. Lee leaned back in her chair, her long legs crossed at the ankles, her feet bare. She blew smoke from her cigarette toward the sky, and handed it to Roland, who took a long, easy drag. Max was talking, his hands everywhere at once. The fact that he was here seemed impossible, and yet it made perfect sense. Ursula was married to Erno, an architect who happened to be friends with Roland, whose London gallery was hosting a show of Max's work. But Leonora didn't buy into coincidence. The reason he sat here was simple, irrefutable. Her love for his art had somehow pulled the man himself to her.

On a blue-and-white china plate, Leonora arranged the short-bread cookies she and Ursula had baked. She scooped the lemon sorbet into a bowl, stealing a heaping spoonful for herself. She smiled. Just enough lemon to balance the sugar. She tasted a cookie. Her Irish grandmother's recipe, it was buttery and crumbly, just as it should be. She popped the rest of it into her mouth. At her tiny apartment, she had been living off of eggs, all she could afford as an art student, and so Ursula had been tonight's culinary benefactor. Ursula had been Miss Blackwell, of Crosse & Blackwell, the makers of marmalade, and both she and Leonora had come from money. The main difference in their circumstances was that while Mr. Blackwell had encouraged his daughter in the arts, and he allowed her to marry as she wished, Mr. Carrington would dole out only as much money as Leonora required to live like a pauper, for to his mind that's what artists were—paupers and beggars and gypsies— and the sooner she learned this the better. She'd fought to come to London, and she knew he didn't think she could make it without his support. He expected her to come home, marry well, and give the family the title his money alone couldn't buy them. She could think of no worse a fate.

Outside, Max was laughing, the corners of his eyes bursting into rays, his head thrown back, his white hair lit and airy, when something smacked the windowpane in front of her, making Leonora jump. She brushed the crumbs from her lips and ran outside to find a bird, lying on its side, its eye shut. "I'll get a dustpan," Ursula said. But without thinking, Leonora scooped the bird into her hand. She hated to see them die like this, flying full speed at a window, death by reflection, by illusion. She touched its soft orange breast. It was a robin, and still warm. So many pairs had nested at the home where she'd grown up in the countryside of Lancashire, but she hadn't seen any since moving to London a year ago. And why had it been flying at dusk? Suddenly, she felt someone beside her. Max reached out and stroked the bird's wing. She felt her hair stand on end, as it did in lightning storms, his proximity startling. This wasn't like anything she'd experienced before. They looked at each other. Was it a kind of recognition? Did he feel it, too, the immediate pull?

Ursula appeared, holding a broom and a dustpan. "You shouldn't touch dead birds."

"It's not dead," Leonora said, sensing the pulse of energy around it, the force of possibility.

The robin opened its eyes, black and shining. She set it in the planter of jasmine and they all watched it fluff its wings and glide to the little park below.

She and Ursula brought the serving bowls to the patio table, which was dressed in a length of white linen and shone in the dusk, seeming practically to levitate. As Ursula set the bowl of smashed turnips and potatoes in front of Max, she giggled. Leonora felt giddy, too, but she wouldn't laugh. She'd worn the men's button-down shirt she liked to paint in, tucked into gray trousers, and her most comfortable pair of loafers. She swallowed any lightness in her head, made an effort to lower her voice. "I do hope you all like halibut." She put the sautéed fish in front of Lee, whose silk sundress clung to her small breasts and hips as if she'd stepped from the pages of *Vogue*, the magazine for which she'd modeled. Cool and glossy, she took a swallow of her drink, something brown. Ice clattered in her glass, and Ursula ferried it to the kitchen for a refill.

Ursula had told Leonora all about Lee, who had, she said, the most famous breasts in Paris. Known for being Man Ray's muse, she'd come to the city from the States to learn from him. As comfortable behind the camera as she was in front of it, she took her place in the darkroom, too, until no one could tell their photos apart. She broke his heart, went to New York City and started her own portrait studio. But after a few years she left it all again and moved to Egypt to marry a wealthy man whose ring still glinted on her finger, though she kissed Roland with her wet lips, and then her whole mouth. Ten years older than Leonora, Lee seemed so confident and free, so in control. She had never met a woman quite like her, and she couldn't stop watching her. When Lee looked right back, her eyes steady and pale, Leonora froze, as though she'd been caught at something. Lee's gaze was somewhere between a challenge and pure, innate curiosity. What did she see in her? Leonora wondered, unable to look away.

As Lee bit into a radish, she studied her lips—thin, elegant as the rest of her. Man Ray had gotten them right. She'd seen his painting at the exhibit, too. Lee's lips, huge, flying through a blue, cloud-speckled sky. "After she left him, he spent the better part of a year painting that," Ursula had told her.

How wonderful it must feel, Leonora thought, to be loved like that.

On the other side of Lee, Max drank his beer. She thought of what Ursula had said that morning: "He has a wife. Of course, he takes lovers. All the Surrealists do." Leonora felt his eyes on her, felt the blood rise to her cheeks. "Won't you sit down, Miss Carrington?" he said, pulling out the chair beside him. She shot him a smile and sat. Was he flirting?

The table shook and she jumped. Ursula's husband, Erno, was pounding his fist like a gavel, exactly the way Leonora's father used to. His voice was emphatic, his Hungarian accent thick. "There's every reason to resist, to take Hitler down now, my friend. When he occupied the Rhineland he broke the Treaty of Versailles. He wants vengeance. You're a fool to think he will stop."

He was talking to Roland, but Lee pointed back at him, her hands large, strong, and articulate. "And if he does start a war, it'll make for some fantastic photographs, won't it? Smoke lends such a mood."

Erno squinted at her, smacking his dry lips. Roland put his hands on her cheeks and kissed her. "The first female war photographer, by God!"

"Enough about war," said Max. "Right now we have summer, which should be enough for anyone."

"Here, here, Loplop!" Roland raised his glass. Loplop, the Bird Superior. She'd noticed the moniker at the exhibition. An ungainly name for a bird.

Ursula gave Lee her drink and handed Leonora a bottle of beer. "Shall we toast?" she said. Her grin, like the rest of her, ebullient, and crafty in the best sort of way, brought Leonora back from somewhere deep inside herself, the place she went whenever there was talk of an impending war. Here she sat, at a moonlit table. Here was Max Ernst smiling beside her. As she reached past him for the bottle opener, her heart skipped like a flat stone across water, sending ripples, she was sure, in every direction. Her head was light. She steadied her hand and pried off the lid.

Her beer foamed, overflowing, and she panicked. The table had been perfect! Why was she always the messy one? Before she could move it, Max sealed the bottle with his thumb. The sudden action surprised her. She held her breath. An electric hum zipped up her spine. *This is how it happens*, she thought. His eyes were ice, a cold, clear fire. "To keep it from going onto the table," he said. The foam sizzled in the bottle. Roland and Lee, pressed so close together they seemed like one two-headed body, Ursula laughing, and Erno, still red in the face—the rest of the party became scenery. There was only them. She clung to the moment, in some futile attempt to see him with an ounce of objectivity. His brown face, his wiry arms and legs, the wrinkles bursting from the sides of his eyes, which were the blue of how she imagined a clear, desert sky might look. It was too late. She held the bottom of the bottle of beer and he held the top. It was as if they were collaborating.

"Food's getting cold," said Lee. "Let's eat."

"But first," Max said, "that toast."

The moon peeked over the row of houses, and the table, the food, and all of them in their white clothes glowed with it. Max's hair brightened, and her eyes watered. Something inside her had given way, the breaking of a dam. He removed his thumb from her beer, but didn't stop looking at her.

"To the future," he said, clinking her bottle with his.

"To the future," the party agreed, clinking and drinking.

Had she seduced him or had he seduced her? She wasn't sure. Even now she felt his gaze sharpening her, defining her with its fierce desire. It was a kind of quickening, as if some part of her that had been asleep were waking. She sipped her beer, spooned the soft, white roots onto her plate. More jasmine blossoms had opened to the night, their smell so strong, the potatoes and turnips, even the fish tasted of jasmine. But the lip of her bottle was salty. It tasted of Max's thumb.

Max, June 1940, southern France

The train lurches.

How long have they been stopped?

It is night still, black and cold and wet. And somehow it is still his shift. There isn't room for all of the men to sit, let alone to lie down to sleep, and so they have settled on shifts. Half of the men in the cattle car sit for two hours while the other half stand, and then they switch. They stand and sit and stand until the night is done. And here he is, still taking up precious floor space, and dreaming.

He's been dreaming! Not a nightmare, like the ones he's had since the Great War, but a dream like he had as a child, the sort with levitation, flying over the dark woods, the sort with a heroine and a hero. It's still here, tickling the back of his neck with its disintegrating fingers. Her voice calls to him. He wants to tell her to stay where she is—he will come to her, somehow—but his lips are too numb to form words. His lungs are sacks filled with wet sand. To catch it! To return!

He shivers, pulling his thin, damp coat tighter around him. Rain drips through the slats in the roof and onto his head. He raises the collar of his coat, tucks his head, and resting his cheeks in his hands, his elbows on his knees, he closes his eyes. If his life is the nightmare, isn't he free to dream? If he can fall back into the swirl of the story she was telling him, her voice warm and endless as her hair, perhaps he can endure—without water, without food—another hour, and then another.

He's been on this train for days. Two? Three? He's not sure. His mind is not right, but then nothing is.

"God of my fathers, God of my fathers, God of my fathers," a man's voice rings over the far fields and into the forest where he is walking, where he is holding her hand.

"May God shut you up, you old fool," someone else growls, and he is awake now. The fresh stench hits him first. The bucket is some-where in the middle of the herd of men, and he is pressed up to the wooden side of the car, as far from the bucket as he could be, but even so the smell is unbearable. No. Not unbearable, he reminds himself, burrowing his nose farther down in his coat. At least he is not one of the wretched souls with dysentery, forced to cling to the metal bucket to relieve himself in this dank huddle.

The man behind him gives his shoulder a shake. His shift is over. His turn has come to stand. He pitches forward, balancing on throb-bing feet.

To stand in the dark, half-asleep, wet and exhausted, is torture. He didn't think life could be worse than it had been at Camp des Milles, sleeping on scraps of hay in an oven where bricks had once been baked, waking with his throat made of paper, his lips cracked like the crust of bread, the bricks having sucked all the moisture from his body. But to lie flat would be such a luxury now that he can't bear to think of it.

When will the day come, the light?

He sways, with the other men, in the rhythm of the train. "What would you give for something warm to drink?" It is his friend, the artist Hans Bellmer, who sways beside him. "For a cup of beef broth?"

He coughs to locate his voice, a craggy whisper. "How can you think of food?"

"Not food. Warmth, broth, marrow." In the dripping darkness, his friend sounds full, sated, as if the words themselves had weight enough to sustain him. He could have been a poet.

"When can we open these doors? I need air!" a man yells.

"Enough!" barks one of the Algerian guards. In the day the guards are friendly enough, but at night they become as ill-tempered as the rest of them. And to open the door would mean they are visible. Should they pass a Nazi motorized column, they couldn't hide.

"This train," Hans mumbles. "It's a ghost train. We are ghosts on a ghost train."

He nods, feeling his eyes close again. Impossible to sleep on one's feet. But he can remember the dream. He can feel it around him. The woods. And how she said she'd find him. Only how can she find him when he doesn't know where he is?

When the train set off from the camp, in Provence, they'd heard the Nazis were coming from the north, the Italians from the east. And so they headed west—no one seemed to know where. Even the engineer claimed he was awaiting further instruction. But then all of France was in chaos, everyone fleeing for the Spanish border. He should have found some way to slip off when the train was being boarded. He should have run. From Camp des Milles, in Aix, he'd have been closer to Saint-Martin-d'Ardèche, to home. Closer to her. Unless the Nazis had made it there, in which case she'd have been gone. Which would mean she'd be running now. She could be anywhere.

Through a groove in the wooden door, he glimpses the faintest gloaming. The sun's return after a night like this is a beautiful, beautiful thing. A miracle.

"Can you smell it?" says Hans. "The sea?" He can almost smell it over the stench. He looks through the chink. The fields are a blur, dark yellow, dark green.

Along with the rain, the thinnest light falls through the slats in the roof. He looks at the men, lit up here and there. They are dressed in gray rags, with bits of uniforms from the French soldiers, green hats and coats, items they bought on the black market, with the hope that they might blend in should they try to escape. But how will they run? Made of ash and shadows, of bones and loose skin, they are broken marionettes, with tangled, useless strings.

Boches, the French called them. Germans. No matter that these Germans are also wanted by the Nazis. Writers, artists, Jews. The ghosts on the ghost train were once men—men who had run from Germany when the Nazis took over, who had crossed the border, legally or not, to France, to freedom. Of course some, like him, had come long before the fascists took power. But the war made enemy aliens of all of them. They were enemies in a country that had welcomed them, a country they'd come to love.

Then the war had stopped as quickly as it had started, and trapped in Camp des Milles they were sitting ducks waiting for the Germans to seize them. The commandant did what he could to ferry them to safety. He'd managed to get this train, he'd pointed them west, and now, in their attempt to outrun the Nazis, they were nearly to the coast.

"Open the door," says a ghost.

"Yes, open the door," another echoes.

The guard groans, and the door slides open.

He shoulders his way to the front of the car, sits beside his friend on the side rail, their legs dangling. He tilts his head back, sticks out his dry tongue. Rain. Each drop a marvel.

Another long train passes, filled with refugees. People sit on the low steps, lie on the top of the cars, the whole world thronging to the border. Searching the blur of faces for hers, he thinks he sees a woman with long dark hair, but then the train is gone, and he finds he is praying. Praying for the first time in years to a god he doesn't believe in, praying his girl has stayed in Saint-Martin and is waiting for him.

He can smell the ocean. "Bayonne Harbor," says his friend, pointing to a bright spot in the distance.

The train awakens with a flurry of questions. They have made it to the coast, but why? There is the ocean—they can see it now—and the masts of ships waiting to take them, where? Overseas? To the colonies? To build the Trans-Sahara Line?

The train slows. A young man shoulders his way to the open door.

"If you don't want to be shipped abroad, now's your chance," he says and jumps, his battered suitcase tumbling beside him.

Outside the station, the train stops. Passengers hop from the car to relieve themselves. Young and old pull down their trousers and crouch on the nearest patch of mud. He unzips his fly beside a low fence and waits. And waits. At last, a slow, ocher-colored stream joins the rain.

Zipping his pants, he stares beyond the fence. The scene is a scumble of black and gray, and then it moves, the sludge a pressing pitch. He realizes he's looking at a highway overflowing with every sort of vehicle, a monstrous procession churning toward the Spanish border; every car with at least two mattresses roped atop it—to shield them from air raids, he realizes with new horror—and he wonders just how far they have come. All the way from Paris? There are towering trucks and pushcarts spilling with people and their possessions, everything they could carry. A chair a grandfather made. A lamp from the last century. A violin. There are people on foot with bicycles, mules, horses. And everyone prodded forward, the air wrung with their hope, heavy as a wet, wool blanket.

A station manager runs toward them, shouting, waving his arms. "Get back on! They are coming! The Germans will be here in two hours or less!" The men pull up their trousers and run to the train. He runs, too, slow motion through a slow-motion world in which everyone is running, but not nearly fast enough. The men pack themselves inside the train. He takes a seat on the side rail, Hans beside him. If the Germans are here, they are here. No good hiding in the back of the train is going to do anyone.

The commandant strides by, dripping with rain, his cheeks red. "We must go back," he is saying over and over, so all of the two thousand men might hear him. But the train does not budge and soon the men convene outside it, their voices rising over one another.

The French have failed, again.

The Spanish border is close. Better to join the stream of refugees? Better to get by on our own?

The Spanish borders are open, but require permits. Only French citizens can pass.

To the French, we will look like enemies.

"Go!" The commandant yells. "You're prisoners no longer."

"Free? We are free!" shout the men.

"You will not live," the commandant says. "Between the Nazis and the gendarmerie. You will be imprisoned, or shot. We have a chance of getting you to a region that won't be in German control when the armistice is concluded."

Men grab their possessions, embrace friends, and head for the highway of people. Other trains—full of soldiers, full of civilians—pull out of the station, and still their train doesn't move. More men leave. Without money, or papers, without water or food.

Hans paces. "The train is obvious. Hitler's men will hear of it. But France is in pandemonium. Disappearing will be easy."

"Stay. You'll die out there," he tells Hans, but he only half means it. Hans is a willful, wily man. He will find a way to live.

The train buzzes with power and the men leap on. Old men are pushed and pulled aboard as the cars jerk back in the direction from which they just came. His heart sinks.

Hans stands on the dirt. "Come with me."

And he yearns to run, to slip with him, somehow, over the border. Together they would find a way. No. He shakes his head no because he has no choice. He must go home. He must try to find her. From the train he watches his friend grow smaller, until the rail curves, and he is gone.

They move through the same blur of green, through afternoon and through dusk. The train slows, and he spots, on a hill, a horse grazing. Lifting its brown neck, it seems to look at him as the train comes to a stop.

"The power's been cut," says the commandant, walking beside the open cars. Sweating, his skin a sickly green, he looks nearly as bad as the rest of them. "Burn your papers—anything pledging your loyalty to France."

A small bonfire fills the car with smoke. He adds his papers to the fire, watches the name *Max Ernst* curl and flare and subside. He watches it turn to ash.

Leonora, June 1937, London, England

Leonora opened the door in her nightdress and ran a hand through her tangled hair. It was morning and here, on the doorstep of her basement flat, stood a man in a black hat, his suit pressed and spotless. He bowed slightly before handing her a small envelope. She knew who it was from without even having to ask. Max. She tore the envelope open and read the note straightaway, as if it might evaporate in her hands.

Come away with me, will you, for a picnic in the woods? If you agree, I will fetch you at two this afternoon.

Before she could talk herself out of it—he was married, after all, and twice her age—she sent the messenger back with a folded note, which said, simply, *Yes.*

It was utterly crazy, she knew, to be alone with him in the woods. Anything might happen. She hardly knew him. And yet it was this wildness, this unpredictablity, that attracted her to him. It was fanciful and romantic; no Brit would risk so bold a proposition. Certainly not if he knew who her father was. Of *course* she would go.

⁓֎

She checked the clock: ten till two. In her dark apartment, the air smelled of cigarette ash and boiled eggs. She sat hunched over her kitchen table, and by the light of the bare bulb she worked on her series of sketches—women without smiles, without breasts, women with their hair short, capped in berets, cigarettes hanging from their lips. All spring she'd kept at them, not at Amedee Ozenfant's art school— where she drew apple after apple in an attempt to render the fruit in a single flawless line—but here, on her own. She spread the drawings on the table and squinted, as if by softening the edges of the paper she could see these women as friends, part of a single scene. Maybe they were lunching together, not planning whom and when they would marry, or what pattern of china they would choose, like the debutantes she'd known, but rather what they would paint, what they would photograph, and how the world would see them as artists and buy their work. Their art would hang in galleries, museums. They weren't sure how they'd get there, but they sure as hell weren't going to settle for the lives their mothers led. It was a group she yearned to join.

If she listened hard, she could hear them talking. *Glimmer*, one said, *but keep the mystery. Put the receiver back on its holster*, said another. *Listen to your heart, your blood.* One woman began smoking a cigarillo, and she crushed the coal of it into the wood, leaving a burn on the table, a dark eye. Leonora squinted more, then let her eyes blur, so the world around the women could come into focus. If she could see their world, she could enter it, leaving her own burn mark on the wood.

Rat-ta-tat. Max was right on time.

Leonora grabbed her bag and leapt for the door. There, instead of Max, stood Serge. He raised an eyebrow, took off his fedora. "You were expecting someone?" he asked, walking past her into her flat. He paced the length of her room, his hands shoved into his jacket pockets. She tried to breathe. *Serge?* What was he doing here?

Serge was an acquaintance of her father's, an architect who had helped set her up at Ozenfant's, and she thought of him as a chaperone of sorts. But from the moment she met him she'd known his real role—to learn what she was up to and report back to her father. He also happened to be her very first lover, one she hadn't ended things with just yet. But usually he'd stop by in the evening, after work, not in the middle of the afternoon. If Max came for her now, Serge would know, which meant her father would, too.

When she came to London a year ago, they had met once a week at a café. Over coffee she'd tell him what she wanted Father to hear. And then Serge started coming by her flat after work. She'd make him tea and show him her drawings. They'd talk. He was seventeen years older than her and in on the London art scene. He was friends with Erno, and was every bit as earnest as he was, though not quite so humorless.

"Ozenfant says you have promise," he'd told her one evening. He seemed truly pleased. And she'd reached across the table and taken off his glasses and kissed him. "Are you going to tell that to Father?" she'd teased. A moment later they were in bed.

The power over her father was intoxicating. Serge might report back, but he would never be able to tell him anything that implied he knew Leonora intimately, and so her father wouldn't know any more about her than she wanted him to. When she told Ursula about their affair, she beamed. "Marry him!" she'd said. "You'd have the most darling children!"

"I'm not going to marry anybody," she told her. "He's my first lover. That's all." So far as she was concerned, virginity was overrated, and she was glad to be done with it.

The affair went on, secretly, for months. But then Serge wouldn't quit hinting at marriage, and he began to look less like a handsome spy and more like a lonely bachelor. He became ordinary, and she started making up excuses. She told him she needed time to think things through. She knew she needed to end the affair, but she couldn't afford to have him turn on her. If he recommended she be sent home, her father would have a car at her flat in an hour.

She laughed, to seem breezy, but it came off flat and forced. "Ursula and I are off to Brighton, to eat oysters, to draw the sea and the pier, or to try to," she said, in as offhand a manner as possible. She sat at the table, took up her graphite, and added a few wisps of smoke to the woman's cigarillo. She didn't have to watch him to know he was looking around her single room, from her twin bed, where they had made what she now felt sure was unremarkable love, to her stacks along the wall—sketches, books, piles of clothes. He seemed to be looking for something, for some clue. Feeling his eyes circle back to her, she looked up. He was twisting the right side of his dark mustache, and she found she was sketching him into a corner, beside the woman with the cigarillo. He was her dwarf servant, his head the exact shape of an egg, to which she added no hair.

He walked behind her, put his hand on her shoulder. She felt her body tense and covered her sketch with her arm. "So, you were at a party last night? Erno said it was a real *Surrealist* gathering. Lee Miller, Penrose, Max Ernst."

So Erno had told him already. *That's* why he was here. She convulsed in a cough, loud and long. Her voice was hoarse. "Yes, well, I didn't have much fun. I'm coming down with something."

He backed away and covered his nose and mouth with his hand. Serge was a hypochondriac, and she knew her fib would keep him away for at least a week. Soon she would tell him it was over, but for now she needed him to go. "They're a dangerous, immoral crew, Leonora." He opened the door. She coughed again. A spray of saliva hung in the air. "Watch yourself," he said, shutting the door behind him.

His steps grew fainter as he climbed the stairs to the street. That was close. At one time she'd lived on adrenaline, sneaking cigarettes at convent school and climbing from her window at that finishing school in Florence so she could wander the town on her own, and stay as long as she liked in the Uffizi. But now she was too old for duplicity. If she were a man, she could live as she wanted, and she couldn't see how the mere fact of her body and its ability to bring a child into the world meant she couldn't. But Father would never see things that way. He wasn't going to leave her alone until she was married.

She heard something like a ball bounce down the stairs and she grabbed her bag. This was Max, she knew, so full of energy that his knock sent ripples of delight through the room. She opened the door to his crooked grin. He surprised her, hugging her right off her feet. She forgot Serge and Father, and she laughed and threw her arms around him. He pressed his lips to hers.

Never had she felt herself dissolve inside a kiss, but suddenly she felt stretched the distance between Earth and Neptune and she floated in space, weightless and spinning a thousand revolutions without coming down for a breath. They walked upstairs and out the door. Never had she walked along the street with a man, but now he took her hand in his, and they were elephants on the riverbank, their trunks locked and swaying, a sign language that needed no interpretation. In the middle of the sidewalk he pulled her to him. She glanced around, worried Serge might be watching, but saw only the faces of strangers, hurrying past. They kissed again. Their eyes closed, they were giraffes, their small heads confused with the stars, their eyelashes touching in the dark.

He let her go and the street came back, its midday bustle a confusion of automobiles and humans. Men strolled side by side, their voices scuffling by. Women walked arm in arm. Their laughter bubbled and splashed. The day had turned humid, and the smell of London in the summer was fecund and voluptuous—cheese softening in the heat, soot and cigarettes, scraps of fat and overripe fruit in the trash.

Roland's Bentley was at a cockeyed angle as if parked in a hurry, with one wheel on the curb. Max opened the door for her, slid behind the wheel, and they were off. He weaved around cars and pedestrians, talking all the while in French, assuming she understood. Though it had been a while since her tutor had taught her French, she found she could follow most of what he was saying to her. A missed word here and there was inconsequential; his enthusiasm conveyed all she needed to know. He'd brought strawberries and scones and a blanket, he said, and he couldn't wait to be alone with her. There was something he wanted to show her.

"Oh," she said, and left it there. What could he want to show her? And what might he expect? She couldn't have spoken more than a hundred words to him, yet he assumed he knew what she'd like? But watching the wind through the open windows blow his white hair this way and that, she relaxed. Too wild for the car with its heft and polish, he looked like the bird he claimed to be—puffed up in his pin-striped suit, his nose like a great beak. She hadn't noticed the avian resemblance until now, his angular grace. His long legs bent, knees by his elbows. He was a crane. Once they were outside of the city, perhaps he would show her his wings.

As they drove, the smoggy sky turned blue and the buildings gave way to the open green of fields. Max turned onto a small treelined road that wound past scattered houses and stopped by a wooded hill. He took a basket from the backseat and a thin, yellow-and-white check-ered blanket. There was a fence, and a gate which he opened for her as if he owned the place. They were trespassing, something she wouldn't normally do, and she liked the feeling of risk and entitlement.

They spread their picnic beneath the canopy of a maple. They slid off their shoes and felt the cool grass under their feet.

A chorus of cicadas galvanized the air. They sounded the way her skin felt—the hairs on her arms standing on end just to be alone with him. To appear calm, she lay back on her elbow, her skirt over her knees. She nibbled a scone. If only they'd had some tea, she thought. Then he opened a bottle of white Bordeaux, tipped the bottle to his lips, and swallowed. "To be sure it's good enough for you." He grinned, offering it. She sipped the wine—far better than tea—and ate a strawberry.

"There are two principles," he said. He had brought a plank of wood in his pack. Over it he scattered leaves, twigs, tiny pebbles. He placed a piece of drawing paper over this and fastened it with clips. He rubbed the side of a pencil over the paper, the edges of the debris appearing in dark lines. It was like dreams, she thought, how they live all day in your body, in the bones of your wrists and elbows, in the spongy tissues of your liver and your lungs. Your logical mind is oblivious to them, and only when you let go and give in to sleep do these dreams dare to show their faces, the way animals at the zoo come out at dawn and dusk, when the light itself is a kind of refuge.

"The two principles," he said, "are chance and intuition—what appears and what you see in it. You and I, we could work off the same frottage and come up with completely different scenes."

"Frottage?" Was this something he thought she would know? Ozenfant hadn't taught them a thing about frottage.

"Friction, rubbing. It's what I call it." He shook out the debris, blew off the excess lead. They studied the image in the sunlight, his hand warm on her back, a wonderful pressure. "Like when you were a child and looked at the clouds," he said, and she knew she wasn't a child, not anymore. She wasn't sitting at a desk staring out the window at the clouds and dreaming of her life. She was here, inside it. She was with Max Ernst, dreaming in a new way.

"There's a queen." She traced the outline of what she saw. "And here's her elephant, see? She's riding away from her kingdom, which is here." She touched the corner of the paper. "On the hill behind her. She's on a cliff, looking at the desert she'll cross. She can't see where she'll end up—it's all vastness, desert and ocean, and on the shore is a ship, waiting for her and her elephant."

He leaned close. "I'd love to see you paint that." He kissed her forehead, an eyelid, a cheekbone, an ear. She could feel her heart pulse in the tips of her fingers and put her hands in her lap. *Steady*, she thought. *Stay calm.* "Will you show me your work sometime?"

"Sometime," she said, though it was impossible to imagine that her painting would ever be good enough.

He lay down, resting his head on her lap, and she forgot to breathe. She stroked his tan forehead, smooth against the tips of her fingers. Go slow, she thought. We have all afternoon. She fed him a bite of a strawberry and ate the rest herself.

"Tell me a story?" he said.

She flicked the berry's green cap into the grass, where it landed beside a mushroom. She was used to writing stories down, not just saying them out loud. Perhaps a true story might be easiest. "Want to hear about the first convent school to kick me out?"

"Absolutely."

"When I was nine, Father shipped me off to the nuns of the Holy Sepulchre," she began, "and I hated the place. During mass one morning, as I approached the priest, my tongue stuck out, waiting for him to place the Communion wafer on it, I lifted my skirt to my waist. I wasn't wearing underwear, and as I watched him, a soft, jowly man, turn red as a coal and walk away from me, I let my skirt down, sure I'd won." A smile spread across Max's face. She had thought he might appreciate the illicit rebelliousness of that act.

"But the days went by and nothing happened. The priest left for a new parish and I was stuck with the nuns. They could make me sit at a desk, but they couldn't make me write forward, so I didn't. I practiced my backward, mirror writing instead." She told him about the nun sending her to her room. Told him how she was ordered to write the sentence "I will not write backward" fifty times, and how, instead, she wrote a letter to her nanny in the mirror writing she had taught her, hoping it would magically transport her home. "When I held the letter up to the mirror on my bureau, I vanished."

"Vanished?"

"In the mirror, I mean. My image faded, and then I couldn't see myself, and I fell to the floor," she said, "my head light as a leaf."

She looked down at him. He was quiet, following the dance of sunlight on the leaves. There was more to the story, of course, but she did not know if she could tell it. There was the strange, underground dwelling, the place she went when she fell, the world that acted as if she'd never left. And the way she'd arrived mid-sentence, as if she had somehow been there all along.

He looked at her, looked *into* her. "What happened then?"

She laughed, nervously, and drank the wine. She'd never tried to talk about the world she'd entered that day, the world of the Sidhe, and she hadn't thought of it in years. She'd never been sure if it was real somehow, or a vivid dream. To tell someone had felt wrong—even Mother or Nanny—like putting a leash around the neck of a horse. But she thought Max might just understand.

"I found myself in another world. But it was familiar. It was a place I knew. One of the Sidhe hovered in front of me and led me through this subterranean maze."

"The Sidhe?" he said.

"You don't know the stories? They're the ancient fairy-folk of Ireland, the good folk. They went underground when the Christians came. But they come up to visit people sometimes. Those whose eyes are open. At least that's what Nanny told me." She laughed to hear herself. Max's face was blank. She'd been right, it was too hard to tell. She was losing him. Best to skip to the conscious part of the story. Maybe she'd tell him the rest when she knew him better, which she felt certain, somehow, that she would.

"And then I came to. There was a cloth over my nose and mouth. It was soaked in something, the smell so sharp I opened my eyes. I was on the bed. A doctor pulled the cloth away, and he and the nun towered over me. 'Concussion,' he said. And I remembered the sentences I hadn't written. My letter to Nanny was on the floor. It hadn't worked. I wasn't a witch, just a disobedient child. The sister shook her head, told me I was hopeless and should pack my things. My nanny would be there in an hour."

She looked down again. Max was there and he wasn't there. He was watching the leaves but was inside himself, far away. She wouldn't tell him about her father and how upset he was at her expulsion, or how surprisingly good his anger had made her feel—solid—as if he were seeing her for the first time. Not because she fit his idea of what a girl should be, prim and pretty, a bow in her brushed hair, but because she'd made trouble for him. She'd felt awful about her mother though, how she'd stood at his side, plucking out one hair at a time. Soothed by the pop of the root coming loose, she'd kept at it, producing a tiny bald spot over her left ear—a spot she could cover with her hair, but which she showed to Leonora when she wanted her to know just what her actions had done.

Leonora bit a fingernail and tore the sliver off with her teeth. Max plucked it from her mouth, flexing the crescent of nail between his fingers. A puddle of sunlight splashed across his face. He tucked a lock of her hair behind her ear. "And Nanny came to get you?"

"She did."

He reached up, took a handful of her hair in his hand, and tugged her toward him. She didn't resist. She couldn't. She was on him, kissing him fully, her open mouth asking—what, exactly, did he want? Whatever it was, she knew she wanted it, too. He tasted of strawberries and wine, sweet tang. Against him, her heartbeat slowed to his. And then he was on her. She felt him through his trousers, against her thigh, and she didn't move. She imagined Ursula standing over them, shaking her head. *You don't get a man to fall for you by following your desire*, she would say. *You resist. You make him want you so much he's willing to sacrifice everything for you.* But this was Max, a man who seemed to know what he wanted. The Surrealists didn't hold back. They trusted their gut, their unconscious appetites. And she knew she belonged with them, belonged with *him*. They understood each other, understood that this moment, this chance, wouldn't come again. She exhaled, loving the weight of his body and how it pressed her to the earth. How could she be other than herself? And she wasn't the passive sort, she reasoned, and reached under his shirt, drawing her nails down his back.

He pulled back and sat up. He tipped the wine bottle to his lips and handed it to her. She took a long swallow. He held her foot. His fingers fit her arch, and squeezed. His hand moved to her kneecap, her thigh. She felt her cheeks, her whole body burn. The tips of his fingers were under the lace hem of her underwear. He slid them to her ankles and off, slowly, in a single fluid motion. He moved her knee to the side.

She had never held this still.

She felt a river turn through her, felt the inside of her thighs cool with the breeze.

All he was doing was looking.

She'd never had sex in the day, only at night, in the dark. And now, as he stared, she could hear her own blood, a tide rushing in, and she felt her nakedness as a new kind of power. He unbuttoned the top of her dress, slipped the straps off her shoulders. He held her breast in his hand, and then her other breast, arranging them so just her nipples showed. She was his model, she realized with a thrill. The pencil still in his hand, he took out another piece of paper, and sat at her feet, sketching. She didn't move.

He looked at her, down at his drawing, and back at her. In that moment, she possessed herself completely. She felt the energy, the ecstatic pull that charged the air between them. If he were to light a match, she was sure they would combust. His voice was a whisper. "Touch yourself."

There? Did he really mean that? She stiffened. If he did, she'd get there when *she* was ready.

She moved a hand lightly across her breasts, brought it down over her dress and let it rest on her thigh. "Here," he said, placing her hand on her pillow of hair. He was sketching again, but she knew what he was asking for. Ursula, funnily enough, had been the one to tell her about it. How you can touch that part of yourself until the acute tickle becomes excruciating and you don't think you can take it and then you keep going and the world collapses, splinters, spins, it rolls shoreward like a great wave and retreats. She'd tried it, alone, and found that Ursula had been right. Light had flashed through the marrow of her bones and she'd lain as if electrocuted, ignited, having flown beyond the margins of her skin.

Would she give him what he desired? An explosion of light, here in the woods? Were these really even woods? It was country, sure, but the land belonged to someone, and there was a house not far down the road, just past the bend. Could anyone see them?

He was sketching, looking at her without apology. She looked at him the same way. His eyes were close-set, fiery and exacting, housed deep in their sockets, and she wondered if they could retreat just as easily, the way turtles could hide their heads in their shells. He hardly blinked. But under the quick nerve, there was someone quieter, removed. There was, she saw, a boy—lost and terribly alone.

She slipped a finger into the warm gloss inside her, moved it slowly over her, up and down. He blurred in her vision, seeming to her like a teenager now, lanky and awkward, his conscious ease a cover. His eyes glimmered. He was more alive than anyone she knew. And what he wanted more than sex was to watch her, to draw her. He wanted her rapture to spill onto his page. And she wanted it, too. She wanted his vision to make her new.

On the blanket in the sun, she let her eyes close. "Keep them open," he whispered. "I want to see you. I want to follow where you go." His voice moved through her like warm whiskey. She lay back, listening to his pencil scratch the page. She watched the leaves shake above her, watched the sky turn white and swallow everything. And she cried out, even if someone at that house around the bend could hear.

~&

It was her first night in a week without Max. Ever since the picnic they had been inseparable. But tonight Leonora sat at her kitchen table in the dark. Her scrambled eggs were rubbery, but she managed to choke them down with a gulp of cold tea. Max was dining with a group of art collectors—just men, he'd explained, as if that made all the sense in the world. Her body ached for him. How could she miss him already, she wondered, when it had been only hours?

She missed the clean, citrus smell of him on her skin, the sound of his voice, his low, nearly inaudible laugh. She missed the taste of his breath, smoke and moss, and something spicy—was it cloves? or cinnamon? Since their picnic she'd been to her flat just to change her clothes and to shower, and now it seemed tiny and stale, and she wondered how she'd sleep without the even keel of his body beside her. She thought of the way their limbs interlaced and how, when the horrors of his dreams rushed through his veins, making him tremble and moan, she held him to her, cooed to him as though he were a child. He'd wake in a sweat. When he needed her most, she became a stretch of calm, stronger than she'd known she could be. More.

And there was the way he looked at her. How, in his eyes that seemed capable of seeing magic, she became a sorceress. *Femme-sorcière* was the term he had used. One of Breton's categories for women, he'd explained, in so much as they were, she realized, muses for men. There was also the *femme-enfant*, the woman-child, so close to her childhood unconscious she served as a conduit between the artist—the man—and his own unconscious inspiration. She supposed, since she was twenty, Max saw her as this, too, but she didn't dwell on it. She would be whom she wanted to be in this life.

She finished the egg with the last swig of tea, thinking of what she hadn't been able to tell him the day of their picnic. About the time when she was nine, when she'd passed out at the convent and the Sidhe had taken her into their earthen dens and shown her the process of alchemy. They'd fed her a pale soup made of roots and rose petals to be sure she would return. But then Father had sent her to more convent schools, to finishing schools, one after the other—and she'd forgotten all about that first, strange lesson until Max tasted its peculiar residue in her.

Femme-sorcière. She liked the sound of it.

She washed her dishes and set about priming a canvas—one Max had helped her to stretch. She wanted to paint something she could show him. Her first real work. She lined up her tubes of paint, poured turpentine into a jar. She held the brush in her hand and stared at the blank canvas. All she had to do was to dream with her eyes open and to paint what she saw. And what she saw was the Sidhe, moving through the blue walls of her childhood nursery as if through air. So she painted a blue room. She wasn't sure yet who might inhabit it. You have to build the stage for the drama to happen.

She heard a knock, loud and firm, and she didn't move. Serge! It had to be Serge. He'd slipped a note under her door a few days ago, asking if she was feeling better and saying he'd be by again soon. If she was quiet, perhaps he would leave? But there it was again—the insistent pounding. She wiped the paint from her hands. She knew she had to end things with him, but what would she tell him? She was in love with Max Ernst, a married man? Her taste of freedom, her time living in London on her own would be up before she finished the sentence. She took a deep breath and opened the door.

Serge hung in the doorway, pale as a potato and trembling. "You are a whore." He spat the word as if to make it stick. A *whore*? She was stunned. His stare pinned her to the floor. He knew. Had he seen Max kissing her on the sidewalk? Had he followed her? Did he know she'd been spending the night with him? She'd hurt him, that much was clear. But a whore?

She swallowed her anger, wondering what she'd ever seen in him. "Serge, let's be civilized. Let's not ruin everything." He stared into the air above her head—by way of dismissal, she realized, hating him—and marched up the stairs.

She paced the room. How dare he come to *her* flat and tell her she was a whore. If they were being honest, she had a few things to tell him. What kind of man sleeps with the girl he's supposed to be keeping an eye on, for instance? She dashed up the stairs into the rain to find him. The pavement wet and cold on her feet, her arms a startle of goose pimples, she bolted up, then down the street but she didn't see him. She stood still, dug her nails into her palms. Next time, she'd be ready. She would unleash her response like a whip.

Under a streetlamp, she glimpsed herself in the glass of a hat store. The image surprised her. Was this the same girl who just a few years ago had been presented at the court of George V? You wouldn't know it to look at her. She was wearing her painting clothes, what she'd been in all day, blouse off her shoulder, torn skirt, her long hair uncombed, ferocious, by God. And here she was, in public! A couple behind her, umbrellas swaying above them, had slowed to look at her, too, a woman they must have thought mad, or poor, or a streetwalker who had seen better days. She laughed—she couldn't help herself—and the people looked away and hurried down the road. She was just the sort of woman her father most feared she'd become—an unmarried artist. The worst was done.

In her flat, she stared at the blue room of her painting, and Serge's voice quivered inside it. *Whore.* She could feel the fear, its wobbly jelly quality. Squinting, she saw it now take the shape of an elaborate court chair, with a skirt, high heels on its tiny feet, and a gleaming, scarlet tongue for a cushion. The sort of chair the queen of the whores might sit upon. She would wear riding clothes, the most androgynous clothing she owned, and sit with her legs apart—not crossed, as a lady's would be. Her stomach and thighs would be womanly, full and inviting, so the viewer would want to grab that extra bit of flesh, there, near her crotch. She wanted that region of her body to tantalize. And her black shoes would be the high-heeled, lace-up sort—a bigger, more brutal version of the chair's feet—which would make one imagine all kinds of sexual deviancies, things involving pain, inflicted by the one wearing those shoes. Yes, she thought, with a fearless, newfound determination. She imagined Serge glowing with subservience, ecstatic as a worm, and went to work at once.

But she couldn't manage to shake off her worry. If he knew, so would her father, if he didn't already. And what would he do? How much longer would she be free?

Max leaps from the side rail into the dusk and the mud, into the blur of drizzle. Stumbling toward the gloaming, following the shadows of men disappearing into the half-light before him, he hears the commandant's far, rasping call. "Come back! All is not lost!"

"Come back! Come back!" the men yell to one another, though some keep walking, the dusk dissolving the edges of their bodies, erasing them entirely. They are doomed men in Nazi territory, but no more doomed than the train, he thinks, climbing aboard. The Nazis could be anywhere by now, but at least the train will take him east, and closer to her.

When it lunges forward again, there are fewer men, but not few enough for everyone to sit. They will endure this night the same way they have endured all of the others. "Shut the door!" someone yells.

"Keep it open!" yell a pair of young Austrians.

"No!" says the scientist among them. "I haven't come this far to die!" He clutches his spectacles as he sways, for to lose one's glasses is to live in a nebulous world for who knows how long. He rubs the spectacles on his shirt, then carefully puts them back on. Poor man. Poor *old* man. But he can't be much more than fifty, and Max will be fifty next year. Which means he, too, is old, with nothing to show for his years on this cursed and beautiful planet—not unless he can make it back to Saint-Martin, back to their home with his sculptures on the walls and her paintings on the cabinets. Not unless he can take all he can from that house and run with her as far from the Nazis as they can get.

"Shut the door," more men plead. A struggle on the other side of the car turns to a scuffle, but no one yells for them to stop. The Algerian guards, they realize, are gone.

The door remains wide and the night begins with a cold, gray blur and a frenzy of stamping and smashing. The luggage the men fought for the right to bring with them from Camp des Milles, the luggage that had been piled as neatly as possible in one corner of the car is being hurled about and opened, its contents dumped on the floor and trampled with such wild delight, it reminds him of Dada, and the rage the young men of his generation felt after the Great War. The two Austrians lead the demolition, destroying their own suitcases and moving on to everyone else's.

They get it. These young Austrians get it. In the face of war, logic has no place. There is only anti-logic. The desire to destroy the workings of a world that gave rise to such purposeless slaughter. He smiles, their mania for destruction contagious. It gives him hope. But then, he has no luggage to lose. It was a month ago when he was handcuffed and dragged from their house to Camp des Milles—for the second time—and retrieving his things was impossible. The Nazis had invaded France, and Camp des Milles was filling with more "enemy subjects" by the day.

The scientist shrieks. "My glasses, my glasses!" They've been knocked off his head and stomped upon like everything else. He retrieves the twisted metal rims and sobs.

He is quiet then. They all are. No good wailing will do. What is gone is gone.

The night is as miserable as the last, only Hans Bellmer isn't here to whisper his jocular asides. There is nothing to lighten the darkness. Max stands for hours, swaying on numb feet.

In a tunnel the train grinds to a stop and he topples, along with the other standing men, onto the sitting ones. But no one curses. They are silent. Overhead, on a hill above the train, a motorized column rumbles.

This is how the Nazis travel. No one breathes. They listen.

When the last automobile has passed, the men close the door without protest, and the train presses eastward into the night. Hour after hour the ghost train stops and starts and stops again. It plods across the same fields, through the same towns as before, but slowly, so slowly the fear that he won't find his girl stretches inside him, monstrous and endless.

Why didn't they leave before France was at war? Leonora had wanted to. She had begged him. It was late August. Friends had visited Saint-Martin en route to their own exits—Lee and Roland heading for the port of Saint-Malo, for a boat to ferry them to England, and Leonor Fini on her way to Monte Carlo. They had insisted he pull his head out of his art long enough to read a newspaper. Germany had occupied Czechoslovakia in the spring, and Britain had begun their conscription. Of course he had known all of this. But the summer light in his studio in the old church was perfect—strong and clean. He'd been in the middle of a large painting. A forest scene. *A Moment of Calm*, he had called it. Perhaps it was the painting itself that wouldn't let him look away. Had he thought it would save them? That the moment of calm would go on so long as he kept painting?

No matter how many times he asks the question, he cannot change the facts. He refused to listen to reason. He and Leonora had made their home, patched the holes in the old stone buildings, made wine of the grapes, and it was too beautiful to leave. How—he still does not know—can anyone willingly leave their idyllic life? It was the closest he'd come to perfection. And then August turned to September, and within the space of a week the Nazis took Poland, Britain and France were at war with Germany, and he was an enemy alien.

He sucks the rain from his dirty shirt, but his mouth is dust, his thirst pure and terrible. The night is interminable. And yet, when it's his turn to sit, he closes his eyes and the patterns behind his lids, the pulsing prisms, become a forest he's inside, primeval, with giant succulents and ferns. Walking the geometry of shadow, hearing the growls of the half-hidden animals, the groaning rage of the plants,

he realizes he is inside his own painting—the moment of calm riddled with anxiety. He can hear the animals and the plants inch closer.
And he holds very still, because he is surrounded. He knows they are
watching him, these animal omens, these manifestations of his fear.

Of course he was afraid. Of course. And now he's tired. So very
tired.

Behind his eyelids, the patterns shift and change color, becoming
the sunlight through the leaves of the maple that first afternoon with
Leonora in the English countryside, their picnic of strawberries and
scones and wine. He's alone with the girl he's waited his whole life to
meet. She's too beautiful to look at without gawking, so he watches a
breeze stir the leaves above him, the light cadmium yellow, viridian,
and all the hues between. She's telling him a story, and the sound of
her voice, the easy rhythm of her words is a river's constant, silver
song, at once young and ancient.

Before the first great war, there was a boy, she says, and he realizes
the tale she's telling isn't her own, this time, but his. Watching the
shifting gems of light, he listens, remembering *the boy who lived in a
house so close to the forest he could hear the trees mumble to the wind as
he lay in bed before sleep, and in the day he would sometimes wander from
the house into the shade of the trees to play hide and seek with the squirrels
while the birds called to each other from the treetops, and he knew their
song meant "hello" and "I love you" and "yes."*

*One Wednesday in autumn his mother washed him in the basin in the
kitchen and she planned to wash his hair the way she did every Wednesday, but when she bent down to reach for the soap, he slipped her grasp
and ran dripping out the door and into the forest, where he buried himself
in leaves. Though he heard her call, he did not answer. She sent his three
brothers and his three sisters to look for him, but they didn't think to look
under the leaves, and when it was time for lunch, they went back to the
house because they could smell chicken roasting and they were hungry.*

The boy brushed off the leaves and followed a path he hadn't seen before, having never been this deep in the forest. He could no longer see his house, only trees on all sides. The path was soft with crushed leaves, a brown and orange and yellow carpet winding through the trunks of the giants who protected him and the birds who called down to him, "where? where?"

"I don't know," he told them. "I am following this path because it leads away from home where I am told what I must do, where I must sit with my mouth closed and listen, where I must wash my hair because it is Wednesday." And he wondered how it felt to be a bird, to be free, but when he asked them they only said "yes, yes." As he walked he imagined his arms turning to wings, he imagined wind beneath a full sweep of feathers, his feet lifting from the ground. He climbed to the very top of a boulder and stood on its edge. He shut his eyes, held out his arms, and when he could no longer feel his feet and was sure they had risen off the rock, he looked.

People had gathered in front of him. One man held in his hand a cross as big as the boy. They were kneeling before him, their palms pressed together, whispering. "It is him? Could it be?"

"Yes," said a woman, "the baby Jesus!" And she climbed to where he stood, carried him down, and wrapped him in her white scarf.

The people processed along the path into town, and the boy with his blond curls and blue eyes was the baby Jesus swaddled and held up by two men in long white robes. The boy laughed at their mistake, but he liked being on his high perch, so he stayed very still as the townspeople gazed up at him, pointing. With his brothers and sisters always beside him, he was never unique, never apart, and now as he held one hand up, blessing the people who stood below him, he knew he would never be one of many again, or if he were, he would only be pretending.

But when they arrived at the church and the men set him down, he snuck away when no one was looking and ran. Jesus was nailed to a cross, and it was fine to be worshipped, but he didn't want to die just yet. In town a policeman scooped him onto his horse and took him home to his mother, with her red, wet eyes and cheeks, to his father, his face pinched and stern. When his father raised his hand to strike him, to punish him for run-

ning off, the boy cried, "But I am the baby Jesus!" And rather than beating him as he had planned to, his father set him on a wooden chair so big it seemed to the boy like a throne and he placed a cross in the boy's hand and painted him as the baby Jesus. As his father worked, looking from him to the canvas, back and again, the boy had the feeling he was being seen by his father for the first time, and he knew that kind of looking meant "hello" and "I love you" and "yes."

Leonora, June 1937, London, England

In the airy dining room of the Savoy, Ursula sipped her tea. Sunlight haloed her loose bun. Her friend Catherine had joined them. Wearing a blouse with rolled-up sleeves and trousers, she had the self-contained confidence of a woman who has lived for a time on her own. She was visiting from Paris, which, she said, was heaven for an artist, a place women could live as they liked. Her angles and eyes sharp, her smile easy, she smoked a cigarillo, as if she were one of the women from Leonora's drawings come to life.

Ursula bit into one of the tiny cucumber sandwiches. "I told her all about Max," she said to Leonora. "I hope you don't mind."

Leonora added cream to her steaming tea, stirred in her usual lump of sugar. "Why should I mind?"

Catherine snapped her jaw, blowing perfect smoke rings over their heads. "Max has a reputation, always more than one girl at a time. Be careful, that's all."

Leonora shrugged. She wasn't going to let herself worry. Not yet. And where *was* Max, anyway? He and Roland were an hour late.

Just then, Roland came hurrying toward them. Sweating, he took off his derby hat. "Plans have changed."

Leonora could feel her heart throb in her fingertips, in her toes. "What happened?"

"Come with me. Max is in the car. I'll explain as we drive."

Roland opened the back door to the Bentley and there was Max, smiling as though nothing at all were wrong. She ducked in beside him and he took her hand and kissed it. As Roland slid into the passenger seat, his driver pulled away from the curb. Roland turned to her. "Your father—" The word cut through her and she felt herself harden against her fear. Her father had wasted no time. He'd done something devious, something terrible. "His government contacts," said Roland. Max sat up straighter at that word, *government*. His hand shook as he lit a cigarette. "They're saying Max's work is the product of an immoral mind. Bad influence on the good people of London."

"It's insane." Max chuckled, but she could hear the catch in his throat, as if a tiny spider had fallen inside it.

"The police came by the gallery, looking for Max. They closed his show. If they catch him, they'll throw him in jail. He has to leave London."

"*Mon dieu.*" Max scooped her onto his lap. "I'm going to miss you."

"I know!" Roland sang. "You'll come to my brother's house, in Lambe Creek! Both of you! Lee is there already, and Man Ray and his gal Ady, Nusch and Paul are due any day, and Eileen Agar and Joseph Bard. The more the merrier! Everyone is staying for two weeks. There are woods and a tidal creek. It'll be absolutely pagan. We'll leave this afternoon."

Max buried his face in her hair, nuzzling. "What do you think?"

Two weeks with Max and the Surrealists? The thought delighted and terrified her. If word of this reached Father, who knew what he would do? But what option had he left her? She thought of the wreck she'd been the night before, hardly able to be alone after she and Max had spent just a week together, and she wondered, if they were together for two, how she'd manage to live without him. But here he was, holding her tightly. Wide with asking, his eyes were the blue of a butterfly's wing. Two weeks with Max.

"Well," she said. "Why not?"

—❧—

Leonora had never cared what women thought of her, not the girls in the finishing schools or in the debutante scene. But the women at Lambe Creek were different. Lee had an air of independence she longed to emulate. Paul Éluard's new wife, Nusch, and Man Ray's girlfriend, Ady, a dark-skinned Caribbean dancer, were so beautiful and exotic she felt like the ordinary one. When they watched her, she faltered, suddenly shy and nervous. But soon she realized everyone watched everyone, and their stares insisted there was nothing at all to hide. Life was a series of jests, the more absurd the better.

"I'm fine with everything being inside, for orgasms and the rest," Nusch said in French. "What I envy is peeing with your pants on. Can you imagine?"

"Well," said Lee. Speaking English, she turned just her eyes to Leonora. They were far eyes, cool and curious, and she felt her face warm under their scrutiny. "I'm glad you don't have testicles, Leonora, for then I'd have to seduce you."

Stretched on a blanket, they were naked in the afternoon sun, and Leonora's breasts were pink. She rolled onto her stomach, unsure of what to say. For Lee, seduction seemed anything *but* a chore. With her small, high breasts and the tuft of dark blond hair between her legs, she made a perfect Venus. But her elbows were raw, defiant. Lee bit a green grape in half and fed her the rest. Feeling her whole body flush, Leonora ate the grape, which was slightly sour, and became one of them. One of the chosen few.

Nusch was asleep, a branch of grapes still in her hand. She had this wonderful ability to nap wherever and whenever she pleased—perhaps, Leonora thought, from her days as a hypnotist's stooge. She'd come from a circus family, Max had told her. Her father would lock her in chains, and she'd slip from them with such ease she'd dazzle the audience. With her blond curls pulled back, her high, smooth forehead golden from the sun, she reminded Leonora of a child, oblivious and untroubled. She could see why, after Lee, she was the most famous of Man Ray's models.

Lee pulled her oriental robe around her body and cinched the waist. "I have an idea."

Nusch opened her eyes. "Yes?"

Lee told them to dress as if for tea at the Ritz. So they rushed to their rooms, emerging in wool jackets and skirts. Ady joined them in one of Lee's button-down dresses, whose pale yellow was even more striking on her, setting off her tawny skin. Lee brushed their faces with makeup—eye shadow, blush, translucent powder.

She arranged them close together, on canvas chairs in the court-yard, Leonora's arm resting on Nusch's leg, Ady's thin, dark hand touching Nusch's tight curls. Nusch laughed, a trilling, contagious laugh that set them all off. And then Lee slipped into the scene and they settled. Lee and Nusch held saucers, the demitasse cups perched atop them, delicate and proper as they must have appeared.

The camera in his hands, Roland was in awe of Lee, rapture all over him, as though he'd been dunked in red wine.

"Now, everyone, close your eyes," she said. "And sleep."

He was the one to click the shutter, but it was Lee's idea. In the middle of a tea party, mid-sentence, they fell asleep. Through Roland's lens, with their eyes closed, they were the dreamers and the dreamed.

That night they danced under the moon, the air full and easy. *Pa-pum, pa-pum, pa-pum.* Max beat a hand drum and they moved to its rhythm. Like being inside a heart that held them all, like being a tribe. Her hair wide and wild, Leonora pulsed, her hips moving as they hadn't dared to before. She spun and stamped her bare feet on the stone patio, forgetting how she might look to anyone, even to Max, who watched her and grinned. Bottles of champagne lined the patio, and she brought one to her lips, drank the last of it. Nusch's sheer dress caught the moonlight. An emerald scarab beetle clung to her hair and shone. Paul swung her in his arms, this way and that, though she made it all look like it was her idea.

Eileen Agar and her partner Joseph Bard, who had arrived just that evening, found a way to waltz to the beat. She was thin, with a boyish body, and wore a tie with a button-down shirt and trousers. At thirty-eight, she was the oldest of the women, and Leonora thought her re-strained, until she slipped off her tie and shirt and pants to dance only in her bra and panties. In a single move, Paul took her hand, pulling her in as he swung Nusch out, and Joseph, with his dark, wavy hair and his smile, caught Nusch. They were laughing, all of them. Nusch whispered something in Joseph's ear and led him by the hand into the woods.

Leonora had never seen anything like it. Nusch seemed fine with the situation. More than fine. She seemed to fly a little as she led him away. Leonora thought of Max giving *her* to another man for a time, loaning her out to Roland or to Man Ray. Would she do it, because she loved Max and it was what he wanted? Would she want it because he did? She watched Paul and Eileen kiss, and her stomach twisted with some streak of puritanism she must have inherited, she reasoned, from her father's side. She should be more open, she thought, more free, but she felt nauseated.

Man took Max's place at the drum and Max stood and stretched and wrapped her in his arms. He had told her about Paul's penchant for loaning his wife out to the men he most admired, an *homage*, Paul called it. And now, her cheek to Max's bare, salty chest, she hugged him close. Turning the question in her mind, she reversed it. Were she to give Max to Lee as an homage, because of her great respect for the Queen of the Surrealists, and because she wanted Roland for herself, were the women to share their men as though they were black Chanel dresses, one size fits all, exchangeable, how would *they* respond?

She wasn't so sure Paul would take it at all well were Nusch to lend *him* out.

Max pulled her closer, locking his arms around her. He pressed his lips to her forehead, and she relaxed. He wouldn't let her go, at least not anytime soon.

In bed, the night hot and close, they made love with a new abandon. Inside and over her he moved like water, with a fluid weight that claimed every ounce of her, and she forgot the snarl in her stomach. But afterward, under her quieting pulse, it was back. If she were Nusch, what would she do? The sheet was twisted around them, and she pried it loose and kicked it off her. Turning to him, she asked, what did *he* think—of Paul and Eileen, Nusch and Joseph, and the easy trading of partners.

Moonlight fell across his sun-darkened face, a shadow complicating the smooth lines of his lips. He sighed. "Paul and I shared his wife, Gala—Dalí's wife now. For three years, in the twenties, we lived together." He spoke softly, with the calm dreaminess of a memory from the distant past. "It was a light thing, at the beginning. It had felt like play. We'd been collaborating. I was illustrating Paul's poems with collages, and Paul had liked me so much he wanted to share all he had, Gala included. He hadn't expected me to fall in love with her, to leave Lou, my wife, and our two-year-old son, Jimmy, in Germany, and to follow him and Gala to Paris, to live with them, to share their bed indefinitely. Paul was okay with it for years. And then, one day, he wasn't."

Astonished, she lay on her back, staring at the ceiling, an empty, white field. There was so much about him she didn't know. He had left his first wife when their son was just two? How had Lou felt? How had she survived? She could hear her father. What sort of man does that? Walks away from his responsibilities because he wants to be free?

Max took her hand in his, their fingers interlaced. What was past was past. Hadn't he done what he had to? Who was she to judge him? "Paul went on a long boat trip to Saigon," he said. "And Gala and I met him there." For a time, he was silent, sorting details, she supposed, and keeping them to himself. "They returned to Paris," he said at last. "And I followed ten days later. That was the end of it. Gala and Paul were together, and Paul and I stayed friends." His eyes were shining—with love for Gala, still?

"I might have lost him," he said, "and for something so trivial as a woman."

Fever flashed through her. Something so trivial as a woman? Now she really would be sick. She didn't know him, nor did she want to. This had all been a mistake. She'd call Ursula, who would send a car.

She'd pack her suitcase and set out on foot, meet the car on the road. Max could go to hell. She stood up, took a pair of pants from the closet, a blouse, her suitcase. And then he was behind her, pulling her to the bed.

"What did I say? I didn't mean—"

"What?" She was too loud for so late at night, with the others and their easy mixed partnerships simmering in the nearby rooms. His hand was over her mouth, and she bit it, hard, and just as quick regretted what she'd done.

He didn't flinch. He got up from the bed, and she panicked, thinking *he* might leave. If she'd bit anyone else they'd have been done with her. But he lay down on the other side of her, so they were face to face. "I didn't mean women are trivial. I meant—"

"Yes?"

"There are different kinds of love. I love Paul. Gala was fascination. My muse."

And what am I? she wondered, turning from him so he wouldn't see her sweaty face, her tears. He held her tighter, smoothed the hair from her forehead with his cool palm. He talked into her ear, his voice low and even. "I was so swept up in our beautiful experiment in freedom, I couldn't see his pain."

—❦—

It was Sunday, and the bees kept busy, seeing that every hollyhock, every primrose was kissed. Barefoot, she walked the dirt path to the creek. For days since she'd come here, she kept expecting her father or one of his men to show up at the door with the police, to haul Max to jail and her back home, but it had been a week and nothing had happened. She knew her father would certainly withdraw his financial support. And he'd never agree to her staying in London, not after this, but where would she go, and how? Max hadn't said a word about what might happen after they left Lambe Creek, but for now, this was enough. More than enough.

She could hear the creek before she reached it. Lifting her skirt, she walked right in—the water cold and clear, the sun shining through to its sandy bottom. Birds called, darting from tree to tree, and the creek sang. She watched tiny dark fish swim past her calves. Her toes spread wide in the mud, she imagined she was a tree, the way she had when she was a girl in the woods outside their home and she'd felt her roots spread through the earth, felt her arms, her hands and head reach to the sky like branches. Her face lifted to the sun, she was still that girl, she realized happily, only now she wouldn't have to come in from the woods, not if she didn't want to. She would find a way to stay free. Maybe she'd go to Paris even if Max didn't ask her to. Though it would be better, much better, if he did.

On the way back to the house she ate blackberries for breakfast, and when a branch clawed her wrist, two tiny rivulets of blood ran down her arm. Her hands were overflowing with berries, the dark juice merging with her blood. She licked it—sweet and salt, iron and the sour tears of fruit taken from the vine. She wanted to taste it all.

Later that morning Lee and Eileen were in the kitchen, making a chicken salad for lunch. Talking over each other, they collapsed with laughter. "But Paul?" Lee caught her breath, looking out the window to where he and Joseph were playing chess on the patio. "He's really nothing to look at compared to Joe."

"Oh, but have you seen, I mean really *seen*, his hands. The long, thin fingers. Hands of a poet. Quite nimble, I'll tell you."

Leonora lingered, wanting to join them but not sure of just how. The door to the darkroom being open, she slipped inside. It was a pantry, but now there were tubs of chemicals beside the cans of beans, the jars of peaches. In the acrid air, photos hung from a string. There was the tea of sleeping women, and, beside it, one Man must have taken. Ady and Nusch, naked, their nipples and lips almost touching. She'd never seen anything so beautiful, so charged.

At convent school the girls had shut their eyes and practiced kissing, but their kisses were clumsy, ending in laughter. They were nothing like this.

And here was a photo Lee had taken of her and Max, kissing. She looked closer, to see who it was she'd become. Dripping from the creek, she was topless. He had seaweed wrapped around him, making him creaturely, mythic. If Father ever saw this photo, he'd choke on his own tongue. His daughter with her breasts out for all to see, cavorting with amoral artists—the thought made her giddy.

A wave of laughter came from the kitchen, and she popped her head out to see. Roland stood behind Lee, his arms around her, a breast in each hand. She turned to him, kissed him. "Here." She handed him a blanket. "Make a picnic for us."

He spread the blanket in the grassy shade of an alder, and Leonora helped him arrange a low table on top of it. They set it with a lace cloth and china. He poured champagne and she dropped blackberries into each glass. Soon they were all at the table, eating grapes and cheese and chicken salad, clinking their flutes of the pink sparkling wine.

"I always think I won't drink," Lee said. "And then afternoon comes."

Roland stood, his camera in his hand. He studied the group. "I must say, the scene could use a bit more of something."

"Or less?" Lee suggested, unbuttoning her blouse.

Sitting beside Leonora, Max spoke into her ear. "You know she invented it." Leonora looked at him, not sure what he meant. "Tossing the top, donning the bust."

"I refuse to be the only one," Lee said, but Ady and Nusch were already pulling off their shirts. Man and Paul sparkled to see their girls topless, and Leonora wished she'd beat them to it. But why? What were these women Surrealists? The entertainment? And then Whitman came to mind, a line or two from *Leaves of Grass*, which Lee had loaned her. And as she drank the champagne, her head swimming with his words, she found she was reciting.

"I will go to the bank by the wood, and become undisguised and
     naked;
I am mad for it to be in contact with me.
The smoke of my own breath;
Echoes, ripples, buzz'd whispers, love-root, silk-thread, crotch and
     vine."

Man and Lee, Eileen and Roland applauded. She wasn't sure Max understood the English, but he grinned, surprised by her pluck, she thought.

"Better not quote him around Breton, unless you want to start a quarrel," Paul said, finishing his champagne. Nusch filled his glass, and Joseph's, too.

Leonora had a hard time not looking at her breasts, two scoops of ice cream with cherries on top, and she found herself wondering how they might feel against hers. "But why?" she asked.

"Whitman was homosexual," Man said. "And Breton has taken a stand."

"He doesn't think Surrealism will gain the respect it deserves unless it's flawless." Max opened another bottle of champagne and the cork landed somewhere in the alder, sending a few sparrows flying.

Eileen lit her cigarette. "And homosexuality is a flaw?"

"Unless it's two women." Nusch sent Ady an impish smile.

"I'm not saying I agree," said Max.

"Mr. André Breton could use a bit of buggery, if you ask me," said Lee, standing, brushing off her pants. "Loosen him up a bit."

Roland held out his hand and Lee helped him up. "Nap time," he said.

"My favorite exercise," said Lee.

"Your only exercise," Man corrected, but Lee and Roland were tripping up the lawn toward the house and didn't hear him. "Poor Aziz," he muttered, "poor fool."

Lee didn't speak of her husband, who'd agreed on her going to

Paris and London when she'd grown bored in Egypt. But she was still married. She was Mrs. Aziz Eloui Bey, and she wore his giant diamond on her finger.

Eileen put her cigarette in Paul's lips and stood. She opened Edward Lear's poems, a book he had given her, and read.

> *"There was an Old Man with a beard,*
> *Who said, 'It is just as I feared!—*
> *Two Owls and a Hen, four larks and a Wren,*
> *Have all built their nests in my beard.' "*

She spoke with heightened articulation, gesturing a long beard with her hand. Everyone applauded, and Leonora's cheeks burned. Lear, whose poems she'd grown up with, was a better choice by far than Whitman. So perfect for the occasion—innocuous, delightful as an acrobat. Not that this was a competition, she reminded herself.

"I have an idea," said Paul. "Let's switch names. I'll be Paul Bard. Good name for a poet, don't you think? Nusch, you can be Nusch Bard. Ady, you'll be Ady Agar, rather nice alliteration. And Man?"

"Man Éluard."

"I'll be Eileen Fidelin," Eileen said. Taking Ady's last name, she held her hand and kissed it with the enthusiasm of a silent film actor.

"Joseph Penrose," said Joseph. "Roland won't mind."

"And if anyone forgets their names, they'll be fined five francs!" Paul said, not so much as glancing at Max and Leonora. All the couples with their mix-and-match names wandered toward the house, arm in arm with one another's partner. And she imagined their napping all six together—arms and legs, fingers, even lips anonymous.

They lay on the grass. Her head on Max's outstretched arm, she watched a cloud turn from a whale to a rooster. Max had a blade of grass between his teeth. She didn't want to break the easy silence, but she had to ask. "Did you mean what you said about André?"

He nodded. "You can't talk him out of it."

"So, you and Paul, then, you never . . . ?"

He twirled her hair around his finger. "Would it matter to you much if we did?"

"It wouldn't matter at all," she said, truthfully. "But how did André take it?"

"I can't say he liked it," Max said. "But what could he really say? For him to pry would have meant some sort of condemnation. And Surrealism was just starting out, it was all about breaking rules, living as no one had dared to live. This political nonsense, censorship for acceptance in the political scene—it doesn't have any place in pure art."

Roland rang the bell that summoned them all to dinner, and to any other event he deemed important. "Come on, everyone," he yelled. "Lee is taking a bath!"

They took their time walking to the house. They were learning each other. She was seeing how far she could probe, which doors would open if she twisted the knob and pushed, and which would always be locked away in his storehouse of secrets.

In the crowded bathroom, Lee leaned against the back of the tub, the bubbles rising to her breasts. Nusch stripped off her flimsy dress and joined her. Ady followed. Leonora watched from the corner as Paul and Man dropped their trousers and stepped in, wedging themselves between the women. Roland took photos as the water sloshed onto the floor and they laughed, smearing suds onto one another's face and hair. Then they left for the creek to rinse themselves.

Max took her hand. He gave her that close-lipped smile she already knew so well and led her to their bedroom. They fell into bed, and she had the feeling he was making her as he touched her. Before she'd been air, a light, dry wind. But with his fingers moving over and inside of her, she was earth, and the roots in the earth were her roots, and the rain they drank was inside her, too. It had been there, somehow, all along. And she burst into leaves, into flowers, into tiny stars, burning.

She was crying. On his side he faced her. "Come to Paris," he said, brushing her hair from her damp cheek. And she kissed him again and again.

———✦———

Their last morning at Lambe Creek, they woke to a photo in the *Daily Telegraph*, someone having slipped the paper under their bedroom door. "HITLER DECLARES MODERN ART DEGENERATE," the headline read. And there stood the Führer himself at the exhibition the Nazis had created. *Entartete Kunst*. Degenerate Art. Hitler with his armband and his mustache had his arms crossed against the offending work. Max squinted at the image, his face white. "*Mon dieu. That's mine. The Beautiful Gardener.*"

In the photo his painting was no bigger than a postage stamp, but she did her best to decipher it. A woman stood in a rather typical pose, with one hand behind her head. Looking closer, she saw that the woman wasn't typical at all. A dove perched on her thigh made for a sort of codpiece, and half her face appeared to be skeletal. There was a figure sketched in behind her, too, a dancing jester. She could hardly make him out in the photo, and she wished she could see the painting itself. She was sure it was marvelous.

"Works by Picasso, Chagall, Kandinsky, Klee, Ernst, and Kollwitz," the article said. The paintings crowded into rooms with such labels as "An insult to German womanhood and Revelation of the Jewish racial soul." It reminded her of her father's view of artists, that they're poor, homosexual criminals. The thought of her father judging works of art petrified her. "Thank God you left."

"Yes. With Paul's passport," he said quietly. "That's how I got into France. I'm still a German citizen. A degenerate one, apparently. Enemy of the state."

They brought the paper downstairs to the breakfast table. While Lee laughed at Hitler's combed-over hair, and at the other paunchy, serious Nazi so disgusted by Max's painting, Leonora read an excerpt from Hitler's speech. "Works of art which cannot be comprehended and are validated only through bombastic instructions for use from now on will no longer be foisted upon the German people." It seemed a direct reference to Dadaism and Surrealism. Why weren't they all more frightened? The tea in her cup shook as she sipped it. "But why does he hate artists?"

Max took her hand in his, steadying it. "He's a failed artist himself. He tried to get into the Vienna Academy of Fine Arts and wasn't accepted."

"Damn school should've let him in," said Man.

"I say it's an opportunity." Roland crossed his legs, stirred sugar into his tea. "We'll have a show at the Mayor of the very artists Hitler is denouncing. After this business with Max blows over, that is. Who knows, all of Cork Street might join in. Peggy Guggenheim phoned me up this morning. She wants me to look for an opening, an empty gallery space on the row."

Lee arched her brow. "An opening, huh?"

Roland chuckled. "She's a compatriot, darling. A degenerate along with the rest of us. She wants to champion modern art. Apparently Duchamp has been coaching her on the subject. We should welcome her with open arms."

"Should we?" Ice rattled as Lee tipped a glass of whiskey to her lips. "She sat for me once in the studio. We're very much alike, the two of us. We go after what we want," she said, studying Roland.

Roland leaned over, resting his head on her shoulder. He kissed her cheek with a kind of glee, as if thrilled *she'd* be jealous of *him*. Lee poured herself more whiskey. It smelled good, right for this morning. Leonora reached for the bottle. Soon they'd all spiked their tea and coffee. But a distinct heaviness had settled over the party, as if the air itself were oppressive. Hitler was here, in the kitchen, the newspaper with the dreadful photo covering the table.

Paul picked up the paper and crushed it to a fist-sized ball. "Let's have a bonfire! For the eclipse! It'll do us good to see the bastard go up in flames."

That night, as the bonfire surged with twigs and branches and the *Daily Telegraph*, flames rising toward the moon that would soon vanish into shadow, they shed their clothes and danced, swapping partners, men dancing with men, women with women. Delicate Nusch lifted Leonora into the air like a circus strongman. Lee locked her bony elbows with hers and they spun. Eileen kissed her on the lips, with just a touch of tongue, and Ady sang to her in French, her voice like syrup.

The fire quieted and they settled beside it. The Earth's bloody shadow was eating the moon, swallowing it slowly as they watched. Max pulled her onto his lap, talking of Paris, how she'd be there before they knew it. And then, too soon, the fire was embers.

She'd have to face her parents. She'd spare them the beautiful details, but give them the truth. She was leaving school and joining Max in Paris. And he would return to his wife, Marie-Berthe. He would return in order to leave her. "I can't promise you anything," he said. "She's a devout Catholic. She might not grant me a divorce."

"It's okay." She leaned her head against his chest. "I have no intention of marrying you. We'll be lovers, artists. Shouldn't that be enough?"

He squeezed her so tight she could hardly breathe. "We'll see."

The slim sickle of light gone, the sky was starry. The moon hung red and round, and she shivered. She knew how cold it felt, with the fat Earth blocking the sun's light.

⟿

She gathered her things. All that mattered—her good clothes and her art supplies—fit into a few bags. She gave notice on her flat and told Ozenfant she was leaving.

"Paris?" he said, removing his glasses and wiping the thick, round lenses with a handkerchief. They stood outside his academy, a converted stable in West Kensington, in the muggy, afternoon air. A drop of sweat skated down her back. She hadn't thought that saying goodbye to him would be hard, but she'd been his first student, and while she didn't much care for his Purist movement in art, he was a kind man, a fine teacher, and something of a grandfather to her. She realized she wanted his blessing. "Paris is wonderful, *ma chérie*." His brown eyes were soft. "But who will you study with?"

Max Ernst, she thought. But knowing he wouldn't approve of Surrealism or of Max, she told him she'd study with no one. He would be her only teacher.

"You are ready?" Though his question was a good one, she couldn't let herself consider it. It had no bearing on her situation. Either she left now or she never would. She kissed his cheek. He smiled at her, sadly, she thought, and placed his rough palms on her face. "We will miss you, Miss Carrington."

She took one last look at Ozenfant and the stable where she had learned to draw the perfect apple, and she turned and started toward the road.

"Don't you want your work?" he called after her.

She spun around, grinning at him. "Keep it. Something to remember me by!"

Her wild heartbeat told her she was free, but before she could leave for Paris, there were things she needed from home. And there was the business of saying goodbye.

She asked her mother when her father would be away on business. As it happened he'd be out of town at the start of September. Imperial Chemicals—the company he was quickly turning into a kind of empire—had extended its talons to the mainland, and he wanted to see for himself how the office in Madrid was getting along. Leonora told her mother she'd been homesick, and she planned her trip so that her stay at the house and her father's presence would only just coincide. She hadn't heard a thing from him since Lambe Creek, and while she dreaded their inevitable confrontation, his silence meant he was busy with other matters, and so long as she acted with speed and resolve, their conflict would, she hoped, be brief.

—✣—

As her train pulled into Lancashire and the blur of green slowed, she saw a mare and a foal on a far field, grazing, and she thought of her own horse, Winkie, whom she couldn't wait to ride. She had been a gift from her father, a birthday present, the year before he'd sent her off to school. It had been an afternoon like this one, cool and bright, when he'd blindfolded Leonora and led her out of the house and onto the lawn. When he took the blindfold off, there stood Winkie, so young and shiny—her own gorgeous, brown mare. She had thrown her arms around her father. In that moment, she had loved him completely.

She spotted Henry on the platform, lanky and a little crooked, in his dark suit and his cap. He'd been their driver for years, and when she stepped off the train he grinned. It seemed he hadn't heard a thing about the Max scandal, or else he didn't care. "We've missed you, dear." He picked up her bags. "Something about you is different," he said, looking her over. "I believe you've grown up."

—✣—

September was ripe and green, her favorite time in the country. She rode Winkie every chance she got, mornings and afternoons, out from their house on the hill into the fields overlooking Morecambe Bay. She rode alone, her mother too busy with the charities and their functions to ride with her.

Stopping to let Winkie graze, she watched the shadows of clouds drift over the glittering water. She would miss this bay, these fields. But mostly, she'd miss Winkie. In a day she'd be gone. She gave her reins the slightest tug, squeezed her ribs with her heels, and they were off, racing through fields under the blue sky. Winkie wasn't so young anymore, but she ran as if she knew it was now or never, as if her heart had the sun in it, and only by flying through these meadows could she let it shine.

Too soon the clouds thickened, low and dark, turning the green to gray. She turned back. Moving through the colorless landscape of erasure, she felt like a ghost. Though she'd ridden this path a hundred times, she no longer belonged to it. It was an odd feeling, being partly here, as if most of her were already in Paris, and just her body was left behind.

She missed Max in a visceral way. It had been a month since she'd seen him, and though they'd spoken on the phone a few, brief times, her body had forgotten him—his smell, the taste of his kisses and his skin. But the feel of his weight on top of her, this she remembered. She longed for him to pin her to the ground. Without him she was hollow, a shell of a girl, a balloon filled with helium, waiting for him to take hold of her string, to tug her back to earth. Since she'd been home, her mother hadn't so much as mentioned him, as if by not speaking about it she could pretend the affair hadn't happened. And Leonora certainly wouldn't bring it up in front of her father, who'd just arrived home and would be dining with them that evening.

─ஃ─

At dinner they spoke of the British destroyer attacked by the Italian submarine, of Imperial Chemicals, and how it would benefit from a war. Of course, Father wouldn't want the war to continue for *too* long. Already there was talk of conscription, but there were Father's government contacts and his money—which meant her brothers would be spared.

"I *want* to fight for England," Gerald said, leveling his fork at him. A little younger than her, he was the brother she liked best. He was at college, but had come home for the weekend because she was visiting. "Really, Father. I'm strong and healthy, why shouldn't I fight?" He looked so earnest, his thick eyebrows raised, his green eyes dancing. He took a bite of carrots, sent a wink and a smile her way, and they were playmates again, sneaking from the nursery to the woods to mix their potions and chant their spells. How she wished they could go there now so she could tell him of her plans, so he could know this was goodbye.

Mother changed the topic to Christmas, although it was months away. Which stuffing went best with Cornish hen, the sort with chestnuts or the sort without?

Gerald caught Leonora's eye and she grinned. Their mother was always worrying about these kinds of things. It had been in the midst of a topic much like this one, a few years ago, when Leonora had announced her intention to go to art school, to become an artist. Mother had gone quiet and plucked a hair from that spot over her ear. Father had pounded the table. "Nonsense," he'd said, his face red as a tulip. He'd sighed then, as if her very existence exhausted him, and proposed his alternative. Always a bargain to be struck. She could stay here and paint in the house. Of course she'd need a real profession. He wouldn't have her living off his hard work, squandering her time on something so idiotic as painting. *Why not breed fox terriers?* he declared, as if it were bloody eureka.

She had gotten her way in the end. But his words still rang, too loud, too clear. At least now, she thought, she wouldn't be living off his *hard work*. She'd be free to work hard herself. But watching Father at the head of the table, she almost felt sorry for him. He should have had a daughter who was happy to marry well, happy in her luxurious subservience, happy to behave as a woman ought.

~&

The moon, full and high, held her room in a pale blaze. Her suitcases huddled in the corner resembled sheep, but they didn't help her sleep. She looked at everything as if to memorize it. Her books on the shelves—*Black Beauty, Don Quixote, Gulliver's Travels, Alice's Adventures in Wonderland*—their gold lettering faded on their worn spines. So many days she'd disappeared into the brilliant lands of their pages. And what was so different now? Wasn't she stepping into the book of the life she was meant to live, becoming Leonora Carrington, the artist? Only she couldn't close this book and go back to her old life. Tomorrow she'd take a boat, then a train to Paris, and her course would be set.

Above the books, her porcelain horses shone in the moonlight. Always in her imagined scenarios the horses were trying to escape, to leave the stable and find the wilderness that meant freedom. What, exactly, did they think they would find there? She'd never gotten that far. The leaving itself had been the thing.

On the top shelf were the photographs, evidence of the life she'd made a flimsy attempt to belong to. She'd gone through the season, fulfilled her promise to Father, and here was the proof, the parade of parties, kicked off with her debutante ball. Here was her face, her anesthetized smile. There had been the smell of lilies, a room stifled by it, where a woman, cursing in Scottish and drinking whiskey, had combed all the wildness from her hair. When she reached her scalp, a black bird had flapped about the room. Had he come through the window or out of her nest of hair? She wasn't sure. But he had perched on the curtain rod and watched the woman tuck her waves into a bun and dress her in a gown of white silk. Or was that something she had dreamed? The woman tugging at her scalp, and that bird? In the photo she was a grown doll, a statue, holding Father's elbow at the top of the staircase. Below them the dance floor had teemed with men. In tuxedos they'd resembled penguins. How she'd wished it had been a ball of penguins!

She touched the photos of this other Leonora. The Royal Garden Party—tea in a great, white tent at Buckingham Palace. Ascot, the races. Her presentation to the court of George V. She picked up the frame and brought it close. It was a photo of her and her mother, their Cecil Beaton satin gowns melting over their hips, cooling in folds at their feet. They stood side by side, and looked, she thought now, like reluctant actors in a play written by someone long before they were born. But her mother hadn't been reluctant, she had wanted this for her. And yet there was a distance to her gaze, as if she were peering into some blurry future. It was resignation, Leonora saw now. She had already known her daughter would vanish from their lives.

She took the photo from the frame. She had no idea when, after tomorrow, she'd see her mother again. She took one of Winkie, too, her twelve-year-old self on her back, sitting tall, reins in hand. She'd need a book to read on the train, so she slid *Alice* into her satchel, and tucked the photos inside.

~⸹

The next morning she sat at the long table, a full English breakfast before her. Poached eggs, ham and an English muffin, stewed tomatoes and beans, and a cup of tea. It was her last English breakfast, and she wouldn't leave hungry, no matter her nerves. Gerald having returned to school, she was alone with her parents. Her father had finished eating, but he liked to sit in the late morning sun, reading the paper and smoking his pipe. Her mother read the paper and drank her tea.

Neither of them said a thing about her affair. Was Father willing to forgive it? To let her stay in London and make art? Since he'd been home, he hadn't really looked at her, which made her think he hadn't decided what he would do with her. No matter, she thought, taking a bite of the egg. She soaked up the yolk with her muffin. From now on she would be the one to decide.

Her mother smiled at something she was reading. Father tamped his pipe. Leonora nibbled her ham. It tasted sad, as if it had been cured in tears. She hadn't imagined it would be this hard. But thinking of her life here, or in London—if he allowed her to stay—making art that was safe, art that reinforced the establishment, thinking of how he would insist she marry soon, she knew she had no choice.

She couldn't eat another bite. She should tell them, get the words that were choking her out into the air. But she wasn't ready to stop looking. The way the smoke from her father's pipe swirled in the sunlight. How his face was shadowed with the stubble of his dark beard, since he never shaved on Sundays. How pretty Mother was, in her pale blue silk robe and her bare feet.

Leonora pushed back her plate and stood, waiting for them to look up. "I have something to tell you." Mother's face was suddenly paler, even, than usual. She knew something horrid was coming. Somehow she always did. They put down their papers.

Father bit his cheek. Mother plucked a hair. The ground felt as if it might fly away. She gripped the table. "I am leaving. I'm going to Paris where I will be an artist and live with Max Ernst. We are in love."

They stared, their mouths ajar, like the mouths of dead carp.

"But he's, he's married," Mother stammered.

"He is leaving his wife," Leonora said, with all the confidence she could summon.

Father pounded the table with his fist and stood. "You do this and you'll not get a pence. Not a pence."

Mother rushed to her, her robe fluttering. "Darling, you haven't thought this through. You're throwing away your life for a man who's been married twice, a man old enough to be your father. And if he doesn't leave his wife? What then?"

"My life is in Paris," Leonora said, loud enough for Father to hear. "I'm going for me, not for him. I don't plan on marrying—him or anyone. I have my ticket. I leave today."

Father huffed. "It seems you have decided," he said. His face assumed a mask of utter indifference, but as he pointed at her, his thick finger trembled. "May your shadow never darken my door again," he said, measuring each word. "You will die penniless, in a garret." He left the dining room. The door swung in the air behind him.

Mother wrapped her arms around her, and she hugged her mother as she never had before, feeling the bones inside her. "I have something for you," Mother said. "I've put money aside."

In Leonora's bedroom she pushed a change purse stuffed with rolled bills into her hand. "You can rent a flat with this."

Leonora nodded, not sure how to say goodbye. She carried her bags to the front door herself, and though the car was waiting, she dashed to the stable to see Winkie one last time. She threw her arms around her neck, wept into her mane. She kissed the white star on her forehead, and her soft nose.

She walked away without looking back. Her youth was gone. It was over forever. She'd never see her horse again. She'd never gallop these paths in the spring, when the hills were glossy green, the world rinsed with rain.

Mother and Nanny watched the car pull away and she waved to them like a movie actress, though with real tears in her eyes. Father, however, had had his last word. He would not stand there like another father might have, and not know what to do with his hands.

⟶❧

As other passengers slept, she stood on the deck of the ferry, her wool coat buttoned to her neck, her arms crossed against the cold. The wind numbed her cheeks. It felt real—bracing and head-on—like the future she was moving toward. She'd reach the dock by morning, and from there she'd catch a train to Paris.

She knew a little of what to expect, having lived in Paris when she was sixteen, when Father had sent her to the final finishing school. It had been similar to the school in Florence, only without horseback riding, which made it a cloistered affair. There, she had combed her hair with a fork, and eaten lamb with her hands; drawing a greasy finger across her cheek, she had marked herself with war paint. They exiled her to her room, then told her to pack.

She was going "someplace tough" her father had told her over the phone, and a taxi dropped her at Miss Sampson's. The woman was a spider, with skeleton limbs and buggy eyes. Every night she locked Leonora in a room over a church graveyard, a tiny, stone room like a prison cell, and one night she made a break for it through the window. A girl at the school had given her the address of a couple she was sure would take her in—the Simons.

She fell in love with them straight off, and they asked her to stay—she never knew just why, but she had been thrilled, and called Father and struck a deal. She'd play the good daughter and be presented at court if she could stay with the Simons until that time. "Fine," he'd said. At least she was someone else's nuisance.

By day, she'd sit on the rooftop reading Baudelaire, Zola, Proust. Or she'd sit at a sidewalk cafe and sketch people, writing stories of their lives. A woman with a hook nose became an alligator wrangler; a plump fellow, master of a traveling circus. She'd never felt so alive. She was sixteen and allowed to go where she liked.

Still, she always came home for supper. Mme. Simon was a remarkable cook, her soufflés airy, her sauces smooth and rich, and M. Simon was a professor of beaux arts. Over an after-dinner cognac, he'd look at her drawings and comment on the elements that struck him, the outlandish details. He said they reminded him of Arcimboldo's portraits of people whose faces were made of fruit and flora. And he took her to the Louvre to see them for herself. A pear nose, a peach cheek, skin of bark, hair of ivy and roots. They'd dilated her perception of what was possible in art.

A gust of wind whirled around her. She tightened her grip on her coat. Now she was returning to the city of freedom, of artists, and this time she wouldn't have to leave. She was done with Father and he was done with her. She'd been fighting him for so long, it felt strange to be on the other side of the conflict, oddly disorienting. Had she won, or only walked away? He might have said he was washing his hands of her, but she knew him—and it wasn't his way to give up. Unless he saw their push and pull of wills as a game of tug-of-war? Letting his end of the rope go, he figured she'd fall on her face in the mud, come groveling back. He had no idea just how stubborn she was. She imagined herself dying in a garret, an anonymous artist, starving and sick. Even *that* would be a triumph.

She looked for the horizon, but couldn't see a clear line. The clouds and the sea were one black mass, the lights of the ferry turning the closer water ice-gray. The sound of the ocean smacking the hull made her drowsy, and her thoughts turned to Max. Soon she'd curl up beside him and sleep. What better way to spend an autumn? She tried to hear his voice, his laugh, but the slap of the water insisted on only itself. It had been a week since she'd called to tell him what train she'd be on. Twice, his wife, Marie-Berthe, had answered. "*Bonjour,*" she'd said, her voice tinkling, and Leonora had been quick to hang up. When she'd talked to Max at last, he'd seemed ecstatic, but what if he'd changed his mind, met someone new, or decided he should stay with his wife? Even as she thought it, she could feel his hands, long and powerful, pulling her toward him, and she knew it wasn't the case. Hadn't he told her he needed her as he needed air, water, food?

—⚶—

When she arrived at the Paris station, Max hugged her off her feet, kissing her whole face, as if to be certain she existed. He took her bags for her, and then they were walking, already part of the city. He'd arranged everything, he said. She was to stay with his friend, the artist Leonor Fini, until she found an apartment of her own.

"My own?"

"Our own," he said, and talked about his work, big canvases he couldn't wait to show her, how marvelous Paris would be now that they were together.

Watching his mouth move, she could think only of hushing it with hers. She wanted him pressed against her in some corner of the station, the world disappearing, as it had in the countryside. How singular and elegant he was, hair radiant against the black of his wool cape, which flapped behind him as he walked. His long legs moved with a slow grace, even as she ran to keep up. Here was the man who would be her companion in this new world, who would stand beside her, a regal, angular guide.

People hurried by—couples, families with children, men walking on their own, bags and briefcases swinging from their arms, hugging and kissing hello and goodbye—hello so much better, she thought, glimpsing the face of a woman lifting her bags, trying not to cry. Suddenly, she saw a line of French soldiers in their tan uniforms and hats filing toward the trains. She felt her spine stiffen, until she looked at Max's eyes, blue and shining. He would keep her safe and close. She didn't need to worry about a thing.

He pushed open the door, and she stepped into the cool evening. He hailed a taxi. They were on their way to Leonor's, he said, and then to a party thrown by the courtier M. Rochas. "But I have nothing to wear!" she insisted, certain her wool trousers wouldn't do.

He laughed. "These things have a way of working themselves out."

⁓ℬ

M. Rochas's flat occupied the entire top floor of an old building off the Rue Balzac. The high, molded ceiling glittered with chandeliers, and the tall windows—glowing with the lights of Paris—were like giant, shiny boxes she couldn't wait to unwrap.

Bright birds from far off islands, the guests posed and strutted and preened. Men wore tuxedos, or suits with flashes of color, shiny ties or handkerchiefs, and the women's gowns shimmered and swept the floor. She looked down at her white sheet and might have headed out the door if Max hadn't wrapped his arm around her, moving her through the crowd and the music. Earlier in the evening, she had been dressed in the makeshift gown by Leonor and her friend, the designer Princess Maria de Gramont. Leonora had felt plain and naked in the sheet, but the princess assured her that she was beautiful and young and didn't need to wear a thing, so Leonora brushed her hair until it shone and strapped on a pair of black patent high heels.

A three-piece band jumped. It was jazz, unlike any she'd heard. The guitarist strummed and plucked, his fingers so quick she found herself staring. On his left hand his pinky and ring finger were bent, fused, and yet, for him, the mangled digits seemed an advantage. "Django Reinhardt," Max said, and he swung her to the swirling beat.

As the party progressed, names came to life as people she'd only heard of introduced themselves. Dalí with his waxed mustache and his lit eyes fell to one knee and covered her hand in kisses. Gala, his queen (and, Leonora was acutely aware, part of Max's old *ménage à trois*), smiled down at him, stroking his head like a dog's. She'd imagined her as a great beauty to have held Max's love for so long, but she seemed ordinary, her dark eyes deep-set and so close together she appeared almost cross-eyed. They were visiting from Spain, and Gala said she missed the ocean, the light. "You'll see. One can only take Paris for so long. It's a small town, *n'est-ce pas*?" She sipped champagne and smiled, her eyes staying on Leonora's too long. Did she see her as a threat? Did she imagine she still held some claim on Max? Leonora took a long sip of her own champagne.

"Leonora!" Paul appeared, embracing her so tightly she felt her body tense. "You're here!" He held a bottle of champagne in his hand and filled her glass. He gave Dalí's back a few pats, and then he kissed Gala on the lips—his hand, she couldn't help but notice, squeezing her breast. Gala was Dalí's wife now, but she didn't seem annoyed in the least. In fact, with Paul and Max and Dalí gazing at her, she glowed. This was exactly what she wanted. Her black dress had a fuchsia flower on the shoulder and she pulled it down her arm, exposing a sturdy collarbone.

Nusch turned to Leonora. She was dressed as a jester, striped tights under high frills. "You've not met Marie-Berthe yet?"

"She's here?" Leonora felt a tremor move through her, a fissure of fear, opening. She hadn't prepared herself. And she was tight now, what would she say or do?

"*Mon dieu*, no!" Nusch's laugh jingled, along with the bells on her wrists. "She's too pious for parties. But whatever *merde* she slings, be ready to duck."

Leonora felt a fingernail rise up her spine. She turned. It was a woman in a dark red corset and high boots. She wore a mask of white and gray feathers, a mustard-yellow beak over her nose. Her dark eyes glittered sharply. "Don't you recognize me?"

Of course. They'd met all too briefly, but those ignited eyes—she'd know them anywhere. "Leonor!"

"What do you think?" She touched her mask. "I made it." The band struck up a waltz, and she took Leonora into her arms. The music made the party a carnival, sometimes too slow, then fast in the oddest places. She was dizzy with it. In the owl mask, Leonor was her dream twin, wise and otherworldly, and so confident she felt, somehow, ordained as they swayed.

Suddenly, Princess Maria de Gramont took Leonora's place in Leonor's arms, her turquoise turban and gown the color of shallow seas enveloping her. They danced off, leaving her alone. As couples spun past, she looked for Max. The music pulsed and swirled, the beat wild. She moved through the bodies trying to avoid elbows and flailing hands. Someone splashed her with champagne. Max was in a black tuxedo like every other man and now they all looked the same. (If only they could have been penguins!) There wasn't a single person she recognized. She found a wall, let it hold her up. She tried to breathe. She was free, she reminded herself. She was at her first Paris party. Why should she need him beside her?

Because he brought her here, she reasoned. And it was their very first night in Paris together! Where was he? She pushed off the wall and searched. A dancing couple collided with her and didn't pause to apologize, but then no one seemed to see her. The music slowed and the floor cleared. She glimpsed a shock of white hair. There was Max—swaying with Gala, her head on his chest. She felt lightheaded, too warm in the sheet. And with the words of the princess, *you don't need to wear a thing*, ringing in her head, she loosened the sheet from under her arm. We'll see who wants to dance with me now, she thought. She let it fall to the floor.

Max let out a whoop, and once again she was in his arms, the room whirling around them. More than a few people stopped talking and dancing and kissing, and stared. In a moment, a man in a tuxedo, his soft, white glove on her shoulder, ushered her to the door.

Outside, Max gave her his jacket, which fell to her thighs. "My bride of the wind," he said, his eyes still dancing. They laughed all the way to Leonor's.

While they were certain she'd still be at the party, they made love on the kitchen table, the cats rubbing against them, throbbing and thrumming. As he cried out her name (*her name!*) his eyes found hers, and he seemed to fall into her, to tumble, headlong. He was hers. She knew that. Why had she worried?

They bathed in a claw-foot tub, steeped in the steamy water. "Soup of the evening, beautiful soup," she sang as Max soaped her all over. He dried her with a towel, carried her to the sofa, and curled up around her, pulling a blanket over them.

He hears the door to the cattle car unfasten with a click, hears it whine as it slides and cool air hits his face. Max opens his eyes to the gray, bleary dawn. Has he slept? If so, then barely. But the men let him sit for longer than his shift, probably because of his age. He inhales, heaves something between a sigh and a groan. A low growl. At least this accumulation of years is good for something.

The train has slowed. They are approaching a town. "Lourdes," the sign reads. The torturous night has taken them a hundred and fifty kilometers at most, and for what? For all they know, the Nazis might have them surrounded. The train stops and the men spill out. They stretch and breathe the open air and relieve themselves. Slow and stiff, half-dead, they climb back on the train. *How many more days can this go on?* the men mumble, too exhausted to complain very loud or long. They will endure because they must.

And then, in the station, they are met with a miracle. The commandant wired ahead, told them to have provisions ready for two thousand Germans. He did not specify what *sort* of Germans. They are brought food and water and newspapers. It is June 26, the paper says. A cease-fire between France and Germany has been signed.

Fresh bread, hard cheese, and salami make a feast, but water is what saves them. They pass the metal cups from one man to the next, fill and refill them with the gallons of fresh water. He wants to gulp it, they all do, but they can only sip. Too much at once and they'd be sick from it, so they share. They pass the cup and come to life again.

"Look!" A man points to a train as it pulls in. "It isn't possible," says another. The men scramble on top of the car to see. Three platforms over, the train has come to a stop and it is full of women, their women. The men whoop and holler. "Mady!" "Rachel!" "Isa!" The women echo. "Karl!" "Franz!" "Klaus!" Names and voices overlap in a rising tide of elation, and now the men flood toward their train.

Between them are two freight trains guarded by French soldiers, but the men don't care. They're climbing the bumpers of the freight cars, even as the soldiers shout for them to return to their train, even as one levels his rifle but does not shoot. Again and again the soldiers send the men back. The freight train is carrying war supplies and the soldiers have orders to guard it. So wives and husbands shout to each other. They send notes which one of the French soldiers ferries grudgingly from one train to the other. The train came from the camp at Gurs, a sister camp to des Milles. The women were released just as the men were, without mandate or protocol, and now they are here. Nearly all of the men's wives are here. It has been almost a year, but they have found each other.

Since his girl, being English, is not here, he sits on the side rail of the car and reads the paper. It seems an old, Fascist general, Marshal Pétain, took over the French government, told the soldiers to stop fighting, and asked the Germans for an armistice—the terms of which are yet to be determined. Which means his return to Saint-Martin might be possible. It all depends on which areas of France the Germans will occupy, which they'll leave alone, and where their train will be when it's finally decided.

"Max Ernst?" The man's officious tone startles him. His mouth goes dry. It's over. They've found him.

"*Oui?*"

The man hands him a paper airplane. *For Max Ernst*, it says on the wing.

He recognizes the tiny, meticulous scrawl belonging to his first wife, Lou. She's alive! Thank God. He unfolds the airplane. *Have you heard from Jimmy?* Jimmy, their son who begged them to come to America three years ago, their son who had seen the future when they had refused to. Two days ago, he turned twenty, Max realizes, with a pang of the old guilt. He borrows a pencil from the man beside him. *No,* he writes back. *As soon as we are out of this mess, we will write to him. He will help us get to America. For now, you must stay alive—for him! Love, Max*

He gives the note to a soldier who shuttles it to the women's train, where someone has begun to sing. To sing in the midst of this gray, rigid world. He recognizes the tune. It's the aria from *Madame Butterfly.* *"Un Bel Dì."* When Butterfly imagines her husband's return. The song is perfect, and he finds he is crying. But then so are most of the men.

He looks at the train, trying to see inside the windows. Shapes, blurred shapes.

All women are muses of one kind or another, and these women, even from this distance, send him in a whorl of recollection—not of Lou, his first love, but of his dark-haired girl. She is just twenty. She thinks he's sleeping and she gets up, covers him with the blanket. It's their first morning in Paris together, and they've spent the night on Leonor Fini's sofa. This song is playing. *"Un Bel Dì."* And he drifts back to sleep.

Bride of the Wind

She woke on the sofa, cold and groggy from the champagne, to a black cat nuzzling her chin. Their blanket had fallen. On his side, Max seemed far off in a dream. Watching him sleep she could see the child he'd been, a calm recalcitrance pulsing through him. Without his eyes quickening, his face looked older, his skin sheer and pale, a vein at his temple. Pulling the blanket up to his neck, she stood, slid into his jacket, and buttoned it up.

Somewhere a phonograph played Puccini. *One fine day, we shall see a thin trail of smoke over the far sea, and then a ship appears.* She'd listened to this, Farrar and Caruso, as a teenager, and this aria was her favorite. The hope in Butterfly's voice so potent and sad, until her husband brings his American wife when he returns and Butterfly slits her own throat. Now Leonora felt a new emotion stir inside her—the terror that comes with loving someone and knowing he could leave.

She followed the music down the hall and stood in the doorway watching Leonor paint. The flat was hers alone, and it doubled as a studio, this room given entirely to her art. The smell of the oil paints was heady, earthy, a touch sinful. It made Leonora long to paint. Soundlessly, she entered the room. Paintings of women covered the walls— women in armor, holding shields, swords, women in headdresses, naked beneath veils, or just naked, and there was a series of sphinxes, one was two-headed, one pregnant, and one was arching her back, her breasts bare—all of them with dark, curly hair and with faces that resembled Leonor's. Masks hung on the walls, too—the mask of an owl, a lion, a panther. From the window a cold light washed over the canvas where she worked. Outside, rain dripped from the eaves. Leonor squeezed paint onto her palette, mixed it with her brush. The painting, another self-portrait—black and white with brief shocks of color—had a nakedness to it, the eyes so dark and pure. Seated on a stool, Leonor held her brush like a wand as she worked on her hair, on one of the vibrant specks that clung to it—a butterfly. Her own hair was down and she wore a loose, red robe. From the folds that reached to the floor, cats emerged and retreated, weaving in and out, pulses of gray and orange and black.

Leonor glimpsed her in the windowpane. She set her brush down and sipped her coffee. "Want some?"

"Please," she said, and followed her to the kitchen. Leonor's robe trailed behind her, satin, stitched in gold. Touching the glossy fabric, Leonora realized it was the robe of a cardinal. Such sacrilege made her bones tingle. "Where did you find this?" she whispered, as they crept past Max still asleep on the sofa.

Leonor poured her coffee. "There's a shop that will sell them to anyone. You don't have to be Catholic or a man or anything." She spoke French with a Spanish accent—or was it Italian? "I wear it when I want to feel especially naughty. And besides, I think my body makes it happy. The robe gets to live a little." Wondering just what, if anything, she was wearing underneath, Leonora tasted the thick, bitter brew and tried to not make a face. She preferred tea, but did not want to offend by refusing.

Leonor looked her over, as if examining her. "You've not met Marie-Berthe yet?"

She shook her head. Max had hardly even described her, just to say she had once been fun and pretty, but now was religious and tiresome. "You'll meet her soon enough. Let's hope she grants him a divorce. You know she's Catholic. Thinks Surrealism is the devil's work. And did Max tell you? She's an illegitimate descendant of Louis XVI and never stops talking about it!"

She forced herself to down the coffee. She didn't want to think about Marie-Berthe. "I should let you get back to work."

Leonor grabbed her hand. "You don't mind?" She searched Leonora's eyes. What was she talking about? "Us," she explained.

It took Leonora a minute. "Oh." It was a small syllable, yet her mouth was still open.

"I thought you knew, I thought he told you."

Leonor was looking behind her, so she looked, too—at Max, standing shirtless in his crumpled pants, his hair wild, his cheek creased from sleep. "Told her what?"

Leonor took her hands in hers. "We had something, briefly, a long time ago. We've been just friends for years, but I wanted you to know."

She squeezed Leonor's hands. "Thank you."

Leonora walked toward Max. Stopping just out of his reach, she unbuttoned his jacket, let it open, and watched him take in the naked length of her. "Is there any woman in Paris you *haven't* slept with?"

—☙

With her mother's money she rented a flat on Rue Jacob in Montparnasse. From another century, with high ceilings and tall windows and even a tiny balcony, it was a third-floor walk-up, but the rooms had been renovated with indoor plumbing and hot water, a true luxury for Paris. She was certain her father would have seen it as a garret, but to her it was paradise. Her very own place in the city of dreams.

Max helped her fill it with all she would need. They roamed the flea markets of Montparnasse until her new home was furnished with a sofa from the nineteenth century, a sturdy table and chairs, and a simple four-poster bed, which she slept in, most nights, alone. His days were hers, but his nights belonged to his wife. He'd leave soon, he insisted. But he would have to remove his art in a single sweep, so she wouldn't have a chance to destroy it—which meant he had to wait for his chance.

Leonora did her best to sleep through the hours he was away. She'd read and sleep and dream of him. But when she'd wake in the night—her heart fleeing, trying to hide itself in her ears as something waited for her in the darkness, watchful and hungry—she couldn't move. She was paralyzed. She tried to summon the Sidhe her nanny had told her so much about, so they might protect her in a circle of light, but it seemed they'd stayed in England. Along with her soul, she thought. She didn't recognize herself. Where was the girl who would make Paris her own? The girl who could take or leave a man, who knew she had all she needed inside herself?

In those purgatorial hours without Max, she'd never felt so alone. Until the mornings, when she would open her eyes and there he would be, asking for all of her. But she wouldn't tell him. She refused to be fragile. If she didn't need him, he would come to her. Live with her. Belong to her.

And then, one rainy Tuesday morning, with Paul's help, Max removed his paintings while Marie-Berthe was at mass. When Leonora saw them that afternoon, paintings in hand, Max was limping. He had scratches on his face, tooth marks on his arms. It had taken longer than they'd thought, he explained, and when his wife came home and realized what they were doing, she'd been livid, feverish, ravenous.

Leonora kissed his wounds. He had moved in. He had left her.

—&—

They climbed the stairs to the Café de la Place Blanche and opened the door, stepping into a cloud of cigarette smoke. There was an open table in the back, where they sat and ordered the house wine. This was her first Surrealist meeting and her body pulsed with excitement. Through the smoke she assessed the men's faces. Yves Tanguy, whom she'd met on the street just that morning—his wide eyes boyish, his thin hair on end—was so engrossed in what André Breton was saying that he seemed not to notice their arrival. But Paul Éluard smiled at her and Man Ray tipped his hat. Tristan Tzara, whom she recognized from photographs, with his ubiquitous monocle, regarded her with an indifference so absolute it made her keenly aware that she was the only woman in the room.

Breton sat beside Tzara, but he might as well have been standing before a blackboard, pointer in hand, given the resolute tone of his speech and the way the men faced him, listening to his theories as they spiraled out, gaining momentum as he spoke of "the independence of art for the revolution" and of "the revolution for the full liberation of art." She sat back and lit a cigarette. He'd come by the apartment just last week, kissed her cheeks and been gracious, and he greeted her now with a nod and, she thought, a hint of a smile.

"Don't call him André," Leonor had warned. "Breton. You must always call him Breton," she'd said, as if spitting his name onto the sidewalk. "The pompous prick! What gives him the right to tell every-one what they can and can't do? I mean, what has *he* created anyway, except for his almighty manifesto?"

She and Leonor had been walking arm in arm, on their way to Café de Flore for an aperitif, and she'd noticed the way the men they passed on the sidewalk looked at them. It was a new feeling, the power women have in numbers, and she liked it. "Of course, there's his novel *Nadja*," Leonor said. "But have you read it? She goes crazy and it's all about how it affects the artist, the *man*. It was inspired by a real woman, too. And where is she, the real Nadja? Locked away in a mental institution for the last ten years. If she's only a muse, what does it matter what happens to her?" She'd stopped on the sidewalk and squeezed Leonora's arm with her elbow. "That's how he sees us all, dear, as muses. And I refuse to be anyone's muse. Except for yours. That is, if you'll have me?"

"Absolutely," Leonora had told her. "But from now on I'm calling you by your last name. If Breton is Breton and Dalí is Dalí, then you shall be Fini."

Leonor nodded, smiled. "And you, my dear, will be Carrington."

She tried to imagine Leonor in this smoke-filled room and couldn't. There was no way she would waste an afternoon listening to a bunch of men talking. But this was new for Leonora. She was seeing the inner sanctum of the movement firsthand.

Paul challenged Breton and they began to argue, although if asked, she was sure they'd have called it simple discussion. To back Trotsky and the Revolution was to splinter the Party further, Paul insisted.

Breton pointed at Paul. "When Stalin exiled Trotsky, he contaminated Communism."

"It's the same reason you condemned homosexuality, for the argument of purity."

"Absolutely. Homosexuality is tolerable in the *individual*. But Surrealism, if we want to be taken seriously, must be immaculate, incontrovertible. Homosexuality is a stain."

She didn't intend to interrupt. She was well aware she was a guest. Women were never allowed to fully join *the movement*. Breton's old boys' club, Fini called it. But wasn't he being vague? "You mean *male* homosexuality?" Max squeezed her arm, a signal to leave it there, but he looked amused.

"*Oui*," he said. "For women it's a natural outgrowth of their anatomy. It goes back to Freud. Girls suckle at their mother's breasts, the same way boys do."

"You might recall that Dada prefigured Freud," said Paul, swirling his wine. "But how about being with a man, if the woman you were with desired it?"

"I would never be with such a woman."

Scribbling in a small notebook, Max tossed in his question. "And buggery?"

"Fine, if it's with a woman," Breton declared.

"Would you enjoy being sodomized by a woman with a dildo?" Paul smiled as he asked the question. Breton's face flushed. He pressed his lips together and said nothing.

Yves was sketching something, etching it with a knife in the smear of a dark, thick liquor on his plate. He looked up. "I would! That is, if it gave her pleasure. Nothing to do with homosexuality," he added, glancing at Breton.

"How could it possibly give her pleasure?" said Breton. "It's a dildo." There was a great deal of discussion then, the men talking among themselves. Was her desire conscious or unconscious? And how important was that distinction? Breton clapped to regain order. "Please, men! Don't you see? Surrealism must be uncontaminated!"

Max stood up so fast his chair fell backward. "What does purity have to do with art? The whole point is free thought!"

A small man tapped her on the shoulder. He looked familiar, but she couldn't place him. Regarding her with fierce, brown eyes, he pulled something from his jacket pocket, reached out, and held her hand. Was he flirting with her? Suddenly, she recognized him. It was the Spanish painter Joan Miró. She'd seen his paintings at the Surrealist show in London. She had liked them, and was thinking she'd tell him so, until he pressed some francs into her palm. "Fetch me a pack of cigarettes, will you dear?"

That was what he wanted? Cigarettes? "You can bloody well get your own cigarettes!" she said, loud enough for everyone to hear. She slapped his money onto the table. "Do I look like I'm your maid? Or perhaps your mother?"

His body tensed, and she thought he might strike her. The room was silent. She'd upset the meeting. Had she also upset Max, or embarrassed him? But he was grinning, thrilled by her defiance. He grabbed her hand and they strode to the door. "It's a lovely autumn day," he announced to the men, "and we have art to make."

"And love," she added. "With an enormous dildo."

~~~

She set up an easel in the corner of their living room near the window. Her unfinished canvas had arrived from London at last, sent by Ursula, who was pregnant, *hardly feeling the need to paint*, her note read. *Just nesting happily.* Their lives had gone in such different directions, and Leonora felt at once lucky to be free—of England, of her family and proper society, of motherhood—and also terrified of tripping, as if she were running so fast the ground beneath her had melted away, leaving only air, and if she so much as stopped to catch her breath, she might plummet to some inconceivable depth.

She opened the box and took out her painting, which was wrapped in brown paper. She wasn't ready to look at it just yet. She'd make tea first. Her painting had to be not just good—showing promise, or talent, what might be expected from a student—it had to define her vision, to claim her place among the Surrealists. It needed to shock the viewer, to penetrate him, or her, in unsettling ways. But mostly, it needed to amaze Max.

He was at his studio now, and would be for the rest of the morning. She had time to work on her own, time to let it start working on her. She sipped the tea she'd begun to take black. Outside a cold rain fell, and she held the cup with both hands, savoring its heat. She wore a silk robe, hoping its oriental pattern and slippery feel might inspire her. But it wasn't nearly warm enough, and she pulled a blanket from the sofa around her.

She tore off the paper. There she was, dressed in riding pants, sitting on a chair whose red cushion shone like a wet tongue. The legs of the chair were proper, covered by a blue pleated skirt. It was the tongue, so sexual and lewd, that most pleased her. But what came next? She screwed the canvas to the easel, turned it so it caught the light.

She'd begun to pay attention to clues the unconscious is always leaving about—love notes, Max called them—the shapes of shadows or of a smear of shampoo foam left on the tile in the shower. One day she saw nothing but cranes, the next, horses. Animals walked through her dreams, too. Twice she'd dreamed of a hyena, and so it had also entered her story of a reluctant debutante. This sort of aliveness felt like listening. The whole world took on meaning—not a meaning that's been agreed on by some gossiping majority, but a private meaning, the seed of one's art.

She stood by the window and stared at her painting, at her *self*— the fierce self she had made, with the wild hair and the straight gaze— and it stared back. *This is you now*, the woman said. *You are me—in a room, a windowless room.* Of course! Painting the walls sky-blue wasn't enough, the room needed a window, an *open* window. If she didn't have a way out other than through the front door (where she'd doubtless be watched and trailed, her lack of decency written into the tomes), she'd certainly go mad.

Leonora let the blanket fall to the floor. Her tubes of oil paint were stuck shut, having not been opened since London. She took a rag and muscled them open. Their noxious, beautiful smell filled the room. At last she was painting again, and time dissolved as it always did when she worked. Golden ocher for the drapes, cadmium yellow and green for the English countryside beyond it, with cypresses and a pine.

Wiping her hands on the rag, she stepped back and looked at the painting. She saw the hyena from her dream, with a sweet, haunting face and full udders, standing in the room and looking at her with her knowing, oval eyes. Hyenas were practically androgynous, the females in possession of a false penis, a fact which pleased her—not *or*, she thought, but *and*. She mixed burnt sienna with a darker brown and umber. She saw just where the hyena would stand and was dipping her brush in the paint when Max burst through the door. Quickly, desperately, she turned her painting toward the wall. He'd see it when it was ready and not before.

"The Éluards are seeing *Guernica*. I told them we'd come. You have to see it."

"I'm working," she said, her throat tight with frustration. She wanted to get the hyena down, while it was still so fresh in her mind she could smell the stink of it.

"Please?" he said, wrapping his arms around her. She sighed. How would he feel if she were to interrupt him? She wiped her brush, swished it in a jar of turpentine. Her painting would have to wait.

～❧～

They paused outside the German pavilion on *Rue de la Paix*, Peace Street, so named for the exhibition. Flanked by Nazi flags, blood-red against the gray sky, the square facade was trimmed with cut-stone columns meant to evoke ancient Rome, but to Leonora the building seemed to be the very embodiment of fascism. All thrust and force. She felt as small as an ant, and as easily crushed. Squinting at the golden ornament at its top, the giant eagle with a swastika in its talons, she had the sudden notion the bird might swoop down, lift Max by the collar of his coat, and ferry him straight back to Germany, to its Führer who hated him.

Max must have been thinking the same thing, because he laughed. Of course the German pavilion had to tower above the Russian pavilion, they agreed, and the rest for that matter. They made their way to the Spanish pavilion, where people had already formed a line. The rain had stopped, but the wind was sharp. Leonora sunk her hands into her jacket pockets. Nusch huddled close. "You're going to love *Guernica*," she said. "We were just here and *had* to come back." Leonora nodded, smiled. All she could think of was her hyena and how eager she was to paint her. Blue. Her eyes would be blue, and they would look human.

They inched up the line and moved inside. There was such a crowd, she could see only the top half of the painting, even when she stood on her toes. Max pulled her to the front, right against the bar. Picasso's painting was massive. All in black and white, like the news, it covered the wall. The heaped, twisted bodies of the villagers, of the poor trapped horse. The open mouths, arms reaching for a sky that should have been clear and blue, but was raining fire. The figures were flat, representational rather than realistic, and yet she could hear their screams. Here was a leg, a flexed foot—but which face did it belong to? She swallowed, tasting bile, as if *Guernica* were reaching into her gut and squeezing. The crowd pressed. She was weak, dizzy. She grabbed Max's arm. "What is it?" he said. "You're white."

She was panting. "I'll meet you outside."

"I'll come with you." She watched him talk to Nusch and Paul, who followed him toward her.

"It's too crowded today anyhow." Paul put his arm around her as they made their way out. She inhaled the crisp air, her stomach starting to settle. But when she thought of her hyena all she could see was the face of that horse, his open mouth, his tongue sharp and distended. Automobiles chugged past them, but she heard only the horse's wails.

"Is *Guernica* not great art?" Nusch was breathless. "It's got us all worked up."

"Great? Maybe," Max said. "But it's ceased to be recognized for itself. It's timely. A political statement."

"It's all about the horror, the enemy unseen," Paul said.

"It's about Germany testing its bombs. Seeing what it's capable of," Max said.

Everyone was quiet. She wanted to talk about anything else. And she had a sudden craving for ice cream, despite the chill in the air.

"Can art stop a war? Can art stop bombs, can it stop Hitler, or Franco?" They'd arrived at Café de Flore and still Nusch wouldn't let it go.

They sat at a sidewalk table. Leonora faced the sun, closed her eyes to soak it in.

"Art is art; bombs are bombs," Max said. "Let's order. I'm famished."

She ordered chocolate ice cream and Max got a bottle of champagne and oysters, none of which they could pay for. They'd gone through her mother's money and he hadn't sold a single painting— not since Marie-Berthe's parents turned the Paris socialites against him. But he insisted you must act as if the money were coming and it would. And besides, Paul had plenty. Perhaps he'd pay.

She ate the ice cream slowly, letting it melt over her tongue, feeling it cool her throat. Her shoulders loosened. She was breathing normally again. Nusch was talking about the big Surrealist exposition she was planning with Marcel Duchamp. "We're including women in this one," she said, catching her eye. It would open next January, in only three months.

Leonora had nothing to show them yet. But she *would*.

She was envisioning her hyena again, when she saw the woman on the sidewalk. She wore a black dress fitted at her waist. A red ribbon held her dark hair back from her pretty face. She'd stopped and was staring at Max. It was her. It had to be. Her eyes narrowed and fixed themselves on Leonora, and then she charged, like a cape buffalo. She was at the table in seconds. "Marie-Berthe!" Max yelled. "Stop! You have to stop!"

She knocked Leonora's ice cream onto her lap and pulled her up by her hair. *"Putain!"* she screamed. *Whore.* She swung around and slapped Leonora's cheek. Marie-Berthe let go of her hair, but rather than retreating, Leonora clawed her cheek with her nails, leaving red bleeding streaks. Marie-Berthe burst into tears. Max stepped between them, facing his wife. Leonora watched him put an arm around her and walk her down the sidewalk. His wife of ten years. She sat back down, trembling. Thinking of all Max had told her—how they'd long ago fallen apart, how she hated his friends and he hated her small-minded piety, her neediness, her jealousy—Leonora watched his wife rest her head on his shoulder.

Max, June 1940, southern France

Traveling east on the ghost train, Max is heading home. And when they turn the corner from the Pyrenees and leave the rain behind them, a dry night opens onto a dry day, and they pull into the station in Toulouse, where the newspapers have black borders, meaning the war is officially over. France's small war is over. In a chess game, France's queen has been toppled after ten moves. Still, it's the terms of the armistice everyone is talking about—which regions of France are free and which aren't.

The commandant hands a few papers around. The scientist grabs one, squints as he tries to make out the text without his glasses, and with a sigh hands it to a rabbi. Max scoots over, making a place for him on the side rail as everyone huddles behind him. The rabbi flips the pages with shaky hands. He stops at photos of Hitler and his men in Paris. They all lean in. Nazi troops march down the Champs-Élysées. Hitler and his entourage pose before the Eiffel Tower, like movie stars or royalty. "Turn the page," someone in the back shouts. The unthinkable has happened. No use in gawking.

The map of France is near the back. The occupied zone is shaded, the unoccupied zone plain white. Their train is in unoccupied territory. It seems all of the south of France, other than the western seaboard, is unoccupied—which means she should still be in Saint-Martin. She would stay as long as she could, she had said. He can't remember her words, not exactly, but he knows they were lying on their land, her head on his arm, staring at a starry sky.

He tries to picture where she is now, tries to see her at the farmhouse, feeding the cats and the peacocks, tending her vines. He tries to feel her presence, but all he can feel is an emptiness in his stomach. An awful, swirling dread.

The train lurches forward and he holds to the side rail, his legs hanging over the edge. The rabbi grabs hold of his arm to keep from falling. There are shouts, men running to catch the train, the same men who'd left in Bayonne and after, more ragged than ever—but Hans Bellmer, sadly, is not among them. It was terrible, they say, impossible to find shelter or food. So they'd explained to one station manager after another that they'd lost their transport, and they had at last caught up to them.

The trains they pass brim with passengers, their faces open, soaking in the sunlight. The France they love might be dead, but the fight is over. They are going home. Even the half-blind scientist sits in the sun, smiling.

The men who returned tell stories; they fill in the blanks. The Germans, it turns out, did not come to Bayonne Harbor after all. Their train's own whispers had started the rumor. Their commandant had telephoned ahead in search of food. When one place couldn't comply, he called another. And always he told them, "I'm arriving with two thousand *Boches*. Can you feed us?" So it spread that the Germans were coming. The ghost train had frightened itself—but in the right direction, he thinks, grateful he didn't run for the border.

The air smells of dried grasses, of fields, of distance and old heat, and soon they can see the Mediterranean, deep blue and shining. But where are they being taken? Back to Les Milles? The south of France is unoccupied, but if the Nazis find out about them, the French will be forced to hand them over. The men debate, but soon let it go. There is sun and warmth and sea, and when it is their turn to sit in the train car, a few men even play cards, balancing the deck on their knees.

Max keeps his plans to himself. He will not return to Les Milles if that is where they are going. He won't return to any camp. He has crackers, lumps of cheese, and salami in his coat pocket. He lets his eyes close. He will save what energy he can. Slip off in the night.

At the junction to Les Milles the train keeps on, north, toward Nîmes, and closer still to Saint-Martin. It circles Nîmes and stops on a siding, in a field a few kilometers from the town.

The men stumble from the train, the sky blazing above them. They scatter in a field strewn with stones. He lies down and stares at the colors, absorbing them like nutrients. The cobalt of the sky as the clouds turn. Indian yellow. Cadmium orange. Crimson lake.

Tomorrow, says the commandant, they will make their camp. But for tonight, they are free to sleep under the stars. And there is a farmhouse just up the road where they can find water, milk, wine. "But don't try to run," he croaks, his voice hoarse. "The gendarmerie know we are here. They'll bring you back as soon as look at you."

Max rambles up the road with the rest of the men. Milk and wine cost money, but the water is free, cold from the well. He drinks his fill.

The heat of the day having gone with the sun, the men wrap themselves in blankets and lie in the field. He lies down, too. He will wait until they are sleeping. But lying flat on the ground is too wonderful, and each time he forces his eyelids open, they shut on him.

~&

He wakes to a luminous sky and bolts up, sure he's missed his chance.

It's only the moon, a blind white eye, a beacon. He buttons his coat, leaves his blanket in the field, and creeps between the men. He steps on a stick and snaps it. He freezes, watches a man sit up. He's one of the young Austrians, and he yawns with such conviction Max feels the pull of the Earth, a wave of vertigo, and wonders if he shouldn't lie down and sleep some more. "We're going?" The boy's voice is groggy, like a child's.

"Just off for a bit of privacy." Max points away from the train, vaguely, and the boy rolls onto his side and is out again.

He doubles his pace, and soon he's following a footpath in the direction of Polaris and up a steep hill. If he can keep heading north, he'll find the Loire, their river, and from there he can reach Saint-Martin.

He looks at the long, gray train once more, at the flimsy cattle cars that ferried them on the worst journey of their lives. All to take them back where they began. All for nothing.

But above him the sky is clear. He's alone for the first time in a month, breathing the sweet, bracing air. And when he hears the distant bugle, the sound that woke them every morning at Camp des Milles, he's already crested the hill, and is entering a valley as it fills with birdsong.

The sky brightens. In summer, the farmers rise early, so he has less than an hour before he will have to hide. Quickening his steps, he trips on a stone, scrapes his palms, a knee. He gets back on his feet and keeps moving, squinting against the sun as it rises, keeping to the edges of the fields. He eats a cracker, slowly, then nibbles the cheese, sucking on it like hard candy, making it last. He is tired, so very tired, and already the day is hot.

In the shade of a sycamore, he spreads his coat over the soft, old leaves. He lies down, covers himself with leaf litter as though he were tucking himself into bed—a trick he learned as a boy when he'd run from his house to the woods to hide—and he sleeps.

⚶

At sundown he heads north, toward Saint-Martin. It could take him four days to reach their home, he figures, or maybe three if he can walk through the nights. He's eaten the rest of the crackers and the salami and still he's weak, and thirsty now, too, terribly thirsty. The air is dry, and all day, as he dozed, it sucked the moisture from his mouth.

His foot is cramped, and so is his calf. He stops to rub them, then presses on, finding a fallen branch of a plane tree to use as a walking stick. Its gnarled end in the palm of his hand, he takes a path near a road, an animal trail, and when he sees headlights, he crouches in the shrubs until the cars pass.

He follows the stars north across fields, up and then down hills. Looking at Ursa Major and Leo, he thinks his girl was right. The bear seems more like a great cat, and the lion looks like a snail. And since he is far from any town, a shadow drifting through shadows, he can even make out the little horse, Equuleus, tiny and faint and alone in a dark corner of sky. He's not seen any gendarmes, but any citizen of France could turn him in. A skeleton in tatters, he looks like a refugee, which is what he's become. A man seeking refuge, a man who wants more than all else to be home.

Leonora and Max marched up Montmartre's twisting streets on their way to the outdoor market to shop for gifts for Christmas, just a few days away. The sky was ultramarine, the sun glinting off the windows of shops selling hats and coats and shoes. On the window of a watch store, something caught her eye. She shielded her face to see. "PARTIR," and under that, "JUIF," were scrawled in rough block letters in paint the dull red of bricks, or, she thought, of blood as it dries. Max stopped too to look, and then quickened his pace. She ran to catch him. They said nothing. This wasn't the first time they'd seen this sort of thing. The fascists weren't confined to Germany. As Jewish refugees flooded into Paris, more fascists had emerged from the shadows, airing their ugliness. Leonora linked her arm through Max's. She tried to catch her breath, but something had caught in her throat. She coughed, swallowed, and slowly was able to breathe again. As they entered the push and pull, the swell of the market, she found herself thinking about the *art* inside *partir*, the *if* in *Juif*. Art and if. If art. If art can stop a war. If it can stop hatred.

They pressed against the crowd. The stalls were packed with antiques and oddities—a stuffed barn owl, the wooden mask of a Pygmy, a blue butterfly between panels of glass in a golden frame. She hurried Max past the cages of finches and canaries, of parrots and macaws, since he would buy all the birds he could afford, just to free them. "Oh!" She stopped when she saw it. The hairs of her arms stood on end. It was a white, wooden rocking horse, exactly like Marzipan, whom she'd loved more than any other toy in her nursery. They didn't bother with bartering. Having just sold a painting, Max paid the man, who slid the bills into his baggy trousers, and he carried the rocking horse home, an early Christmas present.

She dubbed him Marzipan the Second, and on his back she became a child again. He stayed beside her easel in the living room, and she painted him hovering behind her in the blue room of her self-portrait. Still, the voice that had taunted her ever since she'd seen *Guernica* persisted. *Why bother painting a personal work, a self-portrait no less? What's the point of imagination, when innocent people are being slaughtered by war? You should do something important, something that might make a difference. You're wasting your time.*

But she painted in spite of it. Marzipan the Second gave her courage. And the longer she painted, the more faint the voice became, until it was little more than a whisper. She painted not only the rocking horse, but a real, white horse, too, leaping out the open window. As Max slept she painted late into the night. Perfecting the small horse and its shadow, she lost track of time.

It was well past three when, out of the corner of her eye, she saw something move. She saw it in the window's reflection. Just a flash of white dashing across the room and vanishing into the wall. A chill traveled her spine. It was just as it had happened that night in the convent school, when she'd read her letter in the mirror and glimpsed one of the Sidhe. She could still smell the underground tunnels, the earthen walls. The milky sweet taste of the soup was in her mouth. And she could hear the voice of the Sidhe who had fed her. "You'll be back, dear. You drank the soup."

She rubbed her eyes, opened them to a field of white—titanium-white mixed with Indian-yellow, glowing like a glass of champagne in sunlight. It was her ceiling, she realized, her eyes focusing on the old chandelier, its crystals twinkling as if there'd been a gust. Had she fallen asleep? She turned onto her side. She had white paint on her fingers. Her brush lay against the wall as though it had rolled there. She pushed herself up and stood, slowly, feeling her feet against the wooden floor, letting gravity balance the lightness in her head. She glanced around the room, which was exactly as before. The Sidhe had always been a slippery folk. But in waking life, she recalled, you can only glimpse them in a reflection. She searched in the mirror of the window, but the pale flash was gone.

When had the air become so cold?

She wrapped herself in a sweater and studied her painting. She knew just what she would paint, and the thought of it thrilled her. She picked up her brush. There was still a touch of white on the tips of its bristles, and she sketched the Sidhe quickly, a wispy figure beside the hyena. She painted a heart, like the hearts she'd seen throbbing through the skin of the good folk, under their breastbones. She painted the colorless blood in its veins.

When she looked up, the windows were gray with dawn. She covered her painting with the sheet and slipped into bed beside Max. Fini would be here at noon and she needed to get some sleep.

***

Standing in the doorway, wearing the robe of the cardinal and with a basket in her hand, Fini looked like Little Red Riding Hood. She offered her the basket. From inside it came a muffled roar, and Leonora lifted the lid to find a tiny tiger, an orange kitten. "One of Athena's litter," said Fini. "I couldn't keep them all, no matter how much I wanted to."

"Girl or boy?" She lifted the kitten from the basket.

"Girl, of course. Not that I have a thing against boys, but female cats are best."

"I'll call her Woolf."

"*Loup?*"

"Woolf. After Virginia."

Leonora touched her nose to the tiny, cold nose. The kitten caught a claw in her hair and shook it to get free. "I know you don't read in English, but you'd love *The Waves*."

"You should translate it for me."

"I'd never be good enough!"

"Tell me the story, then."

Leonora smiled. "It isn't the sort you can tell." Woolf batted at her arm and leapt under the sofa.

Fini peeled off the robe and stood in the kitchen naked in her heels. "These robes are hard to wash and chicken splatters," she explained as she pulled the hens' plucked bodies from her bag. "Give me your sharpest knife." Leonora handed her the butcher's knife and she slapped a chicken on the cutting board and hacked into its rubbery flesh.

When Leonora had first come to Paris, Max had made a delicious paella for them. But that, she learned, was a special occasion, and soon he'd begun to expect dinner.

Fini had begun the cooking lessons then—*boeuf bourguignon, confit de canard, iles flottantes*—and Leonora looked forward to those afternoons they spent drinking wine and concocting magic, just as Max looked forward to the dinners in the candlelit company of the two Leonors, as he'd come to call them. "I don't see how women do it," she'd confided to Fini. "How do they clean and cook and still have time to paint?"

"Look at it creatively," she'd said. "When you clean, you are dressing a set on which a marvelous play will unfold, the story of your life, *ma chérie*. When you cook, you are an alchemist. A witch. The pot on the stove is your cauldron. Max comes and goes, yes? But this is your realm, one *you* control. Of course I live most of the time with a caravan of men and cats, so no one can expect much of anything from me."

Leonora didn't mind. And besides, whenever she and Max went out to eat, there was the possibility of Marie-Berthe turning up and spoiling things. She had a sixth sense which rooted out his whereabouts the way a pig roots out truffles. Leonora thought of her that way, like a pig sniffing at the dirt—or else a jailor, holding Max with an ugly desperation. It had happened again last week at Les Deux

Magots. Marie-Berthe, screeching, threw coffee cups at her. Max had put his arm around Leonora, firmly, as he told his wife to go home. They watched her limp away on her heels. She should have felt pity, but in the moment it was impossible. Marie-Berthe had been shaking, as if she might break free, grab her by the hair, and do—what? Of what violence might she be capable?

"You know, he still sees her. Marie-Berthe," Leonora said, pouring a good Bordeaux into two glasses. She swirled the wine around, the way Max had shown her, and brought it to her nose. Leather, chocolate. Sipping it, she tasted blackberry and smoke. "He's afraid if he doesn't look in on her, she'll take her life. She has a gun—"

"Maybe you should take over," Fini said, offering the knife. "It feels good to whack away."

Leonora pulled off her white blouse and her skirt and hung them over a chair. She brought the knife down hard into the chicken. Fini was right. It felt good. A leg launched across the counter, a wing careened to the floor. Fini put the pieces in the frying pan, melting butter and adding *lardons*, cubes of pig fat, for flavor. She doused the chicken in red wine, sending steam over their faces and chests. "As long as I've known him, he's always had more than one woman at a time," she said as she added mushrooms. "It's his way."

"He says he loves *me*." Leonora knew she sounded desperate, and tried to laugh it off. "In any case, it's nothing more than some bourgeois notion of love that makes me want him for myself."

Fini covered the chicken. She turned to her, took her hand. "We want what we want. Now show me this painting." The windows had misted over with steam, and the flat was thick with the smell of chicken and wine. Lifting the sheet that covered her self-portrait, Leonora held her breath. She'd shown it to no one, not even to Max.

Fini nodded, putting an arm around her, and the two of them looked at the painted woman, this other Leonora whom Carrington had given birth to, the one who stared straight back and seemed to not need anything from anyone.

Suddenly, she heard the jingle of keys. Max opened the door. She startled, as if caught, though he hardly looked at them, rushing into the bedroom with something in his hands. She covered the painting quickly with the sheet. She hadn't planned to show it to Fini before she showed it to Max, and she wondered if he'd be hurt. But why had she jumped when he came in? Why had she felt like a child?

Fini put a hand on her back, right on the back door of her heart. "Carrington," she said. And Leonora felt the sun there in her chest. Bright and warm, even in December. And breathing that light, feeling it radiate through her and out into the apartment and Paris and the world, she remembered who she was. Sure-footed. Fortified. She was a horse who, walking a cliff, focuses on the path and does not even notice the precipice. Carrington, she thought.

Max reappeared in a fresh shirt with cuff links. When he saw them, naked and nearly naked, he took in the scene, grinning. He opened a bottle of Pernod and poured them each a glass. "To the two Leonors! And to *my* Leonora, my love, my girl."

They drank the green liquor and kissed. Her tongue was numb, which made the feel of his tongue new. It was all shape—like drawing or painting in black and white. She might have kissed him for hours, but Fini was close, watching with an intensity that made Leonora's cheeks hot.

Max cranked the Victrola. Josephine Baker's voice shimmied out of it, quick and careless. *Everybody loves my baby, but my baby don't love nobody but me.* The kitten ran out from the curtains and Leonora scooped her up. "Max, meet Woolf." And he gave Woolf a kiss, draped her over his head, and the three of them danced, like a little family, she thought.

The doorbell rang. Fini slipped into her red robe and Leonora pulled on her shirt and skirt as Max ushered in a woman, tall and striking, a feathered hat low over her brow. "Rose!" he exclaimed. He hugged her stiffly and patted her back. Leonora had thought she'd met everyone in the group, but she'd never heard of Rose.

Fini led the woman straight to Leonora's painting. She pulled off the sheet and Leonora felt the blood leave her face. She looked at Max, who was filling another glass with Pernod, but he seemed not to care a jot that they were seeing it before he did. Wasn't he even the least bit curious?

"Remarkable, *n'est-ce pas*?" Fini asked.

"Indeed," the woman said, her voice low, her accent American.

"Carrington, this is Rose Sélavy," said Fini.

The woman took her hand in her white gloved hands and kissed it. "You simply *must* hang your art in our show, dear." Leonora was intrigued. Just who *was* Rose?

"Oh, I'd like that," Leonora said, still watching Max, who looked at her painting and said nothing. She tried to read his expression, but his face was blank.

He handed Rose the glass. "Drink up. We're going out."

"But we made *coq au vin*!" Leonora protested. They had cooked all bloody afternoon.

"It will make a wonderful breakfast. It's Christmas Eve! Everyone will be out."

"Including your wife."

"Everyone *but* Marie-Berthe, who will be at mass with her parents."

"I'll come for a while," said Leonor, "but then I'm meeting my Italian. It's our first Christmas together, and he has some surprise for me."

"Ah! Yes! A surprise," said Max. "I have one as well. Would you like it, darling?"

"Shouldn't we wait for morning?" It had been her family's tradition. Presents Christmas morning.

"Presents," he said in English, "are best in the present."

An English pun. She had to smile. She sat, closed her eyes, and he put a large canvas in her hands. "You can look," he said. Two horses leapt from a mountain. They spun in a twisted, frenzied embrace. And in the corner hung a white and gold and green circle. It was a ring, she realized.

"It's ten years old, but it belongs to you. It always did." His eyes were bright. "It's *Bride of the Wind*. Like you. Only I didn't know you existed."

She kissed his damp cheeks. "It's the best present in the world," she said, wanting to stay there with it, to study it, but Fini and Rose were already out the door. She and Max grabbed their coats and hurried after them.

"What do you think of Marcel?" Max whispered, nodding at Rose as she descended the stairs in front of them.

"That's a man?"

Max's full-throated laugh, the kind she usually found so contagious, boomed in the stairwell. "That, my dear, is Marcel Duchamp."

This was the man who'd dared to put a urinal in a gallery and call it art? How wonderful, she thought.

The stairwell spun. Dizzy, she grabbed Max's arm. On her empty stomach, the Pernod had gone to her head. "Are you okay?" he asked.

She nodded. But as they walked into the cold, clear night, she brooded. She wanted to be happier than she was. Her art, after all, was to be in a show, and Max had just given her a painting with a ring in it. Yet all she could think about was why he hadn't said a word about hers. He'd told her just yesterday he couldn't wait to see it, but now that he had he was silent. "Are you angry?" she asked him when the others were too far ahead to hear.

"Why would I be angry?"

"I let her see my painting first."

"It's Christmas Eve. No one can be angry on Christmas Eve."

"That's not a real answer," she said, and might have well left it at that. But she had to ask, "What do you think of it?"

"I need to have longer to look, but I love it!" He squeezed her to him so they were walking in step. His answer, though, was too quick.

⁓❦⁓

Les Deux Magots twinkled with champagne and candlelight and the laughter of red-cheeked artists spending all the money they didn't have. Paul wore his derby hat low, and in his dark, pressed suit, he struck Leonora as the perfect companion for Nusch, in her gown of cream satin, her eyes rimmed with kohl. "Rose!" Nusch said. They kissed cheek to cheek as Max, Fini, and Leonora slid into the booth.

They ordered smoked salmon and oysters, foie gras, stuffed turkey with chestnuts, *buche de Noel*, and bottles and bottles of champagne.

"Darling," Rose said to Nusch. "Believe me when I tell you, I've just seen true art. Leonora's self-portrait with horse and hyena. It *must* be in the show. You'll love it."

"You have another piece?" Nusch asked. "You must have two in the show."

"I'm working on something," Leonora replied, although she wasn't, not yet.

Breton stood by the entrance, his mane slicked back, a tall blonde on his arm. Paul jumped up and kissed them. "Jacqueline, André, join us, please."

"*Bon soir*," Breton said, not looking at Fini, or at Rose, whom Leonora imagined he preferred as Marcel. "We don't want to be any trouble. We'll get our own table."

Leonor stood. "I have to go. There should be plenty of room."

"Not enough homosexuals for you here?" His smile was fixed, his eyes shone.

"André, why don't you go blow yourself?" Fini said sweetly, and she turned her magnificent head and strolled into the evening, her robe sweeping the ground behind her.

Breton and the blonde—"My wife, Jacqueline," he said, introducing her to Leonora—squeezed in around the table. Max filled their glasses. They toasted and drank, but the champagne did little to lighten Breton's mood. His intensity was the wrong hue for the evening, too saturated for the balance, so that all eyes went to him. "That woman. Tell me her paintings won't be in the show."

"Well?" said Nusch, and drank her champagne.

"She's shown with you before," Rose said. "I don't see why she shouldn't."

Max emptied the champagne into Leonora's glass. "Let's order another," he said.

Breton's cheeks were pink, his eyes burned. "If that woman is in the show, I will have nothing to do with it, and neither will the Surrealists." Because Leonor challenged the headmaster of Surrealism, because she wasn't docile like his pretty wife, she couldn't be in the show? But Leonora couldn't bring herself to say anything. What could she say when more than anything she wanted her own work to hang with theirs? It was either opportunity or integrity. Women, it seemed, were more often pressed to choose between them.

"Fine," said Rose. "I'm certain she'd prefer not to collaborate with you either."

⁓⸲

The exhibition, as it turned out, was less than a month away. Leonora painted her second piece quickly, before she had time to doubt her vision—horses in a tumultuous landscape, one of them stuck in a tree. Before she knew it, opening night was upon them.

The room was dimly lit and stank of coal. Coal bags stuffed with newspapers hung from the ceiling like foul stalactites, and now and then the fine black powder sifted down. Duchamp's idea, to make the room feel like a cave, a womb, only dirty and ominous. Menacing. The floor was covered in mud and dead leaves, and in a corner a bed sprouted ferns and fronds. It was a bed at the bottom of a swamp, the bottom of a dream—enclosed by shadows that held Leonora inside them, too, squeezing tighter by the minute. Max put his arm around her and she exhaled. This was the Exposition of Surrealism, and her paintings were part of the show.

She stood in a line of artists—Dalí, Miró, Giacometti, Hans Bellmer, Remedios Varo, Man Ray, and Meret Oppenheim, who, Fini had told her, was another of Max's old flames. They leaned on a wall, waiting. Delirious laughter, which Breton had recorded at an asylum for the insane, blasted in riotous peels from a hidden phonograph. The smell of roasting coffee made the air close and acrid. It was nearly ten p.m., and the doors were about to open. Soon, people would be passing Dalí's *Rainy Taxi*, parked right in the entrance—the mannequin chauffeur wearing a shark mask, and the mannequin passenger wet in her gown, real snails on her neck—and walking through the hall of mannequins, each designed by a different Surrealist.

Her pulse thrummed as the first women and men trickled in, waving their flashlights from one wall of art to another. Man Ray's lighting with soffits hadn't worked, so he'd gone out just yesterday and bought all the flashlights he could find. It would add to the feeling of trepidation, he'd said. A light hit her face and left her in the dark just as quick. Max had warned her it would be packed. The invitation had promised a sky of flying dogs, hysteria, and other curiosities. And there was a buzz around Paris—people wanted to see what these degenerate artists were up to now. Max squeezed her to his side. "Any minute," he breathed.

"There you have it. Forced lunacy, darling," she heard one loud woman say. A light was aimed at her painting *The Horses of Lord Candlestick*. But what she saw was the painting beside hers, Remedios Varo's *Las Almas de los Montes*. Souls of the Hills. The spires in the mist had human faces, and a line wound through them, a twist of smoke, the breath of the mountain souls. It made Leonora wish she'd kept the wispy image of the Sidhe in her self-portrait instead of wiping it out, angrily, on Christmas morning, after Max told her he didn't think it worked. Why hadn't she trusted herself?

"*Maintenant*," Man said.

Max nudged her and she clicked on her flashlight. In unison they aimed their lights at the bed. An actress leapt up. She pulled at the chains wrapped around her body, and loosed such a long, piercing cry Leonora was afraid a coal bag would fall. The actress ran from the room, silence in her wake. They turned off their flashlights, and in the darkness Leonora shivered in her low-backed gown. She could hear her own heart, which was so loud she was sure Max could hear it, too, but when she reached for him he was gone.

Someone bumped her from the wall, and soon she was moving with the spectators—so many she felt suffocated. There wasn't enough air and the coal made her nostrils sting. She started to cough and sweat, and she reached out, feeling as if she might fall.

And then a cool, small hand took hold of hers. A woman's hand, her mouth to her ear. "Leonora." She recognized her smooth voice, her Spanish accent. "You look like you could use some air." It was Remedios. They'd met, briefly, when they'd hung the paintings, but now a real warmth moved between them. They wove through the crowd toward the door. Her hand in hers, Leonora felt her heartbeat steady. She took a deep breath.

They passed the actress, entering in a ripped evening dress as the room exploded in applause. They moved against the press of the people, past the avenue of mannequins. Leonora noticed a red bulb pulsing in the jacket pocket of the figure Duchamp had designed. "Rrose Sélavy in one of her provocative and androgynous moods," the sign said. She hadn't seen the name written before, the double *r*'s. Eros *c'est la vie*. Love, that's life. She smiled. Though Duchamp himself was in London, helping Peggy Guggenheim, the American art collector, with the first show of her new gallery, Rose, Rrose, was here. Her upper half clad in a man's suit, her lower half naked, she was Leonora's favorite.

"The Surrealists and their dolls," Fini liked to say. How Leonora wished she were here. Fini had pretended it hadn't bothered her, pretended she'd been better off not being in the show. But she'd been hurt. Breton had won. All the other women seemed to meet him halfway—part muse, part artist. But not Leonor. And maybe not Remedios either.

"I love your painting," Leonora said, leaning in so Remedios could hear her above the chatter of the crowd. "I've always thought that mountains had souls."

"I love yours! That hyena visited me in a dream." Before she could ask Remedios to tell her more, they were in the front courtyard and Benjamin Péret, her poet lover, was pulling her aside. "*Chérie*, you must meet—" she heard before they vanished into the throng.

The line for entry wound down the street and around the corner. Police were directing pedestrian traffic. She'd never seen anything like it. Paris chic, exiled Germans, a clutch of American women, their voices bald and brash—all of them jumbled and so expectant it made her want to leave. Dalí was posing before his *Rainy Taxi* and the cameras flashed. Above the clamor she could hear Breton talking, reporters gathered around him. "This is the first exposition of its kind in the world. In which the show itself is a work of art. Tonight, my friends, you are witnessing the future of art!"

She glimpsed Max's white hair and felt the thrill she always felt when she saw him, followed just as quickly by a rush of relief. Then she saw that he was talking to Meret. He spoke with such animation and intensity that watching them made her ill. She turned away. What was wrong with her? She'd never been jealous before she'd been with Max, hadn't even known what it felt like. A camera flashed. She saw herself in the reflection of the taxi's window. Her face hovered, moonlike, over her dark blue dress. And she could see right through herself. She was diaphanous.

She lit a cigarette and made her way through the crowd. She needed air, and soon found she was walking away from the show, down quieter streets. Why would Max want to be with her, when he could be with Meret? She was brilliant, covering that teacup, saucer, and spoon with the fur of a Chinese gazelle. It had made them so sexual, so warm. Her work was revolutionary, Leonora thought, shivering, wishing she'd grabbed her coat.

But nearly at the Seine, she couldn't turn back now. She had to go down to the river. Water had always made her feel peaceful and whole and she needed that now. She descended the cement stairs, through the stench of urine, to the river, where the lights from the nearest bridge skipped across the slow, gray water. *It's a dead river*, she thought, sadly. *No birds or reeds or snakes along its banks.*

Paris wasn't supposed to be this way. She was free from her father. She was making art and showing it with the artists she most admired. She should be happy for whatever Max could offer her. And what he couldn't she'd make do without. She crushed her cigarette butt with her shoe and lit another. She paced and found she was hoping he would miss her, would wonder where she'd gone and worry.

She was as bad as Marie-Berthe. *And I'm the one he's in love with*, she reasoned. *He hasn't left me yet for a woman ten years younger.* How might she feel a decade from now, when, after she'd completely lost her sense of self, he left her? But this was ridiculous. She was behaving like a petulant child. She'd go back. Max could talk with whomever he wanted.

Turning from the dirty river, from a rat running alongside it, she thought of Lambe Creek—the lush freedom, the long summer days, and how they'd played, how Max was all hers. What if they were to leave Paris and make a life together somewhere else? The thought thrilled her and she headed back, up the stairs and down the sidewalk. She trotted past a man sleeping on a bench, his trench coat pulled over him, a sweater under his head. She slowed. His unshaved face was so young, he had to be a refugee, a man without a family. Perhaps she should take him home, make him tea, and let him sleep on their sofa. But the streets were empty. It must have been past midnight, and she needed to get back to the show.

After a few blocks, she heard footsteps behind her. It sounded like the stammer of high heels, a woman fast approaching. She quickened her step and so did the woman. She turned a corner and the *click-click-click* followed. It had to be Marie-Berthe, she knew in a flash, her skin crawling. She didn't have to see her face. She could tell from the pace of her stride, her steps close together and urgent. Marie-Berthe had her pistol in the pocket of her mink coat, her finger on the trigger. Leonora could hear the clack of the metal as she took the pistol off of safety. If this was the end, she decided she would face her. She would stare death down.

Defiantly, she turned around. Behind her, the sidewalk was vacant. There was nobody there.

By the time the moon rises, Max's throat is so dry he can't swallow. The muscles in his calf have twisted to a hard, painful knot. There's a hole in one of his socks and a blister has formed on his heel. He's shuffling, eyes half-closed, when he gives in, the tug of gravity too strong for him, and falls. On his knees, he presses his forehead to the soft earth.

And then he hears what sounds like an owl's call. Lifting his head to listen, he smells water on the breeze. Could it be? He stands, and then somehow he is walking, running, in the direction of the smell, down a valley through knee-high grasses. The owl dives and lifts into the clear sky, something hanging from its beak. He follows its trajectory and the smell—a whiff of wet clay and crushed leaves.

The sound of the river is more beautiful than freedom. Even faint, it shines in the ear, polishing every nerve, every cell. And then he sees the water flashing in the dark, the structure of longing, called across the continent, singing as it flies over the low rocks. From this distance, it looks like a girl's black mane, glinting with silver fishes, with stars and fragments of moonlight.

The river is slow, shallow at the edge, and the water is clear and cold. He peels off his stinking clothes, wades into the current. It takes him off his feet, surprising him with its force. It pulls his body with it as though he were nothing more than a dead, fallen limb. He swims, angling toward the bank, where his feet reach bottom again. He holds to a stone in the shallows, drinking the water until the airless, crowded rooms of Camp des Milles and the swell and stench of the train dissolve into the mud of someone else's nightmare, and he climbs out, shakes his hair, and tells himself he is a new man.

Some things make sense. The river shines in the night because the moon shines, and he traces its shining curves upstream. He follows the river, even as it veers from true north. Beside it, he doesn't feel so lost. He drinks whenever he needs to. But mostly, he stays because he can feel her presence. Rivers remind him of her.

The bank is rocky. His shirt catches on the thorns of a wild rose and tears. He's wet and bruised and tired, a scarecrow of a man, who has been through war, but this is nothing compared to the last time.

For years, if anyone asked, he'd tell them Max Ernst died in 1914, and in 1918 he came to life again. He had tried to forget the smell of the smoke, all that white smoke, and the way sounds moved like phantoms, like hideous birds inside it. The screams, the explosions, far off as childhood, and then so close his ears howled for days after, leaving him dizzy and numb, and so far away, in a white room inside himself, huddled and shivering, sure he was dead. The smoke breathed around them, making them part of a single body as they limped across the fields. But he fell behind. He kept to the edges, looking for an exit, a way out. *If only he had wings*, he thought, when a shell exploded. He woke alone, the bodies around him still as stones, and he stumbled along a dirt road until he found a town, where someone gave him bread and let him sleep with their horses. They bandaged his face, his hand, but he needed his troop and the doctors who would give him medicine, so he wandered, searching with his one good eye until he found them. They changed his bandages but didn't let him go. Even a one-eyed man can do his part.

And then there was a moment of beauty, a moment of wonder. One wonderful thing among the shit.

They gave him a sack of food for the troops and sent him back toward the battle. He rode trains for days, the sack sealed beside him. And then, in a station, waiting hours for the next train, he watched children, mothers, fathers, grandparents, everyone limp in their seats, staring into the numb and endless distance between them. Everyone dull with hunger, and not one smile. *Why not?* he thought, untying the sack. He handed out sausages and cheese and crackers. Someone opened a bottle of wine and there was a party in the station, laughter and singing, someone strumming a guitar.

⚬

The river widens. Overhead, clouds blush, pink and peach in a color-less sky.

He climbs a hill to see where he is and a town appears with the sun. A bridge reaches over the river and on both ends sit gendarmes with their rifles. From here they are no more than squiggles of gray, but he knows they are there as surely as he knows his feet ache. Every bridge is guarded. He scrambles down an animal path. To walk through the town is risky, but he's too ragged to go back or around. He needs food—any kind of food.

He hears the groan of an engine. It's a tractor rolling toward him down the dirt road, a cloud of dust rising behind it. If he shows him-self, the farmer could report him, could grab him and turn him in—but not without a chase, and, Max sees, he's not exactly young.

He has to try. He climbs the bank and waves. The farmer pulls over. He wears a wide-brimmed straw hat, and Max must shield his eyes to meet his—one brown, the other milky as the sky. They regard each other. They are strangers with a silent understanding.

"*Bonjour.*" Max's voice is hoarse. "Can you take me to Saint-Martin-d'Ardèche?" he asks in French he hopes is free of any accent after so much time around other Germans.

The farmer nods. He is going to Aiguèze, he says, the neighbor-ing town, and he offers Max his hand and hoists him into the tractor. He must notice Max's frailness, the scratches on his face, his soiled, threadbare clothes. He takes off his straw hat and puts it on Max's head. The farmer walks around the tractor and gestures for Max to scoot behind the wheel. He gets in beside Max and nods again, asking no questions, needing no explanation.

Max drives, and the gendarme at the start of the bridge lifts his eyes, which remain on them, as if taking a long time to focus. At last he decides they are peasants, not worthy of his scrutiny. Maybe it's just too early in the morning to be officious. He leans back, reading the paper, smoking his cigarette. The gendarme at the other end, slumped over his rifle, is sleeping. He's young and has a fragile quality about him. Max has the urge to paint him, when he realizes how remarkably he resembles his son. Jimmy.

Soon the farmer takes over at the wheel, and Max gorges himself on apricots from a burlap sack. Drunk on the sugar and the heat, he dozes. The tractor is impossibly slow, and listening to the giant wheels grind over the dirt road like the onset of war, like time, he dreams that this farmer with his furrowed skin and his ancient, gnarled hands has thrown the damn thing into reverse and the months and the war spin back, too, and he listens to reason this time, listens to his girl, and leaves while the leaving is easy.

~&~

The tractor arrives on the outskirts of Saint-Martin at dusk. Heat rises from the fields, and he can smell the Loire on the air—a sprig of mint on a bowl of curried rice. He thanks the farmer, tells him he can walk from there. He wants to say more, but finds he is unable to talk. Like being pulled under water, for a moment he can't breathe.

Nostalgia, hope, dread? He's been gone for only weeks—six? seven?—but with no word from her, it feels like years since he's been home. She said she'd stay, said she'd wait—but with all of France in tumult what right has he to hope? And yet, stepping from the tractor onto the dirt road, shaking the old farmer's hand, he pictures her in that black shawl soft as cobwebs, in her dress of lace, drinking wine and concocting something strange and vaguely disturbing in the old stone kitchen, playing at cooking, at homemaking. His English girl who knows propriety and its rules well enough to hurl them squarely into the wind. They devised their own rules. When to work (from ten to two), when to swim (before ten and after two), when to make love (whenever the spirit struck), when and how to clean (naked, in summer the cleaning was always naked). It had all been play, so removed from the world he's afraid that he only dreamed it. And dreams are tricky rooms to reenter, their doors rearranging themselves when you aren't looking.

Watching the tractor roll down the road toward Aiguèze—which is empty, as if nothing has changed—he realizes he's still wearing the farmer's hat. It might not be a bad thing to be somewhat disguised, he thinks, turning toward Saint-Martin. The cobblestone street that runs through its center is largely empty, too. No gendarmes in their uniforms and their stiff caps. He has time. He can get Leonora and leave for the border.

An old couple sits outside the bar drinking and playing cards. They look at him, lifting only their eyes, and return to their game as if there were nothing to see after all. Do they not recognize him in the hat? But then, they were barely acquaintances. In the two years that Max and Leonora lived here, the townspeople watched them from a safe distance. They might have tolerated him with less indifference had Leonora been another sort of woman—wide in the hips, with ample breasts and thick ankles, and, more than all else, closer to his age. He stumbles over a cobblestone, a fool for thinking he can walk along the road like the man he once was.

The skin at the back of his neck prickles. The town is too desolate for June. In the apartments above the shops, windows click shut. Behind the lace curtains, shadows shift.

He looks ahead, the incline of the road and the smells—rosemary, basil, oregano—all so familiar. For a moment he is back, in the summer of '39, as if this last nightmare of a year hasn't happened. He might be returning from a trip to the store, a bag of flour under his arm. Picturing her face, he walks faster. Her eyes, quick, dark as woods at night.

Her lips upturned, as if she were thinking of something that would shock and amuse you if she deemed you worthy enough to hear it. Her hair, long and wild, tucked behind her ears, ears that gleam like the shells of tiny abalone and make him wish he wrote better poetry.

Their house is at the edge of town, near the river, where the last slant of sunlight still holds it. The olive trees, the stone steps, and the walls with the grimacing cement guardians that had, when he formed them with his hands, made him feel like some demented god, all of it—the whole beautiful place—flickers in the light, as if made of pale fire. She's in there. So long as he doesn't go in, he can be sure of it. Slowly, he climbs the stairs to the house. He shuts his eyes to taste the light, and finds it has a slaty, mineral quality, like a good white Bordeaux.

The sun squints on the horizon. The river is a deep brownish-green, and the fields are blue fields of lavender, yellow fields of sunflowers. He's always stood at the window of his imagination and painted what he saw, but now he wants to capture this. He wants to bring an easel and a canvas onto the patio. He wants to paint the light.

He pushes on the wooden door. Unlatched, it swings into the house.

"Nora," he yells, "Leonora!" And his voice bounces in every direction at once—up the staircase, down the hallway, through the rooms of stone—as he waits for her to answer.

Leonora opened the door to Pablo Picasso, who had brought with him a jar of Spanish wine and a friend. "*Feliz cumpleaños,*" he said, and hugged her, his face nestled, for a long moment, between her breasts. "*Por favor,* this is Renato Leduc."

Renato had a smooth, dark face and hair as white as Max's. "*Mucho gusto.*" His voice was low and quiet. He took her hand in his long fingers and kissed it.

"He's the Mexican ambassador to Portugal, here for diplomatic talks," Picasso explained, tasting the wine himself before handing her the jar. "But all that is dull, and Paris is not, I told him." She sipped what tasted like someone's homemade juice and passed it to Renato. "And I brought him to your birthday to prove it."

"In that case you must have some Pernod," she said, pouring them each a splash of the licorice liquid. They clinked glasses, and Picasso fixed his dark, glittering eyes on her. She laughed. What else was there to do? He really was incorrigible.

For her twenty-first birthday, Max had filled their flat with the blooming branches of cherry trees he'd snipped at dawn in Luxembourg Gardens. He'd splurged on foie gras and tapenade and champagne, though she had no idea where he'd gotten the money. He'd invited everyone, including Breton. Leonor had refused to come.

It was warm for April, everyone agreed, the dusk drunk on the smell of magnolias. She wore a sheer white dress, and into her hair she'd clipped a real, dead butterfly Leonor had given her, its wings a brilliant orange. Max was in the kitchen, cutting the baguettes, arranging the food onto platters, when there was a quiet knock on the door.

She knew it was Max's son, Jimmy, before she opened the door. He knocked the same way he acted around Max, with a painful hope for acceptance. A year younger than her, he was tall and slim, with eyes as blue as his father's, but bigger and sweeter. He was shy and quick to blush, so she was usually reserved around him. But tonight she must have been feeling the Pernod because she threw her arms around his neck and gave his soft cheek a kiss. He turned crimson and grinned. "Happy birthday," he said, handing her a yellow rose.

They understood each other perfectly, she thought. They both had fathers who, though radically different, loomed large.

"Jimmy's here! Time for champagne!" Max said, she noticed, with forced enthusiasm. But then he was always awkward around his son, as though he were perpetually getting to know him. Ever since Lou had fled from Cologne to Paris in '33, Max had seen Jimmy every six months. But Jimmy was already a teenager by then, and Max had left when he was two. Apart from the vacations they'd spent together, Max hadn't known him as a boy.

Max filled their glasses. "To Leonora, who outshines the moon," he said. Their glasses rang and Jimmy drank his champagne in a single swallow. He looked happy for the alcohol. She imagined he was even more nervous with Picasso here. He'd seen *Guernica* seven times, and when she introduced them Jimmy shook his hand too long and had to cough before he could speak. "*Ravi de vous rencontrer.* Pleased to meet you," he said, formally, and bowed a little, though she was sure he didn't realize he was doing it.

Soon Nusch and Paul arrived, as did Breton, who had just returned from Mexico and couldn't stop talking about the indigenous people's bizarre and wonderful beliefs, about the lush colors, the warm jungles, and the artist Frida Kahlo, who was a Surrealist without knowing it. The whole country, he declared, was *Surrealiste par excellence.*

Max had been quiet, not the easy raconteur he so often was, and she sat on the sofa beside him and held his hand. He had blue paint under his nails from the day's work. He pulled her onto his lap, wrapped his arms around her, and kissed her neck. She knew it was Picasso—more rival than friend—that made him sip his wine and say little. When he announced to the room that she must read her story, "The Debutante," she was surprised to hear his voice. Paul and Breton clapped and hooted.

"You write, too?" said Picasso. "My dear, what don't you do?"

"Well, I didn't make much of a debutante." Leonora read them the story, in which the debutante convinced a hyena to go to the ball in her place. She'd written it in French, and Picasso translated the few slang words she'd used into Spanish for Renato. Renato gasped when the hyena tore the face off the maid to wear it as a mask to the ball, and he looked at Leonora as if she really might be a hyena wearing the face of a girl. "It's completely autobiographical," she said. He laughed uncomfortably and lit a cigarette.

Nusch applauded. "I'd like a copy of that." Curled on the sofa with Woolf, she looked like a cat herself, with her slender body and her mysterious green eyes making the room more beautiful.

"It belongs in the next issue of *Minotaure*," said Breton.

The air in the room had grown heavy with smoke, even with the windows open, as if somewhere a wind had died. Jimmy stood, about to give a toast it seemed, but seeing that his glass was empty he sat back down. Max poured himself another drink, whiskey on ice, splashing some into Jimmy's glass, too. "You should tell them about the show you saw on your way back to Cologne."

Jimmy swallowed the whiskey and coughed, clearing his throat. "Well, I had to go back to Germany for a physical, for the visa to America. Anyway, I got off the train in Hamburg," he said, softly. "And there was a traveling Degenerate show."

"The first time he'd seen my work in public," Max said. "Can you imagine?"

"Best collection I've seen in years." Jimmy nodded at Picasso. The alcohol, it seemed, had done its work.

"My primitive pieces, I'm guessing."

"It was wonderful," said Jimmy, animated now, brimming and electric. "And *Guernica*! My God! It made me see Dürer and Goya in a whole new light." His excitement charged the air. Nusch stirred from a catnap; Renato polished off the jug of wine. Leonora felt ill. She couldn't remember the last gathering when talk of impending war hadn't reared its grotesque head. "Oh, and Da Vinci!" he exclaimed.

Max swirled the gin in his glass. "Nothing more recent?" he asked, pointedly.

"You, *your* work, of course." Jimmy blushed. Why had Max made him self-conscious? Did he need to be the center of adoration, even when his son was in the room?

Breton paced. "This is what I've been saying." He stopped. There was something about him. Everyone listened when he spoke. "Art is powerful. *Guernica est formidable.* You can feel the anguish. And the people are sympathetic, no one can talk of anything else."

Max sipped his drink, brooding.

Picasso lit a cigar. "The sympathetic ones are not the ones waging this war."

"This is why the Surrealists must align themselves with Trotsky." Breton's index finger pointed skyward in emphasis. "He believes in the power of the artist for change."

"Enough of Trotsky." Paul was slumped on the sofa beside Nusch, his words garbled. "Why can't you just *make* art? When is the last time you wrote something that wasn't some sort of manifesto?" It was the first thing he'd said all night.

Breton crossed the room. He stood over Paul. "You shouldn't talk about things you don't understand." His chest was filled with air, but there was sadness in his eyes.

Max slid between them. "*Mon dieu.* It's Leonora's birthday! We don't need to talk about war."

Breton hung his head and shuffled backward. He looked so humbled, Leonora felt sorry for him. "Forgive me, Leonora." With the briefest of bows he left the room in a dull silence.

She stepped onto the balcony. The party had been ruined. Why couldn't they all go?

Renato leaned on the rail beside her and lit a cigarette. Somewhere down the street two stray cats cried out. A siren and a wail, harmonizing. Was it a fight over love or was it love itself, she wondered, and thinking of a dream she'd had of Marie-Berthe, she shivered. Marie-Berthe had slipped into bed beside her and took her hair in her hands. Gently, so gently. Her whispers like silk rubbing on silk. *He belongs to me, he's my husband, and you are mine now, too,* she'd said. Marie-Berthe put her lips over hers, sealing her mouth. They were deep under water. She was trying to swim to the surface but Marie-Berthe held her down. Raising her arm she showed Leonora her gills. She could stay down there as long as she liked. Leonora had woken gasping and pulled Max's arms around her, wanting to obliterate his past. She'd wanted to crawl inside him and live there, sharing his eyes and fingers, his heart and lungs.

Renato draped his jacket over her shoulders. "It really is pretty here, isn't it?" he said, but she could only nod.

⁓⚮

A month later, she sat with Max and Jimmy at a sunlit table at Café de Flore. Chestnut blossoms sweetened the air. A waiter poured champagne and they clinked their flutes. "To Jimmy," Max said. "*Un voyage merveilleux.*" Jimmy had passed his physical and was leaving for America tomorrow.

As if they'd planned it, Man Ray and Paul came strolling up the sidewalk. They pulled up chairs to join them. Max's first wife, Lou, lived around the corner, so he phoned her and she joined them, kissing Leonora on both cheeks when they met. With her ruddy cheeks and her earthy, easy manner, Lou seemed unshakeable. It had been years since Max fell in love with Gala, and though Lou had initially threatened to not let him see Jimmy again, it seemed that now all was well between them. Leonora had thought she might feel sorry for her, but she found herself, instead, envying her independence.

When Leonora had entered the picture, Lou and Marie-Berthe became fast friends. They had a great deal in common, as the wives—the women Max had married and abandoned. But Lou didn't seem to mind Leonora's presence here. She was bigger than that.

She raised her glass. "To my exceptional son. May you travel far and wide and have *un bel temps*, and then come straight home."

No one spoke of why he was going, of Germany annexing Austria, of Jews being rounded up and sent to "re-education" camps, how being half-Jewish in Germany was even more dangerous than being all Jewish, since your very being was evidence of what Hitler referred to as "weakened Aryan blood." No one spoke of the things Jimmy had told them, what he saw from the train that night on his way to Cologne, floodlights in a field, prisoners in striped uniforms, gaunt and digging. It was easier to pretend it was a choice, not an attempt to save his life. "Come with me. Come to America." Jimmy's voice wavered as he looked from his mother to his father, and to Leonora, too. "All of you. Before it's too late." A breeze through the plane trees made the sunlight dance over their faces, and Max smiled at Jimmy, his boy who somehow still loved him.

"Oh, Jimmy," Lou said. "Don't worry. It'll all be over soon. You know this sort of thing can't stand. Dictators always fall." Leonora marveled at her resilience, her unflagging hope. She had fled Cologne after the Reichstag fire and the suspension of civil liberties, when three SS officers had shown up at her and Jimmy's door and ransacked their flat, leaving with her passport. Being a journalist, she might have easily been taken, too. Lou finished her champagne. "And besides, this is France," she said. "Not Germany."

They ate piles of steamed mussels, soaking up the broth with good bread. "How's your English?" Leonora asked Jimmy.

He turned red and cleared his throat. "Pleased to meet you, miss. Can you tell me, please, where is station for train?"

She laughed. "Well, it's a start. Repeat after me."

"No, no," Man said. "You'll have him speaking like an Englishman, saying 'bloody hell' and 'rubbish' and 'poppycock' and 'time for tea.' For God's sake, they'll put him right back on the boat and ship him off to England!" And he took over, giving him a lesson in American slang. You were *all wet* or *dizzy in love*, a policeman was a *copper*, a regular guy a *joe*, you could get the *low down* or the *kiss-off*, but now that Prohibition was over, at least you wouldn't have to drink any of that *rot gut*.

As the English lesson continued, Paul ordered more champagne. "André kicked me out," she heard him tell Max. "My poem in *Commune* was apparently the last straw. He called me a traitor. I said I chose the journal for its left-leaning readers, not because it was Stalinist, which was more or less true. Tanguy told me he announced to the group that anyone who doesn't do all they can to discredit me and my poetry is a traitor, too. I guess it was Tanguy's way of explaining why he's going to ignore me next time he runs into me at Les Deux Magots."

Max held his hand up to stop the news. "I don't want to know the details. If you are out, so am I. The Surrealist meetings are as bad as morning mass. I'm not going to make the sign of the cross or go to confession, and I'm not going to allow Breton to confer some sort of benediction on me, or else to deny it. He might have been a true friend once, but I'm too old for that."

It was as if, at the mention of morning mass, he had summoned Marie-Berthe out of the bright air. She stood before them. White as the tablecloth, her fists clenched. "Oh Lord," Max muttered. "Not again."

Leonora's stomach turned. Too many mussels and now this. It seemed so clear. Max loved Leonora and she loved him. But his wife refused to see it, refused now to even look at her. If Marie-Berthe attacked, Leonora wasn't sure she'd be able to restrain herself. She might claw her even worse this time.

"Jimmy's leaving for America," Max said. "Don't ruin his farewell."

"Jimmy?" she said, taken aback. Silently, the boy got up and went to her. Lou was up, too. They both had their arms around her as she sobbed.

"That's right," Lou said. "He's terrible. We know he's terrible, but this just isn't the place. You're better than this. Stronger."

Marie-Berthe nodded, holding tight to the silver cross that hung over her chest. "I'm going to join the sisters of St. Anne," she said to Max. "Is that what you want?"

Max's face hardened. "That sounds perfect." Leonora had never seen him this cold and it frightened her. Shaking Lou and Jimmy off her, Marie-Berthe teetered down the sidewalk. They ran to her and walked her around a corner. Man poured more champagne, but the very air had been spoiled, tasting now like sour milk.

When they returned, Lou looked at Max with a sad and sympathetic understanding, and it filled Leonora with a tight, hot feeling she recognized, grudgingly, as jealousy. Lou had known Max since before Leonora was born, knew him in ways she never would.

And then she realized—everyone at the table was staring, not at Lou or Jimmy, but at her. It appeared that she was clutching a knife, her knuckles white. She laughed and set it down. Seeing Max's pained expression, she looked away. She realized it then and there. If she became as needy as Marie-Berthe, he'd decide he was done with her. He'd fix her with that icy stare, and she'd crumble to a handful of dust.

That night Leonora dreamed of her again. In a crowded room Marie-Berthe fired her gun at her and no one tried to stop her. They only stared. She woke in a sweat.

"I can't stay here. I can't stay in this city," she said.

His eyes were closed and she thought he was sleeping, but then he stroked her forehead. "The light in Paris doesn't suit my new work. There's a town I've been to in Provence. The blue of the sky against the cliffs is like nowhere else."

"Really?" she said, wiping the tears from her face. "We can go?"

He kissed her eyes and nose and cheeks. "There's nothing I'd like more."

The Meal of Lord Candlestick

Leonora, July 1938, Saint-Martin-d'Ardèche, France

That summer, with the help of a hefty wire from her mother, Leonora bought an enclave of abandoned stone buildings in Saint-Martin. She and Max lived in the farmhouse. He took the crumbling church for his studio—sublime heresy he called it—and she took the old post office for hers.

In the mornings, she dipped in the river first thing, and though the rest of the day yawned, slow and warm, she was awake inside it, hungry, as if she could go on forever without stopping. She swept away the cobwebs, and bought beds and dressers, armoires and washstands, tables and lamps to fill the house. She bought two goats, Sophocles and Plato, two peacocks, Orpheus and Eurydice, and a gaggle of chickens, which ran about the acres behind the old farmhouse. Every morning she milked the goats, gathered eggs in a basket, and cooked up omelets which they ate with strong coffee and tea.

Woolf gave birth to four kittens—Lizard, Cricket, Beetle, and Arcimboldo, Archie for short. They lived in the closet for weeks, but then they ventured down the stairs and leapt about the garden as Woolf napped in the dirt and Leonora planted sage and thyme, tomatoes and basil, parsley and cucumbers and eggplants, hoping it wasn't too late in the season.

Max patched the holes in the ceiling, mended the walls, and with cement he formed sculptures on the outside of the house—heads with horns and grimacing mouths. He smoothed cement over a stone wall and she painted the slab with a monstrous bird, its snaking body bigger than hers and its dragon mouth studded with ragged teeth. Like the gargoyles on Notre Dame these would keep the world's evils—including Marie-Berthe—away. They were still married, but at least she was in Paris, and he was here.

The last of Max's sculptures was a bas-relief. A giant, long-necked couple. The woman had a circle for a face, flowers in her hand. The man had a beak, his arms raised in surrender—to love, Max said. In the folds of his robe a winged homunculus danced. Loplop was happy at last.

~❦~

It was late September. Their picnic of dandelion greens and her fat, homegrown tomatoes, of bread from the bakery in town and grapes, cheese, and wine was spread on a slab of river rock, but she wasn't hungry. By this time tomorrow he would be gone. She told herself she'd be fine, but already she had thrown up twice, in secret. To let him know this would have made her manipulative, no better than Marie-Berthe. She sucked a grape. They'd hardly spoken all day. A week ago Marie-Berthe had shown up on their doorstep. Her threats of the convent turned to threats of suicide, and now Max was taking the train to Paris. If he could convince her that they didn't belong together, she would have to let him go.

"It's fine," Leonora said, breaching the silence. "If you have to go, you have to go. But why must you *stay* with her?"

"She's my wife."

"You don't love her."

"When has marriage ever been about love?" He turned a dull, flat stone in his hand, skipped it on the smooth skin of water. Ripples blossomed each place it touched.

One. Two. "Three," she said, feeling cold as the limestone cliffs. It was the number of weeks he'd be gone. She would say nothing more. He'd sworn he'd be divorced by now, that they'd be free to love each other. So what use was talking?

She closed her eyes to feel the dwindling sunlight, to soak it in.

If she didn't swim now, the water would be too cold. She stood, brushed the pebbles from the back of her thighs, and walked into the river, slowly, feeling each inch of flesh as it was taken by the cold. She slipped under, letting the current take her. She could stay in the river and Max would only be a detail in the dream of being human. She could be a selkie if she willed it, if she wanted it enough. It was a story Nanny had told her, about the woman seal who falls in love with a human and hides her skin to be human, too, for a while. She knew if Max left her for long enough she'd slip back into her seal skin and muscle her way to the ocean. He'd never see her again.

She came up for breath. He stood over her, out of breath, too, having run along the rocks to reach her. "You were under too long, *ma chérie.*"

She squinted at him, her eyes tearing in the sun. She didn't tell him she could stay in the water forever if she chose to.

—❦—

9 October 1938

Dearest Fini,

Max is in Paris (perhaps you have seen him?) and I am alone in Ardèche, if you can call taking care of goats, chickens, cats, and two peacocks being alone. I have been thinking of you, my friend, and how much I miss your laugh.

I've begun a new painting, one I think you would like, or at least find humorous. I call it "The Meal of Lord Candlestick." What if the food were alive and the people were dead? I thought. And by people I meant my father (Lord Candlestick himself) and the sort of women I endured at Ascot and the other coming out nonsense at court. In my painting my father has a giant potato for a head and no mouth because I didn't want to hear him say another word. Let him watch these thick-necked women eat his precious baby boy! I painted them eating strange birds, too.

(Nothing to do with Max leaving me here, I assure you.) After a week alone, working on it night and day, I heard one of the women declare, "A flamenco tastes like cherry taffy," and then all of the women chortled, like donkeys.

I've been talking to the cats. What do they think of the direction my painting is going in? What should I have for dinner? Zucchini or rosemary potatoes? (Since Max left I have lost my appetite and eating has become a dull chore.) And then one afternoon, when I asked Cricket (who is the spitting image of Woolf) if she thought it too early in the afternoon to open a bottle of wine, she leapt onto my lap and tilted her head to one side. "When in France," she said with a wink.

Tell me your paintings and your cats speak to you, too, and that I have not lost my head completely. Tell me you have seen Max and that he's sick with longing for me. Tell me you love me and miss me, and that you will come to visit when the weather is fine again, and we can swim in the river like twin mermaids.

Yours,
Carrington

P.S. It's so beautiful here I'm afraid you will hate me. This place will make anyone new if they stay here long enough.

After she sealed and posted the letter, she went for a walk by the river. Max's words repeated themselves, as though they'd been trapped there by the high walls of rock. *She is my wife.* What an ugly word, she thought. *Wife.* It brought to mind barbed wire or an anchor dragging the water.

She lay on the riverbank, letting her body sink into the warm stones and feeling them take hold of her like little gods of permanence. She filled her hands with pebbles and spread them over her body. She'd begun to feel she was made of air, that she could pass through walls like the Sidhe. She thought of how they lived under the ground and she wanted to live there, too. She dug a hole the length of her body and lay in it, then covered herself to her neck with earth and stones.

The cool weight was comforting. She belonged to the darkness, to the mystery of the stones. She forgot about the talking cats and fell asleep.

Marie-Berthe stood over her, looking like a saint with white lace over her dark hair, her silver cross over her injured heart, her tears. Leonora felt a weird prickling in her hands and feet, and realized she couldn't move them. She looked. They had turned to hooves. She tried to speak, but whinnied instead. She shook her hair and felt her neck grow thick and strong. Marie-Berthe held up her cross, as if to ward off a vampire. Leonora reared, and Marie-Berthe fell to her knees, praying a fervent rosary.

And then Leonora ran—over green hills, past her early childhood home, Crookhey Hall, and alongside the sea. At a rowan tree she stopped to catch her breath, and a jackdaw perched on a branch and sang, and she knew it was Max.

She woke with the feeling he was with her, and she brushed off the earth and dipped into the river, which was lit by the moon now and very cold. She dried herself with her dress, pulled her sweater around her, and walked into town along the empty moonlit road. She wanted a beer and more than that she had to speak to someone, anyone, to see if she was still human.

The bar at *Motel des Touristes* was empty save for a ruddy barmaid drying glasses with a dishtowel, and another woman, her silver and black hair drawn up in a knot, who sat at a corner table with her newspaper, her wine, and her cigarette. Leonora ordered a beer and the barmaid eyed her with a mix of disgust and trepidation. "We close in twenty minutes," she said, filling her beer, and with a swish of her hips she vanished into a back room.

The other woman, who had looked up from her paper, waved her over. "Don't mind Madame Barbin," she whispered. "Etienne's wife? You won't get so much as a smile out of her. She despises all beautiful women."

Leonora grinned. So she was still a woman, apparently. She took a sip of beer but it was all foam. "Sit, please," the woman said. "I don't believe we've met."

"Leonora."

"Ah! So you're one of the crazy artists everyone's talking about! I'm Alphonsine. I own the inn down the street."

"The one beside the bakery?"

"That's the one. My husband is the baker. I married him for his croissants." She raised her glass. "It's nice to get a break—from the husband, not the croissants—if you know what I mean."

"I wish I knew." As soon as she said it she wanted to take it back. It wasn't like her to be so forthcoming with a stranger. But as they drank in easy silence, she knew Alphonsine would be her friend. With certain people, you don't have to try. You can just be. She drank the beer and told her all about Max and Marie-Berthe and how alone she'd felt at the farmhouse.

"You must come by the inn anytime you want company. I'm always there. Or else here," she said, finishing the last of her wine.

─❦─

For the weeks until Max returned, Leonora worked on *The Meal of Lord Candlestick* in a kind of fever dream, the way she had worked when she was a student living alone in London. The more she painted, the less she worried what Max or anyone would think. Her anger was on the canvas, becoming clearer by the day. The bird at the center of the cannibal's feast was all bones, picked clean by these women, pale and ravenous, their necks thick as the necks of horses. And when they laughed too loud and long, she cleaned her brushes and visited Alphonsine. She helped her cook meals for the inn, and they shared bottles of wine and talked until the sun went down. Alphonsine filled her in on the town gossip, and Leonora told her all about Paris, about Nusch and Fini and Lee—her wonderfully peculiar friends.

"But don't you miss it?" asked Alphonsine, stirring the béchamel sauce.

"I'm happier here," Leonora said, "with the river and the stars and my animals." She touched her finger to the sauce and tasted it. "When Max returns I'll be right as rain."

Alphonsine didn't ask what she would do if Marie-Berthe refused to divorce him, and for her silent amity, Leonora was grateful.

~&

In Paris Max had sold a few paintings, and Marie-Berthe, at the end of his stay, had agreed to *consider* a divorce. "It's something," he said to Leonora's silence.

"I don't care about marriage," she said. "I'm just glad you're back." It was true. With his snores evening out her breathing, the fears that had racked her stomach and nerves went dormant. They were silent, and so small they could reside in her toenails.

She and Max didn't leave the bed for days. "My kumquat," he called her.

"Yes, my little bird?" she replied, and he bit her all over and she screamed like a child being tickled, like a rabbit being chased. There was no end to their games.

Cricket still regarded her quizzically. Leonora knew she was thinking things through, but with Max around the cat kept her reasoning to herself. Only when Leonora was painting would she cock her head and mutter asides. *Time for wine,* she'd say. Or, *Perhaps a touch more red?*

Leonora was finishing *The Meal of Lord Candlestick.* Against the green tint she'd given the wall and the tabletop, the yellow of Lord Candlestick's bloated face, of the flowers and the flames, appeared jaundiced. The painting delighted and sickened her. She added a filly with flowers on her head, but the horse disappeared beside the fork stuck into the belly of the live baby boy whose screams she couldn't quite hear for the women's ravenous laughter.

Looking at her painting, Max took his time. He was always quiet when he was really taking a piece in. She stood behind him and tried not to gauge the shifting angle of his stance as any indication of his thoughts. All the confidence she'd had while she was painting was gone. If this was a reflection of her, of the world that went on inside her, what did it mean? He'd know how far she'd strayed, and into what strange territory, without him here to ground her. He'd see her weakness, her need for him. And he'd leave.

At last he turned to her. Something in his eyes had changed, as if he'd thought she was someone else, someone different, as if he were seeing her right now for the first time.

And was there a hint of disquiet? Of queasiness?

Yes. She had surprised him.

"You've gone there," he said. "Stepped into your nightmare and painted it so exquisitely it will frighten us all." He shook his head and grinned. "You're amazing."

Max, June 1940, Saint-Martin-d'Ardèche, France

"Leonora!" Max's voice echoes off the high ceiling, and he is home, in this house he knows like his own body. "Hello lizard," he says to the giant cement sculpture on the wall in the foyer, the lizard he gave ragged wings and a crown of spires. Every time he passed it on his way out the front door, he straightened his spine, standing a little taller, as if receiving a blessing from the king of the cold-bloods. In the time he's been away it seems to have shrunk, and now it refuses to look at him.

Has he changed so much? Is he unrecognizable?

A mirror hangs crookedly in the entry, and a man stands crookedly inside it. He stares at him without mercy. His skin is sallow, a sickly gray-green. Huge, sunken eyes swim in his sharpened skull. He attempts a smile but his teeth are dull and gray. His cheekbones poke at his skin. Max turns from him. He's never liked old men or fools, and this man is both. What would Leonora want with a man like this?

"Leonora?" His voice stretches, thin and high. If they hurry, they can pack tonight and leave tomorrow, before they come for him, as someone is sure to. He moves past the foyer calling her name, past her sculpture of a horse's head, which swells, openmouthed, from the stone wall. *You won't find her here*, it drawls.

There are voices, men's voices, men's laughter. He can smell cigarette smoke and something else. Roast chicken. Maybe Leonora is hosting a gathering, maybe they have visitors fleeing from Paris, on their way south, out of France, toward Spain and Portugal and freedom? He doesn't want to see anyone, only her, but he pulls his shoulders back and walks to the kitchen.

Before he turns the corner, he knows he was wrong. It is the wrong sort of laughter.

Farmers sit at their table, eating chicken, playing poker, cards in their greasy hands. Men from the village, men he's seen in passing, and each of them, he notices, is missing a pinky. One wears a bandage around his hand. Max's stomach turns, hollow and sour. He doesn't believe in war. He understands the desire to maim oneself to stay out of the horror, to stay at home and protect those you love, and yet it sickens him, seeing these men at his table, their mud-caked shoes soiling his floor.

A man tilts his chair against the wall, his bare feet propped on the table beside the chicken's decimated carcass. He sucks the joint of a chicken leg. Max can almost remember his name. He owns the other bar and inn down the street, a few doors down from Alphonsine's. *Motel des Touristes* it is called. His wife so despised Leonora—for her beauty and her youth—that she refused to speak to her. The man rights the chair, Max's antique wooden chair, which creaks, as if it wants him to get the hell off it. His eyes on Max, he gets to his feet, puffs up his chest, and strides toward him, hands clenched at his sides. "It's not your home anymore." *Etienne*, that's his name.

"But Etienne," Max says, attempting a soothing tone. Etienne relaxes his fists. He still has all of his fingers. But then, he is too old for conscription. He huffs, and coughs, and opens a drawer in the bureau. Handing Max a small stack of papers, he shakes his head, as if unable to believe his good fortune.

Max recognizes the top paper. It's the deed to their house. My God, what did she do? He flips through the papers. She signed them only weeks ago, scarcely a month after the gendarmes took him away.

What happened to her? She'd been working at her vines, planting tomatoes and basil, scattering last year's hollyhock seeds. But then she didn't write to him as she had when he was taken before. When they took him this time, she gave up, he knows, looking at the man's name in her jagged script, *Etienne Le Blanc*, the man who owns their house, and therefore their sculptures and murals. And where is she? Where is Leonora?

"Mademoiselle left with a woman and a man," Etienne says, as if Max had asked the question out loud. He takes a scrap of paper from the drawer and gives it to him. *Dear Max, I have gone with C., and will wait for you in Estremadura. L.*

She left him only a note, only a sentence? He clamps his teeth, slowly, seamlessly, every tooth fitting together. He will not yell. He won't upend the table, send their platter of chicken flying. He doesn't have the strength. And anyhow, that's never been his way. He examines the flimsy remnant. Her scrawl is more slanted than on the deed, her *e*'s more like headless *i*'s, like she was rushing, not bothering to breathe. *Estremadura*, she wrote—Portugal, where you could still leave for America if you were lucky. It was like her, to be cryptic, choosing to name the entire region rather than specify Lisbon, where they'd agreed to meet should he be taken again, should she *have* to leave. But why wouldn't she have waited longer than this?

I have gone with C, the note says. C? Who is C?

The man offers him a chair and nudges the rent carcass of the hen his way. An offering. The men have pulled her apart with their dirty fingers, their dirty nails. Even so he reaches for a thigh, which is delicious, gristle and all. He sucks the bone clean and adds it to the pile. Which of their chickens, now Etienne's, is this one? Leonora named them all. Is this Celine, Agatha, Gretchen—*Catherine*! That's it! That's the woman's name, Leonora's English friend, the one living in Paris with a Hungarian. Catherine, who must have been fleeing, heading south like everyone else.

"Join us for a hand?" says the dealer. Max shakes his head. His eyelids are heavy, his body exhausted.

A man pushes a bottle of wine toward him. It's their wine, the dry white they bottled last year, the wine Leonora named for Winkie. He takes a swig—lemons, green apples, hay, with a finish of despair that lingers on his tongue, catches in his throat. Thinking he might weep, right here in front of these men, he closes his eyes, swallows.

Beetle, Leonora's black cat, jumps onto the table and licks a chicken bone, and Etienne takes him onto his lap and strokes his shiny back. He nods at Max. "You can stay tonight," he says, gesturing toward the ceiling. "There are rooms."

"Yes. I know." After all, the house is *his*, but he is too exhausted to make a scene. He pushes in his chair, some vestige of civility left over from his youth. The four-fingered men keep their eyes on their cards.

In the living room by the empty hearth, Max's chessboard is still on the table. Their paintings are on the walls—the two pieces they'd finished just before he was taken away. They are, he realizes now, companion pieces, and they seem prophetic. The portrait she made of him shows a frozen land. He wears a coat of auburn feathers, a fish tail dragging the ice behind him. If he moves fast enough, he thinks, he can still get away. He can fly or swim, before the ice clutches his tail, crippling his feathers. Why hadn't he seen it before? How the painting calls for motion, for sudden heat to melt the ice. On the wall opposite hangs his piece, *Leonora in the Morning Light*, small and intricate. He'd wanted it to be perfect and he worked for days, hardly stopping, as if they might come back any moment and tear him from it, from her. He'd meant for it to make her happy, but it scared her, she said. She was alone in a jungle. A wonderful, mythic jungle he told her.

So why the tiny skeleton? Why the minotaur with his open mouth?

No matter what he tries to make, something else always comes through. Only he's too stupid to see it, to read what it means. But she knew. Somehow she always does.

He takes the stairs one at a time. Best to be in the present, to not think ahead, and not to dwell in the past either, but how can he manage that, when the past is all that is left? He hears her voice, calling him to bed—*Max? Max!*—and he wants to move up the stairs as he used to, two at a time, flying toward his name. He loves how she says it. In her accent it sounds like she is eating something wonderful—

mmmm, ahhhh—and might even give you a bite. *Max!* he hears, but it's just the wind against a window. And the stairs go on forever, gravity an awful pull. He grips the railing and climbs.

He opens the door to their room, to the sour smell of sweat, their sky-blue sheets rumpled, darkened by bodies—not his, not hers, other bodies in their bed. The closet door is flung wide, her clothes stretching across the floor as in some anguished attempt at escape. The bottom drawer in her bureau hangs open like a mouth, aghast at such indecency. Closing it, he sees that the box in the corner, where they always kept their passports, is empty. Well, of course she took hers, but his? Not that it would do him any good now—but if she meant to get him a visa, why didn't she leave more details as to where she was going?

Sweating, blood rushing in his ears, he opens a window. There's a breeze off the cooling fields, a low moon, orange and bloated, sinking. He lies on the bed, too spent to throw off his clothes. Rolling onto his side, he hugs a pillow to the hollow of his stomach to stifle its growls. He feels the anger leave him, feels a wave of sleep break over him as he imagines it is her thin back, warming him all the way through.

His mind refuses to rest, seizing on one fear after another. She could be anywhere by now. How on earth will he find her? And the Germans. They might not be here, in this portion of France, but they will force the French to comply with their desires. If he's found, they'll ship him back to Germany, to the camps where the *undesirables* are kept—in what ghastly conditions he can't begin to imagine.

⚬

He wakes damp with sweat, the room still and hot. He is on the floor, having moved there sometime in the night, the bed too soft to sleep in after the weeks on hard ground. And for the moment before he opens his eyes, he is back in Camp des Milles, the air thick with the dust of bricks. He hears coughing, it must be Hans Bellmer, he thinks.

But Max is alone, in his own room, in a patch of sun. Outside, cicadas buzz, a peacock cries, but in the house there is not a moan, not a creak. In the lit air, the motes of dust dance and glow. Over the candle Leonora burned their last night together, a spiderweb shines, thick with golden dust. May and still cold. The night they—why can't he remember? Did they read to go to bed, as they often did, since they made love in the day, preferably out of doors, and best of all beside the river?

He can picture her reading by candlelight with her good, young eyes, reading her childhood copy of *Alice*, which, she said, if she read right before bed, would help her to wake with visions, and to paint with a peculiar curiosity. But what had come instead? Gendarmes with handcuffs, and it was back to Camp des Milles.

Now he is a stranger in his own house.

And here comes Etienne stomping up the stairs to remind him. Max is on the floor still, and Etienne glowers down at him, hands on his hips. He is dressed for the field in his cap and boots, his shirt-sleeves rolled to his elbows. "Up and out with you!" Etienne's eyes cast about the room for what might be missing. "I'm not running a boardinghouse." He softens, shakes his head, as if he just hadn't seen this coming. "You have somewhere to go?"

"I have to arrange things."

"I can't have you here. They could take the house. Harboring an undesirable is a criminal offense." He sighs. "You have one more night."

Max sits. He rises slowly, but his knees buckle, and he's back on the ground. Etienne helps him to his feet. "You'll come down and eat now. Eggs, bread, coffee."

Coffee. He can smell it brewing and it fills him with something like hope.

At the table, Etienne and a farmer Max recognizes from down the way hunch over their food, speaking to each other in grunts. The grapes are looking healthy. The harvest should be plentiful. He'll sell the wine at his bar, slap the bottles with his own label.

Etienne goes to the stove and returns with an omelet. "Sit," he tells Max.

The omelet is cheese and potato, with fresh chives sprinkled on top. Max cuts off a corner with the side of his fork. He eats a small bite, taking it all in—the smell of the steam, the melted Gruyère, the potato. He could cry from the beauty of such simple food.

Etienne puts a cup of coffee in front of him.

"*Merci.*" Max takes a sip. Thick and bitter, it is a holy thing.

Can he feel grateful to a man who has stolen what was his?

At this moment, he can, he does.

Etienne opens the door to a cloudless sky, a balmy breeze. As he and the farmer leave, he glances back at Max. "You can do the dishes as payment for your bed and board."

Max watches him go. Tonight. He will leave tonight, as Etienne sleeps. He checks the pantry. A few jars of Leonora's olives are left. A dozen bottles of her wine. He grabs two bottles, wishing he could carry more, and both jars of olives.

In the sunlit living room, their paintings glow. He'll remove them from their stretchers, roll them inside each other and take what he can.

Upstairs, in their closet, he finds his old knapsack, the leather soft from years of use. He's had this since before the first war. Amazing he's managed to hold on to anything for so long. In a pocket is a small sketchbook, and inside it, a few photos—his mother and father, young and blameless, children on their wedding day. Looking at the photo, trying to imagine them now, he wonders if they're still alive. It's been twenty years since he's seen them. They came to the Dada exhibit in Cologne, in the Brauhaus brewery, when everyone entered through the men's lavatory, where a young girl in a communion dress read obscene poetry. He smiles at their gumption, and then he thinks of the letter his father sent him after the show. *I curse you*, it said. *You have dishonored our name.* The fallout of Dada was inevitable, but now he swallows—regret? The old Catholic guilt? Or maybe it's just the sadness that comes with living long enough to look back that far.

The other photo is of Lou, with her head of cropped hair, little Jimmy on her lap. He'd just turned one. Looking at her easy face, he thinks of her sharpness, her humor. Far quicker with her wit than he'd ever been. And where is she now? In another camp? Or did she escape like he did?

He walks back into the kitchen and pours himself more coffee. He watches Etienne and the farmer walk among the vines. A cat, one of the orange tabbies, nuzzles his leg and he lifts her into his arms. Is she Woolf or Cricket? Mother or daughter? Only Leonora could tell the two apart. She pushes her head into his hand and he rubs her neck, feeling her muscles under her soft fur. Leonora loved these cats with such ferocity, he can't understand how she could have left them. A claw catches on his sleeve. "I'm sorry she left you. I'm sure she didn't want to," he tells the cat—Cricket, he decides—unhooking her paw and setting her down. And then he's washing the dishes. He's not sure why, except that he likes standing here. He can feel Leonora's presence, how she stood right here, day after day, rinsing these same dishes, looking out at these fields, these olive trees, these vines.

~&

Later that morning he heads into town to visit Alphonsine. Though she was always more Leonora's friend than his, he hopes she'll help him, let him use her phone. Maybe she'll even know something of what became of Leonora.

On the cobblestone street a woman waddles toward him, a scarf around her head, bags of vegetables swinging from her hands. The farmers must be convening for the weekly market, he thinks, hungry again. What he'd give for a juicy peach, for a fresh green salad. It is Etienne's wife, he realizes, as they near each other. He smiles, and then looks quickly away. He showered, changed into clean clothes, and still he's ragged, his trousers hanging from his hips, his shirt too big. He avoids her eyes as they pass, but he feels her watching him, feels her judgment and anger, as though this war were somehow his fault.

At the inn, Alphonsine is helping a maid change the sheets of a bed in one of her upstairs rooms. Her hair looks grayer, wound up in a loose bun, and her face, when she turns and takes him in, is etched with fatigue. "Max! You're back!"

"What happened to her, Alphonsine?"

She links her arm in his and walks him down the hall. On the balcony, they lean on a railing. She lights a cigarette, offers him one. She hasn't always been so kind to him, but she was there for Leonora during that time when he was in Paris. He feels awful about it now, and he'd like to tell her, to ask her forgiveness. But when she leans in, lighting his cigarette, there is sympathy in her eyes, and he knows he doesn't need to ask.

The smoke takes him back. For the briefest moment he's not a refugee, but an artist. He is in Paris again, at Café de Flore, a serene and privileged observer of the world.

"I don't know what happened to her," Alphonsine says, looking out over the fields toward the river. "I've been so busy, with everyone fleeing Paris. There were people sleeping on the floor until yesterday. Pierre said she stopped by, asking about traveling permits and saying something about Portugal I think. I was at the market, and before that . . ." Her voice drifts into silence. "She was different. She was talking to the cats."

He inhales—a quick, shallow breath. If he'd been here, it wouldn't have happened. "I have to find her," he says. "I have such a terrible feeling about where she might have ended up. Can I use your phone?"

"*Mais oui.*" She strokes his hair, smoothing a few strands over his forehead, the way his mother used to. "But quickly. Pierre will be back soon, and he's made a rule."

At the phone behind the reception desk Max dials the number he somehow remembers by heart. It rings and rings, and then there's a woman, her voice throaty, buoyant. "Hello?"

"Lee?"

"Max? Where are you calling from? Are you all right?"

"I can't tell you how good it is to hear your voice. Listen, you have to help me."

"Anything."

"Leonora is gone. She signed our house over to a man from town. It's terrible. But worse, she isn't here. She left a note. She's headed to Portugal, with Catherine."

"Who?"

"Catherine." He was trying not to shout. "Ursula's friend."

"Slow down, dear. You're breaking up."

"Do you know where Leonora is? Has she been in touch?"

"The last I spoke with her, she wasn't making sense. She had a weird laugh, not hers at all. But that was back in December."

"Nothing since then?"

"Not a thing."

Pierre, Alphonsine's husband, ducks inside from the bright street. He's so tall the room shrinks when he enters it. Max turns his back to him and speaks fast into the phone. "I need help. A visa. She took my passport, though the damn thing wouldn't do me any good anyhow."

He can hear her light a cigarette, the sharp inhale of breath. "We'll get word to Peggy Guggenheim, all right?" Lee says. "I'd rather not speak with her personally—you know how I feel about her—but she's financing passage for Breton and his family to America—"

"Yes—" he says, just as Pierre takes the phone from his hand.

───⚓───

No moon, at least not yet, and Etienne and his friends are so drunk their snores rumble through the house, and no one stirs. He wears his black wool traveling cape, the hood over his head, to disappear into the night. He's filled the knapsack with the wine and olives, cheese and salami, with his best jacket, another pair of trousers, and a few good shirts.

He picks up Leonora's photo album, to try to fit it in, too, and it falls, opening to them. She's topless on the bank of Lambe Creek and he's the thing emerged from the ocean, dripping and draped in sea-weed. He's a swampy old man and she's golden. What could she have seen in him, he wonders, wedging it into the sack along with her copy of *Alice*, his collage novel, and the collections of stories she wrote, *La Dame Ovale* and her latest, *La Maison de la Peur*. The House of Fear.

He steals down the stairs. One by one, he lifts their paintings from the walls, standing on a chair to do it, careful to not make a sound. It seems he's become nocturnal—like a thief, mouse, or roach, those unwanted creatures that move in darkness as the masters sleep. He carries the paintings to the old church, his studio.

He bumbles down the aisle between the pews, up the stairs to the pulpit, and lights a candle. It's exactly as he left it. On a table he made from a door, his brushes rise like dried flowers from a jar, his tubes of paint with their shriveled skins lie side by side, and a cup with a ring of dried coffee at the bottom sits where he last set it down. His roll of canvas leans on the old lectern beside the stack of boards and nails. Everything's out and ready, waiting for him. He faces his empty easel and sighs, wondering what he'd give to be able to stay. His pinky would be a small price for another year of such perfect light.

Kneeling on the floor, he pulls the nails from the paintings and peels them from their wooden stretchers. Here's *Bride of the Wind*—the painting he gave her their first Christmas together. Laying butcher paper on top of it, then her self-portrait—*Inn of the Dawn Horse*, her wild eyes, her roiling hair, he stops to look at the blur in the painting where the ghostly creature had been. It was late on Christmas Eve and they were tight on champagne. He'd told her he loved it, but when she insisted he elaborate, he couldn't lie. He said the specter seemed out of place, one element too many. She'd tried to explain it to him. It was one of the Sidhe, she'd said. And then she'd been quiet. When he insisted she keep it, she'd wiped it out. But she'd left the blur and its shadow, and her defiance makes him smile.

More butcher paper and then her *The Meal of Lord Candlestick* with its gluttonous, grotesque women, her portrait of him, the winter-scape, and his *A Moment of Calm*. He covers these with his newest explorations in decalcomania, the paint pressed onto the canvas with a pane of glass, and the organic, accidental shapes enhanced, and then made deliberate. Here are the two of Leonora, *Morning Light* and the other, which is nearly too large to carry, *The Robing of the Bride*, Leonora's body cloaked in feathers and a crane-headed man guarding her with a broken spear. Only he wasn't there for her, he thinks, touching her bare belly. He rolls the paintings and wedges them into his pack, from which they extend like a telescope aimed at the stars.

A beam of light moves through the trees and into the church. He crouches below the window and watches the man with the flashlight pass by. He can tell from the limp and the hunch of his back it's the half-wit who lives with his mother. Is this who reported him? He wants to strangle him, to beat him, to leave him for dead beside the road.

The thought that he's capable of such violence horrifies him. What have they made him into? Is he no better than the gendarmes, no better than the Nazis?

He watches the light disappear around the corner, looks around his studio one last time, and blows out the candle. He enters the night, once again skirting the brambles and bushes, slinking through the fields. He knows a prefect from Aiguèze who used to meet him at *Motel des Touristes* now and then for drinks and rousing discussions, a man he hopes is friend enough to give him an exit visa. He'll have to cross the Loire to reach him, and now he carries photographs, books, and paintings. He can't cross the river on his own, but since bridges are out of the question he follows the riverbank. Sometimes a house has a boat, a little rowboat, out back.

As he walks, the moon climbs, wavering in the river, and his thoughts fall to what Lee said. How Leonora's laugh was strange. How did she put it? *Not hers at all.* And she'd been talking to the cats, Alphonsine said, which means, he knows, that the cats had been talking to her. This isn't new. He'd overheard her conversing with them before. It's the fact that she couldn't hide it from practical, stalwart Alphonsine that worries him. He recalls the look she sometimes has if she's been painting all day and into the night, drinking wine and painting, forgetting to eat. Her eyes turn feral—distant and uncanny, frightened, almost, by what they see.

Up ahead, some shining thing catches his eye. As he comes closer, he realizes it is, in fact, a dinghy, and he pushes it into the river and rows it over the quiet water. The moon smiles at his theft, at what he has become. "*Mea culpa*," he mutters to no one, pulling the boat far up on shore so it won't float away, and he thinks of Marie-Berthe, wonders how many times she would cross herself were she here.

He arrives at the house of the prefect Monsieur de Langelier just after dawn. He stands between the trimmed hedges at a large blue door, uses the brass knocker shaped like a fist.

One, two, three. Six. Nine.

He waits in the birdsong brightness. It's too early, he should come back, he's thinking, when a butler opens the door, his face and jacket creased, his eyelids heavy. Max explains why he's there in as simple terms as he can, and the man lets him in, sits him in the kitchen, where the cook gives him coffee and a hot baguette and he floats on a yeasty cloud of warmth. Monsieur is not at home, and they seem uncertain as to when he might return. "But," the butler explains, "a friend of Monsieur's, Georges, the eccentric prefect of La Roque-sur-Cèze, lives in a castle where he most certainly will remain for the duration of the war." The cook lights up with the sort of secret knowledge all good cooks harbor and she chuckles into her sleeve.

Max likes the sound of him. The Eccentric Prefect of La Roque-sur-Cèze. He belongs in one of Leonora's stories. Wonderful, he tells them. But night is better for travel and he's tired. Can he sleep here? Is there an extra bed? And if they have a phone, can he make a quick call?

The butler puckers his mouth at this new inconvenience. The cook, however, taking him in with a single glance, wipes her hands on her immaculate apron and smiles, dimples in her cheeks, mischief in her eyes. The poor artist can sleep in her bed. After all, she won't be needing it today.

The butler shows him to a study, hovering at the door as he dials up Lee. "Don't be long," he says, curtly. Max watches him mosey down the hall, stopping to straighten a picture frame. He doesn't trust him. The man has too much time on his hands.

Roland's man answers, and then Roland is on the phone. He spoke to Kay Sage, he says, Tanguy's new wife, who spoke to Peggy, who plans to be back in Marseille as soon as possible. If he will meet her there—she thought there would be room, come September, at the Villa Air-Bel, the house in the nearby countryside where so many exiled artists are hiding—she'll do all she can to arrange his passage to the States.

"Why would she do so much to help me?"

"Let's just say she has a *thing* for artists." He laughs. She made a point, too, he says, of telling him she had just seen Max's sculptures in *Cahiers d'Art* and loved them. Max jots down her address in Grenoble as Roland tells it to him. "Oh, I almost forgot," Roland says in a rush. "I heard from Ursula. Catherine was on her way to Spain. Which means Leonora might be headed to Spain, too."

It isn't much, but it's something. He thanks him. "Give my love to Lee," he says, and hangs up.

Spain. And then to Lisbon? But how will he possibly reach her? The thought is bewildering. Even if he manages to get an exit visa for France, he'll need an entrance visa for Spain. And he needs money. Why didn't he ask him for some? As a friend Roland would certainly do what he could. He picks up the phone again, to dial him back, and then hangs it up. How would he get the money to him? He needs somewhere to stay for a while, first of all, and then he'll figure out funds.

He glances down the hall. The butler is gone, it seems, and here is yesterday's newspaper on the desk. He flips through it, looking for any news on the armistice. Once again, it's near the back. The terms have been decided. And there it is. Clause nineteen. The French would hand over to the Nazis all "wanted" Germans. Anyone on their list. It's as he expected. The French fascists are complying with the Nazis. Dizzy, he sits for a minute. He thinks of the men on that train, who were most likely in a new camp by now. What would stop the French from handing them all over? They wouldn't have to house or feed them. They'd be the Nazis' problem. He's out of the camp, thank God, but he's going to have to hide for a while. The prefect will let him stay, he hopes, and Peggy Guggenheim will help him.

He searches the cabinets in the study until he finds a map and a compass. He slides the compass into his pocket, rolls the map and slips it into the tube of paintings. He takes a hot bath and, still naked, slips into the cook's soft, single bed, in a room that smells of chicken broth. Dreaming of Leonora locked in a crumbling tower, of her face in a small, high window as he searches his pockets for the key, he wakes to dusk—dusk already!—and a body pressed up behind him, cradling him, a body so substantial he feels small against it, protected, and the hand on him, around him, squeezing, moving up and down, is a hand that has milked cows, a hand that knows its worth is in motion, in work. Turning to the cook, falling into her blue eyes, into her body as into risen dough, he is absorbed. He has no strength to resist this gift. The weeks he's been away from Leonora feel like years. He's forgotten how it feels to be taken, to enter the warm ocean of another, to feel that ocean consume him, to feel it swell inside him, build and crash, wave on wave, God, he's forgotten how it feels to be to alive. "Fuck," he says, "fuck." And she pets his thinning hair, kisses his eyelids and presses him to her breast, and he drifts back into sleep.

From her heavy arms he slips into the weightlessness of the night, taking a loaf of her bread with him. Trotting down the drive, he's light enough to fly. When he reaches the road, he hears a car start up behind him. His armpits prickle. Drenched in sweat, he slows to a walk. He looks over his shoulder and the headlights are on him. The car rolls up beside him. It's the gendarmerie. The butler must have called them. The window is down, a shadow man behind the wheel. "Max Ernst?" he asks. "Get in. Unless you have release papers from Camp des Milles?" He opens the door.

To run would be ridiculous. Max takes a bite of the warm bread before the gendarme can stop him.

⁓⌗

Max is kept in the town prison with the drunks until morning, when a young gendarme puts him in handcuffs and drives him to Nîmes. He doesn't protest. The metal against his wrists is cool, and the gendarme rolls both windows down. He stares at the ancient town and then at the fields moving past him for what might be the last time, this land of Provence that had felt wide and easy, endless as their freedom. He'd thought it had been made for them, for him and his bride of the wind. Looking at a walled village on a hill, he forgets that he's still an enemy to France. He forgets he's a pawn, about to be handed over from one government to another. He tries not to notice the sunflowers, bobbing their heads in a somber *adieu*.

When they arrive, the gendarme leads him to the camp still in handcuffs, like a common criminal. They pass the guards and walk through an old iron gate with the words *San Nicola* tilting across it. This was someone's home once, he realizes, looking at the barbed wire fence freshly and shoddily erected—an attempt to turn this abandoned farm into a prison camp. Inside the fence the green fields are scattered with pretty white tents pointed like party hats. There are a few old stone buildings, too, a farmhouse, and smaller structures for the help, now for the officers, he figures, and the guards. Not nearly as bad as Camp des Milles, he thinks, and then the smell hits him. The stench of the open latrines, the communal furrow where two thousand men are expected to relieve themselves.

They find the commandant in the farmhouse, at a big desk in the study. He tells the gendarme to remove the cuffs, he'll take things from here. Max considers explaining why he left, why he had to leave. But he's hardly unique. The majority of the men here have some loved one they want more than all else to find. The commandant runs a hand over his unshaven neck. He looks exhausted. He shakes his head, as if he doesn't want to do what he has to do, and nods at the guard. "It's only for a day," he tells Max. The guard tries to take his knapsack.

"It's all I have," Max says, tightening his grip on the straps.

"You'll get it back," says the commandant. And the guard takes what remains of his life.

He's put in a decrepit wooden structure that was once the pigsty. The guard locks the door behind him. He sits on the dirt, the slatted roof too low for him to stand. Sun falls through the cracks. And though the pigsty is hot, he lifts his face to the sunlight. A blessing. It means he is still on this Earth.

There's a thin layer of straw on the floor, but when he lies down the smell is rank. It's the smell of human feces. It seems the men who were locked in here before him dug holes with their hands, then covered their shit with straw. One day. He tells himself he can last.

He sits cross-legged and closes his eyes. Flies land on his face and he must continually swat them away. He can hear the men's voices as they pass. They speak to one another loudly, with nerve and vigor. They speak as if what they have to say means something. But it's all chance, isn't it, this business of fate? Yesterday afternoon he was swathed, swallowed in the softness of the cook's bed, in the softness of the cook herself, lusty, smelling of dough, spiced meat, and pitted fruit. And here he is now in a pigsty. But then, had he not stayed for the day, he might not have been caught. This is his punishment, he can hear his father saying. He deserves to be here.

He listens to the men in the camp, Frenchmen from town most likely, hawking their wares. *Leather shoes in fine shape, size ten, newspapers from Paris, wine, whiskey, tomato salad, and roasted chicken. All for a very good price.* Who can blame them? One man's misery is another's profit. It's the way of the world. And right now he'd trade a painting for a tomato, a piece of chicken, and a glass of wine.

The sun inches across the blue. Hot and high, it hangs overhead as if for the sole purpose of making him sweat. His mouth grows so dry he can't swallow. At last a guard brings him a small pail of water, a few slices of bread, moldy and hard. He drinks the water in small sips, savoring each one, making it last. When dusk comes and he's been given nothing more to eat, he scrapes off the mold with his fingernail, breaks off a corner of the bread and chews. As soon as he's out of the pigsty, he decides, he will escape, slip through the barbed wire and blend once again with the shadows.

Leonora, August 1939, Saint-Martin-d'Ardèche

Friends arrived on a hot, dry wind. Fini with her men—André Pieyre de Mandiargues, the French writer, and Federico Veneziani, the Italian. Soon after, Lee and Roland joined as well. It was Lambe Creek all over again, a two-week party, with Max and Leonora as hosts. Everyone worked in the mornings, swam in the Loire in the afternoons, and in the evenings they drank wine and ate their supper under the brightening planets, listening to the throaty songs of frogs.

~✽

Dressed in one of Fini's flowing white blouses and a skirt, Leonora sat in a chair in the garden as the artist draped a shawl over her shoulders. Fini painted wherever she was, and she traveled always with her trunk of clothes—her inspiration. In another week she and her men would be on their way to Arcachon, a French beach town on the Atlantic, to spend a month with Dalí and Gala, and Leonora didn't want to see her go.

"Dalí I understand," Leonora said. "But Gala? Jimmy told me his mother felt like she was this witch who stole Max away."

"And into the life that was waiting for him. Think of it—if she hadn't seduced him, you and I wouldn't be here now. Our lives are entwined, more than we can possibly understand." She unpinned Leonora's bun, let her hair fall. "You know what makes her so powerful? She realized it was a man's world and accepted that fact. She didn't try to defy it, the way we are—making our own art. I'm sure she thinks we're taking the hard, stupid route. Why paint when she can inspire genius? Just watch—fifty years from now it's going to be her face hanging on the museum walls." She moved Leonora's arm so it balanced on a knee. "Now sit still. I'll sketch you. It won't take long."

Fini was working quickly, with charcoal, but not quick enough. Leonora tried to breathe deeply, to empty her mind, but she felt as if she might leap out of her skin and run for the hills. The birdsong didn't help. It sounded false. Right now, in some little town like this, Nazis were rounding up Jews, artists, homosexuals, and Communists— anyone who didn't fit their Wagnerian ideal. She shivered. Most of the time she kept so busy writing stories she couldn't hear the great grinding wheels of the tanks, couldn't hear the gunshots and the screams, but now, sitting here, she couldn't keep them out. Germany had taken Czechoslovakia. The Nazis were spreading their terror like tar from a leaky barrel.

"You've been writing?" Fini asked. Writing and not painting, Leonora thought. Painting opened up that other world inside her, and she didn't feel safe there. Every time she closed the door to her studio, she panicked—the way she was panicking now. "What are you calling your book?" Fini asked. But she couldn't say a word. She was frozen somehow. "Carrington?"

"It's called *La Maison de la Peur*," she said, able to speak again.

Leonor was sketching her eyes, looking at her with such intensity it brought her back. "You've made a piece of heaven, Leonora," she said. "But you need to be prepared to leave if you have to. You know that, right?"

Her eyes filled. The sudden emotion surprised her and she tried to swallow it down. She'd gotten a letter from Mother last week. England was preparing to go to war with Germany. She begged her to come home. And Leonora hadn't said a thing to Max about it. They decided they wouldn't talk about the Nazis, that their home was a safe zone— from even talk of war.

"You know what's happening, don't you? You read the paper?" Fini asked.

"We made a pact not to live in fear. Max says it's the death of creativity."

"You want me to talk some sense into him?"

The portrait, when Leonor finished it, had the feel of a sketch—with Leonora's face as the fulcrum. She stared at it. How had she managed to make her so beautiful? Of course, it wasn't *her*, really, but how Fini saw her.

Looking at it she felt different. Stronger.

⟶❀

She found Max in his church studio. The high sun angled through the open windows, and the room was hot. He was shirtless, working at a new, large painting. An intricate forest under a dawn sky. *A Moment of Calm*, he was calling it. His back to her, he kept working. He hated to be interrupted, but if she didn't talk to him now she knew she'd lose her courage. They wouldn't be alone again until they went to bed, and if they talked then, she wouldn't sleep.

"Max? Darling?"

"*Oui?*" Wiping his brush with a rag, he dipped it into the white squiggle on his palette, making the lightest of greens.

"I hoped we could talk."

"Go ahead."

So that's how it would be. She took a breath. "Leonor is worried for us."

"Is she?" he said, still not looking at her.

"And in her letter my mother—" She sounded like a child, bringing up her mother. "She said England was mobilizing. War is imminent. She begged me to come home."

"You're a free person, Leonora. If you want to go, then go." He said it easily, as if she were no more than his maid.

"If Germany took Czechoslovakia, what's to stop them from coming here?" She waited for his reply, watched him paint in silence. And now she hated that friends had come. They had brought the war with them, and she and Max had no time to themselves. "Max, goddamn it. Look at me." He lifted his gaze, his eyes cold and livid. "*We* should leave, that's what I'm saying. We could go to America, find a place like Saint-Martin, somewhere with big sky and a river. We made this home, we can make another."

He put down the brush. Under his careful calm he was raging. "I'm working, Leonora. Can't you see that?" He spoke too quietly, as if to a child. "I need peace. What about that do you not understand?"

"You can't just ignore this. It isn't going away. We *have* to talk."

"About what? If you need to go then go. Go with Lee and Roland if you want to. I'm staying right here."

She left the church, slamming the door behind her. Maybe she *would* go. He could have his bloody peace until the Germans came and locked him up.

"Wait," he called. She kept walking. "Please." She stopped, let him speak to her back.

"Nora, I'm sorry. I know you're afraid. I know."

She turned. He was that lost boy again, and all the anger fizzled out of her.

"I'd been ruled by fear, like the rest of the soldiers. I did what Germany wanted me to do. I killed men, good men. Paul and I shot at each other across the field in Verdun. What if one of us hadn't missed?" She took his hand, wanting him to know she was here. "When I came back from the war, I promised myself no matter what happened I wouldn't be afraid."

"But we could go. Start over someplace else."

"Nora. Look around. This is our home." She saw the grapes plump on the vines. The giant cement couple loomed from the wall, a wren perched on the man's beak.

She knew they weren't going anywhere.

That night she couldn't sleep, and when she went to the kitchen for warm milk, the scissors on the counter were waiting for her. She took them in hand and cut a small lock of hair. She thought she'd bury it beside the potatoes, which seemed to have no trouble sleeping through both night and day. She remembered how safe and pure she'd felt when she'd dug a hole and buried her body by the river, and she thought if she buried her hair by the potatoes she might feel heavy, starchy, and tired. She dug the hole, covered her hair with soil. The moon was full, and it must have soaked her with its ghostly blood, because she had a wonderful idea.

Shears in hand, she crept through the old house and up the stairs, her heart beating wildly. Roland and Lee slept in the first bedroom. She opened their door slowly, without a sound. Nusch had told her how Roland had a penchant for bondage and could only sleep with a woman whose hands were tied, and now she wondered just what she'd find. The windows were open and the moonlight on the sheets and their naked bodies was dazzling. Lee's wrists were wrapped in a silk scarf festooned with flowers, like tiny kaleidoscopic sneezes. They were over her head, as if she were lounging in the sun. Her hair was short, and as Leonora clipped a tiny lock, just over her ear, she thought of her mother and her bald spot and how she wished she could see her face. She snipped a bit of Roland's hair, and snuck down to the kitchen, where she set their locks of hair in the pantry and wrote their names beside them.

She walked back upstairs and down the hall, the tile cool beneath her feet. She pushed Fini's door open to a rumbling wave of snores from Federico, who slept on his back. Leonor had her arms around André. They twitched at the same time, as if dreaming one dream. She clipped locks of their hair, tucking each into a separate pocket, and added them to the downstairs shelf. Max was next, his hair a shock of lightning, fine as a baby's.

She picked herbs as the sky paled, as daylight erased the shadows—

bunches of oregano, basil, and two ripe tomatoes. Opening the kitchen door, she found Fini in her cardinal's robe, smoking at the table and drinking coffee. For a moment they said nothing, just looked at each other, and she wondered if she were real or if she'd somehow conjured her. Then Fini spoke, and the vision evaporated. "Did you talk to him?"

"We talked." She began to chop the herbs. With the knife in her hand, she was powerful. Why on earth had she felt so afraid? "We're staying. Are you hungry?"

Fini sighed, as if it were just too early in the day to fight. "Not yet. I want to work on coffee and fumes. There's something more fluid about it. It's easier to carry the dream world into this one before you've eaten." And she left with her coffee and cigarette.

While Leonora waited for everyone else to wake, she cut more of her hair and experimented. She wanted her guests to realize they were eating hair, but not right away. She cut her two-inch lock in half and sprinkled it over the herbs in the skillet, careful to cook it over a low flame, so the hair wouldn't burn. When the hairy, herbed butter was sizzling, she whisked in two eggs and, as the mixture darkened around the edges, added a pinch of shredded Emmental and folded the omelet over.

She took a bite. The sinews of hair were tough. The omelet required more chewing. Toward the center the bites became hairier. About five bites in, they would realize there was something furry about their breakfast.

Max came down, and Roland and Lee followed. She wore the scarf on her head, and Leonora found herself searching for evidence of its presence on her wrists, but all she could see were her fine bones as she stretched her body out to the day, out to the singing wrens and the fields of lavender as she stood on the porch in the sunlight to smoke her cigarette.

As Max fetched Leonor, Federico, and André, Leonora sautéed the omelets and, keeping the names straight, made out place cards.

She set the plates on the table—the omelet with the owner's hair in front of each name—and added sprigs of rosemary.

Lee was the first to notice the nametags. "And where is *your* plate, Leonora?"

She drank her tea. "I ate early. I had to test the recipe on someone."

As she predicted, after four or five bites, they pulled a hair, then two, from their mouths. They held the eggy bites up to the light. "What on earth?" said Roland.

"Don't you like the taste of your own hair?" she asked.

Max was laughing. "So Surrealism has made it to the kitchen!"

"Surrealism has *been* in the kitchen," said Lee. "You just weren't there to see it."

"I call it *omelet à la cheveux*," Leonora said, and she took a low bow.

Federico spat out his bite. "*La donna è pazza?*" he asked Max, tapping his temple.

Fini took another nibble. "You know, I rather like my hair. Tastes like—" She thought about it. "Memories softened in butter."

"You want *my* memories?" Federico flipped his omelet onto her plate and fried himself a couple of eggs.

"How did you manage?" asked André, pecking at the edge of his omelet.

"While you slept."

"Perhaps I should call you Delilah," Max said.

"Perhaps you should keep an eye on this one," said Federico.

"He'd best keep both eyes on me," Leonora said.

~⚜~

They were drinking wine in the vineyard, and in the afternoon sun the Chenin Blanc grapes were plump and golden, ready for harvest. It was the end of the party, everyone set to leave the next day. Man and Ady had only arrived yesterday, but even they had to get back to Paris. "Before the war breaks out," Man said, leveling his dark eyes at Max.

"Why Paris?" said Fini. "It has to be one of the worst places you could be when the war breaks out. They've been distributing gas masks."

"Old news," Man mumbled, not bothering to hide his annoyance. But then everyone was irritable. It was hot and it hadn't rained for weeks.

Lee and Roland were heading to Antibes to stay with Picasso. "From there it'll be easier to take a boat to London," Roland explained. "If we have to. We can leave from the port at Saint-Malo."

"But you must stay, all of you, one more week, at least," Max said, pouring wine on their wine.

Leonora must have been holding her breath. When Lee took her hand, pulling her up from the chair, she felt faint. "Come," Lee said. "It's time for that photo."

"But I'm not—"

"Nonsense. You're beautiful. Sit here, on the stairs. You, too, Max," she said, calling him over.

Dressed in one of Fini's lace blouses, Leonora tilted her face toward the sun. Last night she'd had a nightmare. An invasion. Running and hiding. Not knowing when they would find her, only that they would, it was inevitable, she couldn't stay hidden forever. But in the sun with Max beside her she relaxed. His arm around her shoulder, he pulled her close. And when Lee clicked the shutter, Leonora's smile was nothing like the dead, plastered grin from her days as a debutante. It was real.

"I have a fantastic idea," she said. "Let's have a party tonight. A feast!"

"We'll make it the last Surrealist supper of the summer," Lee said.

"Who's to be hung on the cross after?" Max asked.

And then she heard voices in the vineyard, Fini's ringing above them.

They were creating the evening's menu, considering ingredients, conjuring dishes, when Fini charged toward them. "We're having a feast," Leonora said. "Want to help us?"

Fini glared at her. What had she missed? "I've heard."

"Heard what?"

"You still just want to please them, Carrington. You're like a dog doing tricks for her master. When are you going to listen to that voice inside of you?"

Stunned, Leonora watched her rush up the stairs. "Fini!" she called. She had no idea what she'd done.

Lee put her hand on her shoulder. "Let her cool down. Pick some apples. We'll make shrunken heads to float in the sangria. And see if you can find wild mushrooms for the chicken." She had a point. Giving Fini some time couldn't hurt.

The sun was low, the men in silhouette as Leonora approached. Man's voice, usually edged with irony and humor, was blunt. "For God's sake, Max, leave while you can."

Max gestured with his wine. "This is *our* home, *our* land."

"It's French. You're German. You're their enemy."

"We've chosen to not live in fear, which means we have no enemies."

"There's fear," Man said. "And then there's rational thought."

Max stood. "When have we ever aimed at rational?"

She picked the apples quickly and walked past the men, out among the gathering birdsong. It was all wrong. The party wasn't supposed to end this way. And already she could smell autumn in the air, a fact she didn't want to admit. The end of summer had always made her melancholy, but this felt like the end of so much more.

She took the dirt road to a grove of old oaks, where she'd seen mushrooms growing in a furrow. Bending to pick them, to add them to her basket, she heard a car coming from a long way off. She watched its plume of dust rise in the last of the sunlight. The black convertible had its top down, and she thought she saw a monocle, glinting.

Was it Tristan Tzara? Max had said he might swing by. One of the founders of Dada, Tzara was part of the old, *old* boys' club, as Fini called it, and she hated him even worse than she hated Breton, for some reason Leonora had never understood. She hurried back through the dusk—her basket swinging, her heart thumping away. She'd walked so much farther than she'd thought.

Rounding the corner, she saw a car leaving their house—Federico's red Renault—their suitcases and Fini's trunks roped to the roof. Fini sat in the front seat. Arms crossed over her chest, mouth set, she looked straight ahead.

Leonora waved and shouted, but the car zoomed past her as if she were invisible. She ran home to find the table on the patio set, candles winking.

The men sat around it, smoking. Tzara chuckled, adjusting his monocle. Apart from his arrival, everything appeared as she'd left it.

"Better to get it over with," said Roland. "Once England is in, it'll be quick."

"That's what we said about the first war," Max said.

"Did anyone see Leonor leave?" she asked. They looked at where she stood, on the stone steps, but no one responded, not even Max. Her faced burned. She ran up the stairs.

Lee was in the kitchen, humming a tune, turning two chickens on a spit over the fire, a bottle of whiskey half-empty. She took Leonora's basket. "Good. You got the mushrooms. I picked my own apples. You've been gone forever." Sangria filled a vase, and apples, peeled and carved to look like skulls, floated in it. There was a green salad with the petals of wild roses and nasturtiums, with dandelions like tiny suns. She'd smashed potatoes, adding beet juice to them, turning them pink, and now she poured her a spot of sangria. "It isn't ready yet, but tell me what it needs."

"You can see me?" Leonora asked.

Lee squinted at her. She laughed, stirring a pot of blueberries on a low flame. "For the chickens—to turn them blue."

Leonora downed the sangria without tasting it. "What happened with Leonor?"

"Who knows? You know Leonor. She runs hot."

Leonora walked up the stairs, slowly, feeling ill, as if she'd had the wind knocked out of her. The door to Fini's room was open. She stepped inside to find it in ruins. The emptiness hit her with a wave of nausea. Propped in a corner, as if displayed for her to see, was Fini's portrait of her. Only she'd scraped the paint off with a knife. She'd erased her.

But here she stood, in the mirror of the armoire, still wearing Fini's blouse.

Portrait of Max Ernst

Max, June 1940, Nîmes, France

With the sun comes the trill of birds. Max finds he is lying on his side. A rat scuttles into a dark corner. He brushes a fly from his lips. The need to shit overcomes him with a frightening urgency, and he uncovers the muck hole the others made and squats over it. What streams from him is liquid. It's nothing, he thinks. He'll feel better as soon as he eats again. And then he sees the blood.

His stomach seizes and he curls into a ball, slick with sweat. His head pounds, and he knows there will be no escaping the camp, not like this.

By the time the guard comes for him, he's talking to himself. Quoting Rilke to know who he is. "*Ja, die Frühlinge brauchten dich wohl. Es muteten manche Sterne dir zu, daß du sie spürtest.*" Yes—the springtimes needed you. Often a star was waiting for you to notice it.

With the guard's help he stumbles to the communal trench. The cramps are terrible. Beside the others he squats to relieve himself. He tries to stand, and his knees give way.

Someone pulls him up, leads him to one of the tents, where the men glare at him. They move their blankets to make room for him on the straw. "You stink," one of them says. He tries to say he's sorry but all that comes out is a croak. Another man leans over him. Max recognizes his face. He's one of the young, nihilistic Austrians from the train so bent on destroying everyone's luggage. He wants to tell him he appreciates his *hutzpah*, as Lou would put it. "Ahhhhh," he says. The boy puts a glass of water to his lips.

Soon another man is with him, another Austrian, a doctor. As he looks at Max, his face creases with worry. He returns with a bottle of

medicine and spoons it into his mouth—bitterness Max manages to
swallow. They talk, and their faces and voices swim in the swirl of his
fever. The camp infirmary is a dreadful, sickly place, everyone infect-
ing one another. Better to stay here. But will the men in the tent agree
to a bucket? "I'll empty it," the young Austrian says. But why, Max
wonders, when he hardly knows him?

Everyone in the tent agrees, and a bucket is brought. With the help
of the young Austrian, Wilhelm, he hunches over the bucket count-
less times. The day stretches, a monstrous white heat, the suffocating
air filled with the odor of his shit.

With evening come the mosquitoes. They buzz in his ears, land
on his face and arms, too many to brush away. All over camp, bonfires
have started up, one just outside their tent. A man fans the smoke inside with large green leaves. *Leaves of plane trees?* he wonders. Smoke
fills the tent. At first he welcomes the smell, the clean wood fragrance
of it, and then he starts to cough. He turns onto his side and pulls his
blanket over his face.

It's late—after the men have gone to bed—when the doctor
touches his cheek with the back of his hand. He can get opium, he
tells him. But it requires money. Does Max having anything he can
sell? His knapsack is here, the guard must have returned it, and Max
digs out the compass and the map. He won't be needing them. The
doctor returns with opium and squeezes the dropper onto his tongue.

Opium, beautiful opium. How did he manage to find it?

Visions break over him in waves. The cook kneads his stomach.
She forms it into a pie and birds peck their way out and scatter, lifting toward the clouds. His father leans over him. Max reaches up and
touches the wrinkles in his cheek. God is punishing him for being
with her, he says, when it's Leonora he loves. His fever soars as it
hasn't since he was a boy. He can hear his mother crying, her sobs
reaching him from so far away.

He dreams of houses, endlessly labyrinthine, leading him from the
tent into their living room in Saint-Martin, where the plaster horse head

shakes its mane the way Leonora shook her hair when she stepped from the Loire, and he is covered in droplets of icy river water. Stairs lead to one room and then another, to one wife, one mistress after the other.

Leonora left her laugh in the closet of the bedroom of their Paris apartment, the one with the walls painted a dark shade of pink, the exact color of the inside of her labia, and the laugh rattles her lace dresses like a wind that is trapped and set on breaking free.

He closes the door on it. In the silence he hears a woman speaking. It is Marie-Berthe on a throne, a cross in her hand raised as if to strike him, but when he cries into her skirts, she drops the cross and strokes his head. *Where have you been?* she asks. *Why did you never return?* He opens his mouth to answer her and beetles crawl from his throat, over his tongue, between his lips. They climb her robes and she shrieks and runs from him.

In a bathroom, Gala lies in a bath, the water to her nipples, her knees exposed. The water is the blue of the ocean shallows on the beaches of Saigon, where they ended things. He takes off his clothes and kneels beside her, praying "Hail Mary full of grace" like his mother taught him. He dips his finger in the water and crosses himself.

Walking a long hall, he climbs more stairs. It's their old apartment in Cologne, his and Lou's and little Jimmy's, whose wooden blocks and toy cars are strewn over the floor. There are more rooms here, more than he realized, an entire third story, packed with things from his own childhood, or is it Leonora's? There, at the top of a tower of furniture, is the rocking horse from her nursery, the horse she told him she loved from before she could remember. Maybe little Jimmy would want to ride on it, he thinks.

Reaching to lift it down, he sees he has, instead of arms and hands, wings now, and he flies into the morning wishing he could go back to that room, packed as it is with treasures. And what of the rooms that are left? The rooms he hasn't seen?

But first he must rescue Leonora's laugh from that closet. He feels sick for having left it there.

No, he thinks. That's not right. *She* left me. And waking, he is an animal again, a wretched body squatting over a bucket. Wilhelm puts a glass of water to his cracked lips. His face contorts. Max wants to tell him not to worry. His life was never worth that much.

⁓⸙

Another day, another night. Time goes on and on, oblivious to his pleas for it to end. He longs for stillness, for a void, a white void that will wash him clean.

The men's voices come and go. They talk of Nazis and clause nineteen and no time to lose. But what was clause nineteen? He can't remember anymore, and he can't see how it would matter now that they've reached the Sahara. He can hear what sounds like sand pelting the tent when the wind blows. Wilhelm is speaking in the twilight. "Will they turn all the prisoners over or only the politicians, the writers, the artists?"

Artists? But why, he wonders, when art amounts to nothing? Everything he believed in, everything he dedicated his life to—is nothing—less than nothing, it is *merde*. They thought art could change the world, could dissuade men of their greed, their need to destroy. It did nothing. Nothing.

There is a door hovering midair. He can reach it easily, he's no longer touching the floor. The day his bird died his sister was born. He remembers his bird's body on the bottom of the cage, how it seemed, in death, to have shrunk. He remembers the blotched faces of his mother and his sister in her arms. He's close enough to reach the door, but if he so much as touches the handle he knows the door will open. He'll be on the other side.

And Leonora! He'll never again touch her hair, never fall into her dark eyes, never feel her clutching him to her, pushing him deeper inside her. Why didn't he listen to her? He was a pigheaded idiot. He wanted what he wanted. He wanted to stay in heaven and he thought he was God.

Nora, he calls. He knows he's moaning in his sleep but he doesn't care. He calls louder. *Nora! Mea culpa, mea culpa.*

She presses a wet cloth to his head. *Shhhh,* she says. *I'll tell you a story.*

But when he opens his eyes, he is alone, floating in the white haze of her breath. And here is the door, shining. It's okay, he thinks, reaching for the handle.

Leonora, September 1939, Saint-Martin-d'Ardèche, France

Deep in a forest the birdsong deafened, and a snake, blue-green and shining, wound its way up a tree. *Run*, it told her. But which way? It all looked the same. Light through the leaves puddled between the buttressed roots of giants, and everywhere a small rain. And then she heard the terrible crashing of trees, the grinding of tanks. She ran but could not outrun the noise.

Someone was at the door, their knocks loud, insistent. Max buttoned his pants, his white work shirt splattered with paint. "Who?" she said, through the dream's ratty edges.

"Etienne most likely. Why didn't we make our guests pay their own bar bill?"

"I suppose this means caviar for breakfast," she said, but Max was already heading for the door. She pulled on a dress, laughing at the thought of serving Etienne the tapioca soaked in squid ink, which was ready to go in their icebox. And then she heard voices bellowing off the high walls.

"Max Ernst?"

She rushed down the stairs, stopping mid-staircase. A large man held handcuffs, and another, slighter man, held what had to be a warrant. "You were born in Germany?"

Max was pale. His voice was small. "I have been here eighteen years. I am loyal to France." She'd never seen him so scared, and she found she couldn't move. "I have friends, people who can vouch for me."

"You must come with us," the slim man said. The other man had Max in the cuffs and was leading him out the door.

She ran, following them outside. "Wait! He's an enemy to Hitler!" she yelled, her voice odd. Low and raspy, with frayed seams.

"That's not for us to decide," said the big one, jostling Max down the stairs.

"Do you need money? I can give you whatever you need."

"We just need *him*, mademoiselle," said the thin one. "Your husband?"

"No."

"Well then, *au revoir*." He tipped his hat. With a hand on each arm, they dragged Max to the car.

"I won't be long," he yelled, his voice shaky. "We'll figure out something!"

"What should I do?"

"Call Éluard! See what he can do." Inside the car Max pressed his forehead to the window, and they drove away.

Her body limp, her head light, she told herself she would not faint. She would not be one of those women overcome by the brutality of the world. She watched the car until they turned out of sight, and then she lay facedown on the dirt between the potatoes and the green beans, and she sobbed.

She called Lee and Roland, Paul and Nusch. There was nothing anyone could do. France was at war with Germany and Max was a German citizen. But even if he were a French citizen, they would have taken him, now that anyone born in Germany was an *enemy alien*.

She asked Alphonsine to feed her menagerie and followed Max to the town of Largentière, some sixty kilometers away, where he was locked in a prison with a hundred other Germans.

An old stone building high on a hill, it belonged in a fairy tale, only she had no magical powers to break down the door, and his wings had been plucked, the feathers used to stuff the beds of his captors. She knew he was freezing in those rooms of stone because she shivered when she thought of him, her bones ached, and though she layered sweater over sweater, she could not get warm.

She stayed at a small hotel, brought him clothes from Saint-Martin, and food—ripe tomatoes and hunks of cheese, salami and sausage and fresh bread. The guards unpacked her picnic. They smashed the tomatoes and the cheese, stabbed the meat and the bread. She could see him, they said. Briefly.

She sat with Max in a tiny courtyard as a guard stood by, smoking, his rifle slung on his shoulder. They held hands. It had been ten days since she'd seen him, days long as months. He was thinner, his clothes too big. There were shadows under his eyes and he seemed to have aged. And still, he was the sun after a winter of rain. Each second with him was a gift. How had she already forgotten the pure blue of his eyes?

He worked in the office, filing papers for the captain, he told her. A better job than others, than cleaning the latrine, for instance. But if she'd bring art supplies, the captain promised him three hours a day in the sun in exchange for a landscape, a "souvenir" Max said, in the captain's brusque voice. "As if he were on holiday," he added under his breath.

As he ate the sausage, her stomach turned. She'd eaten little since he was taken. Potatoes, tomatoes, some greens when she could get them. The smell of meat—even cold—made her gag, but then so did a slice of cake.

She didn't say she was lost without him, didn't tell him the villagers all looked the same, like pigs. They had done this to him—the pig-faced idiots of the world. She didn't tell him she ate her dinners alone on a terrace crawling with cats, or how they spoke to her of the revolting mediocrity of the villagers, of the pestilence that was humanity. They brushed past her legs as she paced, counting her steps, from one end of the terrace to the other, certain there was a person behind her (she heard breathing), but every time she turned to look she saw only air.

Instead she told him she'd been writing stories, as if to make him proud. "Time is up," said the guard, one of the pig-faced minions.

They couldn't hug, so they lingered. The air between them thickened; the hairs on her arms stood on end, reaching out to him, magnetized.

She took the train home, returned with paints, brushes, canvases. She brought one of his finished paintings, too, a weird little work of plants with buggy eyes, with mouths and barbed teeth. *Don't let them tame you*, the plants said.

Max painted. The sun gave him strength. But he would not paint a landscape. They might have taken everything, but they could not force him to create some vapid work of pleasantry Hitler himself would applaud. A month passed, not as terrible as if he'd spent it in a cold, dark room. And when, one morning in early November, the commander asked for his "petite landscape", Max gave him the painting she'd brought. Its bug-eyes ogled; its toothy mouths jeered.

When she visited, Max told her how the captain exploded. He imitated his outrage. "What do you mean, painting a picture like this? You have no right!" Even imprisoned, he was victorious, though she wished he'd have appeased the captain instead. Maybe then he would have let them picnic on that sunny hill.

In a few days, when she was allowed another visit, she found the building empty, save for a couple of guards. Max and the others had been transferred, they told her, to a larger prison, Camp des Milles in Aix-en-Provence.

She packed her things, caught the next train to Aix.

The train ride calmed her. The autumn trees and fields gave her hope. She bought biscuits from the commissary and ate them all. Maybe at this Camp des Milles they'd see reason. Maybe they would do their research, see that Max wasn't a threat, and send him home.

Aix was a pretty town, a river running through it. She bought apples from an old man at an outdoor market, and when she asked if he could point her toward the camp, he threw his hands up. "Camp?" he said. No one else at the market had heard of the camp either. So she went to the city hall, and here a tired, gray-faced man gave her directions. "But why are you going?" he asked her. "No visitors are allowed."

"We'll see." She threw her shoulders back, tilted her chin, and thanked him.

She ate an apple as she walked a dusty road to the outskirts of town. As soon as she saw Camp des Milles, she knew she'd been wrong to hope. A former brick factory, it resembled a prison, the massive building surrounded by high barbed wire. And though she smiled at the guards, though they took the apples she offered, they refused to let her see Max. She could talk as long as she liked, they said, they weren't going to let her in, and no prisoner was allowed to leave the compound, not even for a minute. "Will you at least tell him I was here?" she asked.

"We'll try," said a young guard. "What was your name again?" He was smiling, teasing her, as if this were a game.

She caught a night train to Saint-Martin and their husk of a house. She fed the cats, the goats, the chickens, and the peacocks, grateful for their warmth, their voices and hunger. Otherwise, she might have tucked herself into bed until Max returned. But she could not sleep. She lay awake, floating, vibrating in the darkness, and when she slept, she dreamed of Max dying, asking for water, asking for her, she heard his voice but she could not find him among the hordes of men.

The days grew short, the nights long, each one a cavernous mouth closing around her, each one an infinity. Every evening she built a fire, curled up beside it with her five cats, and slept as best as she could in the living room. But her heart was too loud in her ears and the cats wouldn't stop talking. *He might be dead for all you know. And if he isn't, they might not let him go. What will you do then? Will you return to England? Will you run?*

She stared at her half-finished canvas, one she had started in Paris. A portrait of Max as a bird-fish in a frozen dream. But she could not pick up a brush. She opened her notebook and could not write, not even to reply to Jimmy, whose letter said he was doing all he could to get Max out, but there was nothing anyone *could* do—no one in America, that was.

Every day she waited for Henri, the old mailman, to trudge up the road. Every day he shook his head. "*Rien*," he said, and kept walking. And then, one day in early December, he handed her an envelope, small and rumpled, a shoe print across it, as if it had lain, forgotten, on the post office floor. *Max Ernst, Camp des Milles*, the return address read. She tore the envelope open. The pages were thick, one side torn—ripped from a notebook.

18 November 1939

Cher Nora,

It is cold here. There is no heat. Prisoners have lost toes, fingers. Wrapped in a thin blanket, I sleep on a pile of straw in an oven where once bricks were baked. There is brick dust in the air, in the food. It has settled into my lungs and my hair and is a fine grit always between my teeth. The red dust has soaked into my skin. I am beginning to think I am made now of only bones and bricks.

At least Bellmer is here with me. We are cellmates and share a single oven. We petitioned the commandant and he has allowed us drawing materials. Hans and I have asked for painting supplies, too. I want to show him the decalcomania process, which I think he will love. For now, we sketch portraits of each other to forget for a while our hunger, to forget the itch of the lice, which we pluck from each other's scalp, to forget the stench of dysentery, and the interminable lines for the filthy, communal latrines and for the food, if you can call what we eat food, laced as it is with bromide to dull our wits and sex drive.

I would tell you more if this letter were private, but nothing in this hell is private. Nothing.

I miss you as badly as I miss freedom itself. Perhaps more.

I have written to Éluard in the hopes that he might write a
letter to the president on my behalf.

I am yours, Leonora, entirely—
Max

He was alive! She wept she was so happy. Rereading the letter, she
lingered over his closing. He was hers *entirely*. She wrote back, sending a story she'd written in Largentière, one she hoped would cheer
him, however unsettling it might have been, with its dinner of the
lovely, dead woman with the goose-pimpled body of a plucked hen
decorated with currants and cooked pears and stuffed with the pick-
led hearts of hedgehogs.

Somehow, the weeks passed. Mornings, she walked along the
Loire, and when the wind called to her to follow it—around one bend
of river and the next—she ran to keep up, she flew. She was made of
air. Vacant as light.

—&—

"Leonora?" It was Alphonsine, here for her usual afternoon call. To
check on her. But she was upstairs in their bedroom, and she didn't
move, didn't say a word.

Standing in the sunlight, she was stuck, as if in a deep groove. She heard
Alphonsine walk across the creaking boards in the living room, heard her
voice ring up the stairs, but she was unable to answer her—her voice hid-
ing somewhere inside her, impossible to find. The clock in the entry ticked.
She heard her cross to the door, heard it click shut behind her, and now
she could move. She ran outside, calling after her, "Alphonsine!" There she
was, descending the stone steps in her sensible shoes. Her long peppered
hair usually knotted at the back of her head—the hair she kept always
tucked away—was loose down her back. It was lifting in the wind. It was
lit. She turned to Leonora. She was wearing the mask of an owl. She was

Leonor Fini at the ball, leaning in, kissing her lips. She was Fini, who had
not answered the letter she wrote to her over a month ago.

Alphonsine peered down at her. "You fainted." Holding her head and
shoulders, she helped her to sit. Leonora's head throbbed. She leaned on
Alphonsine, who guided her down the steps. "Come. I've made soup.
You'll eat. *Mon dieu*," she said, sadly. "You're disappearing before my eyes."

~*~

December brought rain, a thin sleet Leonora braved only on her daily
afternoon dash to the mailbox. In her kitchen she wrung the rain from
her hair, pulled off her wet sweater and slacks. She sliced open today's reward, a box from Fini, who was writing from Monte Carlo.
There was a pink sweater inside it, a pullover. It was soft and fuzzy,
and slipping it on, Leonora felt like a child. She knitted it herself, Fini's letter explained. A gift by way of apology. She was sorry for leaving Saint-Martin as she did, but she couldn't be in the same house as
Tzara. She thought Leonora had invited him and was pleased to know
she hadn't. And besides, what else could she do in Monte Carlo other
than knit and paint and smoke? She was waiting out the war there,
and there really wasn't much of an artist's scene.

Leonora made tea and sat at the kitchen table to write her back. The
pen in her hand had a sharp metal nib, and she tightened her grip on it,
afraid it might fly into the world, an instrument of her anger, attacking
officers and heads of state, stabbing them in that soft spot between their
collarbones. She licked the nib, scribbled until the ink was flowing.

9 December 1939

Dearest Fini,

Your letter comes at a time when I have never been more alone.
To know that you still love me means I can die without dread.

Please. Don't laugh. I can hear your laughter now, but hear me
out. You understand me as no woman does. You have taught me to
not hold back, to unleash my rage onto the canvas. Though now I
cannot paint. I feel nothing, not even hunger, and I have such fits
of vertigo I must lie on the ground to understand the proper order
of things.

 If I do fall from the Earth—if I am licked clean by a white,
radiant horse and cannot return—promise me you will
not abandon Max. Watch over him as I would have were I
stronger.

 I am not without hope. Paul has written a letter to the president
of France vouching for Max's character, declaring his absolute
loyalty to France, and we pray the president will show mercy, and
that by Christmas, Max might be home.

 I send kisses, and all my affection. Please write to Max at
Camp des Milles. It would hearten him so to hear from you.

Your adoring twin,
Carrington

—§—

The morning Max was released from Camp des Milles, Leonora stood
out front. She'd been waiting since dawn. The day was cold, and even
in her wool coat she couldn't stop shivering. She was so hungry and
excited, she thought she might float off, becoming just another dark
cloud in the sky. The night before, in her tiny hotel room in Aix, she
hadn't slept. Though she'd lain on the hard bed, she could barely close
her eyes. Now here he was, limping toward her.

 His smile was wide, but his eyes were tired, his skin dull. He fell
into her arms. "I smell," he said, pulling away. She drew him tighter.
He was so thin, she could have carried him to the train.

 "Max," she crooned. "My little bird." She wiped away tears before he could see. And as they walked slowly, hand in hand, the clouds moved off, and the sun warmed her all the way through.

By afternoon, they were back in Saint-Martin. Ignoring the stares of the villagers, they climbed the road home.

The peacocks perched on the stone wall to greet him, squawking the tale of Orpheus from beginning to end, though no one understood it but Leonora. She lit every candle in the house. She changed into a dress of white lace, combed the dust from her hair, and perfumed herself with dried lavender and rosemary. She cooked lamb in their new stove, a stove her mother had sent the money for, insistent that she *eat, eat*, something so hard to do during the three long months Max had been gone, but now he was home, and the cats, who had become transparent, slipped back into their coats, thick and lusty for winter. It was Christmas, and she drew a hot bath for the man she had lost, the man whose return from the underworld had returned her, too. That essential beast that was her soul had come to the stable to eat and drink, to love again. She burned his clothes, stiff with sweat, stinking of airless rooms, of bricks and chalk and shit, of the beard of an old mule, and the world's doom.

Her mother had sent a package of creamed peas, mushrooms, chestnuts, almonds, dried figs, sugar, and flour—and a pheasant, which rotted over the two-month journey. Leonora roasted the chestnuts, heated the peas and mushrooms, and served them alongside a leg of lamb, and she concocted an almond tart in a *pâte brisée*, a buttery crust her mother had taught her how to make when she was a child. It was Christmas, and they played Django and Josephine Baker on the Victrola, they sang and danced and feasted. It was Christmas, and Paul's letter to the president of France had worked. Max was home.

Her appetite returned. The rations presented a challenge she took on with a fervor. With her own olives and sundried tomatoes, a can of tuna made a casserole that fed them for days. Trading eggs and goat milk, olives, dried apples, and wild mushrooms for butter, flour, and sugar, she baked sponge puddings and cakes with port and raisins, and they grew fat.

Lee sent photos from their week last summer, and Leonora bought an album and spent afternoons pasting photos inside. It was all about her and Max. There was Lambe Creek, and the Parisian cafés, Max on the rocking horse in their flat. And Saint-Martin-d'Ardèche, before they took him. Before. Their faces in the sun. My God, they had been happy.

"You should be writing," he told her when he saw what she was doing. "Or painting."

"I will when I'm ready," she said. "You're going to want this some-day."

Max didn't talk about the camp and she didn't ask. "It's behind us," he said. "Why ruin here with there?" But there was something more distant about him, insular and brooding. With a desperate urgency he threw himself at his work—a new decalcomania. A menacing blob of ocher paint became what looked like a bear, and then it was her naked body stepping from a cloak of feathers. There was a painting in the painting, too. It hung on a brick wall behind her, and in it her image repeated in miniature. Again, she was stepping from a cloak of feathers, only here she was free, standing against a blue sky.

He only stopped for food when she brought it to him, and soon he had another canvas going, this one with a pale sky, and then a jungle, a tangle of roots and vines bursting with clusters of tiny, prehistoric flowers. There were horned creatures—a minotaur, a brown unicorn. She was among them, her face peeking from the leaves. "I'm calling it *Leonora in the Morning Light*," he said, and she saw that it was inscribed to her.

She touched the arm of a tiny skeleton in the bramble. A numb, cold feeling spread from her chest. "It frightens me," she said so quietly she had to repeat it for him to hear.

"But look at yourself. You're strong and calm, like the dawn. You waited for me. You woke me from my nightmare." He took her in his arms and she felt surrounded. She felt whole. For how long had she been only part?

Holding her breath, she entered her studio. She dusted off her portrait of Max. Her tubes of paint, her brushes felt foreign, she'd neglected them for so long. Or not neglected, so much as feared. But now she knew what she would paint, and she worked quickly, before she could worry what Max would think of the painting or what it might say about them.

—⚹—

"Am I keeping you captive, darling?" He studied the portrait of himself, squinting at the little horse he held in a glass globe.

"You're keeping me alive, taking me someplace warm, where you won't need those silly socks and where I can run through miles of meadows."

It was the first real afternoon of spring, and they'd opened a bottle of her wine from the year before, wine she'd named for Winkie. They were on the patio in the sun, eating olives and sardines on crackers. Crouching on the cobblestones, he examined her brushwork, his fine wrist bones and fingers, the glint in his eyes, cool and precise, his face like a falcon's. No woman had painted him before. It was a kind of claiming, she knew.

"But why are you so small? Did I shrink you for easy transport?"

"I shrunk myself." *It's what you do when you love someone,* she wanted to say. *You shrink to fit the picture.* But it wouldn't have made any sense to him. He was a man, the star of his own drama, and the scene shifted to fit him—always, it seemed.

"You didn't paint a ring on my finger."

"It's your right hand, Max." She laughed, ate an olive. "And anyway, you haven't worn a ring for as long as I've known you."

"I'd wear one for you."

She could feel herself pulling away, turning icy—like the horse in the background of her painting. It was dangerous to think this way—that he could be hers, when he couldn't really. Not ever. She knew him too well to imagine otherwise.

"Marie-Berthe signed the papers. The divorce should be final in a month or two."

"You'll be free." Her words sounded hollow. It was just too hard to believe.

"I'm calling my painting *The Robing of the Bride*," he said. And thinking of the painting inside his painting, of how confident and free he saw her against the blue, she turned from her own painting, from the blind, frozen horse behind Max, from the tiny horse he carried, sealed in the uterus of the lantern.

He reached out his hand. She took it and he tugged her to the floor and kissed her. Crushed in his arms, she retreated. It had been years, years of being with him but feeling alone. Those times he left her to be with Marie-Berthe, times she couldn't hold against him because hadn't they helped to make her strong, to make her this woman he now wanted for himself—rings and all?

The wine had made her drowsy and the sunlight had turned golden. When they kissed, she burned from within, and she wanted him to annihilate her, to smash her into jam or pudding. They made love right there, in the open, because they were together again, they were Max and Leonora, and it was spring.

Jimmy wrote. *Leave*, he urged. *Pack your things this moment. Come to New York. Please, listen to reason. Get out of France while you still can!* But on the curtain rod over the bedroom window a pair of wrens were nesting—five eggs tucked tight, and the mother and father took turns keeping them warm. If Max and Leonora lay very still under the covers, the wrens would hop onto the bed, cocking their heads at them. In the garden the rosemary's purple flowers had opened and the lavender and roses had begun to bud. Chicks hatched, soft and yellow, and Sophocles the goat gave birth to Zeno, a female, who followed the chicks on her spindly legs. Leonora cooked and wrote stories slathered with food—foie gras and puree of duck liver, honey and ice cream and halvah.

April came. Max turned forty-nine. She turned twenty-three. She gave him a white river stone shaped like an egg and a crown she'd formed of feathers. He gave her a choker made of the black and red beetles he'd found dead on the bank of the river last August. They shone in the sun like polished stones.

When the Germans invaded Denmark and Norway, Max painted the beak and eyes of an owl on his bride's—on *Leonora's*—feathered mantle. He painted a man with wings and the head of a crane guarding her with a broken spear. Then the Germans invaded France, and he turned from his canvas, put down his brush, and smoked on the terrace waiting for the *Boches* to roll into town and seize him— degenerate artist, defiler of the motherland.

"But you're safe here." She pulled him inside for dinner. "How would they know?"

"You think our neighbors wouldn't tell them? You think they would hesitate?"

"Not Alphonsine."

"No. Not Alphonsine," he said, taking a bite of duck in figs and port.

~&~

In the dark of a new moon, they wrapped themselves in a blanket, lay on a slope of earth, and studied the stars. "*Ja, die Frühlinge brauchten dich wohl,*" he quoted. "*Es muteten manche Sterne dir zu, daß du sie spürtest.*"

"Rilke?" she asked, letting her eyes close, drifting in his arms.

"Yes—the springtimes needed you. Often a star was waiting for you to notice it."

He pulled her closer and she willed her eyes to open.

"You see the bear?"

She squinted at Ursa Major. "Looks more like a cat. Like Cricket about to pounce."

"And Leo?"

"The snail?"

"Perfect." He was quiet for so long she thought he'd fallen asleep. And then she saw his tears. "If I'm taken, promise me you'll stay here. I'll come back for you."

"And if the troops come first?" She tried to sound calm, but her heart was racing. He had promised they'd leave if things got *really* bad, and here they were still, on their land.

"Then we'll meet in Lisbon. But wait for me. Wait as long as you can."

The Horses of Lord Candlestick

Leonora, May 1940, Saint-Martin-d'Ardèche, France

When Max was taken the second time, there wasn't any knock. The gendarmes strode into their home with their rifles drawn, their boots muddy. Again, it was the French who hauled him away. "You have no right, no reason," Max said as they cuffed his wrists. "The president himself says I'm not a threat. Leonora! Get the letter!"

"Papers do not matter, Monsieur. You are a suspect," said the man, the boy, leading him away. "You've been transmitting information to the enemy."

Leonora could not move or speak. She watched the gendarme push the rifle to Max's back and prod him down the stone stairs and into the car. She watched them drive away. Then she slid on her loafers and ran to the police station in her nightgown, hoping she'd find him there.

At his desk, the chief drank café au lait and adjusted the radio for better reception. Something about the impenetrability of the Maginot Line, the bravery of the French army, crackled through. Static cut in and he turned it off, but she was still trying to catch her breath.

"Gendarmes took Max. Have you seen him?"

He brushed the flakes of a baguette from his wide mouth. "No. It's a different branch of the gendarmerie—specifically for enemies of France."

"You *know* Max, you know he's no enemy. You can say something!"

"It is out of my hands, mademoiselle."

"*Leonora.* Martin, for God's sake, you know me!"

He looked out the window, his cheeks flushed. "We turned over the report. We had to. To not turn it in is as good as colluding."

"Report?"

"Jean-Pierre—the deaf and dumb son of poor Adelaide." She stared at him. She didn't know *poor* Adelaide, nor did she care. "He's taken it on himself to patrol the town. He reported light signals sent from your house. I'm surprised they didn't take you in, too."

"Light signals? Probably Alphonsine out looking for snails with a flashlight. It's what she does when she can't sleep."

"If it *is* a misunderstanding, I imagine they'll send him home."

"Where did they take him?"

He shuffled through papers, pulled one out. "Camp des Milles. You aren't married, are you?" She bit her cheek, hard. "There's nothing you can do." He lit a cigarette. She wanted to strangle him, chief of the pig-faced idiots. He sighed. "You have family? In England? France is no place for an unmarried woman. Go home, Leonora, go *now*."

Instead she went to *Motel des Touristes*, where she ordered a beer though it was not yet noon. The beer was warm and she drank it, to feel heavy and dull, to soften the world's ugly edges. Max had left her once again. She ordered another, and another, and when Etienne refused to fill her glass, she tromped home through a town of traitors. She passed two farmers who stopped talking and watched her with narrow, suspicious eyes.

In her bathroom, she splashed orange blossom water over her face. This was a dream she could wake from. Only, perhaps she should *drink* the orange blossom water instead? Like a potion. She swallowed the remaining half bottle. *Wake up. Wake up!* she thought. There was burning in her throat, in her mouth and head. She would wake, and her body would be pure and new as the flowers of an orange tree.

Her stomach cramped. She doubled over, ran into the garden, where she fell to her knees and vomited—gladly, thankfully. She wanted to be empty, purged of the world and its hateful bureaucracy. If she could purify herself, she could rise above it.

In the days that followed she ate little. She might have traveled to Les Milles, but they wouldn't have let her see him. And besides, he'd said to wait for him at home.

She worked at her vines, which were blossoming and had to be sprayed all over with sulfur. She worked at her potatoes, and the more she sweated in the afternoon sun, the more pure she became. Sanctified. She sunbathed on the hot river rocks and felt stronger than she had in her entire life. What did it matter if Belgium fell? She had the sun. She had her vines and goats, her cats and hens.

At night, she drank at *Motel des Touristes*. Short glasses of whiskey, tall glasses of beer. After a week she ran out of money. "Don't worry," Etienne insisted, filling her glass. "You have your house. You're good for it."

She ended each night by signing another note. It was easy. Her signature was a distant, abstract thing. Leonora Carrington was only a name. It might have belonged to anyone.

─❦─

In early June the Germans bombed Paris, and Saint-Martin flooded with refugees. Alphonsine let her rooms for free, and Leonora swept out the old post office, her studio where she hadn't painted a lick since Max was taken. The roof leaked and generations of daddy longlegs had made an acquisition of the ceiling, but she opened its doors.

Soon every building in town was overflowing.

"You must let people stay in your church," Alphonsine told her one morning.

"The church is Max's studio," she said, scraping last night's dinner of chicken and rice, which she'd barely touched, into the cats' bowls. Cricket eyed her. *Don't do it*, she said. "He'll be back any day," Leonora told Alphonsine. "He'd be furious if I let anyone in."

"People need somewhere to sleep. We might all be refugees before long. We have to help each other." She was angry, her mouth tight.

But she was watching Leonora, too, backing up slowly, imperceptibly. "Do you need anything, Leonora?" her voice soft.

"Not a thing," Leonora said. And she promised to think about the church, which seemed to satisfy Alphonsine, whom she was relieved to see go.

After she'd fed the rest of the animals, she walked out to the old church. At the door, she hesitated. If she didn't open it, Max just might be inside. The notion was absurd. He hadn't been here in weeks. And yet she could feel his presence, and the possibility that he was in there, working, made her unable to go in.

The next afternoon, when Alphonsine came around, Leonora was in a treetop, watching her the way a cat watches a bird. And Alphonsine, not finding her, left.

Norway surrendered on a Monday. The Germans occupied Paris on a Friday. She'd rather not know these things, but she had to go to town now and then, and the headlines on the papers were unavoidable. And the people were always talking. She marked off the days on her calendar. Max had been gone for a month, and she'd heard nothing from him. But then she hadn't tried to write to him. If she didn't write to him, she reasoned, then he might have only, somehow, gone on a jaunt to Paris, he might be home any day.

~❦~

Rising with the sun, Leonora found the nest was empty. "The wrens have fledged," she said to no one, and listened to a wren's song, hollow and bottomless, burble through the open window.

Despair fled to a country so deep in her body she couldn't locate it if she tried. Instead, she moved through the day on a string of chores. Provence surged with life. The rosemary, the lavender, the wild roses exploded with flowers. The ants, the bees, and the butterflies were tireless, exuberant. Today was the solstice. The Earth lolled in its own grandeur as the sun luxuriated, taking its time.

On her knees in the afternoon heat, dressed in one of Max's shirts knotted at her waist and a pair of threadbare shorts she'd taken to wearing daily, she weeded the potato patch. Lizard and Beetle slept on their backs in a sunny patch of dirt. Cricket nuzzled her knees. "I can't pet you, my hands are muddy," she told her, only not in words. She thought it, and Cricket cocked her head, listening.

Leonora hadn't used words in days, hadn't spoken to a single human. She'd stopped going to the bar because she owed Etienne money. When she'd offered him one of her paintings for the balance of the bill, he laughed. "These women look possessed. And anyway, art means nothing in times of war." Then, so close she could taste his breath, he had said, "Give me the deed to your house, dear, and you can drink all you want."

"That's crazy," she'd said, though it hadn't seemed half-bad.

Weeds in hand, she watched a train of dust stir in the distance and move closer. An old yellow Fiat rumbled past the house, turned around, and parked in their drive. She dropped the weeds, brushed her hands on her shorts. A woman got out, and then a man. She wore slacks, loafers, a T-shirt, her hair in a scarf. Was it Nusch? Leonora squinted. No, it wasn't Nusch, and the man was not Paul. The woman shielded her eyes against the sun and looked up at the house. Leonora ducked behind the rosemary. If she hurried down the other side of the hill, she could slink off to the river without their noticing. They'd be gone by the time she returned.

But now they were climbing the stairs. She'd missed her chance.

"Leonora?" the woman called, her voice familiar. It was Catherine, Ursula's friend. She was smiling, waving anxiously. Leonora stepped out from the rosemary.

⁓⦦

For dinner she opened a bottle of her wine. She fed them potatoes with butter from the farm down the street, and Charlotte, one of her fattest hens, with an olive tapenade.

"Paris is unrecognizable. The bombs! The smoke! People escaping on foot, their possessions heaped on their backs, children, old people stumbling. Nazis marching down the Champs-Élysées." As if she were still fleeing, Catherine spoke in a flurry. Her hands shook as she reached for her wine. "Thank God we got out when we did—and with no brakes! Our brakes gave out. Can you imagine?"

"I'll have a look at them tomorrow," Michel, Catherine's lover, said. He chewed slowly, like a hippo. He was Hungarian, sturdy, with a straight, practical nose, a clean part in his dark hair.

They seemed not to notice Leonora's silence. The smell of the food was too strong for her to eat, so she drank wine, watching them slice into Charlotte's body, her skin and muscles, and take her into their mouths. She'd never realized how sensuous the act of eating another animal was. Porous, she thought, chewing a strand of her own hair.

"We have to get our exit visas," Catherine was saying. "Everyone will be thronging to the borders. Leaving will only get harder." Their words were strange—the squawking of chickens. And when Leonora looked at them, they were waiting, as though they'd asked her a question. "Well," said Catherine, "do you?" Leonora took the hair out of her mouth. "Do you have a plan?"

"A plan?" Repetition was easy. The words so smooth they rolled off her tongue into the cooling air. Catherine and Michel put down their forks. They stared. Did they expect her to say something more? Out the window, the sky was yellow ocher. It was vermilion, cadmium-orange, indigo. The sun had set on the longest day of the year and she missed it!

She took her glass of wine to the vineyard and watched the sky pulse. Her bare feet on the warm soil, she looked west, over her garden, her apple trees, her vines. Eurydice stood on the stone wall in perfect silhouette and unleashed her plaintive call. The cats slunk about Leonora's legs asking for dinner. How could she leave this— her home?

Catherine stood beside her. "You don't know what you'll do, do you?"

"I'm waiting for Max." She blurted the words she so wanted to believe. "If France surrenders, they'll have to let him out. It isn't as if they can keep him. Unless—" But she wouldn't say the thought out loud, to speak was to give it power. What if they handed him over to the Nazis? Maybe they already had, packed him onto some train bound for Germany. It would mean she might never see him again. Her knees gave a little. Catherine's arm was around her, holding her up, and Leonora turned to her, kissing her mouth, impulsively, needing human contact and pressure, something to keep her on her feet.

"I've been alone for so long," she said.

"You'll come with us. We'll fix the brakes, get our exit visas, and we'll go."

"But what about this?" she asked, with a small sweep of her hand. "If I'm not here, the Nazis will take it."

"They will take all of France. There's nothing you can do. And it isn't safe for you here. A woman, alone?"

She thought of her recent powers, but she couldn't put her knowledge into words. Not yet. It was too new, too easily crushed, like a baby wren. So she drank her wine, tasting the sun in it, the soil—her *terre*. Her voice, when she heard herself speak, sounded small. "If I go, how will I find Max?"

"Everyone's leaving from Lisbon. We can wait for Max there. And then we'll all take a boat to America."

"Lisbon," she said, thinking of that night with Max, and what he said under the stars.

~⚬~

Walking to town beneath a moon just shy of full, she felt like she was floating. She was a ghost, not really there at all. The town drifted in and out of sleep. Maybe she *was* dreaming, she thought, passing the dark buildings—the *commissariat de police*, the inn where Alphonsine with her true smile and her rough hands was both queen and servant. She wouldn't leave, wouldn't run away like Leonora.

Motel des Touristes had its lights on, its windows open, a round of laughter coming from inside. How could anyone laugh at a time like this? Unless it was Nazis? She looked through the window. No uniforms, just men from the village, hunched over their beers. And she could use a spot of whiskey. Then she would go home, pack what she needed—the essentials—and they'd be off. She could feel the pull of distance, a gust crossing her face as she opened the door, and she longed to let go, to be taken by the wind, to free herself of all she loved.

She sat on the open stool at the bar, between farmers in their field clothes who grew quiet in her presence. The man beside her rested his hand on the counter, a bandage where his pinky had been. Done to avoid conscription, she realized. Looking at his smooth face, she thought of her brother, Gerald. Her mother's letter had said he'd joined the army, *chosen* to join. But Leonora wished he'd listened to Father and stayed out of the war and safe.

Behind the bar Etienne wiped down the counter. "Lovely to see you," he said, "but how will you pay?"

"Just a whiskey, please. I'm off for Portugal. I've come to say goodbye."

"Come for your whiskey, you mean." But he was smiling, pouring her a finger full. He slid the glass in front of her, watched her tilt the amber liquid to her lips. "You are leaving your house for the Germans?" He pulled at a long, gray hair in his eyebrow. "You might as well gift wrap it for them, no?"

"What choice do I have?" She set down her glass and he poured. Two fingers.

"Turn your house over to me. We'll call it even."

"I can't have had that much to drink!" In the mirror behind the bar the room pitched one way, then the other. The whiskey burned going down, and the night was vague and curvaceous. "And anyway, what good would that do you? The Germans—"

"—want an amicable takeover. They won't seize a property so long as a Frenchman owns it. A non-Jew. Sign your deed to me and your house will be safe." The men were loud again. They were laughing.

What had she missed? "I'll even throw this bottle of brandy into the deal." Etienne wiped the dust from an old bottle. He sliced the wax seal with a knife, pulled out the cork, and poured her a glass. "After the war is over, you can have your house back."

She wasn't sure she believed that last part, about giving it back, but the brandy was the best she'd tasted—warm spice and vanilla. It was real, and words were made of air. Oh, but her babies! "You'll feed my cats and goats, my chickens and peacocks?"

"*Mais oui*, Leonora. But we must make it legal. Otherwise they can take it just like *this*," he said with a snap.

~§~

She didn't sleep. There wasn't time. In the armoire, under heaps of clothes—Max's trousers, her shirts, a few lacy items Leonor had left behind—she found her suitcase. It had her name on a brass tag and the word *Revelation* engraved above it. A present from Father when she went off to convent school. Revelation had been her favorite chapter in the Bible, with its dragons, angels, and beasts all cavorting in a cosmic, end-of-times dance. But now the word meant something else. It was what she was moving toward, what was moving toward her. It would recognize itself in her, would stand naked and strip off its skin to show her its bones, its bulbous heart. She had begun to see things already. Her senses had sharpened.

Her hand on the armoire grew warm, then hot. The wood had stories, and closing her eyes, she could sense the tree it had been, how it felt to grow, to eat light, to breathe in a forest of its kin. She could feel its anguish on being chopped down. How it felt to be dead, and still here. Its sadness paralyzed her. Her vision blackened, filling with stars.

She started, startling herself awake. She jerked her hand away from the armoire as though from a flame. Moving fast, she threw skirts, shirts, trousers into the suitcase, wedged in a hairbrush, a toothbrush.

She slipped into Leonor's blouse—the one she'd worn the day Leonor left—hoping it would give her courage. Around her neck she fastened the beetle necklace Max had given her last Christmas, a lifetime ago. She stroked a red beetle's shiny back.

How it felt to fly through air, how it felt to die on a riverbank, to sur-render to the earth.

She shook off the sensation. "No more," she said aloud. She closed the suitcase and set it by the door.

If Max were here, he would know what to do, and she would trust him, the way she always had. Now such faith seemed a weakness. She'd forgotten how to rely on herself.

In the bottom drawer of the bureau she found her passport, Max's beneath it. Holding it, she was holding him, and if she brought it with her, she'd be taking him along, to Portugal, where she'd secure exit visas for them both. *I'll* save *him*, she thought, and tucked the pass-ports into a zippered pocket in her skirt.

─❦─

In the morning she met Etienne at the notary. How light she felt, sitting in the office. With a pen in her hand, she was a balloon wobbling somewhere above her body. She thought of Woolf and Cricket, Beetle and Archie and Lizard, of Plato and Socrates and Zeno, Eurydice and Orpheus; she thought of the morning light over the vines and the olive trees, thought of her wine, clear and crisp, of her paintings and what she might have painted had she stayed; she thought of Max and his possible return. If he came home, how would he find her?

A note. She'd leave him a note.

On the desk was a slip of paper, and on it she scrawled, *Dear Max, I have gone with C., and will wait for you in*—here she paused. She wanted to tell him Lisbon, but that would be a giveaway. Should the Nazis find this, they could scour Lisbon for him. Instead she wrote *Estremadura*. It was the province where Lisbon was located, too big to search. Max would know what she meant. She tucked the note into her pocket, glanced up to see them watching her, waiting.

She bent toward the deed, unable to read a word. It was a tangle of terms, legal horseshit. What did it mean? It could not begin to define her or Max or the Eden they had made. Etienne tapped the bottom. There was a line, a ledge, waiting for her to skip her pen across it. "You'll feed them tonight?" she asked. "All my darlings?"

"I will. Your pets are safe with me." He placed a sweaty palm on her hand. His face was a bloated mask of wax, melting at the sides. Airless and hot, the room spun. To leave, she had to sign. The thing was to keep moving. Motion was freedom, and freedom was all that mattered. She moved her hand and it appeared—that name again.

Leonora Carrington.

Max, July 1940, Nîmes, France

Max opens his eyes to whiteness, the tent glowing above him. It is morning and he's famished. Wilhelm brings him two crackers and a cup of tea. He helps him shuffle outside. Max squints against the brightness, finds a spot in the sun where he sits and eats the crackers slowly. Food is strange, as is the business of chewing and swallowing. He's gone so long without eating, even this insipid cracker swells with taste.

Closing his eyes, he watches the sun pulse red behind his lids. He listens to his breath, even and strong. He has reached the other side. He's alive.

In a week he's eating small meals. In another he's convinced he is strong enough to escape. Wilhelm, however, is not so sure. Men come and go through gaps in the barbed wire; they go to town or to the countryside for a walk, or even just outside the camp to relieve themselves in the woods instead of in the stench trench. But if a man goes farther than town and he's brought back by the gendarmes, he's thrown in the pigsty like Max was. The thought of the place sends Max into a panic. He can't endure it again.

"And without discharge papers you won't be able to get a food card," says Wilhelm, reasonably, as Max tucks a few crackers into a pocket in his pack. "Every day more are being issued. You should wait."

"German commissions are visiting the camps," Max says, repeating the newest rumor. And *Leonora*, he thinks. Already he's lost weeks. He can hear her trapped laugh in his dream, how desperately it rattled the door, and he knows he has to do all he can to find her.

But first he must see the eccentric prefect of La Roque-sur-Cèze for an exit visa.

"But you cannot walk that far, Herr Max," says Wilhelm. "You will need a ride."

⟶⟿

He hardly sees Wilhelm for a couple of days. Then, one evening, he's in the tent sketching the men playing a zesty game of poker when Wilhelm ducks inside. "Tomorrow," he says. He'll take Max to a nearby lake, where he will wait for a woman in a blue Renault. She'll be driving north and can take him to La Roque-sur-Cèze.

He spends the morning before his journey drawing Wilhelm, the barbed wire fence behind him. He signs the portrait and gives it to him. "In case it's worth something someday." Wilhelm hugs him, like a son hugging his father, Max thinks, wishing he could feel this much himself with Jimmy.

After lunch, as the midday malaise begins, they duck through the barbed wire. Wilhelm insists on holding his pack, and he straps it in front of him, so if they are being watched from camp it will look only as if they are going for a stroll. They are just past the woods and are nearing the road when he hears someone running toward them.

It's a guard, too close for them to outrun him. But how is it possible? They've hardly gone far enough to risk suspicion. Max reaches for the pack. He's the one who should be punished, not Wilhelm— but the boy won't let the pack go.

The guard is out of breath. He has to spit before he can speak. "Max Ernst?" he says. He doesn't have to show his gun. Were Max to run, he'd only have to call the gendarmerie and they'd pick him up in no time. There isn't enough wilderness out here to hide in.

They pass that lovely old gate and are again inside the wire with the drove of men. If only he had a dose of prussic acid, he could end things right now. Maybe Wilhelm can get some? But how can he ask him? The boy is crying, he sees, as he hands Max his pack.

Inside his office, the commandant tells Max to sit. He wipes his brow, drinks his tea, searching through a stack of papers on his desk. With each second of silence Max suffers more. Why can't the man announce his fate and be done with him?

He will beg, he decides, falling to his knees. "Get up!" says the commandant. "For the love of God." What does God have to do with any of this, Max wonders, rising. The commandant offers him a document. "Your discharge papers."

His papers? It's too good to be true. "Bless you," he says in spite of himself.

On his way out, stunned by his luck, Max flashes his papers at the guards and walks through the gate in the other direction. Wilhelm meets him on the road. "We must hurry," he says, throwing the pack onto his back.

Coming around a clump of rosemary, Max sees it, the blue Renault. The woman rolls down her window. "Get in," she says, smiling. He slides in beside her, her perfume smelling of jasmine and the sea. She drove down to pick up her husband, she tells him, through small pops in her chewing gum. But they decided to wait for the discharge papers. Any day now, they are saying. And why is Max going to La Roque-sur-Cèze?

He tells her about the eccentric prefect, who lives, they say, in a castle, and about Leonora giving their house to the barkeeper. As he tells her about Peggy Guggenheim, how she might be able to help him, he notices the way he says *me* rather than *us*. It's the smell of her perfume, he thinks, making him vague.

He finds the address on the slip of paper, somehow still in his satchel.

"Oh," she says, as they pull up to the house. "It really is a castle."

—❦—

"Built in the twelfth century," says the prefect of La Roque-sur-Cèze. "There's a moat, a tower, and a ghost, the Lady in Blue, who wanders the halls at night, reciting Baudelaire." The prefect is portly, red-cheeked, with thinning hair and a thick brown beard streaked with gray, and he shuffles about in slippers and a quilted, satin robe, as if he were abbot of some glorious church of decadence. Max likes him immediately. He has a dog named Milton, a cross between what must be a beagle and a sheltie. Long of nose and hair and body, he follows Georges everywhere.

That night Georges cooks a grand meal. He loves to cook, he insists, and at last he has a guest. Max sits at the long dining table in the great, empty hall, as Georges, still in his burgundy robe, carries a milky soup from the kitchen, crème of mushroom, in ruby-red bowls that twinkle in the light of the dusty chandelier. The soup is delicious. Max can taste the soil the mushrooms have grown in; he swears he can taste the summer sun and the rain. Savoring his glass of red wine, he feels almost human again.

Georges takes the bowls away, and in an instant he returns with more red bowls, this time filled with a salad of endive, walnuts, and apples. Next comes a course of chicken and hazelnuts and a sauce that sings to his every cell of sleep, the sleep of the dead and the sated, and again in identical red bowls. He marvels at how slippery clean they are, how with each course they appear more lustrous. Apple tarts and three types of cheese conclude the meal, though he's too full to have more than a bite.

"*Plein du la grâce de Dieu,*" says Georges, refilling their glasses with wine. He leans back, a hand on his bulging belly.

"Please," he says when Georges rises with the last set of bowls. "Let me help."

He waves Max to sit back down and returns with a bottle of cognac and two glasses. "No dishes," he insists, lighting his pipe. The dog trots in and sits at his master's feet, licking his lips. "You see, Milton and I manage quite well."

So this dog, then, is his kitchen frau? Max bites his cheek, and then he laughs, a real belly laugh. It's been so long since he's laughed like this, he doubles over, unable to stop. How he wishes Leonora were here. The fat, lusty, beautiful man laughs along. "Stay if you want," he says. "As you can see, I have only Milton here, in our little Paradise Lost."

"I'd love to," says Max, yawning. His body warm and dense from the meal, he sniffs the cognac and floats on its perfume toward a sea of torpor. He savors the amber liquid, his first taste of liquor in months.

Georges shows him to a room with a window on the dark hills, a desk, a wide feather bed. It was his son's room, he explains, before his wife died, before Europe lost its sanity and his son left for the States. *Like mine*, Max thinks, but he doesn't say the words out loud. He doesn't feel right laying claim to Jimmy in that way, when Lou was the one to raise him.

Georges bids him good night, and he settles in, hangs his few garments in the wardrobe, dusts off the desk. Thinking of Peggy and how he must write to her, he opens the top drawer and finds a pen, ink, paper, and envelopes monogrammed with what must be the prefect's son's initials. BEM. A letter won't make sense coming from him on this paper, but then nothing makes sense anymore. Emboldened by the meal and the cognac, he takes the pen in hand, making breasts out of the B, drawing a snake between the E and M to reverse them.

28 July 1940

Dearest Ms. Guggenheim,

Roland tells me you have agreed to help me get to America, and for this I owe you no small debt. And now you will find me on my knees once more, begging for another favor. I recently returned to my home in Saint-Martin-d'Ardèche, or, I should say, my former home. You remember Leonora—whose painting you kindly purchased a few years ago? While I was incarcerated in Camp des

Milles, in a fit of what must have been madness, she signed our house over to a crooked Frenchman.

Roland mentioned that you had seen my sculptures in the journal Cahiers d'Art, and I wonder if you'll send a letter for a lawyer, testifying that you've seen them, and that they are worth at least—

Here he pauses. What are they worth? They are priceless. The home and the life Leonora and he made there are priceless. But he needs to assign them a value if he's to try to get them back, or be compensated for their loss.

—at least 175,000 francs. And if you might be able to send me six thousand francs, to secure the lawyer, this would be a tremendous help as well.

Most humbly and gratefully yours,
Max Ernst

He takes off his clothes, switches off the light, and slips between the cool, smooth sheets. Perhaps he should have told her more about Leonora—how he means, somehow, to get her to America, too? How he's hoping Peggy will be able to help?

No. There will be time for honesty later, once he has her on his side.

Leonora, June 1940, Saint-Martin-d'Ardèche, France

When Leonora left Saint-Martin, it was afternoon, the light turning golden. She didn't look back, didn't peer into the rearview mirror. She was squeezed into the Fiat between Catherine and Michel, and they crawled ahead, when she longed for speed to pull them free. Too slow, far too slow. She shouldn't have left. She'd filled her cats' bowls with food, but when night came they'd try to find her, and she wouldn't be there. What if Etienne didn't feed them? What if they starved? She should ask Alphonsine to check on them.

She wanted the car to stop. They couldn't have gone more than twenty kilometers. She'd walk back. But now they were hurtling downhill, gaining speed, and when Michel pumped the brakes they jammed, throwing them all into the dashboard. "It's my fault," she heard herself cry.

Michel shifted into neutral, then threw the car into gear. It lurched, and the brakes let up. Catherine was sweating. "Leonora, how could it be your fault?"

It *was*. She'd wanted the car to stop and it had stopped. Who could say how?

They bumped along the road. Catherine's head on her shoulder, Leonora dozed, woke to a dark sky and a convoy of trucks ahead of them. The back of the last truck was covered in burlap, and in its taillights' glow, she saw something dangling. *Things* dangling, she realized as they approached. Or, not things, but legs, feet, arms, and hands, limp and flapping. She turned to Catherine, whose chin bobbed on her chest, then to Michel, who had to see them, too. Or did he? He said nothing. "Do you see the trucks?" she ventured.

"We can fit beside them," he said, accelerating. As they passed, she saw swastikas painted on the doors. *Max*, she thought, *where are you?*

—❦—

She stretched, blinked, yawned her ears open. They were winding through the Pyrenees and it was a new day. On the mountains, red poppies blazed. There were old stone buildings, women and men, their possessions in bags they hauled over their shoulders, on bicycles and in baby strollers. It was the last town before the Andorran border. Michel parked the car and stopped at the only hotel, which, it turned out, was full. He whispered to Catherine, who threaded an arm through Leonora's and led her to a café.

"Darling." Catherine pressed a few francs into her hand. "Eat something, and don't talk to anyone, okay? Let us figure this out. I'll be back soon." Watching her scuttle off, Leonora knew she was wrong. It was up to *her* to find the guide who would show them the route through the mountains and across the border. As Catherine and Michel tried their channels, she would seek true knowledge among the people, where it was always found.

Her baguette and tea arrived steaming. The waiter had dark curls and dark, smooth skin. He winked at her as he set the plate on the table, and her heart danced wildly, certain he would tell her where they should go. She spread the bread with butter and jam, and as she took a bite he eyed her, lifted a cigarette from his apron, and went outside. She followed his lead. He stood in sunlight, his eyes closed, basking. When he saw her, he took the whole of her in, unfurling a plume of smoke into the cool air. "We are hoping to get to Andorra today," she said in English. He only nodded in reply, so she repeated it, this time in French.

"*Bon chance, mademoiselle.*" He dropped his cigarette, crushed it beneath his shoe, and went inside. Had she misread the signs?

No. Here was a man crossing the road, walking toward her. He wore the thick pants of a mountain guide, his broad felt hat adorned with a feather. "Monsieur," she said. His eyes flashed. He tipped his hat. She followed him around a corner, where a bootblack waited for her on the sidewalk. "Can you tell me how to cross the border?" She offered the francs Catherine had given her, and he patted his bench for her to sit.

"Leonora!" Catherine took her by the arm and wheeled her around.

Michel pulled the car up to the curb. "Get in," he said. "The guides are waiting." Already? she thought, amazed by the way information traveled here, so fast, and without the need for words. Michel and Catherine didn't thank her for arranging the guides, but she was all right with that. She knew what she knew.

Michel took a road south, toward the higher peaks, and soon they were winding up a narrow dirt road, navigating furrows and jutting rocks, a sheer drop below. Near the hilt of the mountain, where the road ended, two Andorrans sat on a rock. Michel stopped the car. He handed Catherine's keys to one of the men. This was the deal— safe passage in exchange for the car. They hoisted the bags onto their shoulders and started up the steep incline.

"*Adieu*, old car," Catherine said, laying a hand on her Fiat's battered hood.

The men they followed were short, their skin dark from sun. They reminded Leonora of Picasso, quick and to the point. She started after them but found she couldn't stand, her knees were too weak, and the world was rolling over and over again. She couldn't tell which way was up—although the bald sun helped, so hot and close she was sure she'd combust if she stayed still too long. She crept sideways in a swaying motion. Like a crab she crossed the craggy pass, using her hands for balance. She must have appeared ridiculous, but the men didn't look back. They maintained their pace, with Catherine and Michel close behind them. She could barely keep them in view.

Why wasn't Max here? He would have taken care of things. Everything would have been fine. She froze with the thought of him, stuck again. Feeling his passport in her skirt pocket, she willed herself forward. He was with her. She was carrying him to freedom.

The sun set. Swifts rose and dove. Reaching the top of the mountain, she met a sky of purple and orange. In the valley, a town glowed. They walked by the light of a full moon, a witch's moon. It was beautiful here, clean and pure, and she wished she could stay here in the mountains and sleep on a bed of sand. But when she lay down, Catherine tugged her up, and soon they were stumbling down a dark hill toward distant lights.

The men left their bags on the steps of the Hotel de France—the only hotel in the town. After trying the bell, Michel pounded the locked door with his fist. When no one came, they found the servants' entrance in the back, which was open, and climbed the stairs to the lobby. The hotel was empty save for a single maid, a girl who couldn't have been more than fifteen, who screamed when she saw them, wept in apology, and found them rooms. Leonora's was the size of a closet, bare, with a washstand, a window, and a single bed, which she fell onto, not bothering to undress.

⁓☙

Sunlight pulsed through the dirty windowpane. It was dusk. She'd slept an entire day and she was starving. She knocked on Catherine and Michel's door, knocked harder but no one came. Refugees bumped past, carrying suitcases. Down the hall a baby screamed. She needed fresh air, needed to be out, under the sky. Men jostled her on the stairs. Flattening herself to the wall to let them pass, she found she couldn't move. The wall was made of smooth stones, river stones.

Water rushing, singing. These stones tumbling and alive! Then quiet on the riverbank, warm in the sun.

She opened her eyes. A girl stared up at her, frightened. She must've looked a mess, her hair a nest of knots, her face puffy from sleep. She pushed off the wall, moved sideways, slowly, as though she were at the bottom of an ocean, weighed down by a mile of water.

The lobby was tight with people. She weaved through them, around the heaps of luggage, and shouldered her way out the door. Across the street was a café, where Catherine and Michel were eating. She couldn't see them, but she knew they were there. She could feel their hot breath as they colluded at a corner table.

Crossing the cobblestone street she found she had to shuffle, as if she were ninety-nine years old. A car honked and she scuttled out of its way.

Inside she saw she was right. They sat in a corner, huddled. Michel waved her over. He bit into a baguette. "Visas are harder to come by than I thought," he said, a pale paste on his tongue, his teeth. "And we need them to get into Spain."

"What about your father?" Catherine spread pâté on a slice of bread.

Leonora covered her nose to not gag. "What about him?"

"You're not well?" Catherine pushed a bowl of tomato bisque toward her. "Eat. I'll order another."

"Can I wire him about the visas?" said Michel, pointedly.

The soup smelled good. Picking up the spoon, Leonora's hand trembled and it fell. She'd always hated spoons. She lifted the bowl to her lips and drank. "Father?" She thought of his fiery eyes, his cheeks ruddy with anger, thought of his parting words, *May your shadow never darken my door again. You will die penniless, in a garret.* "Is there any other way?"

Michel leaned in, his voice low. "We can't stay here long. The town's already overrun. Imperial Chemicals has offices everywhere. He can make things happen."

That was what worried her. Catherine put a hand on hers. "Leonora, he will do it for *you.*" She resembled a goose, her long neck craned, her eyes hard, dark beads.

"You've already wired him, haven't you?" It was a fact they didn't deny. Leonora set the bowl on the table. "Do what you need to," she said. "I'm going to the mountain."

Moving through the packed café, she touched the backs of the chairs to remember which way was up. On the street she kept close to the shops, the old stone buildings, and soon she was free, away from the crush of people, out among the rocks and trees. She tried to climb the mountain, but gravity was too strong. So she gave in and lay on her stomach on a slope of dirt, her forehead on the ground. She exhaled and let the earth take her. The sky darkened, the moon rose, and she became nothing, forgetting the war and Hitler, Catherine and Michel, forgetting herself, and even Max. She slept. When she woke, she got to her feet, moved slowly higher, and soon she could scale every vertical slab of rock, strong as a lizard, now that she was in the mountain and the mountain was in her.

Cresting a rise, she saw a band of wild horses, white and brown, mares and foals, grazing in the moonlight. In a slow, steady zigzag she approached them, walking among them. A white mare was so close she reached out and rubbed her neck, soft as ocean air. She stayed very still and calm, and the mare nuzzled her ear. She'd always understood the language of horses, but now it seemed they understood her, as if she were one of them. Another mare nudged her. Brown with a white star on her forehead, white socks on her legs, she looked exactly like Winkie. Her eyes shone in the moonlight. She was Winkie! Leonora's chest swelled, and she knew Winkie was free now, the way she was finally free. She placed her palm on her star and held it there. The squeeze of birth, the cold air, licked clean by love. The warmth of milk, the body of the mother. Hay. Legs wobbling. Running through fields. "Leonora!" a woman yelled. Mother! she thought.

Squinting, she saw the woman on the hill was wearing trousers. It was Catherine, Michel beside her. They stumbled over the rocks, sending pebbles down the slope. The horses bolted into the night.

PART II

Shepherdess of
the Sphinxes

Peggy, August 1940, Grenoble, France

Peggy lights a Pall Mall and slices open a letter from Max Ernst.

She met him in Paris in the winter of '38. She'd seen his paintings in London, at Roland's house, after Max's show closed unexpectedly, his paintings having been declared immoral by some British official or other, all because of Leonora Carrington, Max's newest pet, and her controlling father. At least that was the story Roland had told her in bed one night, before he slid off her silk Elsa Schiaparelli dress, tied the thin silk belt that had hung all night at her hips around her wrists, snugly, and made love to her with a single-mindedness that had surprised her.

When she had met Max at his Paris studio, Leonora was a cat curled at his feet, warming the room with her quiet beauty. They were an unlikely, fairy-tale couple—the wizard with his white hair and his black cape, and the girl he had bewitched. She half expected to see a thin gold chain looped around her ankle, the magical device that kept her by his side. Young enough to be his daughter, she was one in a line of many pets—women Peggy had heard about—Leonor Fini, Meret Oppenheim, and his wife, Marie-Berthe.

But then again, despite his age, there was indeed something about him. The great beak of a nose, the blue eyes. There was a rightful kind of majesty, as if he were accustomed to holding court. And it made sense. Cats are always drawn to birds. They eat their heads, crunch their bones, bat their carcasses about like toys. But Max was the Bird Superior, cat tamer of the Surrealists.

She was drawn to one painting of Max's in particular—blue with a white circle in the corner, and two horses tangled in a dance, or a power of wills, ecstatic and vicious, one horse with its teeth bared. She asked him what it was called.

"*Bride of the Wind*," he said. Then he was silent, something about his eyes making her babble on about her collection of paintings, her gallery in London where she hoped he'd hang a piece in the next group show. She talked on and on, unable to stop herself. All the while, he stroked Leonora's dark, shiny hair. When Peggy said she'd like to buy the painting, he told her it wasn't for sale. It belonged to Leonora.

Turning to go, she saw another painting of horses. Not in Max's rough, expressionistic style, but more colorful, more lucid, it pulsed with sexuality and terror. One of the horses was stuck in a treetop, unable to get down, as if, earlier in the scene, it had had wings, as if it had been a bird and a trickster god had turned it into a horse. Its eyes bulged, wild with such height. Like the horse in *Guernica*, she thought. Such palpable fear in its eyes. "And this one?" she asked.

"Mine." Leonora's voice was soft but sure. "It's called *The Horses of Lord Candlestick*. I painted it."

Startled to hear her speak, having forgotten that she was a girl and not a girl-shaped cat, Peggy felt a thrill turn through her. It was an electric sensation that meant she would buy the painting, no matter the cost.

She reads Max's letter quickly. Yes, of course she will send the letter for the lawyer and the money. And she will ask for a painting in return.

Max, August 1940, La Roque-sur-Cèze, France

The morning sun warm on his back, Max sits at the breakfast table with Georges reading the paper, sharing it between them. Vichy is passing new laws, reexamining the citizenship of immigrants, cooperating with the Nazis. "You're on their list. You're wanted by the Gestapo," Georges says, as casually as if he were saying it might rain today. "Even in the south of France you are wanted. I got a letter saying to report criminals at once." He looks at Max over his glasses. He wouldn't turn him in. Not Georges.

He pours Max more coffee. Max takes a sip. It's too hot and he's inhaled it. He's coughing.

Georges is on his feet, patting his back. "If I got it, so did all the other officials."

"But Leonora," Max says, as if the mantra of her name might retrieve her from wherever it is she has gone.

Milton, who is lying at Georges's feet in a patch of sun, lifts an ear, but doesn't bother opening his eyes. Georges leans across the table and places his hand on Max's. "You aren't going to be any good to her in a German camp. Stay here," he says, "until you have a safe place to go."

Peggy writes back, sending money and a letter for the lawyer, whom Georges secures for him. He'll instigate the lawsuit, the lawyer tells him, but it will take time. France is a mess and everything is taking longer than it should. Peggy's in Grenoble getting her own things in order, extricating her life of twenty years from Europe, trying to find a way to ship her art collection to the States. She won't be in Marseille until the spring, and that space for him at Villa Air-Bel is postponed until December. He calls Roland, but there's been no more word from Catherine. Leonora might be anywhere.

—⁂—

Autumn comes. On the grounds of the castle the leaves of the chestnut trees turn fiery and fall, and he stays with Georges.

Most days Georges only leaves his study for the kitchen, or to walk the path to the mailbox and back. His larder is full enough, he figures, to wait out the war—another year, two at most, unthinkable it should go on any longer.

When he does go to town, he brings Max paints and a huge canvas. He's given him room and board in exchange for a painting. Max begins at once. Soon there's a blue sky, and against it, the orange-red sinews of decalcomania. It's post-apocalyptic. The earth pulled and stretched. Not a stitch of vegetation. But there's a woman, looking out, across an expanse. She's waiting. She has her back to the viewer, but even from behind, it looks like Leonora. He might have painted her face, only he can't remember it, not even when he closes his eyes.

Occasionally someone knocks on the door, and whether it is a citizen in need of his prefect services or merely a friend, Georges lets the visitor in, but not before Max is tucked out of sight in his upper bedroom, curtains drawn.

Never has Max been so quiet, so still. And as the nights lengthen and the days grow cold, he sleeps as he hasn't in years. He dreams, as if it's the most natural thing in the world, as if he'll never stop. But night after night Leonora refuses to visit him. And then, early one morning he hears her laughter. He follows it down an endless hall, where he finds it flapping its wings against the ceiling, frantic for escape. A dark thing, delicate and vicious. Then it falls to the floor, still and small, a blackbird he scoops into his hands.

He hears a woman speaking in verse. *Moi, mon âme est fêlée.* Me, my soul is split. Baudelaire. The Lady in Blue walks toward him, beautiful, radiant—her Prussian blue sleeping gown rising up her long legs, her white hair moving above her, as if she were underwater.

~&

December. Dawn. The light dull and directionless. Georges sits at his desk, barricaded behind stacks of books and towering piles of paper. He stamps Max's exit visa, loudly, with every stamp he can find. His beard has grown in the months Max has stayed with him. It has also grayed, Max is sure of it. Georges stands, moves around the desk. Giving him the visa, he surprises Max with a hug. Max squeezes him right back, thinking how, if he ever paints an angel, he will look just like Georges. He thanks him, for everything, but Georges insists he is the grateful one, for his company and for his painting, already hanging on the wall.

They look at it, at the tattered landscape, the ruins war leaves behind. "I'm afraid it isn't very hopeful," Max says.

"Hope isn't something you can see," Georges says, smiling a little, as if amused.

Max wraps himself in his black cape, hangs his knapsack over his shoulder. Georges and Milton walk him down the drive, where Georges's friend sits in his shiny, black Citroën, waiting to take Max to Marseille as if he were some sort of dignitary.

Leonora, July 1940, Andorra

Leonora was dreaming of the wild horses—the horses she hadn't seen again, though she'd wandered the hills every day for weeks—when she was woken by knocks so loud they shook the walls. It wasn't yet dawn, and she lumbered from bed and opened the door to Michel, who shoved a slip of paper into her hand. Holding it to the sputtering light of the hallway, she saw it was a visa for Spain, with the words "Imperial Chemicals" stamped across it. He snatched it back. "Pack," he said. "The train for Madrid leaves in an hour."

The station brimmed with refugees, with families. A grandmother held a baby; too tired to bounce, or to soothe, she let it wail. There was a line to reach the customs officer, and when they did, he shook his head, pointed at some detail on the paper. "Good for two."

"I'll stay," Leonora offered, thinking of the horses, of how she was bound to find them if she kept looking, and then she would ride one into the wilderness.

"He is *your* father," Michel insisted. "I'll find another way."

Leonora and Catherine took window seats. Catherine flattened her right palm on the window and Michel met it with his left. Their mirrored hands pressed, fogging the glass.

As the train pulled away and Catherine dabbed at her eyes, Leonora pulled Max's passport from her skirt pocket. Warmth spread through her. He was with her. He wore a suit, his tie askew, and his eyes were clear and cold. He was young in the photo, in love with Marie-Berthe, and yet he was here, in Leonora's hand. He was *hers*. She touched the stamp, its eagle and its swastika. She would find him before the Germans did. But somehow she couldn't put him back in her skirt. He'd suffocate. So she slid him into a side pocket of her purse and snapped it shut. She'd keep him close and safe.

~&

In the Madrid station, refugees pressed and churned, the air thick with tears and sweat. In the jumble of languages, of hands clasped to all the suitcases they could hold, children overflowed the arms of their parents. They ran to keep up. A small girl held the foot of her doll, its head dangerously close to the floor. In a corner lovers kissed with such fervor Leonora knew this was goodbye. The summer heat had its hands around her throat. Or was it something about Madrid? There was a suffocating sadness, from which no one was free.

Outside, she and Catherine pushed through the crowd to the street. Catherine hailed a cab. Looking at Leonora, she put a finger to her lips. "Hotel Roma," she told the driver.

~&

At the hotel's sidewalk café, Leonora tipped an oyster to her mouth. She ate her salad with her fingers, a leaf at a time. Like everyone in the buzzing café, Catherine kept her voice low, in case someone at the next table was listening. "We'll stick to the plan. Wait for Michel, then go to Portugal, the three of us."

A man at the bar swiveled on his stool, looking at them as if he'd heard. He was new, not one of the regulars Leonora had come to recognize in their three days at the hotel. He reminded her of a reptile, she was thinking, when she realized the stool was actually stationary, and he was turning just his head. And then he was strolling to their table, a young man beside him. With a stomp of his boot and a stiff bow, he introduced himself as Van Ghent. "And this is my son. He works for Imperial Chemicals, the English division."

Leonora glanced at Catherine, willing her to not say a word. These men were spies, sent by Father. Or perhaps they were here to help? Michel had to cross into Spain, and they all needed visas for America—Max, too, she thought, tightening her hold on her purse.

When the men pulled up chairs to join them, Leonora didn't protest. They were in public. What harm could they do?

The son had thin, blond hair and pale skin. They were Dutch but he'd been living in England. And now he was here, as an attaché of sorts, he explained, smiling weakly, as if apologizing. The father ordered gin and tonics all around. "You must like gin," he said in his Dutch accent. "British girls always like gin." His chest puffed like a pigeon's, he put a pack of cigarettes on the table. "Go ahead. You can share it."

Cigarettes were a black market item, and since Catherine was already putting one to her lips, inhaling as he lit it, Leonora joined her. The smoke tasted of Paris, of her old, audacious life. But this was exactly what this Van Ghent wanted—for her to let down her guard, to relax. "You are here—*why*?" she asked.

He smiled, the way a snake might smile, or a lizard. Pulling out his passport, he slid it across the table so she could see. It was stamped with a swastika, just like Max's passport. But then Holland was German now. He took it back, slid it into a jacket pocket. "I am a Jew, but they leave me alone. You see, I *help* them."

On the sidewalk a gypsy pushed her cart toward them, walking more slowly than the rest of the passersby, who looked to Leonora like automatons, controlled by Van Ghent, she realized with a shiver. But the gypsy was not one of them. Dressed in vivid rags, she was old as the earth, her dark skin creased, like the smeared paint of Max's decalcomanias. Leonora waved her closer. Jewelry filled her cart. Sifting through the bracelets and rings of colored glass, Leonora chose a brooch of plain silver, a spiral. Slowly, she traced the spiral inward, feeling the sadness of Madrid spin into her stomach, as into a cauldron. It was the sadness of the world, and by taking it in she could transmute it. She could liberate mankind. But of course! Her skin prickled, her pores opened with insight. *This* was her purpose.

"I could arrest her now." Van Ghent laughed. Scales gleamed under his skin.

Leonora ignored him and offered the gypsy a handful of coins. The gypsy smiled, toothlessly, took a coin, and rolled her cart away. Leonora fastened the brooch to her blouse, the very one Leonor had left her in, and the transmutation began. It happened in an instant. Her stomach churned, she tasted bile, and her intestines groaned so loudly she was sure everyone could hear. Doubling over, she ran to the loo, where she vomited long and hard.

When she returned, they were on the next round of drinks. Catherine's cheeks were flushed. She'd given away every secret. "Gin?" said Van Ghent, pushing a fresh glass toward Leonora. "What happened to your brooch?" he asked, smiling. She felt for where she'd pinned it, just above her heart, but it wasn't there. How could he have taken it from her? And then she felt him clammy and soft, under her skin, twisting, constricting her organs. What did he want with her? If she became his puppet, what would he force her to do?

"You will find it in your purse," he said, calmly. She opened her purse and her pin was right on top, coiled on Max's passport, which she didn't remember having put there.

If he was so interested in her things, he could *have* them. She dumped the contents of her purse on the table. She wanted none of these trappings—lipstick and perfume. Even their passports seemed flimsy now, filthy and contaminated. "Take it all," she said. And she left the café, rode the lift to her room, and lay on the bed.

The doorknob twisted. She'd forgotten to lock the door. Standing over her, a cleft in his chin, Van Ghent was her father. He was Hitler, Mussolini, Franco. It was not enough to rebel, she had to stop him. He had enslaved Madrid and she was the only one who could liberate it. She knew this, and yet she couldn't move. He set her purse on the nightstand. "You should be more careful with your things," he cautioned. "Your passport is here. You don't want to lose your identity."

She blinked. Slowly. Had he drugged her? When she opened her eyes, he was gone.

She looked in her purse. Everything was there. Everything she no longer needed. She would find someone else to take it. And she would get Catherine away from Van Ghent. Clearly, she was oblivious to his terrible power. She slung her purse over her shoulder, its heaviness a burden she couldn't wait to give away. She hurried back to the café to find their table empty. However, the bar was bustling.

A group of Spanish Requetés officers, with their red berets and their mustaches, called her over. They'd fought on the side of Franco, but they seemed convivial, and she wasn't ready to return to her room. They bought her orange *aguardiente*. The clear liquid burned going down. Heat radiated from her empty stomach, warmed her hands and face, a fiery purification. She told an officer about Van Ghent, and then another, but no one would listen. When she urged them to take the contents of her purse, they laughed. One placed a lit cigarette between her lips, another traded her empty glass for his full one. She drank and smoked and the bar melted around her.

Everyone had left, it seemed, except for the officers. One helped her to stand. Another took her free arm. They led her down the road and into a car. But who was driving? And where were they going? She would have asked, but her lips were numb, paralyzed, and anyhow she'd find out soon enough. They drove, one street so like the next she didn't try to keep track. Her eyes closed. In the backseat, her body swayed between the men as the car sped up, slowed down, turned right, and left. Their voices and laughter drifted through her.

She was made of air, hardly there at all. And then she heard thumping, faint at first, then louder, constant and deep. It was the heart of Madrid. They were taking her to the city's heart, to the very seat of its sadness.

The car stopped. An officer got out, held the door. "Mademoiselle," he said. She saw the house, the Spanish balconies, all the windows dark. The man beside her scooted her off the seat. She was moving with them, up stairs and into a room with Chinese vases, a bed with a red silk quilt. She was on her back. The men in their red hats whirled with the ceiling. One had his knee between her legs, her skirt up her thighs. Sweat dripped from his face onto hers. She clawed his cheek and the marks filled with blood. Her wrists over her head, tight. The swamp of breath, her body slick with sweat. Sharp nose, hard eyes, the scar across his eyebrow like a tear in fabric. A bald, jagged interruption in a life. The face she'd never forget. Her blouse torn open. Buttons hitting the tile. So many pieces of herself scattered she'd never find them all. Searing thrusts. The room a red scream. Hers. His hand over her mouth. She bit. Another on her, in her. Dead flesh. A rag doll, she saved her energy. He shuddered, pulled himself from her, and she twisted, kneed his groin. He cried, cursed. She was up, then yanked back down. His eyes wide, pointing to her necklace of beetles, he backed away. "*Bruja*," he said, and ripped the necklace from her neck. The beetles scattered. She crawled to pick them up, and then thought better of it. A *bruja* would leave them as a curse. She pulled down her skirt, closed her ripped shirt with the remaining button. Here was her purse, the strap over her shoulder. Someone poured a bottle of cologne on her head. *Of course*, she thought, because now she was ready for the city, having endured the worst it had to offer.

Not the worst. Here was her body, breathing.

Two men took her in the car, stopped at a park, pushed her out. She stumbled, wandered. She lost a shoe, so she kicked off the other. Grass cooled her feet. Once she'd been a girl on the lawn of Crookhey Hall, chasing sparrows. Who was she now? In a fountain she lay down, her head under water. She held her breath, and the heart of Madrid, pulsing in her ears, behind her eyes, consumed her. She screamed under the water, high and long. Gasping air, dripping, she sat on the fountain's edge.

A flashlight crossed the grass, landed on her face, blinding her. A policeman wrapped her in a blanket. He drove her to the hotel whose name she somehow remembered. *Roma.*

In the lobby, she didn't look at the man behind the desk, though she felt his eyes on her damp skin as she made her way to her room.

On her bed lay two silk nightgowns, pale green and pink. A gift from Van Ghent? An apology? Or, perhaps, an offering, an acknowledgment of her powers. The nightgowns were freshly laundered. To wear them she, too, needed to be clean. She filled the tub with cold water and dunked. Like the river in winter. She leapt from the bath and rubbed at her skin with a towel until she was rosy. She slipped on the green gown, took it off, plunged into the icy bath, dried herself, and slipped into the pink one. She alternated, green and pink, with baths between, until—her skin raw— she could no longer feel where their fingers had pressed, could no longer feel her flesh at all, and she drifted on the bed, dressed in shiny green, like a caterpillar.

───❦───

In dream after dream Van Ghent followed her as if through the rooms of a house. She locked a door to escape him, vanishing into a new dream, and he moved right through it. In a convent school, he was a priest, offering her a poisoned host. In Saint-Martin he was a villager whispering to the others, lighting their torches as they circled her and closed in. "*Sorcière,*" they chanted. "*Sorcière!*"

The morning sky, an insipid blue, was a flimsy and treacherous facade. She splashed her face with water.

In the mirror over the sink, her reflection had begun to fade. She was vanishing again, into the mirror world, the way she had at the convent. But the pupils of her eyes glowed—they shone so she could hardly look into them. They were suns, two burning suns, and around them were planets, orbiting. She blinked, looked again. The solar systems were still there— one in each eye. Her stomach groaned with the anguish of Madrid, but it

no longer devoured her. It couldn't. She embodied the totality. One with
the cosmos, she could feel the pain at the same time she was beyond it.

She pulled herself from the mirror, put on a clean white dress and sandals, and buried her clothes from the night before in the trash. Even the blouse that had been Leonor's, the blouse that had given her courage. She didn't need it anymore.

In the café, Catherine read the paper. She folded a slice of *jamón* into her mouth. Leonora ordered tea. "Aren't you going to eat?" Catherine said. The *jamón* was vulgar, mottled with fat. It made her gag. Catherine sipped her coffee, a dark, thick brew. "Did you end up with my nightgowns? I had them cleaned and I think they might have sent them to your room by mistake."

"Yes, yes, I have them," Leonora said, but she was thinking of her pupils, of the cosmos inside them. "Do you notice anything different about me?" she asked, leaning toward her. Catherine looked up from her paper. "Do you see my eyes?"

"You look exactly the same," she snapped.

"*Really* look." Leonora widened her eyelids. "Can you see the planets?"

"Darling, *please*," Catherine whispered, going back to her reading.

Leonora let her read because now Van Ghent was in the lobby. She didn't need to see him. She could feel his slippery presence.

Catherine peered at her over the paper and sighed. "What was it we wanted, do you remember? When you and Ursula and I had tea that day at the Savoy?" She paused, waiting. Did she really expect her to answer? That was another life. Leonora had been someone else then.

"We wanted to make art," Catherine said. "We wanted *our* art to be in the world." How could she be so oblivious? How could Leonora make her see?

"There isn't a world anymore. It's been hypnotized by Van Ghent." She nodded toward the lobby, where he and his son were planning their next move. "Do you see this?" she pointed at the headline,

"*Nazis Ataque Inglaterra Por El Aire.*" "This was his doing." Hearing herself say it, she knew it was true. "The newspapers are his instruments of hypnosis."

Catherine lit a cigarette. "Perhaps you should go to your room and rest."

Leonora picked up the pack—two left—and she knew why Catherine couldn't understand her, why she refused to help. It was the cigarettes Van Ghent had given her. Leonora slipped them into her purse and strode right past the fascist Dutchman and his son.

Outside, she took a stack of newspapers from the newsstand—as many as she could hold—and standing in front of the hotel where she knew he would see her, she tore them up one at a time and threw them to the wind. The people gave her space. As they stared, she felt herself gaining strength. She would dismantle his powers, but she couldn't do it alone. She hurled the remaining papers into the street and ran inside to convince Catherine.

In the lobby Van Ghent and his son were deciding her fate. Van Ghent grabbed her arm, shouted, "You are mad. You have to stop. I have contacted your father." The son slinked back, guilty and weak. It wasn't his fault—she knew—it was the fathers she had to free herself from. She gripped Van Ghent's hairy forearm and plunged her teeth into it. He howled and let her go.

From a corner Catherine watched. "Come on," Leonora urged, but she shook her head and looked at the floor. She was of no use anyhow. Leonora would find help elsewhere.

She ran to the street and hailed a cab. "British Embassy," she told the driver.

The drive jostled her this way and that, like it had the night before, but this time she knew where she was going.

Max, April 1941, Marseille, France

The night cooler than he'd expected, Max pulls his black cape over his shoulders, hoping it will make him invisible. He's been staying at the Villa Air-Bel for months with the other artist refugees, and though it's just outside Marseille, he goes to the city as little as possible, to keep risk to a minimum, but tonight he's drinking wine at a sidewalk café, waiting for Peggy Guggenheim.

The Vichy government, organized now, and frightfully systematic, has begun to enforce the *Statut des Juifs*—Statute of the Jews—rounding up and deporting Jews to camps. The black market is full of plain-clothed informers, and everyone is vying for visas and dreaming of America. If Peggy arranged Breton's voyage, perhaps she will secure his as well.

Breton was still at the villa when he arrived. For days they barely spoke. And then one night, after they'd finished their supper of cold potato soup and green salad and lamb, Breton pulled out a jug of praying mantises. The tiny green monks crawled over their empty plates, over their hands and up their arms and necks and into their hair, clutching their skin as they went, and all at once the lines of bravado struck Max as idiotic. They'd known each other for two decades. They might not see eye to eye, but that no longer mattered here, at the end of the known world. They laughed and were friends again.

After Breton left, Consuelo de Saint-Exupéry, the wife of the aviator writer, took his room, though she spends her days in the branches of the plane trees, reading. The painter Victor Brauner, who has one glass eye, is living at the villa indefinitely, having been denied an American visa, since the quota for Romanian visas has been met, and won't open again, he's been told, for at least two years, and Chagall comes and goes, hoping for his own visa to come through. And still, there has been no word of Leonora.

In two days Max will be fifty. Never in his life has he had less, or lost more—the sculptures and paintings still on the walls of the house in Saint-Martin, and yet more paintings burned by the Nazis after the Degenerate Art show closed. But surrounded by artists and enlivened by the longer days, he's begun, at last, to work in earnest again, painting women as monoliths, as giants, cloaked in decalcomania—a ragged, disintegrating fabric of oranges, umbers, reds—all of the women naked, all of the women half-hidden from view, all of the women—*her*. Leonora.

Suddenly, here's Peggy, stepping from the back of a dark car, her hair swept into a loose bun, her pressed white shirt tucked into a tailored skirt. The conservative exterior doesn't fool him. He knows—doesn't everyone?—she's a wild thing, falling into bed right and left, a little like himself. She approaches him smiling, her narrow hips swaying. She wears flirtation like a perfume he can smell from a distance. He smiles, kisses both her cheeks, the smooth cheeks of his savior.

Having parked the car, Victor Brauner joins them. He wears his fedora low in the front as much to keep his bald head warm as to shield his face from view. A Jewish Surrealist, he does his best to blend, to draw no attention.

As Max orders a bottle of champagne he is sure Peggy will pick up the tab for, she lights a cigarette. Leaning back in her chair, she breathes a swell of smoke into the night, lets loose an easy laugh. Victor, however, is quieter than usual. His real eye refuses to look at them, but his glass eye can't stop staring. It is the eye he'd painted missing years before he lost it to a shard of glass, one night when an argument in a Montparnasse café turned violent. Max was there. He saw it happen. And after he'd lost it, Victor told Max, he was seized with inspiration.

Peggy touches Max's hand lightly, drawing her manicured fingertips across his knuckles. The gesture, at once absentminded and forward, sends an electric pulse through him, and he turns his hand over, offering his palm. She traces his lifeline, the tickle delicious. "I hear you've been painting," she says. "When can I see your work?"

"Tomorrow." Well, why shouldn't she come tomorrow? He pours the rest of the champagne all around. "You must come to Villa Air-Bel tomorrow."

She turns to Victor. "Darling, can you fetch me at the hotel? Let's say at noon?"

"It would be my pleasure," says Victor, who looks anything but pleased.

"I want to see it all. Perhaps we can work something out—a painting for the price of your ticket to America." Her eyes flicker with the candlelight—a lovely shade of green. "Victor told you, didn't he? I'm opening a gallery when I return to New York." Her laughter trills into the spring air. "All of those New Yorkers who think they know art." The tip of her tongue emerges between her pressed lips and retreats just as quick. She arches her brows. "Together, my dear, we're going to blow their cocks off."

⁓ஃ

He spends the morning covering the walls of the living room of the villa with his paintings, arranging them as he would for an art show, with attention to composition, color, and size, and how one painting will lead to the next. Beginning on the left side of the room, he moves clockwise, mixing his newest paintings in with the old ones he managed to carry from Saint-Martin. The afternoon light should show them off well. He owes Peggy a painting, promised her one to compensate for his passage to America, but perhaps she will agree to buy more. He needs money of his own. Living off the generosity of others has grown tiresome.

Peggy is all business. She wears trousers, shakes his hand the way a man might, and hardly looks at him. Smoking her cigarette, she moves from one painting to the next in silence. Only she starts at the end, moving counterclockwise, exactly opposite the way he envisioned the spectacle. And he doesn't have the nerve to stop her. He feels foolish, pretending this is an art show, when what it more closely resembles is a pawnshop. He is a desperate artist and she is an American heiress; she can take what she wants and he will give it to her for pennies on the dollar.

Might as well play the part of a pauper then. He asks her for a cigarette, and she takes one from her silver case. Pall Mall, American cigarettes. Crouching in the corner of the room, he smokes, watches her cross her arms against the new paintings, against, particularly, *Leonora in the Morning Light*. "To Leonora," she says, reading the inscription, and he flinches to hear her name in Peggy's mouth. She lets out a huff and then coughs, to clear her throat, apparently. She sucks in her cheeks at *The Robing of the Bride*—Leonora in red feathers, a muse with an agenda all her own, a queen mid-stride, on her way to Lisbon. If Peggy gives him enough money, perhaps he can make it in time. Perhaps his girl will be waiting for him still.

Victor trails Peggy, standing close enough to her that when they speak it sounds like murmurings, dull and cruel, reminding Max of his parents, so long ago, deciding what to do with him when he defied their wishes. Victor nods, shuffles over—a wingless, one-eyed Hermes. He winks, and for a second, it is just the glass eye, watching. "She likes your old stuff, but if you'll give her those, she'll take a few of your new ones too."

"She'll *take* them?" Max spits into the palm of his hand. The coal of his cigarette sizzles as he puts it out. He stands, his face hot. "Which old ones?" he asks, wondering why he hung *Bride of the Wind* with the others. Perhaps he did it out of spite? Or because he wanted to see it again, to remember?

Peggy is looking at it closely, and when she turns to him her eyes are wet. "But this was the painting that wasn't for sale. You told me it belonged to Leonora."

He walks to her, taking his time, and stands close enough to smell her perfume, bright as spring, persisting through the cloud of smoke.

"That's all over now," he says, and though he has a hard time believing it, as her eyes shine with tears, he has the urge to kiss her, to become someone she will need.

"Forgive me." She turns to wipe her cheeks. "I don't know what's the matter."

Victor taps him on the shoulder. "Should I fetch your collages, too?" He is too kind. Too selfless. And Max, apparently, is the sort of man who will save his own skin at his friend's expense. He feels mired in shit—as if he were back in that pigsty. Only this time, he deserves it.

"Of course," he says. Whatever she takes from him has a better chance of getting out of the country. In his hands, the collages are a death sentence—an *aberration* the Nazis called them—but in hers they are art. They are history, evidence of Dada and the fact that Germany once gave birth to a movement free of rules, made of reckless happenstance and the absurd belief that a life without war was something you could choose.

Victor fetches the collages and spreads them across the floor of the living room. On her knees, Peggy looks them over, these fossils of a lost world, a continent sunk. A doctor with the head of a raven listens to the heart of a sleeping girl through a stethoscope. A lion-headed magician suspends a deck of cards in the air. And Peggy Guggenheim leans over them. She is buying dreams on the black market. His dreams.

"Take them all," he tells her.

Peggy gets to her feet, as business deals, it seems, cannot be conducted from the floor. Smoothing her trousers, she agrees to give him two thousand dollars, minus the six thousand francs he owes her, and he will give her all of his old paintings, and a few of his new ones, not *Leonora in the Morning Light*, which makes her nauseous, but *The Robing of the Bride*, which, she says, she believes she can get used to.

The Robing of Leonora, he should have titled it.

But hasn't he always been adept at moving on, at letting go? And besides, he reminds himself, *she* was the one to leave him.

They shake hands and Victor gathers the collages, takes the paintings from the walls. Outside the sun glints through the leaves of the giant plane tree, and he suggests they celebrate with the last bottle he brought from his vineyard. *My vineyard*, he says, rather than *ours*, or more accurately *hers*.

They toast to the rousing air of spring, sweet with cherry and apricot blossoms, and to the summer that will follow, to America, a word that—when Victor goes pale—makes Max wish he hadn't said it. Their glasses ring to their health, and as they drink the sunlight of 1939, he closes his eyes, as if the wine were a potion that could send him back to Saint-Martin, to that irretrievable year, and this time rather than entertaining friends and making art and wine and love, they would pack and leave paradise for America.

"It is *her* wine," he says, though neither Peggy nor Victor hears him. Leonora trimmed the vines, and with the help of a couple of workers, she picked the fat grapes and crushed them with her bare feet, the way they make wine in Sicily, and now he sips her toes, her sweat, the salt of her neck and her collarbones and beneath the curves of her breasts. The others are drinking wine, while he drinks Leonora.

~❧

Max's fiftieth birthday is lobster and steamed clams at Marseille's *Vieux Port* as the sun sinks. It's wine and grappa, and a stroll with allies and fellow degenerates past the fishermen unloading their boats, down alleyways teeming with exiles—Italians and Spaniards and Germans, Czechs and Belgians and Poles—and through the back door of a black market restaurant where there is bread, lamb with rosemary and mushrooms sautéed in real butter, chocolate soufflé and strawberries for dessert. He feels better than he has all year.

Varian Fry, head of the American Rescue Committee, raises his glass. Fry's dark eyes glimmer behind his spectacles. Jimmy has been in touch, he says, he's involved his boss, the head of the Museum of Modern Art, and an American visa for Max seems at last to be in reach. He should stop by his office this week to get it underway.

Poor Victor Brauner raises his glass, too, his real eye brimming. "I will miss you, my friend," he says, and he swallows his burgundy, orders more grappa, and sings along with Édith Piaf. *Moi j'suis malade, j'rêve à ma fenêtre.*

Max is dreaming out the window, too, but with his appetite boosted by the salt air and Peggy's bare leg pressed to his, he's no longer so sick with sadness. Closing his eyes, swaying with the music, he can picture the shoreline of New York, the Statue of Liberty peeking out of the fog.

She sticks a cigarette between her lips and he lights it. Fry is talking, but Fry is always talking. "So Chagall has a proposition for you," he tells Peggy. "He needs to get eight thousand dollars to the States. He wants to give it to the Rescue Committee and have you pay him back when he gets to New York."

"Who does he think I am? Rockefeller?"

Fry laughs and runs a hand through his hair. "A Guggenheim, I suppose?"

"Yes. But a *poor* one," she says, and orders more champagne. Glass in hand, she levels her eyes at Fry. "Tell him I can do a thousand for him."

"Much obliged," he says, relaxing visibly, and lights a cigarette. "You *know* what they're doing now, right? They're sweeping the hotels for Jews. Even the best hotels, even the Grand Hôtel du Louvre et de la Paix."

"But I'm American."

"Yes. And you're also Jewish."

Taking Peggy's cigarette in his fingers, Max puts his mouth to the red smear of her lipstick, takes a drag, and hands it back. "You are absolutely right," he tells her. "If the police question you, you must insist you are American."

Fry pours them all champagne. "What I'm saying is that you have to leave here as soon as you can."

"And I will. Of course, there are my children to get home, too, and

Laurence, my *ex*-husband," she explains to Max in particular, "and his wife and their children. It isn't so simple. But then, what is these days?" She sends a plume of smoke over their heads. "It's all in motion, trust me, Varian. But first I must take Max's paintings to Grenoble, where the rest of my collection is—squirreled away in the basement of the museum there. What sort of a collector would I be if I let something as fleeting as war deter me?" She plunges her cigarette butt into a dollop of chocolate sauce. "Someday I'll have a museum, and it will be around long after this egomaniac Hitler is food for worms."

Under the table Max rests his hand on her leg, on the knobby wool of her skirt. She has a kind of androgynous allure. She can hold her own in any company, utterly self-assured, like Leonora. Unlike her, Peggy didn't turn her back on her family's money—but then, when her father went down with the *Titanic*, it was given to her outright, no strings attached. And she put it to use. Max has no doubt she will have her museum, and his art will hang on its walls.

"Did I tell you how my collection was in Paris when the Nazis were closing in? I had to find somewhere to put the paintings. The Louvre was going to send them to one of their secret vaults in the country with the rest of their work, but when they saw them they thought they were too modern. Not worth saving. Can you imagine? So I put them in my friend's barn, in a tiny town near Vichy. Luckily the Germans were only there a couple of weeks and had no idea all of that *degenerate art* was stacked behind bales of hay in her barn."

After the dinner is over and Peggy has taken care of the bill, he links his elbow in hers. They stroll under the stars and he puts his mouth very close to her ear. "Where will we meet?" he hears himself ask.

She stops and looks him in the eye. "At the Café de la Paix, tomorrow, at four in the afternoon. I'm in the hotel there. My nap time is at five, without fail, and I do so hate to sleep alone."

Leonora rang the bell of the British Embassy. She wouldn't hold back. She'd tell them all she knew. A proper English butler, tall and gray-haired, opened the door. "I'm a British citizen," she blurted, and shoved her passport into his hand. Stepping aside so she could enter, he tried to give it back. "Keep it. And this, too," she said, giving him Max's passport. "I must see a consul, immediately."

"You have an appointment?"

"I have information, very secret information. He will want to meet with me."

He squinted at her over his spectacles. "Very well," he said, and led her upstairs, to a room with a wide window that overlooked a plaza where fruit and flowers were for sale. Behind the desk a bald man looked up from his paper. His eyes lit on the butler, and then on her. She jumped right in, told him about Van Ghent, the Jewish Dutch Nazi, who was controlling all of Madrid with his mind, and she tossed the partial package of cigarettes on his desk as evidence. "His hypnotic device. As well as this," she said, taking his newspaper from him, wadding it into a ball. "The war is a metaphysical war, waged by Hitler and Mussolini, of course, but Madrid is Van Ghent's terrain." She hurled the newspaper from the window.

The consul looked at her differently now. He knew she meant business. He took her hands in his and walked her to a sofa. "Who is this man? You met him where?"

Finally, someone was listening! And his eyes, when she looked at them closely, had planets and suns, just like hers. "At our hotel, the

Hotel Roma. He claims to know my father. And his son works for Imperial Chemicals, so perhaps he was telling the truth."

"Your father is?"

"Harold Carrington."

"Of Imperial Chemicals?" He jotted the names in a little pad, but was he truly hearing her? He seemed not to understand the urgency of the matter. She did her best to simplify things. "The only way to end this war is for every human to realize their power. If we meld our power, Hitler doesn't stand a chance. You must confront Van Ghent. Once he knows we're on to him, his hold on the city will be broken."

He dialed the phone. Was he calling the police, or Hotel Roma? Was he trying to track down Van Ghent? "Dr. Alonso, *por favor.*" He watched her. The planets danced in his eyes.

~&~

She emerged from the hotel bathroom when room service arrived. "*Por favor, señorita,* wear a robe at least." Dr. Alonso put an arm around her shoulders and led her back to the bathroom. They were in a room at the Ritz and he wouldn't let her leave. So she bathed in the claw-foot tub as he sat in a chair by the door reading and smoking his pipe. "I don't mind your being naked, but the waiters! They could kick us out, and we're not ready yet."

"To meet with Franco?" she asked, for this was the first step. She would wake Franco from this dream of tyranny, and Spain and England would sign an accord. England and Germany would be next, and soon she'd return to the house in Saint-Martin.

Dr. Alonso poured her a flute of bromide. "Drink it all before you come out, clothed this time," he said, and he closed her in the bathroom. Clothed? She'd been vanishing into the mirror a bit more each day. She didn't see why clothes should matter much. As she sipped the bitter medicine, a sense of calm spread through her muscles, through her blood. Her body was hers but it was not *her.* She draped it in white towels, searching for the right ceremonial style for her visit with Franco.

Days passed and she was not brought to Franco. Dr. Alonso had not understood the urgency of the situation, so she went over it again and again. She had to meet with Franco, and then with Hitler. And if Hitler would not cease, she'd assassinate him. Dr. Alonso paced. He poured himself a glass of bromide and phoned another doctor, Alberto, who arrived that afternoon to take his place.

Alberto was different, a magnetic ease in his long limbs. When she walked about the hotel room naked and theorizing, he did not object, nor did he avert his gaze. He turned on the radio. "*Los ojos verdes*," a man sang, and Alberto swung her around the room in a waltz, his eyes green as the Loire, green like her brothers' eyes, and Michel's, and she knew it was her brothers who had come to rescue her from the fathers.

She wanted Alberto as much as she'd wanted anyone. More. He was young and hungry, and she could feel blood returning to regions in her body that had been bloodless for too long. They ordered room service and made love in every inch of the room. She'd been a shell, but now she was a woman, an animal in heat. He gave her flowers and fruit, dresses and perfume, and he took her dancing and to sidewalk cafés.

Then, one afternoon, Alberto brought her along to an appointment with Mr. Gilliland, the head of Imperial Chemicals in Madrid, and told her to wait in the lobby while they spoke. He had come for Father's money, that much was clear. How else could they remain at the Ritz?

In the waiting room she sat in a stiff-backed chair. It was August and warm. She was wearing her white sundress, but even that was too much, and she could feel sweat run down her back. In a mirror on the far wall she could barely see herself. Her image had grown very faint and she had to walk closer to get a look. The angles of her face surprised her. Her hair was swept into a tight bun, like a flamenco dancer's. The last time her hair had been pulled back in this fashion, she was being presented at court to please Father. Today, Alberto had spent the morning brushing her hair, twisting it up, and at lunch he'd stuck a hibiscus behind her ear. She plucked out the flower and dropped it. Wide open, the petals were a livid pink. She'd been hypnotized once more, this time with beauty and longing. She'd been tricked.

At her desk a secretary typed, looking up at her frequently. Perhaps she'd been told to watch her, told she might run? Smiling, Leonora stood slowly. She didn't bolt into the hall. Rather, she opened the door to the office. Calmly, she stood in the doorway and looked from Alberto to the man behind the desk, Mr. Gilliland himself, another lizard man, with the same cold eyes, the same long fingers as Van Ghent. Alberto was a traitor. He'd gone to the fathers for help. "I see you for what you are, Alberto. A snake. No, you are not that good. You are a worm. A maggot," she said, pulling the pins from her hair, wrecking the bun he'd worked so hard to smooth. "You are here for my father's money, not to bring me any closer to Franco, or to Hitler. And you—" She turned on Gilliland. "You are a trifling moron—working for my father no doubt, doing just what he says."

"Leonora, please." Alberto was up. His hand on the small of her back he tried to get her to leave. "I understand you're upset, but listen—"

"To whom? Two hypnotized fools? Have you explained anything to him?"

"Why don't *you* tell me," said Gilliland, ensconced behind his desk, smiling. "What is it you want to explain, Leonora?"

"The state of the world. The truth you are unwilling to face." Sitting where Alberto had been, she started at the beginning.

Soon a certain Dr. Pardo was in the office. "Leonora," Gilliland said, "would you kindly enlighten him on these affairs of state?" She repeated it all. She was used to explaining things over and over, since no one seemed capable of understanding her. Dr. Pardo was an old man, his hearing faulty, so she shouted. She sounded like someone on a street corner, standing on a wooden crate, talking to anyone who would listen, but she couldn't stop—to stop was to give up on mankind. And if she could convince even one person, then maybe there was hope.

When she paused for breath, she was standing in shadow. The sun had gone down, or else ducked behind a building. She looked for Alberto, but he was not in the office, and when Gilliland and Dr. Pardo led her out, he wasn't in the waiting room either. He'd left without a word—the sort of man who was easily bought, easily sold. The secretary was gone, too. There was no one to see her vanish.

Gilliland opened the passenger door of a big black car and she slid inside. "I am going to see Franco?"

"Yes, dear." His eyes focused on her cleavage, he closed the door.

Dr. Pardo sat beside her. And Alberto was behind the wheel. He hadn't abandoned her after all! But he wouldn't return her smile. "Why so dour?" she teased, because she was going to see Franco, *finally*, and Alberto ought to be happy for her. Watching the city give way to rolling hills, she hummed the song she'd had stuck in her head for days, *"El Barco Velero,"* the sailboat, taking her into the great unknown. She scooted toward the window, glimpsing stars—the cat and the snail low on the horizon. *Max*, she thought. But she was going to solve everything. She was going to see him soon.

The hills rippled like the dress of a giantess, and she was thinking how she'd like to paint a giantess one day, an earth goddess presiding over the land, when she felt a sting in her arm, an ache, as if she'd been slugged. Dr. Pardo pulled a needle from her flesh. Everything blurred—Alberto's face when she tried to ask him what was happening, words she couldn't form—and blackness pressed on her, soft and watery and warm.

Peggy, April 1941, Marseille, France

Late in the morning someone knocks on the door to Peggy's room. "Max?" she calls. Was there something he forgot? There's no reply, just a barrage of knocks.

It's too early for the maid, and room service would wait for her call to clear the dishes. She cinches her robe. "We're not quite done," she says loud enough that she hopes whoever it is will hear her through the door and go away. She wants to shower. Leonor Fini is coming for lunch, bringing a painting Peggy purchased (on Max's ardent recommendation) after having only seen a photograph, and as Leonor is ten years her junior, and rumored to be a great beauty, she means to look her best.

She opens the door to a man in a dark suit. His odor hits her like an insult. No one who works for the hotel would smell like that. "*Vos papiers, s'il vous plaît.*"

"Excuse me?"

"Your papers, madame."

He pushes open the door. In her robe, her feet bare, she stands tall, assumes her coldest gaze, and peers down at the smelly man. This is clearly a mistake. "Why should I show you my papers? I don't know who you are. You should leave immediately."

She phones the front desk. She will remain calm, outraged. But with each ring of the phone her heartbeat quickens. She presses the receiver to her ear so her hand won't shake. At last a woman picks up. "There's a man here, who pushed his way into my room."

He pulls a badge from his coat pocket and holds it up for her to see.

"*Oui, madame*," says the woman. "No need to worry. They are only rounding up the Jews." She hangs up the phone.

"I am an American," she tells the man. "I'm leaving very soon for America."

"Your papers." He smells of fish and old alcohol and has the body odor of someone who hasn't showered in a month. She walks to the window to crank it open, and he stops her, gripping her hand. "You are stalling. Perhaps I should take you in now?"

"One second," she says. Her purse—where did she leave it?

She moves around the bed as the man watches her. Here is the heap of last night's clothes— her silk dress, Max's hat and tie, his trousers and his shirt. He has no permit to be in Marseille, and if they find that he stayed with her, they will not only take *her* in for questioning, but they'll wait for him, detain him, or worse, send him off to Germany.

"Please, could you open the window? I have a terrible headache." She presses her palm to her forehead. He sighs at the inconvenience, but opens it, giving her time to pull her dress over Max's things as she grabs her purse. Inside it, along with her papers, is the bundle of black market money she secured the night before—enough to get Laurence and the children by until their passage to America, which she now realizes isn't nearly soon enough. She closes her purse, hands the man her passport, her travel papers folded inside it, and sits on the bed, because now her head really does throb. She altered her travel permit herself, changed the date months ago. But she couldn't have possibly left when it ran out—there was still so much to arrange. It would have meant leaving her art, art she had spent years collecting.

He holds the permit up to the daylight. "These are no longer valid. You must come with me."

"What do you mean? Why?"

"You have changed the date."

She stands. The room spins. "No."

"No?"

"I didn't change it." She thinks as quick as she can. "The officials in Grenoble changed it. See? Their stamp." She points to a stamp faded past recognition.

"Why have you not registered in Marseille?"

"I only just arrived. I planned to go today."

He looks around the room, walking slowly, and picks up her red dress. She flinches to see the fabric in his filthy hand. Throwing it aside, he grabs Max's clothing, his hat and his tie, evidence of her crimes. "Who are you hiding? A Jew, perhaps?"

"These are my husband's. He left for Cassis this morning, but he'll be back in a few days." As soon as it is out, she knows she said the wrong thing. While it's true that Laurence, her ex-husband, is in Cassis, it is also true that Cassis is where the Jews are being segregated and sent off to God knows where.

"Cassis?" He opens her passport again. "Guggenheim is a Jewish name, no?"

"No. My grandfather was Swiss. He came from St. Gallen."

"I don't know where that is," he says. And he begins to look in earnest, under the bed, in the bathroom. He points to the armoire. "What is in there?"

She throws the door open. "Look! You will find no Jews in here."

He stiffens, scowls at her. "Your papers are not in order. You must come with me to the police."

"In this?" she says, shoving her hands into the pockets of her robe.

"Madame can dress, I do not mind." He leans on the door, watching her.

"I, however, do. You can wait in the hall. I'll be out in a minute."

She holds the door for him. Her passport in his hand, he steps outside.

She shuts the door, tries to think. She pulls on slacks and a shirt, fastens a belt, draws a brush over her hair. She should hide Max's things, or at least leave a note for him in case she doesn't return, but where is a pen?

"I can't imagine you require any more time than this, madame!" he calls, rapping on the door. She grabs her purse and a hat, stuffs the bundle of bills into a sock, and buries it in a drawer—not much of a hiding place, but the best she can do—and she opens the door.

The hall is empty. Where could he have gone? She could flee down the back stairs, but the man has her passport. Without it, she is lost. She might be anyone. And besides, running would make her guilty. She has no choice but to meet this head-on. She walks down the hall, her heels clicking on the wood floor, and she presses the button for the elevator.

She insisted she was American—just as Max told her to—and it got her nowhere.

She's sweating under her hat and dress when she steps into the elevator—the Narcissus lift, Max calls it, the walls covered with mirrors. In his tan suit and matching pillbox hat, the operator looks the same as always, red-cheeked and round enough to bounce, and he smiles when he sees her. "Lobby?" he says, latching the metal gate.

"*Oui. Merci*, Paul."

He pulls the lever and the cage lurches. The arrow presses to eight, seven, six. With each passing floor she is descending into the hell of a war she has somehow managed to skate above, and her sidelong reflection descends with her.

She tries not to look at her face, at her nose in particular. Years ago she attempted to have it done. The surgeon was supposed to narrow the sides and give it a tilt. But he managed to botch the job and she was in such terrible pain she told him to leave it. Now, watching her nose reproduce itself in ever smaller versions in the opposite mirror, she wishes she'd endured the pain a bit longer.

She adjusts her hat to hide her nose and the gesture hurtles itself toward the minutiae of infinity. She wonders at just what point she can no longer be seen by the human eye but goes on nonetheless, in some intangible realm of substrate and postulate. She thinks of love, and of memory, which also belongs to that realm, and of the story of

Echo, that luckless nymph in love with Narcissus, who in the end has nothing left but her voice, cursed as it is with mere repetition.

She loves Max too much. She swore after Beckett and Tanguy that she wouldn't do it again, wouldn't fall in love with an artist who would love his art and himself and his beautiful *femme-enfants* before he loved her. She would always be their backup, their standby, and yes, their benefactor. And yet she couldn't get enough of them. She never felt so alive as she did in their presence. When their attention, however brief, was fixed on her, she became—there was no other way to say it—a work of art.

She pities the mirrors their nakedness. They seem obscene to her now, like lidless eyes. She focuses on the arrow until it falls to zero. Paul pulls the lever, opens the folding metal gate. "Madame Peggy," he says, bowing slightly.

She can see the detective speaking with another, larger man, who has the distinct demeanor of one in charge. He holds her passport in his hand. She walks straight toward them. She will let them take her. Max will see how it feels to be in Marseille on his own, without the rich American who would do anything for him.

Max, April 1941, Marseille, France

Lou is already in the office of the American Rescue Committee when Varian Fry's secretary ushers Max in. Varian, who is single-handedly helping as many refugees as possible leave for the States, has been in touch with Jimmy about the possibility of Lou leaving on Max's visa, and here she sits, with her purse on her lap, staring out the window at the sky, an empty blue. Dressed in a gray tweed skirt and coat, with small holes along the sleeve where moths have nestled and eaten their fill, she looks worn, and thinner. The circles under her eyes have deepened. Her time in Gurs aged her, just as his time in Camp des Milles aged him.

Dear Lou. When was the last time he saw her? Could it have been at Jimmy's going away party? How different they had both been then, foolishly hopeful, drinking champagne and toasting their marvelous son.

She smiles, her brown eyes warm. "Max," she says, and stands to kiss his cheeks. Her smell is the same, coffee and cigarettes and something that is her own, tart and sweet and surprising, like the smell of tulips. He thinks—*why now, after all this time?*—of their midnight picnics along the Rhine, before the first war. They were students then, drunk on Goethe and moonlight. Just touching her hand was electric. His eyes fill and, bewildered, he blinks away tears.

He might have been so much more. He might have been the man she thought she was marrying—the one who would stand by her until death itself parted them, the one who wouldn't abandon her and their small child because his art, his soul, required freedom.

He has failed her. And there is nothing he can do about it now.

"Coffee? Tea?" Fry says in an attempt at breezy cordiality. They decline, politely, and sit. Fry's forehead furrows. He shakes his head. "I called you in because, well, we thought—*hoped*—it might work. We only just got word, you see."

Max reaches over and squeezes Lou's hand. An instinctive gesture. He's here for her. He'll help her now any way he can.

Fry clears his throat. "As you know, we have an American visa for Max Ernst and his wife," he says, looking from him to Lou. "And when Jimmy contacted me, with the suggestion that you might still be, more or less, his legal wife—at least as far as the French government is concerned—your divorce legal only in Germany—we ran it by Mrs. Roosevelt, who, these days, seems to be more and more involved." Fry takes off his glasses, rubs his red eyes. "To be honest, I wasn't the one to run it by her. I wouldn't have thought it a good idea—she really doesn't know the way the rules, shall we say, *bend* here."

"Tell us," Lou says. "Whatever it is, I'm fine. I can wait. Jimmy will manage something. He takes care of me. He always has." Her words knife through Max—though she didn't mean it that way, he knows.

Fry sighs. He stares at the floor, wipes his glasses, and puts them back on. "I am sorry. You can't pose as Max's wife. When the first lady says no, we cannot go around her, no matter how much we might like to."

"Marry me." Max is on one knee, his hands clasped. "Please, Lou."

"But Marie-Berthe—"

"We divorced. She allowed it finally." He takes her hand in his. "You *have* to marry me, Lou. You don't understand."

"Understand?" She looks down at him, and there is love in her eyes—real love after all these years. "You want me to trade my life for a visa to America? We don't belong together anymore, Max. We've lived separate lives for twenty years."

"I know you don't love me, Lou, I don't expect you to love me. But think of Jimmy. If you won't do it for yourself, do it for him! It would be one thing if you were only an intellectual, but you're Jewish."

She laughs. "You think I don't know that?" She kisses the top of his head and takes back her hand. "It's a lovely gesture, Max. One I appreciate. But I can't. It wouldn't be right. And besides, all this might still prove unnecessary. I'm an optimist."

Peggy, April 1941, Marseille, France

In the lobby of the Grand Hotel du Louvre et de la Paix, Peggy approaches the detective and the large man beside him, who is holding her passport. He nods. "Chief of Police," he says, holding out his hand, which she shakes briskly. Her heart is rushing, but she stands tall.

"That is mine, I believe," she tells him with as even an authority as she can muster.

He looks at her photo, then back to her. "Madame, I apologize," he says, and she allows herself to breathe again. He regards her fragrant persecutor. "You will leave this woman—and all Americans for that matter—alone, do you understand?" She watches the dirty, little man shuffle off, his shoulders slumped. She is lucky. This week Americans are popular, having just shipped France a boatload of food.

The chief gives her back her passport. "But please, madame, you must register with the police today."

"Why of course." She steadies her voice, her hands. "I was on my way to do this very thing this morning. Only I wasn't sure just where it is." If ever there was a time to stretch the truth it is now.

He takes a small notebook from his pocket and is drawing her a map when Max strolls through the door, a petite woman dressed in white lace on his arm. Peggy feels the blood leave her face. Good God, how horribly in love with him she is. *Damn it. Damn him.* The woman wears a white sun hat and clutches what must be a painting wrapped in butcher paper. Leonor Fini has arrived from Monte Carlo looking like she belongs at an Impressionist picnic, and Peggy feels like an ape. Her shirt clings to her back. She wipes the sweat from her forehead and lowers the brim of her hat, willing them not to come over with the chief of police in such close proximity.

Out of the corner of her vision she sees the two of them laughing as they make their way to the café just off the lobby. Max hasn't so much as glanced her way. With a pretty woman on his arm, he's oblivious to the world—from which she is, apparently, indistinguishable.

The chief gives her the map, and she thanks him profusely and excuses herself.

She runs her fingers through her bobbed hair, trying to give it a lift. She meant to look her best, and now it is impossible. All of it, the entire mess of her life, feels impossible.

But aren't I the one he's making love to? she thinks, straightening her spine. What does she have to prove? She darkens her lips with lipstick, takes a deep breath, and walks into the Café de la Paix. It is packed, an anxious buzz in the air, and with her heart galloping away, it takes her a moment to spot them at a table in the back, close and quiet.

Looking up, Max sees her and rises to kiss her on both cheeks. "Peggy, Leonor Fini. Leonor, Peggy Guggenheim, patroness of the arts," he says, pulling up a chair for her. She shakes Leonor's gloved hand. Patroness? Why didn't he introduce her as his lover? The slight stings, but it is Leonor who objects.

"Patroness! What sort of word is that? You know *patron* means father, right Max?"

"Christ, Leonor! Do you have to put such a fine point on everything? After all, she bought *your* painting."

"For which I am exceedingly grateful," she says, smiling at Peggy. "But really Max, *patroness*?"

The word is a thorn in her ribs. Why won't Leonor let it go? Peggy shoots him a look, but he is busy staring at his young protégé, a stupid grin on his face. Her head throbs. She wants to vanish, to run upstairs and take a bath hot enough to obliterate her. Instead, she orders a vodka martini.

"You have no idea what sort of morning I've had, darling," she says. And as she tells them about the man in her room, Max grows pale, shifty.

"Oh, you poor thing!" Leonor touches her hand. "I hear there's more security at the train stations, too. I have nothing to worry about, at least I don't think I do, but I drove anyway. All those men in uniform make me nervous."

Max sips Peggy's martini and smiles at Leonor. "How about showing us your painting?"

Leonor unwraps her canvas, and they gather by the window to look at it in the sunlight. "Oh," Peggy says in spite of herself. "It's beautiful."

Max beams. "Didn't I tell you?"

At the center of the painting stands a warrior woman, clad only in a tiny cloth fastened with thin straps over her hips. Long-haired, topless sphinxes surround her. "It's called *The Shepherdess of the Sphinxes*," says Leonor, and Peggy notices the way that Max can't seem to take his eyes off the sphinx at its center.

"It's her," he says.

Leonor feigns shock. "So now you don't want to share your muse?"

Peggy isn't sure just what they are talking about, but she feels the martini souring her stomach. She stares at the face in the painting, and then she realizes—the soft cheeks, the dark eyes, the black, riverine hair—it is the same woman who appears in all of Max's newest paintings. It is Leonora, and she's bought her once again.

Max touches the hair of the sphinx, he traces the staff of the shepherdess up to her face, which, Peggy sees, is Leonor's. "You're protecting her," he says.

Peggy watches Leonor's face harden, just for a second, and then she's let the anger go. "You've heard nothing, I take it," Leonor says.

Max shakes his head, lightly, his eyes brimming.

Peggy is sure she's invisible. Yet here is her hand on the canvas, her nails with their shell-colored polish chipped at the tips. He told her all *that* was done—all the Leonora Carrington business—hadn't he, more or less? *She lost her head and gave the house away. She could be anywhere.* It had been rather cold the way he'd said it, but now she feels his longing for this lost girl. It's like the longing Peggy feels for him, although he is here, standing beside her.

"Well, thank you for this, dear." She wraps the painting and tucks it under her arm. "I really must lie down. I have a terrific headache."

The Villa Air-Bel sprawls in the midday heat.

"Hey, Max!" Consuelo de Saint-Exupéry waves down at him and Peggy from the tree where she is perched, and someone else is up there, too.

"*Bonjour*," says a woman, looking up from her book. "We're reading!"

Max squints to see her better. Even in silhouette she's recognizable. The wave of thick hair in the bun, her quick curves, her smile. It is Remedios Varo, who showed her paintings in Paris at the last Surrealist show. "I can see that!" he hollers up at her.

"We're taking your room!" she yells down at him.

"The window sticks."

"Good to know."

Peggy pokes his ribs with her elbow. They have only hours. Set to leave this afternoon, he's come to gather his paintings and to say his goodbyes. He's also come for money.

"*Au revoir*, Max," says Remedios.

"*Je te verrai de l'autre côté!*"

"Yes, we'll see you on the other side! Now go!" Consuelo shakes her book at him. "I have two pages left, can I read in peace?"

"You heard the girl," Peggy says, turning him.

He feels like he might cry, but he has to leave. He will see Leonora on the other side, too, or at least he hopes he will. Peggy gives his arm a tug, and he hurries with her to find Chagall, who they're hoping will be willing to loan him fifty dollars—enough to get Max to Lisbon with a little left over for lodging until Peggy can join him.

It will take her at least three weeks to petition the Banque de France for the five hundred and fifty dollars they are each allowed for their passage on the Clipper. The flying boat will take Max and Peggy, along with her ex-husband, Laurence, their children, Laurence's wife and *their* slew of children to America. Peggy's own stash of black market money went to Laurence, who left for Lisbon with all of the children yesterday.

No francs are allowed to leave the country and there isn't any time left to apply for a permit for the cash. To go without money is fool-hardy, he knows, but he'll do it if he has to. Marseille has become un-tenable. The police are out in record numbers. It's only a matter of time before someone asks for his papers and hauls him off.

They find Chagall tucked away in the garden, drawing with cray-ons. It's a picture of a woman on a flying horse, a bird on her head. "Money? I don't handle my finances." He has a smudge of green on his nose, Max notices, feeling jealous that he's making art—even now, as the Nazis close in. "That's my daughter's realm," he says, giving the bird's eye a spark of light blue. "She's gone to the market, but should be back in an hour or two."

Max imagines he has the cash there, in his room, most likely. "I like your drawing," he says. "Especially the horse." And taking Peggy's arm, he leads her out, since she looks like she might strangle the man.

"That. After I more or less gave him a thousand dollars," she says, lighting a Pall Mall. "Now what? I don't see what we can do."

"It's fine," he tells her. "I've gotten by without money before, I'll get by now."

When they arrive in Marseille, traffic is thick. Max has little more than an hour to make the train. The cab drops them blocks from her hotel, and they are sprinting along, Peggy's heels clattering on the sidewalk, when he spots Varian Fry. Walking toward them, he seems to float over the sidewalk like the angel he is. "Max!" he says, smiling.

"I'm going," Max tells him, and Fry pulls him in for a hug.

"I'm sorry, about Lou and all—" he says, when Peggy cuts him off.

"Max needs fifty dollars for the trip." She's so up front about money, Max has to admire her.

Fry reaches into his pocket. He has exactly fifty U.S. dollars in his wallet, and he presses it into Max's hand.

~&

He steps out of the cab. Still in the back, Peggy dabs her eyes. "Well, darling, I guess this is goodbye."

"I'll see you in Lisbon," he says. And she gets out to kiss and hug him properly.

"Oh." She pulls his ticket from her wallet. "I nearly forgot."

He takes the ticket, kisses her again, and walks away. He can't help looking back. Her face is blotched and she's waving a handkerchief. He waves back. Entering the fray of the station, he feels her recede.

Without her by his side, he is colder. Despite the heat, he feels a chill in the center of his bones. Maybe it's her money or the fact that she's American and not subject to the same laws, it seems, as the rest of them. Maybe it's the fact that she loves him, but her presence in his life has given him hope—hope, even, that he might somehow find Leonora. Perhaps right now she is in Lisbon waiting for him. The thought quickens his step as he presses through the throng of people, clutching his suitcase, his knapsack slung over his shoulder. Inside it are Leonora's paintings as well as his own—everything Peggy hasn't bought, which isn't much. His visa to America is tucked into his coat pocket. He gives it a pat to be sure it is there. His exit visa, which expired months ago, is there, too, tucked beneath it.

Passing a gendarme, and another, he keeps his face forward and trusts that his mask of indifference is convincing and that he blends with the crowd. He can't survive another camp—or any form of incarceration—but he has no choice but to risk traveling now. If he were to wait for a proper French exit visa, his American visa would expire, and he'd have to start the Gordian process all over again. He'll have to make do with his old visa. He will have to hope.

On the train, a man punches his first-class ticket—Lisbon by way of Madrid. He stows his luggage overhead, takes a seat by the window, and settles in.

They leave Marseille. Pass fields, horses. Impossible to not think of her. But he can't remember her face, her eyes. Not exactly. If he had his paints and brushes, he would conjure her on canvas, but he doesn't have them, and when he picks up a pencil to draw in his tiny notebook, his hand is shaking.

This is not the ghost train, and he is not a prisoner. He is sitting in a clean cabin. He could buy a coffee from the commissary if he wanted to, even a baguette. But he's not free yet. He's in France and France is controlled by fascists.

At the Spanish border, the train stops. He takes his bags and stands in a line to leave the train through the only open door. "Exit visa," the station manager yells. He takes his from his pocket. It's ridiculous, faked stamps filling every bit of it. This was a risk he had to take, but now he cannot breathe. The line inches along, and he is back at Camp des Milles, waiting again, sweating, one of a horde of humans, and no longer himself. Outside the window, he can see a dove flying inside the station, over the swell of people. It flies out of view, and he leans across the empty seats, presses his face to a window to see. The bird has built a nest in a high corner of the rafters. But why here? If Max could fly, he thinks, he'd go anywhere but here.

At the front of the line he gives the station manager his exit visa. The man scowls, squints. "What is this?" he says, flapping it at him. "And anyway, it has expired. Where is your passport?"

All that work to get an American visa for nothing. What has been the point of any of it? He might as well have let the Nazis take him straight from Camp des Milles. "I don't have my passport," he tells him. "It was stolen."

"Wait in my office, monsieur," says the man.

His bags are heavier now. Infernal pendulums, they swing from his arms. The Spanish customs officer waves him over. Might as well go. After all, he has nothing more to lose. He unlatches his suitcase, but the man is yelling at him to open his knapsack with the large tubes protruding from it. He loosens the drawstring and the man takes out his paintings. He unrolls them one at a time. A few small works are on stretchers and he sets them on the table, making a show of it.

"*Bonito!*" the customs officer says, and another officer agrees, stroking his mustache.

Max's train mates, too, are looking. They seem enthralled. They have never seen paintings quite like these, with their liquid skies, their strange, dark structures of sinew and bone. "Oh, my!" one woman exclaims. Looking at the human eyes of Leonora's hyena, she reaches out and touches the full udders. There's a man looking at *Leonora in the Morning Light,* and Max could swear there are tears in his eyes.

But here comes the station manager. Max's visa in his hand, his belly protruding, he, too, looks over the paintings. He lets out a huff. "I told you to go to my office, monsieur, after you have gathered your things."

Max rolls his paintings carefully, as if to slow the quick pulse of blood in his ears. If this is his last moment of freedom, he will spend it in the service of his art, all he has left in this world. He takes his time, rolling up his life, placing the paintings back in his pack. He closes his suitcase and meets the manager in his office, tiny and cluttered with papers.

"Please," he says, "close the door." He gestures for Max to sit. The chair has a loose leg and wobbles under him. "I admire talent. Clearly, you have exceptional talent, monsieur. I respect that." He hands him back his visa. "Follow me."

Max follows him through the press of refugees and out to the platform, where two trains are preparing to leave.

"Here is the train for Pau. I am sorry, but I must send you back to

France," he says, loud enough to draw furtive glances from passersby. "Without a proper exit visa or passport you cannot enter Spain."

He gestures, then, to the other train. "And here is the train to Madrid." His voice is lower, just loud enough for Max to hear. "Whatever you do, monsieur, do *not* take the wrong train."

And with that he walks away, leaving Max to decide.

Fear

Leonora, August 1940, Santander, Spain

The girl wakes. A room materializes. White ceiling and walls. A high window onto another room, where she hears voices but cannot make out the language. There's no sun, no hint of sky.

She's been in this world, this underground realm, before. But where are the Sidhe, who will teach her the process of alchemy at last? And why can't she move? She's flat on her back on a bed as hard as a table. Leather straps bind her wrists and ankles. There's a tube up her nose, a machine beside her, groaning. Her joints are hot with pain. It must be a hospital, the girl thinks. The automobile must have crashed.

She lifts her head as far as she can, not quite an inch, far enough to see her body naked beneath the straps. She can see a woman beside the door knitting. She looks just like the girl's nanny, and the girl thinks she might be at home, but when the woman looks up, her eyes bulge like a frog's behind the thick lenses of her glasses. She smells of sardines. She is not Nanny.

"Who are you?" the girl asks. The words seem spoken by someone else. Her tongue thick, her voice soft as dry sand.

"Frau Asegurado," the woman says.

Frau? Fear moves through her, slowly, taking its time. "Is this a German camp?"

The woman smiles, sadly. "No," she says.

Thinking she might be dreaming, the girl closes her eyes. Willing herself to wake up, she opens them.

Nothing is changed.

"Where is Alberto?" she asks, remembering. Unless he was someone she'd dreamed?

"*Madrid.*"

"*Where am I?*" *she asks, though she knows the question is too big for anyone to answer. Strapped to the bed she is drifting—on the sailboat in the song she'd been humming in the car as she stared at the stars. By now she could be anywhere. She might have been sleeping for years.*

"*You are in a place where you will rest,*" *the woman says.*

The girl feels her eyelids click shut like the lids of tiny boxes.

She wakes to a fat man in white standing over her. "*Father?*" *she says. But his eyes are darker than Father's. Two dark hollows, two pits, they give nothing back. The girl doesn't flinch, but her liver trembles. Still, she must ask.* "*Why am I here?*"

His eyes take her into their silence, their void. Without a word he leaves the room.

The Frau leans so close that the girl loses herself in the pores of her long nose. "*You must understand. Don Luis is a great man. Like Hitler. He talks to you every night. And you answer him as he desires.*" *Scuttling after him, she closes the door.*

As he desires? The girl shudders, thinking of her father, of his rage when she defies him, and how it fills her with such glee. But in this strange world he is a doctor and she is his patient, his doll to control as he pleases, to hypnotize as she sleeps. As she—sleeps.

She will stay awake. She will guard her consciousness, she vows, as the boxes of her eyes close.

~&

Days. Weeks. Time has ceased to exist. No sunlight enters her room to mark morning from night. Sometimes the Frau sits in her chair knitting. And sometimes a young man with dark hair puts a lit cigarette to the girl's lips and she smokes it, feeling her body lift, as if the straps have loosened. He gives her bites of his apples, his eyes the green of leaves, the green of her brother's eyes. His name, he says, is José.

"*Hermano,*" *she says. Brother.*

When she sweats with fever, he dabs her body with a wet towel. He cleans the filth from her, the shit and the piss, and, oddly, she feels no shame. Her body is only a body. The more restricted it is, the more her mind can soar, gathering all it needs. She will get things straight. She'll escape somehow.

⁓⚬

On one of his visits José plays an out-of-tune guitar and hums so she can almost hear him. She drifts on the music. She's the sailboat following the green eyes of the brother who looks at her between verses with a limpid longing. "It's not your fault," she wants to say. "It's Father's doing."

Opening her mouth to speak, she feels a gust enter her body, a spirit. Darker than death or pain or emptiness, it fills her with its need—to destroy. The birds and horses and cats—all the living things she loves. Her head throbs. Her limbs are heavy and hot. The doctor has possessed her, and she can hardly breathe.

José puts down the guitar. He presses a washcloth to her forehead.

"Please," she says. "Unstrap me. Take me to Madrid."

"But the doctor?"

"Is not here. I'm sure of it. He couldn't do this to me if he were here."

He hesitates. "Sí," he says. Quickly, he unstraps her, helps her to dress, and slips shoes on her feet, which prickle as they awaken. He unlocks a cabinet and she takes her purse, in it all she owns. They move down the corridor, steadily, steadily. They are nearly to the door to outside, where birds sleep under stars. José twists the knob, swings the door wide open to the doctor. Her heart plummets. He regards her calmly, without surprise, as if this were part of his plan. He says something to José in Spanish, and the poor boy looks at the floor. He, too, has disobeyed Father. His cheeks burn the way the girl remembers her brother's cheeks burning when they were caught playing witches in the woods. You should have known better, Father said, his disappointment worse than a slap across the mouth, and her brother went with him. But she bolted, scrambling down an animal path to where no one could find her.

She runs down a corridor—her legs so stiff they won't bend right—around a corner and another. The building is a maze, forcing her to choose. Now right. Now left. Running, she feels the joy of moving. After so much stillness, it feels like flying. She's out the final door, winging through an orchard of apples. The leaves at her feet glow, yellow in the moonlight. How long was she strapped to that bed? How much life has she lost? Or maybe she is dreaming and time isn't as it seems?

"This is my dream!" she shouts, hoping someone in the other world will hear her and wake her. The branches shiver, raining leaves. She twists her ankle on a fallen apple and tumbles.

José breathes thickly over her. She can smell ocean on the air. He pulls her up. "Lo siento," he whispers. Or is it the wind through the branches? As he carries her back, she drags her feet, looks at the full moon, and howls.

⁓𝄕

There is the room, the bed, her naked body, and there are dreams, so many dreams. Horses whinny in the night, and she is one of them, running over mountains. A hawk who is a man calls to her from the sky, where he is a speck in the blue, wheeling. He is a merman and he dresses her in seaweed. They are painters in Paris throwing a party, and she can't find him anywhere, he left her without a word, and she opens a door to see him undressing a woman she met once, somewhere. "Don't you love me?" she asks. "Love is complicated," he tells her, taking the naked lady into his arms.

⁓𝄕

José unbuckles her straps, draws a bath, and changes the sheet on her bed. In the warm water of the bath, she tries to remember her dreams, but cannot. She is empty, the way the light is empty. Water has never felt so good, and she melts into it, slipping under. Her breath bubbles up. *This is how she will get back to the world that must still exist—if she can only find the way to it—by going below the surface of things, by letting go.*

His big hands under her, José hoists her from the bath. She inhales eagerly, like being born. He dries her with a rough towel and her skin is new and pink. She sits on a chair and he combs her hair, like Nanny used to. There are huge knots, but he starts at the ends, working his way up with a beautiful patience. Nanny would have told a story to pass the time, and the girl thinks she might tell one, but what happens when you tell a story inside a story? she wonders. And because she is not ready for the answer, she hums a song instead. José kisses the top of her smooth head.

The bath has made her heavy, like a ripe melon on the vine, and she lies on the clean bed and lets José fasten the straps. How can she reach the other world? What knowledge must she gather? What riddle must she solve? Her questions fall through the ceiling. Absolved, she is ready.

Absolved, she waits.

Here is another doctor, standing over her. "We must test your blood," he says. To see if she's pure enough to be entrusted with the truth, she thinks. But when he comes close, a syringe in his hand, she sees she cannot trust him. His eyes are the brown eyes of the fathers. Her pulse races, but she can't budge.

She'll be clear with him, civil. "I do not authorize your use of needles on me. I signed nothing."

He flicks the syringe with his fingernail. "You didn't have to," says her doctor, standing now, beside the first man. Her doctor holds her hand. He stares at her, into her. She feels pain in her thigh. She opens her mouth, but she cannot scream or speak. The eyes of her doctor are bald puddles of sunlight. Ice picks, they skewer her from head to tail, and she plummets down a tunnel, a well, black, and so cold she cannot stop shivering. Her teeth rattle. She cannot locate herself in the starless whirl. She is no one, no one. She can't find herself anywhere.

Gasping, she opens her eyes to his, terrible and lidless, to his hypnotic spell. Her powers are nothing compared to his. He is a sorcerer and he has eaten her heart. She shuts her eyes against his, but he is inside her, or she is in him, her surrender complete. She belongs to him.

—❦—

The doctor unbuckles her straps. Has she slept for a night or a week? Her legs are so heavy she must fight to wiggle her toes. "You feel better, then?" *he asks, helping her to sit. He places his thumb between her slack lips, between her teeth so gently she feels a warm pulse between her thighs and she closes her mouth around his thumb and sucks. He pushes it deeper, his brown eyes gentle, almost kind, then he slides it out.*

"It seems, young lady, your claws have retreated?" *He offers her a hand—the hand of the father—and she reaches for it.*

—❦—

The sunroom is made all of glass. There's a writing desk, a sofa, a table holding a vase of roses and a bowl of lemons. She sits on the sofa and eats everything José brings her—bread, biscuits, milk, berries. The sun arcs across the sky, as though a day were an hour. Watching the shifting light, flawless as math, she feels it enter her pores. Oh, how she's missed the sun! She resists nothing. Voracious, she eats the lemons, rinds and all. She stares at the roses for hours, runs her fingers over the smooth stems before she realizes—someone has removed their thorns.

There's a purse beside her on the sofa. She flips open the clasp and the dark mouth gapes. She takes out a gold tube. When she twists it, a stick of red angles out. She runs it over her lips and the metallic smell settles on the back of her tongue, reminding her of someone. Just a flash, a passing ghost from that other life which might not have been real. She isn't sure anymore.

There's a pocket in the purse, a secret compartment.

Glancing about, discreetly, to be sure she's not being watched, she unzips it, and finds two passports tucked into each other, their pages like the fingers of interlaced hands. She opens one.

British. Leonora Carrington *it reads. Here is a full-faced girl, brazen, naïve smile, her eyes unflinching and her confidence—why, she looks as if she might take on the world. The other passport belongs to Max Ernst. She stares at the man with white hair and a blank face, eyes narrow and fixed, as if he were frightened of something. She stares at the symbol stamped across the pages—an eagle holding a black spider, a square with four missing pieces in the shape of rectangles. She stares until the missing pieces are all that she sees. They are corridors, each intersected by the other, every direction an impasse.*

Hearing the even footsteps of her doctor, she slips the passports back in the pocket. Her finger hits something sharp—the pin of a silver brooch, a spiral, which she quickly pins to her dress. Tracing, from its center, a clockwise movement, she feels her heart open, thinking she understands. The doctor will reward her with a pat on her head. Perhaps he will put his thumb in her mouth again. The thought sends a charge through her, and she salivates, thinking of ways to please him. He will see she is a good daughter, and he will show her the way to leave this horrid world.

When he enters the sunroom, she curtsies low and long. Seeing her red lips he smiles, but when he notices the spiral, he unfastens it with thick, clumsy fingers. "José should have known better," he says, pocketing the trinket.

~§

Now that she is tame, they let her sleep without straps.

She walks the grounds with the Frau beside her, surprised to find buildings other than her own. She glimpses one through the orchard. The tall windows have no bars and laughter spills from them into the breeze. "What is this place?" she asks.

"It is where you will stay when you are well," says the Frau. "We call it Abajo."

"Below?" This residence of joy and freedom, this Abajo, is calling to her. She runs toward it, sure the way back to her life is inside it somewhere.

She was right, the other world might be above, but she must go below the surface of things to arrive there. The knob of the door is crystal, casting rainbows onto the grass. She holds it in her hand. But when she twists the knob, the Frau stops her.

"You are not well enough yet."

—◦—

One morning a woman who looks just like her nanny shuffles into her room. She wears a gray shawl like Nanny wore, but this woman is older, thinner, and far more pale.

"Sweet pea!" she cries, and she knows it really is Nanny, here in this strange world.

"Nanny, how did you get here?"

She sits on the Frau's chair. "By submarine," she says. "Part of the Royal Navy's fleet."

"Of course!" How else would she have reached her in this land below the earth?

"The journey took days. It was dreadful," she says. Not so dreadful as here, the girl thinks, hoping she will take her back with her, though where back is, what back is, has become increasingly mysterious, a dream she can only remember when she is dreaming.

Nanny's right hand shakes when she takes it from her pocket to pat her arm. "Now, now. Tell me how all this happened." She gestures at the plain white room. The girl holds her nanny's hand so it trembles less, but she doesn't tell her much. How can she when she doesn't know herself?

When the Frau comes to take the girl to the library, she brings the black shawl she's been knitting and wraps it around the girl's shoulders. Nanny scowls at the Frau, at this woman who has replaced her. This pleases the girl, and she walks into the day light-footed, filled with the advice of proverbs. "When in Rome, fortune favors the bold." And "You can't lead a horse to water without gathering moss."

The library is sunlit, with shelves up to the high ceiling and a sliding ladder to reach the books. There is Don Quixote *and* Gulliver's Travels. *There's even Baudelaire's* The Flowers of Evil. *The book the Frau hands her is* The Philosophy of Loyalty.

"Why can't I pick out my own book?"

"You will have to wait," she says, "until the doctor decides you are ready."

The girl takes it, because any book is better than none, and follows her to a sunny hill where the Frau spreads out a blanket, and leaves her alone.

The book is heavy and its words are heavier, and dull. When she nods awake, the sun is low, the air cool. She wonders what month it is—October? November? She could ask Nanny, but time is different here, and she's not sure she could tell her.

~§

She creeps down the corridors into the night, her every step soundless. She's visiting the Prince of Monaco, who lives in a neighboring pavilion. He's assured her she's earned the privilege of walking the halls, but she doesn't quite believe him. At every turn she expects her doctor to seize her, strap her down, and hypnotize her.

In his room the Prince is typing. He has a bowl of cigarettes, and she takes one. "Diplomatic letters," he says, pounding away at a typewriter.

She smokes and examines the maps that cover his wall. Here's a map of France and Spain. A line of red pencil traces a route from southern France to Andorra to Madrid and back north, to Santander, Spain's topmost tip, right next to the sea. Moving her finger along it, she realizes the room is quiet. The Prince has stopped typing. "Familiar?" he asks, adjusting his monocle.

She nods, not sure just why she is nodding. "We are here?" She points to Santander.

"We are. The red line is your journey," he says.

"So small?" she asks, trying to understand.

"Everything looks tiny when it's tacked to a wall."

Beside the map is a blue butterfly, encased in glass. Its wings are like cellophane and are as big as her hand. Staring at the butterfly, she sees her own face reflected in the glass. One eye gleams, and here is the shadow of her mouth. How had she not realized before—this place does not have a single mirror.

Gazing at her vague reflection, she sees the butterfly's antennae twitch. Or was it only her eye, blinking? She lifts the framed butterfly off the wall. The Prince pulls the paper from his typewriter and places it on his stack of letters. "It's a Morpho. From a forest in Mexico." She turns the frame over. The underside of its wings are plain by comparison. They are brown, with seven gold circles like eyes. Adjusting his monocle, the Prince looks at her. "So it can rest and not be noticed."

She holds it to the light so he can see its wings tremble. "Do you see?"

"Of course, ma chérie, but you mustn't talk of such things to anyone else. You must learn to keep the things you see and know to yourself."

"We should break the glass, so it can breathe and be free!"

"It cannot live in Spain. Too cold and dry. Only in Mexico," he says, sliding open a matchbox of old excrement and touching it lightly, the way one might pet a lizard.

"Is it fox?" she guesses. But he only grins.

~❧

The Frau holds a list in her fat, freckled fist. Books the doctor has forbidden the girl to read. But the library is full of books. She ought to be able to find one good one. She pulls Gulliver's Travels from the towering shelf and the Frau finds it on the list. She takes down Don Quixote, which is also on the list. And then she sees Through the Looking-Glass, and she squeals to have found it.

Of course! she thinks, holding it in her hand. She's gone through the glass, she's inside the mirror. That's why no one can help her escape. They don't know how to get out. But this book will show her the way.

The Frau's head ticks, side to side. She shows her the title, first on the list—as if the doctor knew what she would most want to read. It isn't right, *she thinks, or has she said it aloud? From the look in the Frau's bulging eyes, it seems she's shouted it. Well, fine. She's had enough. She marches from the library with the book in her hand.*

Outside her room she hears the doctor talking. Nanny says something about "Mr. Carrington's wishes." The girl stops. Who is Mr. Carrington? The father of the girl whose passport is in her purse—that remnant from the other world? "I can take her back with me," says Nanny.

Back? the girl wonders. Outside the mirror, certainly, but back to—where?

Stepping into the room, she holds the book up for Don Luis to see. "Give me one reason why I shouldn't read this? For Christ's sake," she says to Nanny. "You read this to me when I was six!"

"Exactly," says Don Luis. "You should not resort to childish ways, young lady."

"I refuse to accept your authority over me."

Her voice is clear. It rises from the earth, on which her feet are planted; it rises from her stomach, where her power resides. She will not tolerate this condescension, this insult to her intelligence. He can kill her if he wants, but she won't acquiesce. She will not be anyone's young lady. "My inner life isn't yours to control." The book in hand, she walks away, grabbing Nanny's hand and pulling her along. But the doctor takes the book. He has her other hand, and he's pulling. Nanny is pulling her, too, as if they would tear her apart. Pain jolts through her shoulders. A seam in her dress pops. Nanny is on the ground, and the doctor is taking the girl where he wants her to go. She knows what he will do to her, and she doesn't resist.

She is stronger than that.

He straps her to the bed. Then another doctor appears beside him, the same man as before, and she knows they are really one person—or that her doctor is two. He's the man who smiles and holds her hand, and he's the one with the black bag and the syringe, here to test her blood, to see if she is still only a girl, to be sure she hasn't become a witch. She feels a prick and she falls, as before, into the endless wells of his eyes, but this time she shuts hers against them, praying he won't find her here, in the dark, won't tear her will from the lining of her gut, like teeth being pulled from gums.

Spinning, falling, without a single witness, she senses a thread of freedom in the darkness. It is tiny. A single glowing hair. She reaches for it.

─❧

In a chair beside her bed Nanny weeps. "Sweet pea! What did they do?"

The girl has no words to explain. She longs to cry against her chest as she used to, but when Nanny opens her arms, though she isn't strapped down, the girl cannot go to her. Her warmth is a magnet, pulling her home, back to Mr. Carrington, her father. And she knows the truth. She is the girl in that passport. She is Leonora Carrington, and if she were to go with Nanny, she'd never be free again. "You need to leave me," she says. Nanny's head droops like a dying flower, and the girl feels an ancient guilt leave with her.

She opens the door to sunlight. She is in Abajo at last.

─❧

The Prince has a friend he wants her to meet. His name is Etchevarria. He's been sick, but today he is well enough to talk with her. Walking to the Prince's room, she pulls her shawl tighter around her shoulders. The air is cold. The branches of the apple trees are bare. Walking beside her, José gives her a cigarette, and when he leans close to light it, she marvels at how lovely he is, his hair black as the sweater under his smock.

He leaves her when they reach the Prince's room. His door is open, and inside, a small man with a silver beard and a black beret sits very straight on a low upholstered stool. He has skin the color of rich soil, and the hands of a sculptor, which move as he talks to the Prince, his voice low and easy. Seeing her, he rises with the help of his cane. It is ebony, carved with forest scenes, she realizes, bending to look closely at the monkeys and the birds. "Sit, my child," he says.

The Prince pounds at his typewriter. Perhaps it is the rhythm that awakens something in her, or maybe it's Etchevarria's kind words and the way his hand takes hers—not so tightly she can't take it back, and just enough to convey his sincerity—but she feels as if she were on the crest of a great swell, a hill she's climbed to look farther than before, through air that is very clear. "You will leave here soon," he says.

In her chest, she feels a flutter. How she wants to believe it is true. "But I'm in Abajo now," she says, for she is happy in his presence.

He gives his beard a tug and rubs her hand with his thumb. "Abajo is a pavilion for the insane and you, my dear, are not insane." She tells him of the wild horses in the hills of Andorra, how they let her touch their faces, but he only chuckles. "Of course you speak the language of animals. You're a kindred spirit."

She leans very close to him and, in case someone is listening behind the door, whispers, "But how can I escape my doctor? His sorcery is powerful." She confides her attraction to Don Luis, how his thumb in her mouth made her yearn for him. "Why should I feel desire for someone so horrid?"

"Desire is power," he says, softly. "In this place you have been powerless. But he is swine. A doctor who feeds on his control over his patients."

"But the spells he induces? I have such violent spasms."

"Cardiazol," he explains. "He injected you with a drug. He has no powers."

The Prince stops typing. In the sunlight, she sees plainly. She looks at the wall, the route in red pencil, her journey from France through Spain to here. Seeing Madrid, she remembers her plan to free the world from the despotic rule of the fathers—of Hitler and Franco and that awful man Van Ghent. What if the M in Madrid stood for Me instead? she thinks.

What if the world is what it is, and I am the one who must change?

Beside the map, the butterfly holds still in its frame. The Prince lifts it off the nail and hands it to her. "To take with you," he says, and the room feels sad and small. "Home to Mexico."

"I'm not going to Mexico," she says, but the Prince refuses to take it back.

There's a knock. "Time for lunch," says José.

Etchevarria's eyes glimmer. "You desire him, no?" he whispers.

"Oh!" she titters. "But I do!"

In the orchard she pulls José behind a tree where they kiss until the Frau walks by and clucks her tongue at them, and they wipe their lips and walk, sharing a cigarette.

⸻

Nanny comes to her room that evening, her eyes swollen and red. "I'm leaving tomorrow," she says.

"Oh, Nanny." The girl pats the bed beside her, and Nanny sits, her body like a bag of wet sand. "I've never thanked you. Not enough."

"But it's my fault." Nanny falters, swallows. "This magical way you see the world. I told you the stories when you were too small to know they were just stories."

"You mean the Sidhe?"

Nanny nods. Her tears spill. The sun has gone down, and in the twilight the objects in the room—the chair and the desk, the unlit lamp and the blue butterfly propped against it—come and go, here and not here. Nanny herself wavers. And the girl sees, peeking from her skirt, the little people, transparent and glowing. She hears them murmur, their ancient tongue misty as the shores of Ireland. "Nanny!" she cries, and is about to tell her, when the butterfly's wings tremble. "It isn't such a bad thing," she says. And she turns the butterfly over, so what shows is the plain brown pattern.

At the door Nanny pauses. "Your mother wired. You have a cousin in Santander. A surgeon. I'm meeting with him tomorrow before I go. He might be able to get you out. You don't belong here, sweet pea."

⸻

Despite the protestations of her doctor, her cousin meets her in the library. The Frau brings them tea, and they chat about family and boarding schools and marmalade. He is a little older than her, with dark hair, and eyes the green of José's. Drinking the last of his tea, her cousin jots something in his pad. "I know the ambassador in Madrid. You will be out within the week," he says, and she can hear José, who is shelving a stack of books, sniffle behind her.

~&

Rising before the sun, she brings her butterfly into the garden, where she sits on a patch of grass. She is alone and not alone. When the veil of night lifts, she sees all the creatures that exist only in the half-light. She watches them flicker—ghosts of cat-headed women, ghosts of bird-headed men—watches them recede into the pieces of night caught, still, in the corners of her eyes, so that when the birdsong begins, she is already expansive. The birds call to one another inside her.

She aims the framed butterfly so the glass reflects the sun, and by covering the back of it with the black fabric of her skirt, she can see her face hovering behind the butterfly. A backward face. Large, dark eyes, lips pressed tight, as though trying to keep a secret. She moves her fingertips over her hollow cheeks to be sure they are hers. She traces a wrinkle between her brows that wasn't there before. It looks as though she's been concentrating on a problem for a very long time. And since she can't recall just what it was, she wonders if she didn't somehow solve it.

Leonora, December 1940, Santander, Spain

When he said goodbye at the station, José pressed a pack of cigarettes into her hand. He took something from his pocket. It glinted in the light, and she saw it was her spiral brooch, the one she'd bought from the gypsy in Madrid. "Don Luis took it from you," he said as he pinned it to her dress, under her collarbone.

She held his palm to her cheek. He kissed her with his soft lips, and she felt a small sun growing inside her chest and wished she could take him with her. Why couldn't he be her keeper instead of the Frau, who shifted her weight, sucked her teeth loudly, and sighed? "*Es hora.*"

"*Sí,*" said José, his green eyes bright. "*Adios,* Leonora."

She pressed the brooch to her chest to stop her own tears. The Frau took her arm and turned her toward the trains. "*Adios!*" she yelled, craning her neck to watch him until the crowd folded around him, and he was gone.

It was New Year's Eve, the afternoon so cold her bones ached. She pulled her shawl around her. The Frau might have been her aunt as far as anyone could tell. With their matching black wool dresses, they moved through the crowds wordlessly as shadows. The Frau toddled along with a suitcase, but Leonora carried only her purse, having left her suitcase long ago in some hotel room in Madrid. *Roma,* she thought, remembering. *Hotel Roma,* a lifetime ago. It had been July, the heat stifling. She remembered Van Ghent and his son, and the officers with their red berets, the house with the Spanish balconies and the bed with the red silk quilt. She'd woken to the universe spinning in her eyes, and then she'd lost six months in the asylum.

In the station, people rushed past them. Among the mass of exiles were couples dressed for parties, ready to ring in the new year. The men were sharp in their black suits, fedoras pulled low over their eyes. The women's dresses shimmered like glimpses of moonlight beneath their coats of marmot, muskrat, and beaver, which Leonora had to resist the urge to pet. She watched a young woman rise on tiptoe as a man stooped to kiss her, and she thought of Max, of meeting him in the train station in Paris, how she couldn't get enough of his smell. Now he was lost to her, even the idea of him having no borders. Sometimes she felt him behind her. She heard a faint whistle, like birdsong, but when she looked around, the branch was empty, bobbing in the wake of his flight.

Stepping from the platform onto the train, she had the sense that she was entering time again. They settled into their seats. She took the window, and as they set off she pulled the framed butterfly from her purse, moved it so the blue wings flashed with the light. Mexico, the Prince had said. But how impossible! Or had he meant it as a metaphor? Mexico was warm, full of color and spice, at least that's what Breton had said, how lush and unscripted it was. Maybe some country inside her was Mexico, she thought, closing her eyes, feeling the pulse of her soft, humid heart.

In Ávila the train stopped at the station. The night's chill seeped through the window, and she huddled in her shawl. Across the tracks was another stopped train, whose carloads of sheep screamed in the raw air. Their cries were ghastly, just as the men who packed them up and left them to freeze were ghastly. Her stomach seized with the anguish of these sheep, and she found she was clenching her jaw, her hands. Men were horrid to one another, but they were worse to animals. The Frau snored and drooled. She could slip away and free them, but that would mean chaos, sheep running through the station, and she'd be locked away again, she was sure. So she bit her cheek, dug her nails into her palms.

At last the train lunged into motion and they hurtled through darkness. Such beautiful speed, taking her far from the doctor and his hollow eyes. Far from beautiful José, too, who had given her back a small part of herself. She traced the spiral with her finger and smoked one of the precious cigarettes as the Frau slept.

The train slowed to a stop. They were in Madrid, the other passengers disembarking. She could leave with them. Disappear into the crowd and be free. But she had nothing. No friends, no money without her parents' help, and they had made sure the Frau was with her. She could feel her father behind it. The Frau was the condition of her release.

Leonora woke her. Outside the station, she hailed a taxi.

—❦—

They arrived at the Ritz just shy of midnight. It was the same Ritz from last July, when the lobby had been filled with flowers. Now it was candlelit, chandeliers blazing. Crossing the marble floor to the front desk, she slowed, an icy comprehension moving through her. She was again in her father's domain, and like before, he planned to keep her here, a naïve prisoner, until he could *arrange* things, find a new place to put her away. It really wasn't surprising that nothing had been said about where she was going, or what was to come next. What worried her was why she hadn't thought to ask.

While the Frau checked them in, she wandered into the bar, where there were whoops of jubilation, as if this new year would be better, so much better than the last. Corks rocketed to the ceiling, champagne splashed, glasses clinked. "To 1941!" someone shouted, and everyone was kissing. Couples swung in each other's arms as a jazz band struck up a new song. One man stood a head above the rest. Dark-skinned, with a shock of white hair, he was graceful, a natural dancer, and familiar. She knew him, she was sure of it. He wheeled his partner around and looked right at her.

Renato Leduc! Picasso's friend.

Renato walked straight for her and scooped her up in a hug. He led her to his table, poured her a glass of champagne. "*Dios mio*," he said, grinning. "Tell me. How are you?"

Already the Frau was scuttling toward them, her face more pinched than usual. But the champagne was dry and light, and Leonora felt girlish, and almost happy. "*Plus terrible,*" she told him.

"But where have you been? Where is Max?"

"We have our room." The Frau's eyes narrowed as she looked Renato over. She curled her plump fingers around Leonora's wrist.

Leonora patted her hand as if she were a large, headstrong child. She downed the champagne and explained—in French, so the Frau wouldn't understand—how Father had her locked up in the asylum, how Max was taken, put in an internment camp by the French. "But now—he could be anywhere," she said, trying not to think of him in the hands of the Nazis. "And you—you're living in—"

"Lisbon. I'm at the Mexican Embassy there."

"Oh, Renato, you've no idea how lovely it is to see you." She twisted free of the Frau's grip and threw her arms around him. His cologne, warm and spicy, smelled like home.

⟿

She needed proper clothes. She might have been a nun in her shapeless black wool dress, but clothes required money, which meant going to Father's people rather than waiting for them to come to her. So the Frau and she met with Mr. Gilliland, the same head of Imperial Chemicals in Madrid who had arranged her stay at Santander. They met in his office, where he sat behind his big desk and looked her over.

"You seem much improved. Still planning on assassinating Hitler?" He chuckled, as if her very presence entertained him. "So you need a wardrobe? This should do." He slid a stack of pesetas across the desk, and though Leonora extended her hand, he gave it to the Frau, who folded the cash into her brassiere.

Later, he invited her to a dinner without the Frau in tow. His wife sat across the table, coiffed and prim and so nervous that when the waiter brought Leonora her steak knife she snatched it. "But how will she eat her meat, darling?" Mr. Gilliland took it from his wife, giving it back to Leonora with a wink.

He must have enjoyed danger, because he contrived to see her often, just the two of them. He took her to the zoo, to the Prado to see the works of Goya, and then, on a blustery night, to a restaurant with white tablecloths, crystal, china, and waiters as beautiful as José. They ate paella and drank white wine.

He put down his glass, took her hand. "I like you." He smiled, a shred of something green between his front teeth. "I've been given orders by your father to send you to a sanatorium in North Africa, but I can save you from that. You can stay here. I'll set you up in a *very* nice flat." His hand moved to her thigh, pressing. "Not to worry, you won't be lonely, not lonely at all."

This was something to consider. Another sanatorium would kill her. It was pure luck she got out of this one. If she was sent to Africa, her family would forget about her—which was just what Father wanted—to forget he ever had a daughter. And he could. He had the funds and the means, and what was to stop him, other than this man's lust? Perhaps she should take his offer. She could wait out the war and arrange her escape when things settled.

"I'll think about it," she told him, removing his hand with the lightest possible touch.

After dinner, as he opened the door for her and she stepped onto the sidewalk, a whopping gust of wind whipped her hair over her eyes. It rattled the huge, metal restaurant sign, blowing it clear off its hooks. The sign crashed at her feet. Had she been one step closer, it might have sliced off a hand, or her head.

She pulled back her hair and looked Mr. Gilliland in the eye. "My answer is no."

—❦—

Before the week was out, it had all been arranged. On the curb of the Ritz, the Frau dabbed at tears behind her thick lenses. And Leonora surprised herself by hugging her—her turnip-shaped keeper who'd seen her through the worst of her days.

Gilliland took Leonora to the station and put her on the train to Lisbon. Handing her a folder with the papers she'd need—exit and entrance visas, all of it in perfect order—he let his gaze skim her breasts and hips and linger on her legs beneath her new, knee-length skirt. "What a waste," he sighed. "But then, the orderlies are going to love you."

A year ago she might have slapped him. Now she only boarded the train without glancing back. As they pulled away, she looked straight ahead. She would not be going to Africa. That much she was sure of. She gripped the butterfly, her talisman. Its wings twitched beneath the glass. *Mexico*, she thought, and on its heels, *Renato*.

The door to the cabin opened, and the conductor asked for tickets. She handed him hers, and when he punched it and gave it back, she noticed the date. April 2, 1941. Max's birthday. He was fifty today. Which meant in four days she would turn twenty-four. A page of her life ripped and burned. But Max, fifty? And here she was, at last heading to Lisbon. It was some kind of terrible joke, her arrival so late she felt hollow when she thought of him. As if he were locked away, in some room inside her, and she'd lost the key, or else hidden it from herself. She'd like to find the key, to open the door and let him out, so he could be real again, a person and not her idea of him, faint as a ghost. Yes, she thought, she would like him to come out and speak for himself—though she had no idea what she would say to him.

⁓⊱

In Lisbon she stepped off the train into the hands of a stern English entourage from Imperial Chemicals. Dressed in black suits, the men seemed to shine, like guards. Rigid and efficient, they stood out from the swamp of people waiting and disembarking, crying and hugging. One man took her suitcase, the other her purse, while the woman walked in step with her. Squat and burly, she could have tackled Leonora easily. "You are lucky, my dear," the woman said, pitching her voice over the din of the station and up an octave, as if toward kindness. "You will be staying a few nights in Estoril, a lovely town by the sea."

"How wonderful," said Leonora, playing along.

"Yes. We'll all be there!" The woman gestured at the men as though they were a family. "For a time," she added, and sighed with the weight of her honesty.

They crammed into a taxi. In the backseat she was sandwiched between the two stern men. The woman was up front, with the driver. Sun glared off the buildings and sweat dripped down Leonora's hairline and between her breasts. For all she knew, one of the men had a syringe in his hand and was preparing to sedate her. Her heart galloped. *Think. Think. You're smarter than these people.* She had to get them to stop, to make some sort of outing.

She leaned toward the woman. "Excuse me, darling," she said, assuming an upper-class lilt that would have made her father proud. "The sun will be absolute hell on my hands. I simply must have gloves for the trip, and a hat."

The car dozed in the hot silence. She held her breath.

"You're right," the woman said at last. "A lady must have her gloves."

The men grumbled. They were not being paid enough to shop.

"We'll drop you at the office and *I'll* take her then," the woman declared.

"I don't think that's a good idea," one man barked, and to Leonora's delight the woman glared at him, her face a veritable fortress of gravity and not to be trifled with.

At a boutique, Leonora found a plain sun hat and white gloves. The woman, whose name was Nancy, and whom she'd begun to think of as the Frau's distant English cousin, was trying on hats herself, fancy, ridiculous hats. Leonora told her she was ready, and since Nancy had not yet decided, she gave Leonora the cash to pay for her things. It was just enough, so she swapped the gloves for a cheaper pair. With the change in her pocket, her small victory, Leonora told her she was starving, she hadn't eaten a thing since Madrid. And after Nancy settled on a hat—black felt, with a low, slanting brim and a single red feather, something she could picture Leonor Fini pulling off, but not so much this woman—they ducked into a café that was large enough, thankfully, for her purposes.

As they studied the menu, a waiter brought bread and butter and she gorged herself. She was truly famished. She ate so fast what she did next was easy. "Oh God," she moaned. Convulsing, she gripped her stomach and pressed a hand over her mouth. "Which way is the loo?" Looking terrified she'd heave right there, Nancy pointed behind her, to the end of the café, and Leonora grabbed her purse and made a dash for it.

The windows in the restroom were high and too small for her to fit through. She peeked out the door. At their table Nancy was looking at the menu, the brim of her hat blocking her view of Leonora. It was now or never, Leonora thought, and bolted toward the kitchen, out a back door, and kept on running, down the block, winding through the slow-footed people on the sidewalk, and around a corner where she hailed a taxi.

"*Embajada Mexicana*," she told the driver, blood pulsing in her ears. Too slowly, he pulled away from the curb. It was early afternoon, the traffic light, cars zipping along. *You're almost there, you're almost there.* She repeated the words like a mantra as they drove through Lisbon, moving toward the interior. She'd never seen Lisbon before and the buildings reminded her of Paris, the iron scrollwork of the balconies, the garret apartments with the red tile roofs. Only here some buildings were so old they were crumbling, and others were piles of rubble. She rolled the window down and the ocean wind whipped her hair.

Almost there.

The streets narrowed as they entered the center of the city. People spilled from the sidewalk into the street. Like her, they were refugees, wearing too many layers of clothing for the heat, but they were smiling. Two young women held hands, laughing. They were out of the reach of the fascists. They were free the way she was almost free. The taxi turned onto a one-way street, where traffic inched along. She could walk faster. "*Dónde está . . .?*"

"*O amarelo.*" The driver pointed at a pale yellow building half a block ahead.

"*Bueno. Cuanto?*"

He pulled up to the curb. "*Sete,*" he said, and she gave him her handful of escudos, at least twice what he asked, and all that she had. She joined the crowd, walking quickly to the Mexican Embassy, where she rang the bell. She rapped on the door with her gloved knuckles, peeled off the glove to pound harder. A policeman on the sidewalk stopped to stare. Casually, she removed her other glove and clasped her hands behind her.

Her head throbbed. They would answer. Someone would come if she waited. She looked down. The stoop was a black, yellow, and green mosaic of tiny square tiles. It was a black labyrinth, trimmed in green and yellow, and she stood at its center. She glanced behind her. The sidewalks were a carpet of vivid mosaics, one after the other. How had she not noticed she was walking on art? And that policeman, thank God, had moved on.

The door opened. "Señorita?" said a man, young, mustached, a cap on his head.

"May I come inside?"

"*Por quê?*" He straightened his spine and peered down at her.

"I'm looking for Renato Leduc," she said in Spanish. "Is he here?"

"He is not. Come back later. *Un momento.* I'll get his card." He shut the door.

In his dark jacket and cap, the policeman was strolling back this way. When the man opened the door to give her the card, she stole past him into the embassy. "I'll wait." She perched on a settee by the window. "I won't be any bother."

"But señorita, why not leave him a note? He can phone your hotel."

She watched the policeman light a cigarette and lean on a nearby lamppost. "The police are after me," she said, pulling her own cigarette from her purse.

"Ah, I *see*, señorita." He winked at her. "You can wait for Renato right here."

After an hour Renato came in. He beamed when he saw her. As he led her to his office, she told him about her escape and the place Father planned to send her. Her hands were shaking, and Renato took them in his own calm hands.

"Marry me," he said. "You'll have diplomatic immunity. There will be nothing your father can do."

His brown eyes were steady. They were eyes she could trust. She noticed a fleck of green in the brown. She liked how it glinted in the sunlight. "We'll go to America?"

"Absolutely. America, and later, possibly, Mexico. I think you'd like it there."

She did not pretend what she felt was love, seasoned as it always was with desperation and euphoria. She felt something she needed even more, a relief so immense her whole body went weak. He was one of the brothers, a bear of an older brother who would protect her from the world. He hugged her and she let herself weep in his arms.

PART III

Napoleon in the Wilderness

Max, June 1941, Lisbon, Portugal

Max dresses in the dark of early morning. Never before an early riser, he's come to love this time of cool air and quiet broken only by the faint whistling of a pedestrian or by an occasional passing car.

He has been in Lisbon for three weeks, waiting for Peggy's arrival, and while he has run out of money, he has achieved something like peace, if peace is an emptiness, a clean hollow that light can sometimes fill. Though he's hungry most of the time, he can't say he misses her exactly—not if he's being honest. What he misses is the way she takes care of him, sees that he eats well and that his clothes fit. And now that she's on her way, due this afternoon on the Marseille train, he feels a charge on the air, as if a storm were on its way after a long dry spell and he can already taste the rain.

In his tiny room in the pension, a room he'll be able to pay for when she arrives, he buttons up his unwashed linen shirt and watches the first light set fire to the windows of the apartment houses across the boulevard. He dreamed of Leonora and woke with a leaden ache in his chest. The dream so real, the voice and the laughter hers exactly, it seems to him she must be here, in Lisbon, like they planned. It might be a year later, but he has made it. Why shouldn't she have made it here, too? If she was alive, that is.

He spends his days walking the streets, searching the face of every willowy, dark-haired woman, convinced he will turn a corner and there she will be, radiant with intelligence and mystery, untouched, somehow, by the clutches of this war. Because he cannot imagine her changed. It would mean his youth, even its afterglow, would be gone, and he would live the rest of his days in its shadow.

Yesterday he trailed a woman from a fountain in the old section of town, through a maze of narrow streets, until he caught sight of her face. The woman, who, he realized, was not Leonora, regarded him with the same sort of faraway look Leonora had so often assumed in photographs, as though she were looking at some distant thing only she could see. Then she unlocked a door to an apartment house and closed it behind her.

Pulling on trousers, he watches through the open window as the city rouses itself. A boy on a bicycle scares a clutch of pigeons into the sky who, remembering they are birds and capable of flight, flap their way up to a telephone line, and when a collie pulling an old man along behind him stops to bark at the birds, a woman who has been pushing her cart of tulips stops to talk with the old man in the effortless way people talk to each other when they've been neighbors forever. It seems to Max that she's known him all her life.

The scene makes him smile. And he finds he is thinking of Germany, Cologne, the city of Dada, and the apartment he had with Lou that served as its hub—the all-night parties, the dancing and rowdy discussions and recklessness of it all. Dear Lou. Before this war and the one before it, they had walked beside a field of tulips, yellow and pink, red and white. They were college students then. Floating on the heady scent, they were young and immortal, talking of Dürer and Goya as if they'd been the first two people to discover them. Then he thinks of what Lou told him in Marseille.

After that meeting with Varian Fry, during which she refused to marry him, even if it would have meant her ticket to America, they left the office together. On the sidewalk she took a cigarette from her purse and offered him one. They stood in the sunlight smoking, and the day was too balmy for April, too bright, so that what came next made the whole world feel wrong.

"In case I don't see you again," she said matter-of-factly. "In case I'm caught, put away in a camp for Jews, I suppose you should know. When you left Jimmy and me, I was pregnant. I was pregnant with your child."

He had stood there like an idiot. "Why didn't you tell me?" he managed to ask her.

She shrugged and looked off, down the street somewhere. "You didn't want to be with me. Getting rid of your child was the price of letting you go." There were tears in her eyes.

"But," he started, and couldn't say the rest. He couldn't even tell her he might have stayed. "I'm sorry," he said.

With her characteristic stoicism, she shook off the tears. "Don't you see? Your leaving made room for me. I had a place in my own home again. I found out what I was capable of."

"I've failed you," he said. And she kissed his cheeks once more, smiled her saddest smile, and waved goodbye with a ripple of her fingers, like she always did.

It was true. He failed her as he failed Marie-Berthe and Jimmy and Leonora, too. He has failed them all.

He slides on his oxfords and laces them up. He's headed to the open-air market in a plaza by the sea. There's a fruit vendor there, a woman, who will give him a basket of tiny, fresh strawberries for the price of one of his drawings. Today he has five for her to choose from.

~§

Making his way through the streets in the morning sun, he comes to life again. Lisbon seems at once old and young, aroused by the ocean air and not to be trusted entirely. He likes it here. It's the sort of city he could live in, he thinks, if it weren't for the war breathing over its shoulder. Already the narrow sidewalk is a stream of people. More refugees arrive by the day. A group of children sit on the steps of a boardinghouse. Three small boys in their best suits, creased and worn, stained at the knees. An older girl hands apples all around and they bite into them, lifting their faces to the sun. They are free here, hunted no longer.

At the market, the strawberry lady takes her time looking through his stack of drawings, choosing, at last, a pencil sketch of a man with wings gazing at himself in a puddle and seeing the reflection of a horse. "*Obrigado*," she says, handing him back the other drawings along with a basket of strawberries.

He eats a berry as he winds through the market, past the stalls of flowers and vegetables, tomatoes and oranges and fish, on his way to the sea. The strawberries will not be enough to stop his stomach from growling, but they are delicious, tart and sweet, and he savors each one.

At the edge of the market there's a woman selling eggs and live chickens. If you buy a chicken, she'll wring its neck while you wait and bag its body in a burlap sack, bloody feathers and all. He watches her perform the deed as naturally as if she were tying a child's shoe or wiping a snotty nose. And then he notices the woman she's giving it to.

Loose dark hair thick as Leonora's, but her face more chiseled. She wears a black broad-brimmed hat with netting that covers her eyes, but even so he can tell this woman is older, her profile stricter, like one of those teachers from his youth so skilled with the ruler. Jaw tight, mouth pursed, she doesn't smile. Still, she is beautiful, her skin so pale it could be marble. He watches her pay the woman and put the chicken in her basket. He turns to the beach, where he means to go, and finds he cannot walk away.

He looks back, but she is gone.

Desperately, he rushes toward the market. Turning a corner, he peers down another winding alley of vendors. It's full of people, women mostly, and he weaves past them, looking for her lace blouse, her black skirt and hat, her dark hair. He only looked away for seconds. He can't have lost her.

And here she is, her basket swinging at her side, her skirt trailing the dusty mosaic path, erasing her footprints.

Leonora, June 1941, Lisbon, Portugal

With the freshly slaughtered chicken in her basket, Leonora walks down a winding alley of vendors to find beets and potatoes, which she'll roast along with the fat hen. She'll make a late lunch. Renato will be delighted. She didn't tell him she was coming to the market—he'd only have worried. They aren't married yet, and although when they've been out they haven't seen anyone from Imperial Chemicals, he's wanted her to stay at his flat as much as possible. But today the sky was so blue, the air so light, she couldn't be inside a second longer.

Pressing through the crowd, she feels a prickle at the back of her neck and has the notion she's being watched. She pulls the netting of her hat lower over her eyes and glances about. No one is staring at her. But she'll be quick. She'll buy her roots and hurry home.

At the stand, the beets and potatoes are small. She'll need seven of each, at least. She's selecting the largest of the beets when a man squeezes in beside her. Their arms graze and a charge zips through her. She steals a sidelong glance. His white hair backlit by the sun, he glows. She faces him, squints. "Nora?" the man asks.

She lifts her veil. "Max?" she ventures. He is thinner, his face weathered, its furrows deepened. His eyes are wet. They are the blue of the ocean on a day as fine as this one. She places a palm on his cheek. She must feel him to know he is real. It *is* Max.

The world whirls around them. His face flies open as if she's the one back from the dead. "Ah, Nora!" he whoops. Dropping his basket of berries, he throws his arms around her.

Inside his embrace, she feels herself melting. Her very bones are melting, the scaffolding that's held her together for the whole of this terrible time without him. Her head is light, airy. If she collapsed now, he would catch her. But she won't let herself give in. She worked for this strength, she suffered for it. She feels her skin harden with some invisible shield, an exoskeleton inside which she is fortified, safe from her desire to surrender herself to love. Never again. She will never trust another man so completely, never rely on one the way she relied on him.

"Max," she says again, as if to understand. Pulling away she grasps his arm with her free hand, holding her basket in the other.

He is there, she is here. They are not one.

Max, June 1941, Lisbon, Portugal

After all this time, he has found her.

Her eyes search his. Ringed with the dark, purple-black of one who has not slept well in months, or years, they are the eyes of a witch, a sorceress. His nerves tingle, as if his body has been asleep for a year and is coming to life again. He has the feeling that if she were to blink he might disappear with her, happily.

But there's something so different about her. She remains strangely stiff, as if he meant no more to her than a distant acquaintance. She smells odd, too, metallic, like the air in Provence when the humidity peaks, just before a thunderstorm. He takes a step back to look at her again, to be certain it is her. She is thinner, and though he doesn't want to admit it, she seems frail, and almost frightened of him. Dark with secrets, giving nothing away, her eyes are on his, peering so far inside him he's sure she can see his childhood terrors, the night jungle he is lost inside, the lion who stalks him, mouth watering.

There is nothing he can hide from her.

"I didn't think you were real anymore. I wasn't sure," she says. Her face a shade whiter than before, she is a specter.

Dreaming. He must be dreaming. He bites his tongue and tastes blood. "Nora," he repeats, an idiot in her presence. She blurs and he blots his eyes one at a time, afraid she might disappear any instant, yet here she still is, not a girl anymore, but a woman.

She scans the market and steps closer to him, flips down the veil and tilts her hat forward. "I shouldn't even be here, in public. I wanted to surprise Renato by making lunch."

"Renato?" He stands in the sun, sweating. A chill seizes his neck.

"You remember him."

"Picasso's stodgy friend?"

"I need to get back." She buys her beets and potatoes, fits them into her basket. "Walk with me," she says, taking his arm.

They leave the busy market, descend a flight of old stone steps and walk the empty strand of beach, taking off their shoes, walking arm in arm, the tide throwing itself at them, breaking into beads that catch the sunlight. Her skirt is wet up to her knees and she twists it into a knot at her hip. Talking over the tumble of stones as the tide advances and recedes, she tells him how Catherine came to Saint-Martin with Michel, how they'd fled Paris, bringing their terror with them. She tells him odd details, the way her body refused to move at times, as though it had a mind of its own. The wild horses that let her touch their faces. The doctor who made her his prisoner, who hypnotized her with his black eyes and his Cardiazol. He tries to hear the meaning of her words, tries to follow her journey, but he's lulled by her voice, the voice he's been dreaming of, the voice he couldn't recall in his waking hours no matter how much he longed to. And now she's slipped from the hands of her father's people, she's saying.

"His people?" he asks, because he's listening now. And she tells him about the sanitarium in North Africa, the prison her father wants to lock her in.

"But you're not insane."

"I might have been, a little." Her voice is tiny, the voice of a young girl. She clears her throat and speaks in the earthy way he recognizes. "And anyway, you know Father. Nothing as flimsy as the truth has ever stopped him from getting what he wants. All he knows are which laws he can work around and which laws he can't, which is why Renato and I are getting married."

"A marriage of convenience. A marriage on paper."

"A marriage is a marriage."

He stops walking to look at her. She stops, too, seems to waver just out of his reach. She is changed, utterly changed. "Nora, you haven't thought this out."

She glares at him. It's the look he knows too well from his ex-wives, shot through with its verdict of guilt. She runs, and he chases her, grabs hold of her arm and the bag swings out, sending the roots and the chicken flying onto the beach. He doesn't let her go. "When?"

"As soon as possible," she says with such calm that for a second he despises her. "As soon as he has everything in order. Now help me." She shucks him off of her slowly, with fierce elbows. They gather the groceries and sit on the sand.

Pebbles hiss as the ocean rushes toward them and away. He tells her the horrors of the ghost train and how awful it was to be home without her. She looks at her feet when he says this and carefully wipes the sand from each toe. He tells her about the Villa Air-Bel and how the station manager only let him leave France because he liked his paintings—our paintings, he says. He tells her Peggy Guggenheim is helping him leave for America. Leaving out the fact that he and Peggy have been sleeping together, he says she might be able to help her leave, too.

"Renato's arranging all that," she says.

He is silent. He's in no position to argue.

A gull lands near their feet, cocking its head. "I had strawberries," he tells the gull. "I'd have given you one."

"Here," says Leonora. "I think I have a biscuit." She digs in her purse and throws the bird crumb after crumb, which he gobbles down, walking a little closer each time. When she reaches out to pet him, he flies in circles above them. Landing farther away, he calls to the other gulls, who enclose them in a wide, jagged circle.

She looks past the squawking birds toward the pale horizon. Max turns to her. "Nora," he says. "Don't marry him."

She shakes her head. "If I'm not the property of my husband, I'm the property of my father."

"But *I* can marry you. I can marry you right now. The paperwork went through."

She stands and takes too long to brush the sand off her skirt. When he tries to look at her, he is blinded by the sun. "I need to get home," she says.

"Home?" An orange-and-purple sun dances in his vision, blocking her face.

"Renato's," she says. And as if she were sorry for him, she reaches her hand out to help him up. "You can walk me back if you want. That way you'll know where I am."

Peggy, June 1941, Marseille, France

Peggy follows her porter to the front of the line. "Madame's passport and exit visa?" says the station manager. She gives him the passport open to the proper page, so all he should have to do is glance.

She taps the toe of her Valentino pump. Why is he not stamping her visa? The line of people is waiting. Her porter has pushed ahead and probably has her bags settled on the train by now. "Is something wrong?" she asks. Without a word to her, the station manager nods to an officer who has been standing off to the side, apparently. He steps forward, takes her by the arm, and they are walking. "But my things," she says.

"This will only take a minute." He leads her to a door guarded by two Gestapo.

Inside a windowless cell of an office a French deputy—a large, grim woman—stands with her hands on her hips. "Close the door," she says. Peggy does as she's told. "You will remove your clothes." Peggy pulls her blouse over her head. She unzips her skirt, steps out of her shoes.

"Everything?" she asks. The deputy nods. Quickly, Peggy unhooks her bra, tugs her black, silk panties down her legs. Naked, she looks at her watch. Her train leaves in ten minutes. She watches the deputy search every pocket, turning her skirt and blouse inside out, searching the seams. The woman takes the lining out of her pumps, rubs her panties between her thumb and finger. Perhaps she'd also like to check inside her vagina? Peggy would like to ask, but she's far too terrified to emit any sound.

The woman finds nothing, because there is nothing to find. Peggy only brought the exact amount of dollars she's allowed to carry out of the country, but even so she can't stop thinking that the deputy will send her to a camp in spite of her compliance. She's never been treated like a criminal before, nor has it occurred to her just how easily she might be stripped of her rights and belongings.

"You can dress," the woman says at last, her gaze lingering on Peggy's diamond necklace and earrings. Peggy pulls on her underwear, fastens her bra. She's zipping up her skirt when she sees that the woman has her passport in her hand. "Guggenheim is a Jewish name, is it not?" If she was to disappear from the station, no one would be able to find her. She'd be another Jew France was only too eager to rid itself of.

"I am American, my grandfather was Swiss," she says, zipping up her skirt, pulling on her blouse, trying to still her trembling hands.

With a huff the woman gives her the passport. "You may go."

Peggy runs to catch the train, slipping through the doors just before they close. Safe in her seat, she drinks the remainder of her bottle of laudanum. It isn't until they cross from France into Spain that she feels her breathing grow steady again.

~∂

The train slows and she falls awake. They're pulling into the station, but she closes her eyes to remember the dream. She was being strip-searched at the border between reason—a long stretch of desert—and love—a mountainous, watery state. The officer from the land of reason was a woman in a helmet and a blue blazer. She wore white cotton gloves and ran them over her body lightly, dusting for fingerprints, which she was not permitted to carry across the border. "All evidence of your lovers belongs to us," the woman said.

Opening her eyes, Peggy feels exposed, disheveled, and, oddly, aroused. *Max will like this dream*, she thinks, watching the other passengers gather their hats, their bags, and children. The border of reason and love. But thinking of the real strip search, she must take a breath. She cut things too close this time. And yet she has managed to make it to Lisbon. The last stop. And Max has promised to meet her at the station.

Most of the passengers have disembarked when she rises from her seat and gathers her bags. She's moving slowly, the laudanum still in her blood, but as she steps from the train onto the platform, her heartbeat quickens. Finding Max in the crowd, she thinks she's never been so glad to see someone. His hair is whiter than she remembers, spectacularly so. Staring at the pavement, shoulders slumped, he resembles a fallen angel. Laurence has brought the children, Pegeen and Sindbad—though at sixteen and eighteen, they are hardly children anymore. It has been a full two weeks since she's seen them, and they seem, remarkably, to have grown. She rushes toward them. *All my pretty ones*, she thinks, wondering when she was last this happy.

And then Max looks up, and she sees that something has changed. His forehead is furrowed, the skin around his eyes swollen, as if he's upset. Laurence hurries toward her. "Peggy!" he calls, with his usual exuberance, and they all huddle around her.

Max opens his arms and she tips toward him. "Darling," she says, "you won't believe what happened to me."

Clutching her to his chest, awkward and ardent, he puts his mouth to her ear. His breath smells of alcohol. "No. You won't believe," he whispers. And he tells her.

The station goes silent. She pulls away from his sloppy embrace. His mouth is still moving but she can hear nothing more. This is how the end begins, she thinks. With the words *Leonora is here. I have found her.* Her skin is cold. It's a shell she can hide inside. Her backbone is made of the steel of sunken ships. And yet the station spins. She must squint to bring Max into focus. "I'm happy for you," she manages, flatly, sure she's going to be sick.

Her children hug her with an unusual fervency. They mean to protect her, she realizes, as they turn their attention to Max. He met them once before, in Marseille, and told them story after story, delighting them with the lurid details. Camp des Milles, the ghost train, Saint-Martin, Leonora having run off, the four-fingered men, Georges and his dog. But now they keep a measured distance. Sindbad glowers. Even Pegeen purses her lips, looking from Max to Peggy to Max again.

Taking her bags, Laurence hums, making light of conflict as he always does, so long as it doesn't involve him. "One step closer. Before we know it, we'll all be in America."

"Let me," Max offers, taking the smaller of her two bags. His hand is trembling, she sees, and his lips are chapped. There's a scab in the corner where a crack bled.

She's never seen him so undone. She pushes ahead. Leonora can have him, she decides, walking faster. There was a very nice Englishman on the train who slipped her his card. She'll call him, meet him for dinner. Who knows, perhaps he'll become her next husband and she'll move to England and take a war job. Do something meaningful for once.

When she confesses this latest plan to Laurence over wine in his hotel room, he insists she's being thoughtless. "You have children, for Christ's sake. You might try being a mother to them. Get them to America at least." And though she'd like to fight him on this point—after all, they are his children, too—she knows he's right. She's been traipsing around Europe as if she belonged only to herself and could throw her life around if she wished to. But the time has come to go home.

⁂

Dinner at the hotel has the whole group sitting together like one boisterous family, everyone talking over one another just to get a word in. Everyone, that is, but Max, who eats in silence. But afterward, he asks her to walk with him, and she agrees.

Turning from the main street—so clamorous with the rumbling of automobiles—down a narrow, empty side street, where the streetlights sputter dimly, Max takes her hand. He unfurls his story, telling her all about Leonora. As he describes her plight, what made her resort to seeking out the "boorish Mexican"—whose name Peggy doesn't quite catch—he is so overcome he seems to feel Leonora's anguish as his own. "I should have found a way to get back home sooner. It was my fault. She trusted me, and I left her." He whines this last bit, sniffles, and kicks a small stone over the pavement. "Do you have a cigarette?"

She gives him one, which he lights, offering it to her as they start up a hill. She's never seen him so concerned about anyone besides himself, and she feels herself falling for him all over again. The bastard. "Why are you telling me this?" She will be cold, rational. "Be with her, if that's what you want."

He nods, absently. "She's changed. She's unrecognizable." He's talking to himself, and then he is here, with her again. "Tomorrow," he says, "you must meet her."

"You think that's a good idea?" The road is steep. They stop to catch their breath and he turns to her. His eyes are impossibly blue, and she hates him.

"Maybe—" he says. "Do you think you might? No. It's too much."

"What?"

"Could you help her get to New York?"

Were she a stronger woman, she'd slap his face, tell him it was over, this thing between them. He could figure out his own way to America. Perhaps the Mexican would pay *his* way. Were she stronger, she'd leave him right now and walk back to her hotel alone.

Instead, she moseys along beside him, not quite a puppy. Not that bad. Stopping to crush the cigarette butt under the toe of her pump, she realizes how much her shoes are hurting her, and she takes them off and walks barefoot.

They reach one of the city's upper layers, where they happen on the ruins of a church, and enter through a great hole where the door had been. The roof has collapsed and lies in pieces around her feet.

Above them the sky is aged bourbon, dark and pure. If she could drink it all, she knows she would dissolve, her hair and skin and bones, even her jewelry would dissolve. She wouldn't leave a trace of evidence. Peggy Guggenheim would up and vanish. How lovely, she thinks, releasing something between a sigh and a moan.

~&

The following afternoon he brings her to the home of an English woman, a friend of a friend of Leonora's, from what she's gathered.

Leonora kisses both her cheeks when she shows them in. She kisses Max on the lips—briefly, chastely—and leads them to a back patio of a garden, overgrown with jasmine and climbing white roses. When she goes to the kitchen, Max shifts in his seat like a schoolboy, as if he is afraid she may not return and it's all he can do to not run after her.

But soon she is back, with a steaming pot of tea and biscuits and cherries. She is wearing a formless, blue cotton dress, and her hair, held away from her face by a single bobby pin, is a dark swell. Her eyes are the eyes of a poet, haunted and glossy. And she has the exact tip-tilted nose that Peggy had asked for when the surgeon botched the job. Leonora is, perhaps, the most beautiful woman she has ever seen. Of course he loves her. Of *course*.

She pours them tea. Her slow, steady hand, white as alabaster, seems to glow, *she* seems to glow, and Peggy has the feeling they are floating, that the whole garden is floating, weightless as a spider's web. Watching Leonora arrange a small plate of cherries and biscuits for Max, she tries to be objective. He seems, somehow, like an uncle to her, a dear uncle, of whom she is very fond.

"Peggy can get you a ticket on the Clipper," Max says.

"I can try," she says, squinting at him. She told him she would *try*.

Leonora, who sits very near to Max, pours her own cup of tea and seems not to have heard them. Max reaches out to touch her arm, but then clasps his hands in an attempt to contain himself. His stillness strikes Peggy as entirely uncharacteristic. The man who is in constant motion is arrested by her presence. "But darling," says Leonora, having heard them after all, "that doesn't change my passport situation."

"I would very much like to help you." Drinking her black tea, Peggy realizes this is true. But why would she say such a thing? If Leonora is marrying the Mexican for a passport, why not let her? Nothing so officious as marriage ever stopped a love affair, but it might complicate it slightly.

"You are kind. But Renato has made arrangements. We're going to New York by boat. After the marriage is legal, of course. But please—" Leonora leans so close Peggy feels lit by her incandescence, electrified. "Please don't let on that you know. Renato is very sensitive about it. He'd be terribly upset if he knew I was speaking to you about this."

At the mention of Renato, Max recoils. His silence peevish, he gulps his tea. When he speaks, his voice is pinched and loud. "This Mexican is *un homme inférieur*."

"Max, *please*," says Leonora, more command than supplication.

The garden is too small for the three of them. "Pardon me," Peggy says, getting up, "where is the loo?"

In the bathroom, she looks in the mirror, wipes the makeup from where it has melted under her eyes. She doesn't wear much, but heat always makes it run. She thinks she might let herself out the front door and get a taxi back to the hotel. The situation is too much. Max seething and venomous, and Leonora so detached, yet strangely eager to appease. Christ, Peggy should be glad he's not in love—that way—with *her*. If he were, she imagines she'd run. At least the thought makes her smile.

She washes her hands and splashes water onto her face. *Why couldn't she have been born beautiful?*, she thinks, fixating, as always, on her nose. And then she hears monkeys, hyenas, she hears two prehistoric birds fighting. Their voices rise as she walks through the apartment, not exactly in any hurry to join the commotion. Finding the door to the patio closed she's relieved to stand behind it and listen.

"I saved her, Max. Would you have had her stay? The Nazis were everywhere. Where were you? Where were you?"

"They took me!" It is a child's cry—desperate and helpless. "One week! I missed her by one week! Why couldn't you have waited? God damn it. God damn you."

"Please, Catherine, leave us," says Leonora.

A woman bursts through the door. Pushing past Peggy, she grabs her purse. "I advise you to keep your distance. From both of them." She leaves, the front door slamming behind her.

Max emerges from the patio with a rose pinned to his lapel, his face stunned and rapturous. Peggy takes his arm and leads him out, into the balmy Lisbon afternoon, and to the café on the roof of her hotel where they drink martinis and smoke in silent misery.

"I should go," she says after a time.

"I'd rather you didn't," he says. And because he seems to mean it, she orders another drink. She doesn't try to console him. She simply doesn't have the energy. She will let him founder, if that's what he's set on. As for her, her case is hopeless. She hates three-way affairs, and aren't they all three-way affairs? Unless they are four-way. She supposes that happens often enough as well.

Leonora, June 1941, Lisbon, Portugal

At the café where she and Max lunched yesterday, and the day before, a small place on the edge of town, he is at their usual table on the patio when she arrives. He's smoking, gazing over the Atlantic, an open bottle of wine and a bowl of olives before him. She stands in the shadow of the doorway, watching him behind her veil. Her heart hurrying off without her, her muscles frozen, she is stuck for a moment, as she was in the Pyrenees. She is unable to move.

Seeing her, he smiles, waves. And she is walking again, toward him.

She sits. He pours her wine. She helps herself to an olive. She scans the patio. Couples, mostly. A few women, lunching. No one who resembles an Imperial Chemical employee, no one who looks like a detective. She takes off her veiled hat, pushes the bobby pins further into her bun. Behind her a man and a woman are talking. "How long before Franco invades Portugal?" the woman asks. "How long before he joins with Hitler? We can't get out of here soon enough!" she cries, a strangle to her voice, as though she were a bird pinned by her throat to the ground. There is a chill in Leonora's spine, her palms dampen. She reaches for the wine, takes a long swallow without bothering to taste it.

"I dreamed about you," he says, and he spills the dream onto the table between them. "You said you'd be right back and you were gone. I couldn't find you. The city was labyrinthine. Horrible. I was lost." Why is he telling her this? He's so awkward and ardent, she feels guilty, as if his dream were real. "When I found you at last you didn't seem to care that you'd left me, that I was a miserable heap of a man. You didn't care about *me* at all."

"It's not like that," she says. She rests her hot forehead on her palms, her head too heavy for her neck.

The waiter stops at their table. Max straightens and, consulting the menu, orders for them both. Grilled octopus and abalone. "And more olives, *por favor*," she adds, pressing the cool glass of wine to her temple.

"*Sim, senhorita*," says the waiter. He tips the rest of the wine into Max's glass. "*Outro?*" Max nods, and the waiter leaves, a stiff silence in his wake.

They smoke and drink the wine.

"I'm sorry," she offers. "You're having nightmares again."

"If you're in it, it can't be a nightmare. Not entirely. Were your dreams any better?"

Better? she wonders, remembering the dream she had with him in it. Curious how he'll interpret it, she decides to tell him about it. "I was with you in your studio. I was curled on the rug at your feet, just like a cat."

"Oh," he says, a hopeful smile spreading over his face.

"I was like your tubes of paint, or your jars of brushes and turpentine, I was right where you wanted me to be. You called me your beautiful girl, and a portrait you'd made of me hung on the wall, but when I looked in the mirror there was an old woman staring back at me. She had gray hair and wrinkles, and she was laughing. She found the scene hilarious, apparently."

"But you're so young, darling. You have your whole life ahead of you still."

She laughs. She can't help it. She isn't bothered by the old woman. She rather likes her. What bothers her is the feeling of satisfaction she had at Max's feet. How she dreamt of his painting rather than of her own. She pulls the pins from her bun, letting her hair fall.

She unclasps her purse, sets his passport on the table. He opens it, shaking his head as if he can't quite believe that it's here. "You still have it, after everything."

Though the sun is aimed at him, it's her eyes that water. "You were with me the whole time." She doesn't tell him how she tried to give his passport away. Anyway, it wasn't really *her* that did that. It was her when she'd fallen down the rabbit hole, and the world and its rules were altered, in a way they aren't now.

The waiter opens an Alvarinho and fills their glasses. It's good, bright acid and citrus. "My wine was better."

"Of course it was. It was yours."

She raises her glass. "To the present."

"A present," he says, and their glasses kiss and ring.

And here is the abalone in its iridescent shell. It's breaded and fried, tender and sweet. She's never tasted abalone before, and she eats it slowly, then brushes the crumbs from its pretty shell, which she slips into her purse. The octopus is wonderful, too, especially with the wine, and the afternoon, she thinks, is the best she can remember.

When they finish the wine, Max orders champagne. He's brought pencils and paper, and they sit in an easy silence and draw until the sun floats, low and yellow over the water.

She's so focused on her sketch, she hardly notices Max twisting something in his fingers. She does her best not to see. And then he is on one knee and she can no longer ignore him. "Nora," he says. He's holding up a wire bird he's made from the champagne's muselet. In its beak is a wire ring.

"Don't," she says. But here he is, with his bright, eager eyes, confusing things.

"Will you—"

"Please. Don't."

"Marry me."

How many times has she dreamed of this moment? Now that it's here it seems an awful prank. Her stomach turns and she tastes acid and octopus. She gathers her things and stands, wipes tears from her cheeks. "You've ruined a perfectly beautiful afternoon."

"You don't love him."

"When has marriage ever been about love?"

"Fine then. Marry him, but come home with me. Live with me. I'm no good alone, you know that."

The tide retreats with a hush, a silvery breath.

"Yes," she says. "I know."

Max, June 1941, Lisbon, Portugal

That night Max waits for Leonora. He can't help himself. The night is mild, and he sits at his table drawing and looking out the open window at the passersby, hoping each time it might be her.

When Laurence raps on his door for their usual nightly walk, he keeps still until he leaves. Having known each other decades earlier from the Montparnasse café scene, they've struck up something of a friendship in the last month. But he knows Laurence would talk him out of his single-minded lunacy, and besides, he needs to be alone. If he is alone, she just might come.

Though she is well aware of the Leonora situation, Peggy has given him an allowance, which is how he's paid for the lunches. A fact on which he does his best not to focus. And tonight he bought a bottle of whiskey—Leonora's drink—just in case. But now that it's well after midnight and moving in on dawn, the bottle is more empty than full.

To pass the time he sketches. In exchange for the allowance, he's promised Peggy a large painting in the decalcomania style, which she believes will be well received in New York. Though he never makes sketches for the decalcomania paintings—it would defeat the purpose of the process, the element of surprise—as his pencil moves over the paper, and Leonora's face surfaces again and again, he knows she will appear in this painting. Her presence is as unavoidable as the air.

Her things, the photographs and books and rolled up paintings he brought from Saint-Martin, still occupy a corner of his room. And as the sun rises, Max finds he is gathering it all into his pack. He is stumbling along the sidewalk, past clusters of refugees sleeping in doorways and on benches in the plazas. He is traversing the mosaics with the smattering of other early birds. He is making his way to her. He memorized the route weeks ago, and more than once he's found himself walking toward her apartment when he planned to go anywhere else. Turning onto her street, he scares a clutch of pigeons into the air. In his near somnambulist state, he watches them become sunlight.

The other times he's come here, he was content to stay quiet, to lean on the building across the street and stare at her window on the third floor, the one with the white lace curtains, and wonder if she were inside, and what she might at that very moment be writing or drawing or dreaming. But now he means to leave this bag with her. And so he picks up a stone, jagged and cold, from a planter bed. Her window (how can he think of it as *theirs*?) is closed—otherwise he might just whistle or call her name. He turns the stone in his hand and then he sends it flying in a hard line.

The sound is louder than he imagined it would be. The rock leaves a hole in the glass and cracks reach from it like the legs of a giant spider. Bull's-eye.

But it is Renato who pulls back the curtains, opens the window, and bellows down. "Max? *Dios mio! Eres loco!*"

Insane? Max thinks. Well of course, he is in love!

Renato is leaning out the window, shirtless, his white hair on end. He gestures with his hands, spewing insults. "Come down," Max yells. "Let's settle this like men."

Renato leaves the window. Max puts down the bag, rolls up his shirtsleeves.

Leonora opens the door. She walks onto the sidewalk in her bare feet, a white silk robe billowing around her as if she were a saint riding toward him on a cloud. But no. She is not beatific. Her hair is like Medusa's, her eyes have a violet sheen. He cannot bring himself to face her and stares, instead, at his feet. He's standing on a black-and-white mosaic in the pattern of a chessboard. His right shoe has a hole in the toe he hasn't noticed before, his pale sock peeking through the leather.

What was he thinking, coming here? *"Je m'excuse,"* he mutters.

She is standing on the chessboard, queen to his dispensable pawn. He will call his new painting *Napoleon in the Wilderness*, because that's just where he is, he thinks, raising his eyes to hers.

"Poor Max," she sighs. She takes him into her arms, and he weeps, terribly, his chest heaving. All his running was for nothing. He might have let the Nazis catch him, it was all the same to her. She doesn't want him. She is done.

He heaves her off of him. The buildings sway. He picks up the bag, pushes it into her hands. "Your things. The things you left. I thought you'd want them."

He feels like a child again, given to sulking, to walking away. Imagining just how much his leaving would hurt his parents. Just how sorry they'd be.

Without looking back, he weaves toward the pension, pushing against a gale moving in off the coast, bringing with it clouds, dark and dense, a real storm. *Let the sky open up then*, he thinks. *Let it drown me.* The rain is sudden and torrential, and he's glad for it. Men pass him on their way to work, men in hats and jackets, briefcases in hand, umbrellas spread over their bowed heads. His shirt is soaked and clinging, so he pulls it off. He tilts his face to the sky.

Half a block from the pension, in front of their hotel, he spots Laurence with all of his luggage on the curb. He is hailing a taxi, and Max runs to catch him.

"Where are you going?" he asks.

"Monte Estoril. I came last night to tell you. We're taking a hotel there, Peggy, Kay, the children. We'll wait for our Clipper passage by the sea. It's a better place for the children, a better place for us all."

"Take me with you," Max says. "Please." Because he cannot take himself away. He doesn't have the strength.

"I suppose I can wait." He waves the taxi away, puts his arm around Max. "Come. Let's get your things. Peggy will be happy to see you."

Peggy, June 1941, Monte Estoril, Portugal

Their hotel looks over the water, and Peggy has taken, every day at sunset, to sitting on the little balcony off of her room to watch the sun slide into the ocean, the shameless peach of a sun. Swallowing her wine, she thinks of the roundness of the Earth and tries to feel the motion of it, how at this very moment she is falling with all of Europe into darkness.

The sky and the water, dressed in rolling ribbons of orange and chartreuse, remind her of the painting she loves best by Tanguy, the one she bought from him when they were lovers. *The Sun in Its Jewel Case*. A title almost as luminous as the painting, and as lonely. She wishes she could look at it—it always seems to calm her—but it's in the bowels of a boat, somewhere on the Atlantic, with the rest of her collection, the hundreds of paintings that had better be waiting for her in America when she arrives. She sent them along with lamps, books, and a few pots and pans, and labeled the shipment "household objects," so no one would think to question it, but last night she had a dream her collection sank, the way her father sank into the icy ocean when the *Titanic* went down.

He's just a vague notion now, ghosting her childhood memories. How he'd sit her on his knee and bounce her when she was small, how, when he came home from work, he'd whistle his way up the stairs, and she'd run to have him scoop her into his arms. The time he sent her to her room for asking him at the dinner table if he didn't have a mistress since he was so often away from her and her mother and sisters. It's all distant, as if it belonged to the life of some character in a book she read long ago.

But her collection—she woke in a panic. It's all she has to show for her twenty years in Europe, her time in bohemia, collecting art and artists. Tanguy, Beckett, Penrose, and now Max, the one she most loves and, already somehow, loathes most, too.

He arrived at the hotel this morning. They walked along the shore, and he told her about Leonora and how she refused to leave the Mexican. "It is done." He said it in an offhand manner which couldn't hide the misery that spread from the corners of his eyes. His hand, as it tried to hold hers, had a slackness to it. She dropped it. "It must be very hard for you," she said, and left, making the excuse of some errand or other.

She'll give him space, she decides. Let him go, and if he comes back to her, well, then she'll see, won't she? She shouldn't be so forgiving, she knows, but everything is softer by the ocean. The cheese and crackers on the plate before her, the red lipstick she blots onto her lips before she heads down to dinner.

Max sits across from Peggy at the huge round table, but she does her best not to look at him. He isn't speaking, so it isn't difficult. Still, she can't help but to notice how he's eating all of one thing on his plate before moving to another, finishing first the steak and then the lobster, and ending with the green salad. If only he did that with his women.

Pegeen and Sindbad are discussing their after-dinner plans. There's a club with live music a local girl told Sindbad about when they were on the beach today. *O Gato Azul.* "And if I don't lose my virginity, how can I go back to the States?" Sindbad says. "I'm nearly nineteen for Christ's sake."

"Well don't lose it to a local. Venereal disease is rampant. You want your nose to fall off?" Peggy swallows her wine. It came off more harshly than she'd meant it to.

Pegeen wipes her mouth with a napkin and stands. "I'm in. Let's go to the Blue Cat."

"Me too," pipes up Jacqueline, the other sixteen-year-old at the table. Pegeen's friend from her boarding school in France, who was more or less adopted by Laurence and his soon to be ex-wife, Kay Boyle, Jacqueline tips an oyster into her mouth and looks at Sindbad with such longing it seems she might really melt. She reminds Peggy of herself at sixteen—hopelessly hungry for love. Not that so much has changed since then.

Kay chatters away. To her great relief, she has gotten her "friend"— the man she's leaving Laurence for—off to America, and now she shall see to it that their Clipper passage happens sooner than later, she says with such self-importance Peggy laughs. She can't help herself. It'll be fun to watch her try to do more than Peggy—who has been working at it for weeks—has already done. "It's high time we leave Europe, don't you think? The whole place is crumbling under our feet." Such a trite metaphor. Trite and easily digested, like her awful novels. She can't write with any verve, any voice of her own, and she isn't beautiful either, but plain, with a long nose and small, hard eyes. Though she's four years younger than Peggy, she's already showing her age, her skin loose at the jawbone, her arms soft and freckled.

Peggy fails to see just what Laurence fell in love with. Even now, after a year of separation, he looks at Kay with bruised admiration, a tenderness that sets Peggy on edge. Why should he be so kind to her, when she left him for someone else? He was so horrible to Peggy when *they* were separating—taking Sindbad from her and making her grovel if she wanted so much as a day with her son. She lights a cigarette, blowing the smoke over all of their heads. It was a decade ago, she realizes, and she's not forgotten any of it. Even so, Laurence and she have become truly close this year. They make better friends than they ever did husband and wife—all thanks to Kay's falling for someone else. Perhaps she ought to thank her, sometime when the sound of her voice doesn't make her teeth ache.

"Did you hear?" Kay is saying. "Another French boat sank just yesterday, on its way to New York, I believe."

Peggy has taken a bite of lobster and now it's stuck part of the way down. She gulps her wine, but it stays lodged in her esophagus. "*Which* boat?" she croaks.

"Oh," Kay says. "Why?"

"My collection!" she gasps. "My art!"

This gets Max's attention. "My paintings?" he asks, going pale.

Kay breaks into a laugh. It's one of her appalling gags.

Peggy can't look at her face a second longer. She polishes off the wine and the lobster goes down. She orders a cognac she takes to her room.

She'll go to bed early, she decides. She'll wake with the sun and take a long walk and then, maybe, a swim. She pulls off her clothes, turns off the light, and lies on the bed, but the night is balmy, even so close to the sea, and music has started up somewhere—guitar, trumpet, and drums, long jazzy rifts that stir her. She pulls on a robe and goes looking for Laurence, to say good night and maybe have a nightcap, only she can't remember his room number. And here is Max, coming toward her down the hall, with his slanted smile and those maddening eyes.

"Do you know Laurence's room number?" she asks him. "I want to say good night."

He takes a step toward her, so close she can feel his heat. "To him and not to me?"

"We're saying good night now, aren't we?" She presses her lips into a tight line, an effort to hold some small bit of ground.

"He's in room twenty-six," Max says, still smiling.

"I'll see you tomorrow, then." Walking away, she feels him watching her. "Are you coming or going?" she'd like to ask him, but it's altogether too boring a question—one which, if she's being honest, she doesn't really want the answer to.

She takes the tiny elevator down a floor and knocks on twenty-six. And Max opens the door, a little out of breath. "What a lovely surprise!" he says.

It is *his* room he sent her to. At this she has to laugh. Once again, his charm has reeled her in.

—❧—

They spend the nights in her bed or in his, their days in the sun and the sea. Weeks pass. She watches Max draw with Pegeen in the shade of a beach umbrella, and when the tide is low, skip rocks with Sindbad across the flat water.

And then one day Leonora turns up at lunch and he takes her on a horseback ride through the country. All afternoon they are gone.

When Max knocks on her door that night, Peggy refuses to let him in. Leaving the chain on, she cracks the door open to hear him. "Peggy," he bleats. "Nothing happened between us." He leans on the wall, his mouth very near hers. She smells whiskey on his breath. "I still want *you*."

"None of this changes the fact that you love her," she says, as much to him as to herself.

He's quiet. He will be honest with her. She is thankful, at least, for that.

"No. I suppose it doesn't," he agrees, and she closes the door. He knocks again, harder this time. She unchains the door and steps into the hall.

"How about we go for a walk?" she says, taking his hand and walking with him to avoid a scene. If she loses her temper, if he loses his, she doesn't want to have a row inside the hotel.

Outside, there's a warm breeze, a full moon turning the sea silvery blue. She leads him along the ocean toward a rocky cove she found just yesterday.

Already it's the end of June, their Clipper passage just two weeks away. New York will change things, she's sure of it. Max will have to navigate America and he'll need her. But she'll miss this little beach town. There's so much more she'd love to explore, and she'll miss her daily baths in the sea.

They hardly speak as they walk, but she lets him hold her hand. After all, she's accustomed to sharing her men. Though she can't say she likes it, especially not while she's still so much in love. Perhaps the thing to do is to welcome Leonora into *their* life, hers and Max's. It's the modern way, isn't it? Proof she's civilized, not jealous in the slightest.

"We should have a party before we go. You can invite Leonora, and her Mexican—what's his name?"

"Renato," he mumbles, his jaw muscle flexing.

"Yes. Renato," she says, letting the name sing. "Laurence and Kay can come. We'll throw a soiree at that club the kids like so much. *O Gato Azul*. It would be amusing, don't you think?"

Having reached the cove, she sheds her clothes and runs into the cold water.

"Peggy!" Max yells after her. "What are you doing? Come back!"

He chases her as far as the water's edge. The tide is high and there are jagged boulders on both sides of the cove. There are rocks beneath her, too, and the waves are bigger than she's seen here. But tonight, having added a few fingers of grappa to her usual intake of wine and cognac, she's up to any challenge.

"Get out!" Waving his arms, Max looks like a windup doll. "You could drown!"

"But it's lovely! You should get in, too!" she shouts.

The waves come one after the other. She counts the set as it builds. Four, five, six. The seventh wave dwarfs the others, its torn edges looming over her. She dives under, staying as close to the bottom as she can manage, but the wave tugs her along and she tumbles with the crash. She surfaces to find Max wading out to her, his clothes still on. "Come in!" he shouts. "You could have drowned! What would I do without you?"

It's a good question. What *would* he do? How would he possibly get to America without her? She laughs—at what, she's not sure. Maybe at the futility of it all.

In the shallows he wraps her in his arms and walks her to shore. They scramble up the boulders, find a smooth slab, and, with their clothes as a mattress, make love.

Wet and naked in the open air, she feels brazen, unabashed, and she keeps her eyes open, marveling at his sinuous arms and chest, how they shine with moonlight. He is focused, and altogether too quick for her taste, but she takes her time on the rock afterward, staring up at the moon. And then a smell wafts over them. The wind must have changed. Their most rapturous moment, they realize, laughing, took place on the town latrine.

They rinse their clothes and bodies in the shallows and walk back to the hotel, where they shower, separately. The next morning she leaves the items for the hotel's laundry service along with an extra tip, hoping the whole mess is not a sign of things to come.

Leonora, July 1941, Monte Estoril, Portugal

A tiny place at the water's edge, *O Gato Azul* is packed, tonight being the birthday of a certain illustrious toreador, here with his adoring entourage. Huddled around a table by the dance floor, the couples—Leonora and Renato, Peggy and Max, Kay and Laurence—make their own scene, speaking over the music and one another. Though Leonora hasn't said more than five words to Peggy—*Thank you for inviting me*—and Peggy hasn't said much to her either. Her back to Max, Peggy talks with Renato, laughing loudly when he says anything approaching humorous. Max ignores her, whispering in Leonora's ear about another dream he's had—something about finding himself inside an eggshell and painting onto the shell a door, which as it turned out opened into their bedroom in Saint-Martin. She lets him talk—she's still here for him, after all—but she can feel Peggy hating her. Her jealousy forms a knot between Leonora's shoulder blades. Why did Peggy invite her, she wonders, sipping her whiskey on ice and doing her best to relax. As Max talks, she watches the toreador, a young, swarthy fellow with broad shoulders and a wonderful smile. He reminds her of José. Standing in the center of the dancing bodies, he spins a girl out and back in, and then there is another girl. He is juggling them, and having so much fun that when he asks her to dance, she doesn't refuse.

The band strikes up a new song. "Every honey bee fills with jealousy when they see you out with me," the guitarist croons. The toreador spins her and the room blurs. As they teeter like a boat on wind-whipped water, she glances back at the table. At one end, Max sits alone, sucking his drink through a straw. Peggy is extending her hand, asking him to dance, but he doesn't budge, so she turns to Renato instead. They dance, and Laurence and Kay join them.

The floor is seething. Sweat slips down Leonora's neck to the small of her back. Renato swings Peggy into his arms, but his eyes, she sees, are fixed on the toreador. At the end of the song, he pulls him away from Leonora and exchanges words with him. She can't quite hear them, and they're speaking in Spanish, anyway, but their puffed up chests say it all. She and Renato have not been married a week, and already he's territorial. It's absurd. But she can't bring herself to confront him. She feels too fragile—any amount of conflict makes her panic.

She watches Peggy step between the men. "Come, let's get some air," she says loudly, taking Renato's hand. And since the band is on break, the rest of their little party grab their drinks and join them on the balcony.

Leonora breathes the ocean air. The breeze is wonderful, and she lifts her skirt to feel it better.

"Well, what will we do now?" says Kay, lighting a cigarette. "Don't let's be the boring sort."

"How about a story," says Renato. "Nora, *querida*?"

Max's eyes widen. That was his name for her. Watching him slump, resting his head on his hand, she wishes she and Renato hadn't come. Peggy settles in beside Max, a self-satisfied grin on her face. She threw this party to torture him, Leonora sees now.

"*Por favor?*" Renato tilts his head, draws a finger across her shoulder.

She winces. "I don't know," she says, glancing at Max. He looks so hurt, she feels terrible.

"She finished it just this afternoon," Renato tells Kay. "And it's wonderful, truly. A pure delight."

"Fine." Leonora takes her notebook from her bag. "We'll see if I can read my own writing. It's gotten even worse since—" Nervous suddenly, she laughs, coughs, and then she finds her voice.

Story with a Minotaur in It

They say he terrifies the ladies of the manor. He does not terrify me.

It's true, he does not know how to sip tea from a china cup. The Earl Grey dribbles from his chin, and when he's fed up with the dull idiocy of manners, he eats the cup, and the saucer, too.

He sleeps in the day, and at night he walks between the hedgerows. He is white as the moon, with white horns, and he glows with his own light. I can see him from my window. He moves about the garden in a clockwise manner, and then he turns and retraces his steps. He is searching for someone who vanished—a woman he still loves.

She was the only daughter in a family of all sons, so her parents watched her and paid servants to watch her, too. She'd been prone to headstands since she was a small girl, and too much blood to the head leads to obdurate ways. She was seventeen, and all her mother could talk about was her presentation at court—who would design her dress, and which eligible men would attend. Dreading the party, the girl dreamed of her own naked body on a huge, silver platter, of being injected with a tranquilizer and unable to move while the men took their forks and knives in hand and cut into her thighs and breasts as if she were a broiled bird. When they reached her heart, they divided it in equal portions. "Delicious," they agreed. "The perfect meal."

The nightmares did not relent, and soon she couldn't sleep at all. Instead, she roamed the garden.

She first saw him beside the lake. He sat at the end of the dock, watching his image ripple the black water. He could have done anything with her that he wanted, his dark eyes told her as much, but she didn't scream. And when a tear fell between her bare toes, he knew he loved her.

Every night she came to see him, and he taught her the ways of the occult—how to bring her dreams into the daylight, and how to

journey to the past by sitting cross-legged on the ground, closing her
eyes, and counting backward while peeling a hard-boiled egg in an
unbroken spiral.

   He always woke as the sun set, and then he would look for her.

   It was the end of September and the flowers had shriveled and
fallen. He rubbed his eyes open and saw her with the man to whom
she was engaged. He was old-fashioned with his top hat and his
monocle, and although he was young, he leaned on a cane, coughed
into a handkerchief, and squinted at the garden and the sky as
if nature itself were not to be trusted. The diamond on her finger
caught the last of the sunlight and sent it back to her minotaur. He
thought of the tear between her toes, how it had twinkled, and he
knew this was goodbye. He watched her turn, watched the door
close behind them. And he cried out, but the wind was against him,
and it sent his grief far out to sea.

   It's been fifty years, and still he waits. Sometimes he sits by the
lake and peels an egg. Perhaps, missing him, she will do as he taught
her. Perhaps one night he'll open his eyes and she'll be young, and
sitting beside him.

   Praying mantids nest in his hair. They flutter their dusty wings
and try to console him.

In the wake of her story, everyone is quiet. There's only the sound
of the waves. Max won't look at her. She shouldn't have read it. The
grieving minotaur was too much for him.

   "Breton would love it," he says at last. "You've humanized his be-
loved minotaur."

   She closes her notebook. It's all too painful, too raw. Her chest
aches, and the moon, swaying on the water, is more lonely than she
can bear.

   "Well, I'm off," says Kay. "Fantastic story." She kisses Laurence
on both cheeks, and to the rest she gives a little wave, throwing her

pocketbook over her shoulder. "I'm writing the very end of my novel. I can see it now. Thank you, Leonora!"

If Kay is escaping this sad party, so can Leonora. "I have to visit the loo," she announces, heading back into the club.

"So do I," she hears Peggy chime, as the door swings shut behind her.

In the ladies' room, Leonora and Peggy pee in neighboring stalls. Leonora recognizes her black patent pump, her bony ankle. They say nothing. Peggy's dislike for her is palpable, so why did she need to join her in the bathroom?

At the mirror, Leonora fumbles in her purse for a lipstick and Peggy takes a long time washing her hands. A woman stands between them, dabbing powder onto her nose. As soon as she leaves, Peggy shuts off the faucet, dries her hands with a small white towel, and addresses Leonora with a directness that surprises her. "If you love him, why aren't you with him?"

"Max?"

"You don't think I mean Renato, do you?" Dropping the towel in the bin, Peggy crosses her arms over her chest. "Either return to him and make him happy—or let him have his life with me. Do you know the pain you're causing him, coming and going?"

Peggy's wearing a dress with a pattern of birds and flowers, yet there's something formal about her. She reminds Leonora of the women she met at the various balls. She's made a claim and she means to defend it. And then Peggy blurts "I love him," blurts it sloppily, with such transparency Leonora feels ashamed. She hadn't known they were together. Or had she just not wanted to admit it to herself?

"Leave him to me," Peggy says. "I beg you."

Leonora backs up, toward the door. "Of course. I didn't realize you two were—" She has her hand on the knob. "I'm sorry, I saw him out of pity," she says, though she knows it isn't quite true.

Pushing past her Peggy opens the door and holds it for her. "Thank you," Peggy says, so sincerely Leonora is afraid Peggy's knees might buckle under the weight of her gratitude. She grabs Peggy's hand. Leading her to the patio, she decides she'll give Peggy to Max. And then she'll walk away, leaving them together, and this mess will be over.

On the patio, Laurence is talking loudly, slurring his words. "Just wait. New York will be the next artistic mecca. Breton. Duchamp. And as soon as we arrive," he slaps Max on the back, "the whole scene will explode."

Peering down at Max, Leonora squeezes Peggy's hand. Max looks up at her, with his crumpled shirt, his crumpled smile. She hates to hurt him, but she's doing the right thing. After all, she's married to Renato now. She nudges Peggy toward him and backs up. But she can't bring herself to leave. She has to see how the scene will end. So she lingers in a dark corner of the balcony by a far door.

"What was that?" he asks Peggy, who is crying. "What did you do?"

Renato stands, his chair toppling backward. "Where did my wife go?" he says, draining the rest of his brandy. *My* wife? As if she were no more than a possession? Stunned, Leonora doesn't make a sound. They are lit by the moon, and in the shadow she is invisible.

"Your wife?" Max says.

"We were married Tuesday. Didn't she tell you?"

Max looks like he's been slugged in the stomach. Leaning over the railing of the patio, he vomits onto the rocks below. Leonora feels her own stomach turn, as if this whole, horrible scene were somehow her fault.

Peggy stands beside Max, rubbing his back. "I told her to stop seeing you. If she loves you, she should be with you or leave you to me."

"What?" He knocks her hand off him with such force that Leonora flinches. "What gives you the right?" Peggy bursts into sobs, but he holds her by the shoulders. "You will find her right now. Do you understand? Find her and tell her you were wrong. Tell her I'm lost without her. Tell her she must see me whenever and wherever she can. Tell her, or I won't have a thing to do with you, not a thing."

Hearing this, Leonora feels weirdly disembodied. She had dreamed of his loving her this singularly, above all the others. And now his love is too late.

Peggy nods, dries her eyes, and goes inside to look for her. He collapses in a chair.

"What was all that?" Renato asks. "I missed something."

"It's all wrong," Max says.

Renato drinks the dregs from her glass of whiskey, brown and watery, the ice having melted long ago. "And where is Leonora?" he asks. She holds very still, willing him not to see her.

"Dancing with the toreador, most likely," says Laurence, pouring himself more wine.

"Well, it's time we go. This excitement is not good for her. Not good at all." *Really?* she thinks. *Because he's my husband now, he assumes he knows what's best for me?* But as she clutches her hands together to keep them from shaking, a part of her wonders if maybe he's right.

Getting to his feet, Max blocks Renato from the door. "She only married you to get away from her father. You have no right to tell her what she can and can't do." Renato's fist is clenched, and she's afraid he'll hit Max, but she still can't say anything. Max wants her to be free, but isn't his desire for her freedom itself a kind of claiming? And what does *she* want? It had been her choice to marry Renato, she reminds herself.

Renato takes a step back. He is calm, abruptly sober. "I am her husband, Max. A role which, from what I understand, you have never been very good at. I plan to protect her, to get her to America. Now will you kindly get out of my way?"

Max lets him pass. It wasn't fair, what Renato said, and she'd like to tell Max so, but she doesn't want to make him hopeful. She watches him sit down and light a cigarette. He's looking out at that lonely moon on the ocean when she inches open the door, slipping into the steamy bar.

The band is playing, and she weaves through the warm, dancing crowd. Renato is talking to the toreador again, but now he's relaxed, laughing at something he's said. She puts her hand in his, tugging him toward the door.

"Take me home," she tells him. "I'm spent."

Max, July 1941, the Clipper, Lisbon

Having never flown before, Max didn't expect to be so anxious. When Peggy bought a bottle of laudanum for the occasion, he laughed at her, but the pre-flight whiskey has done nothing to calm his nerves, and now that the Clipper, a kind of boat-plane, is prepared to lift off from the water, he asks her for it.

"One dropper goes a long way," she says with a slow raise of her eyebrows and a dreamy smile. He squeezes the dark liquid onto the back of his tongue and swallows. It's bitter and he coughs as it slips down his throat, but in a moment all of the edges are rounder, smoother. Peggy in the seat beside him is beautiful with her eyes closed. And as the Clipper accelerates, as he feels the thrust of propulsion pressing on his chest, pressing his head to the seat, he remembers his good fortune. How lucky he is that Peggy took a liking to his art and to him. It could have turned out otherwise.

They are off the water, lifting into the sky. He presses his forehead to the glass, the way he did as a child against the pane of a train's window. Had his father been beside him? His mother? There had been a warm, large body, a feeling of protection. And what town had they traveled to? It is lost to him, the way his family is lost, and Germany, too—he ran off without looking back, left it all behind him so long ago that when he thinks of it now it seems like someone else's life.

Up and up, he's flying. For the first time, he's moving through air. The plane tilts and he sees the blue fabric of ocean fluttering, a boat moving through its whipped peaks, leaving a wake like the tail of a giant fish. Peggy leans toward him and peers through the window. "Leonora left today, didn't she? I'd bet you anything that's her boat."

"Yes," he says. "I imagine it is."

She is bringing his paintings with her. It is as if that part of him that is real—his soul and dreams and imagination—were down there with her, safe on water rather than joggling through the flimsy air.

His latest canvas just dry enough to roll, he brought her everything, eighteen canvases—old and new. He entrusted them to her. It was a practical matter. There wasn't room for them on the Clipper, each passenger allotted only a suitcase and a tote, but he likes the fact of Leonora carrying his paintings, shepherding them across the ocean.

In her kitchen, watching her kneel on the floor in her long skirt to fit them one at a time in her trunk, beside her own paintings, the ones he'd rescued from Saint-Martin, he felt himself relax in a way he hadn't in a very long time. Once again, their lives were entwined. She had stood then, and hugged him—a real hug, the first since the long separation. Pressed to her chest, he had wished he could die. It is how he wants to die, he thinks as he drifts to sleep, he wants to be annihilated by her wondrous swamp of a heart.

Leonora, July 1941, en route to America

Leonora stands alone on the deck. Renato has befriended another man, a younger, very handsome French fellow, and he's gone inside to drink with him at the bar. Leaning against the railing, she looks at the great sweep of water, where it bends into the far, low clouds.

West. This is how it feels to travel west, toward freedom. The wind lifts her skirt, lashes her hair into her eyes and mouth. She twists the whole mess into a bun she hopes will hold. She means to see where she is going, to look as far ahead as she can.

High above, a huge plane floats past. The Clipper. It has to be. Following the plane into the bright sky, her eyes fill. For all her insistence on separation, Max and she are leaving for America in tandem. The horse on the water and the bird in the air.

Thinking of the finality of it all, how she might not return, she realizes she has to see Europe once more. She thought she was ready to not look back, thought she was that white horse from her self-portrait, leaping out the window of her nursery into the wide world, but now she's making her way to the back of the ship, weaving through the crowd of men and women and children. She wants to watch the continent retreat, watch it become a speck of brown before it turns into the pure blue of memory. She thinks of Mother and her brothers, and whether she'll see them again. She thinks of Father, who was right about one thing. Never will her shadow darken his doorway. She will live on another continent, an ocean between them.

Having reached the stern, she sits on a bench and takes a pencil, a sketchbook from her purse. Absently, she draws a horse, a pony. At her heart, a sort of flowering star takes shape, and through her high legs, one figure chases another. They are small and light, barely visible forms, with the sort of bodies that can move through walls. One carries in her hand an egg and around the other spheres and spirals revolve.

A gull hovers behind the boat, riding the current of air. It lands on the rail and cocks its head at her. She takes a biscuit from her purse, breaks off a corner, and tosses it to him.

Leonora in the Morning Light

At the LaGuardia Marine Air Terminal, Max is the first off the plane. The Clipper was an air-conditioned nightmare, with Kay and Peggy snapping at each other like dehydrated turtles, everyone tight on gin and tonics, everyone breathing one another's smoke. But now he is free. He's walking on land again.

Peggy catches up with him as they are funneled inside the waiting room. The press of people, the air hot and close. He searches the sea of faces, sees Jimmy before Jimmy sees him. His hands clasped in front of him, his small smile, how like his mother he seems. And yet, he is without her fortitude. It's as if he inherited the fragility at the heart of both of them. Or maybe it has to do with Max not having been there. The boy was fatherless—but no longer. Max waves and Jimmy comes running.

"You must be Jimmy," Peggy says, pulling him in for a hug.

He blushes. "Your paintings have arrived!" he says brightly. Turning to Max, he opens his arms, and Max feels sick with guilt. It should have been Lou who got to America first, not Max.

A man steps between them as another seizes Max from behind. Immigration officers surround them. There are flashes. Cameras shoved in their faces, snapping hungrily. The press got word? He could collapse with the weight of it all. But then, it just might help his paintings to sell, he thinks bitterly.

"What's the bail? I'll pay it!" Peggy cries. But there must be a hearing on Ellis Island. Pan American Air cannot be responsible for a citizen of the Third Reich—*who is therefore subject to their laws*—the officer explains, being admitted into the United States without a hearing.

"You can't hand him over. He's Hitler's enemy! He'd be locked up, he'd be killed!" Peggy shouts as he's hurried away.

In the back of a car, squeezed between two officers sweating in their blue suits, he's a prisoner once more. *But this is America*, he thinks, numbly. *At least that is something.* And Leonora is on her way. This last thought more thrill than consolation. My God, how his body still rushes at the thought of her!

The car turns, and he's sure he'll be sick. "Pardon me," he says. He doesn't know enough English to explain in detail, but the officer must see the look on his face because he rolls down a window just in time. Leaning over him in a rush, Max takes a deep breath of the outside air, and the officer grumbles something in English and switches seats with him.

The city smells of automobiles in the way no European city does. It is a blur of black and white and gray, the people vivid specks like confetti on the sidewalk, coming in and out of the buildings. A woman in a yellow dress, with a wide, white sun hat, who stops to bask in the sun. A man with a leaf-green tie. Children running after each other, lavender and fuchsia and mint. As if a carnival has come and gone and left its merry, faded trash in the dust, he thinks. But then he's feeling sorry for himself. The truth is that these New Yorkers are hopeful, he realizes with a sort of awe. The war is far away from them across the giant pond. It has always been very far away.

He looks up, tries to see the tops of the skyscrapers, which seem to have come from some stark and inevitable future, but they are too high, the sun too sharp on their windows.

The ferry to the island is calmer, peaceful even. He is again immersed in the blue to which he's become accustomed, and the ocean air is cool and clean. He can see the Statue of Liberty as he couldn't from the Clipper, her torch raised in a toast given to the States by the French—the French who interned him. Half a year of his life behind barbed wire. The reason he lost Leonora. What right has he to hope? And yet, he's so close. They can't send him back, not with Jimmy here, working with the Museum of Modern Art, not with Peggy, with her love for him and her money. He's going to be all right.

On the island, he's met by a young officer with a round, pink face who ushers him toward the building. He takes a deep breath of the sea air and walks inside. Dense with people and a mess of languages, Ellis Island is a shock he didn't prepare himself for. A sour smell swamps him. It's hot, and he thinks he must waver, because the officer slows, looking at him. Does he need help? He shakes his head. He does not.

They step inside a great hall. The officer gestures upward, as if showing him the high, domed ceiling and the windows, through which the rays of sunlight stream onto the familiar lines of exhausted people. A child wails. This is where the processing happens, he thinks, resigning himself. But thankfully, the officer leads him out and to a dormitory. He shows him to his bed. "We know who you are, sir," he says. "You are a great artist. We have given you a bed by a window. But first, you must eat."

The long tables in the mess hall are full. Since most everyone is eating already, there is only a small line for the food. Warm food. He hadn't thought he was hungry, but as soon as he stands in line, he finds he's famished. Hearing bits of conversations, he welcomes the languages—Dutch, Spanish, Portuguese, and some he can't place. Soon all he will hear is English, a language with the hard edges of German, and without the romance. He sits at a table and tastes the chicken soup. It might not be Café de Flore, but nor is it Camp des Milles.

No. Ellis Island is nothing like Camp des Milles. He has a bed, an actual mattress—thin enough to feel the springs through, but a mattress of any sort beats a hard floor with scraps of hay. And there are toilets with proper plumbing.

He gets to know other Germans, Italians. He even plays chess—which Peggy doesn't play—and realizes how much he's missed it. In fact, there is a strange peace here, away from Peggy and the world.

If anything, in the days he is held, waiting for his hearing, there is too much time to think. Watching the square of sunlight stretch across the dormitory floor, he wonders whether he loved Peggy at one time. When they were first together, in Marseille? He knows he loved how she made him feel. Visible again. But my God, how lucky he is. What if he hadn't been an artist? He'd probably be stuck in Germany now. But then he wouldn't have been labeled a degenerate. His art both damned and saved him.

~&

On the third day, he's taken to the courtroom for his hearing. Peggy and Jimmy are just finding seats when the judge calls Jimmy as a witness and he takes the stand. Seeing his son's big blue eyes and his sweet smile, Max knows he is saved. He has letters of recommendation from the Museum of Modern Art, and the judge looks them over. "And you, Miss Guggenheim, will provide Mr. Ernst with a place to live?"

"I will, Your Honor." She gushes. She has tears in her eyes.

He swallows and finds he is gripping his seat. He's a kid again, a kid at a fair who has gotten on a ride which, as it starts up, he realizes he doesn't want to be on. But it's too late to get off. He's on it. He will have to wait for the ride to run its course.

The judge bangs his little hammer. "You are free to join your friends."

~&

Peggy and Max take rooms at the Shelton, separate, non-adjoining rooms, at the insistence of Jimmy, who reminds her that New York in 1941 isn't like it might have been in the twenties, and it's not Europe, either. They should play it cool. Which is fine by him.

They explore the city, visiting every museum. Apart from the Museum of Natural History and the National Museum of the American Indian he finds the art stale. Even the newer works belong to the time of realism, the time before the first war—as if Dada had never happened. They visit Breton, who is perfectly pleasant, happy to have

Max back in his fold. They see Tanguy and his wife, Kay Sage, who has put Breton and his family up in an apartment and convinced Peggy to give him a monthly two-hundred-dollar stipend.

Peggy is more sparing with the money she allows Max access to. But already he's sold a few paintings. And when she offers Jimmy a job as her secretary, rather than his working in the mailroom at MoMA, Max is able to press a hundred-dollar bill into his palm and tell him to wait, see what's out there before he accepts. But Peggy loves a contest, and she keeps at Jimmy, who is too sweet to refuse. Now that she has her collection at hand, she's begun, with his help, to make up a catalogue. She's determined to find the perfect space for her gallery, and when she does, her catalogue will be ready.

⁓ஃ

Peggy and Max are having their nightly pre-dinner drinks in his room when there's rapping on the door, rapid and emphatic. He feels his heart seize, sure it's an officer come to haul him off. Peggy opens the door to Jimmy, flushed and stuttering. "I saw her! At the drugstore. Leonora was buying aspirin." Max's face goes hot. His palms sweat. He smiles at Jimmy. He's sure Peggy sees his foolish hope, but he doesn't care.

"She gave me her address." He takes a slip of paper from his coat pocket and gives it to him. "She said you should come by tomorrow morning. For your paintings," he adds, prudently.

With that tight grin of hers, Peggy swirls her glass of gin and tonic as though it were wine. "Yes. We can visit before our lunch with Breton. Which is at one tomorrow, if you'll remember."

"Yes," he says. "Perhaps." And for the first time since they landed, he realizes he is happy.

⁓ஃ

Peggy mixes herself a new gin and tonic. "How was your day with Leonora?" she asks.

He's seen Leonora every day for a week, and though he says nothing to Peggy about it, somehow she always knows. And she seems to
bring it up between her second cocktail and her third.

He collapses onto the sofa in a weary, blissful stupor. What should
he tell her? It was beautiful? Transcendent? Should he tell her when
he's in Leonora's presence he floats at least a foot above the pavement?
But she's talking again. She didn't really want an answer. "You know,
you only wear cologne when you are going to meet her."

That night he sneaks over to Peggy's room and her door isn't
locked. But then it's never locked. Their fucking is wild and erratic.
She digs her nails into his arms, his back, and she wants him to look at
her, to tell her he loves her. He says it to have some peace, to return to
the world behind his eyelids where it's Leonora he's with.

"Let's go on a trip," she says when they've finished. She is answered
by the silence of her dark bedroom. But she has Max thinking. Leonora is here, and seeing her is sublime torture. But when he is not in
her presence, he finds New York as cramped and humorless a city as he
did on that drive to Ellis Island. He likes it less, it seems, each day. And
it's August, the heat and the smell of the trash unbearable. "My sister
wants us to visit her in Los Angeles. We'll bring Pegeen and Jimmy.
Maybe we could buy a car out there and drive it back. See the country."

When he tells Leonora about the trip, she is quiet. "I'll miss you,"
she says, and he can see that it's true. "If there's a river, promise me
you'll swim in it?"

~§

Hazel, Peggy's sister, has a house in Santa Monica where Max paints
on the sleeping porch. They visit Man Ray, who lives in Los Angeles
now, and Max meets with a reporter from *Art Digest*, who asks what
sort of American paintings he most admires. When he tells him he
loves the paintings and pottery of the Native Americans, loves how
true the work is, how full of imagination, the reporter refuses to speak
with him further.

"I'm not sure what I said," he admits, afterward, to Peggy, who phones the furious man.

"He didn't mean it as an insult, or some kind of cruel-hearted joke," she tells him. "He truly admires their work."

Max hears shouting through the receiver. "How is that not a snub to American culture?"

But what could be more American, he wonders, than petroglyphs?

———&———

Peggy buys a silver Buick convertible. They leave Los Angeles early in the morning to avoid the midday heat of the Mohave, which, even before ten in the morning, is scalding. Max doesn't mind. The blue sky over the desert is like a dream, its depth entrancing.

But it's Sedona, Arizona, where Max must pull the car over. He can't believe his eyes. In the distance, giant red-and-orange monoliths rise into the blue. "It's straight out of your paintings," Peggy says. Jimmy agrees. And they're right. It's just like the decalcomanias he painted in Saint-Martin, when he was with Leonora, and after Camp des Milles, when he missed her so. Peggy touches his shoulder. It must be one hundred degrees out and he has chills. His teeth ache. It is fate. All of it—Leonora and the war and Peggy—all of it has led him here, to this Surrealist landscape, this place where he knows he'll make a new life, where *they'll* make a life, like they had in Saint-Martin, but without the war. Far below the road, he sees a river, gleaming. He's walking down to it, Peggy calling after him. "You can't be serious, Max! What are we supposed to do? It's a thousand degrees out!"

"Come swim!" he calls back. "Peggy! Jimmy! Pegeen!" But he's moving quickly. Ducking under a scrub oak, he follows an animal trail down to the water. He strips off his clothes and dips into the creek. Clear and cold, it is only waist deep, but he takes a few strokes, drinking as he swims, the water delicious.

Hot and dry, Peggy doesn't speak to him all the way to the Grand Canyon, but he doesn't mind. He's thinking of Sedona. Even the name is beautiful. At the canyon, Peggy, in the dramatic way a child might behave, insists on standing at the edge of the abyss. "Be careful," he tells her. To which she laughs.

"Because what would you do without me. Am I right?"

He leaves her to her histrionics and wanders into a Hopi shop, which is filled with kachina dolls—the Hopi's carved and brightly painted ancestral spirits—so remarkable he's unable to choose between them. He touches the beak of a bird-headed figure, runs his finger along the feathers of its wings. "Why not just get them all," Peggy says when she finds him gawking. "You always end up with what you want one way or another."

She's right. He wants them all.

The new Buick carrying the four of them and all of their luggage is overly full. Even so, they manage to fill every last nook with kachinas.

They drive through New Mexico and Texas and Louisiana, staying just long enough in each state for Peggy to send Jimmy off to the courthouse to inquire about their laws regarding marriage. Max doesn't protest. There's talk of America getting into the war, in which case, unless he is married to an American, he'll once more be an enemy alien. Other than a marriage license, what's to stop them from throwing him into another camp? One flimsy sheet of paper would secure his freedom.

Leonora's studio is the kitchen of their third-floor walk-up on the Upper West Side. In the mornings, after Renato leaves for work, she makes tea to the sound of horns and whining brakes, to motorists screaming at each other—in English, the harshest of languages. She looks down at the blackened heaps of snow at the edge of the sidewalk, at the people hunched in their dark coats walking fast as they can to keep warm. New York is Paris without the romance. It is Lisbon without the colorful mosaics, without the ruins of buildings that give the city such soul. If it reminds her of anywhere, it is of London with all of its cold formalities. Here everything is ordered, the grid of the city stretching out, not so much a maze as a prison. She wanted to like New York. Give it a chance, Jimmy told her. He hated it at first and now he wouldn't live anywhere else. But she's been here more than eight months, and she's only begun one painting. She could claim there's never enough time, but that's not quite right. She's too far off the earth here. She's painting in air.

Her canvas is small. It's on the white tile counter on the stand that also holds her cookbook open, the one from the sixteenth century with a worn leather binding and pages as frail as dried leaves. She bought it from a street vendor one afternoon as Max and she were strolling, and she seems to spend more time cooking from it than she does painting. It isn't easy, certain items—hedgehogs, turtles, the tails of beavers—being difficult to obtain. Not that she'd want to eat turtles or beavers anyway. She's content with substitutions—calf's head for turtles, rabbits for hedgehogs. André and Jacqueline come to dinner, Tanguy and his wife Kay, Max and Marcel Duchamp. She invites Peggy, but Max tells her she's busy looking for a space for her gallery. Somehow she's always busy.

Renato stays home the nights she cooks. He plays husband. Other nights he gets too drunk at the bar and has to sleep on a friend's sofa. Or else he has to be away, he tells her ahead of time, on embassy business.

She tells herself she doesn't care. She likes her solitude, after all. But she doesn't dare paint at night. She's afraid of where she might go, afraid of who might appear in her kitchen. She's not ready to entertain the little glowing people. The city's so hard, metallic and unforgiving—not the kind in which she can afford such visits.

In the mornings, however, she replaces the cookbook with her canvas. She sips her tea, smokes, and dips her brush in the green of English meadows after rain. She paints a groomed countryside. A woman inside a circle, cocooned in a cloth, the way they wrapped the witches when they hung them upside down and forced them to confess. There's a cauldron with stags inside it, their white antlers branching. And there's a subterranean land of bats, more cocooned women, and a bird protecting her eggs. And finally, as part of the aboveground scene, there are two horses, each collared and tied to a tree that grows from the other's tail. They face opposite directions. They are going nowhere.

When Renato asks her what it means, she shakes her head. "It just is," she says, and he lets it lie. Art is something one does, she decides, not something one needs to talk about. It exists without explanation. Everyone will have their own interpretation anyway.

Of course this new theory excludes the opinions of Max, whom she can't wait to show it to—perhaps today, if she can finish the pear tree before he arrives, it might be ready.

She still sees him often, in spite of his being Peggy's husband now. He married her right after Pearl Harbor. He had to. Then the FBI took him in for questioning, and thank God he was married to an American or he'd have been locked away again. They moved in together—

Peggy, Max, Jimmy, and Pegeen—moved into a three-story house on the Hudson where Max has a big studio filled with light.

The bell rings. She puts down the brush. Christ. She's every bit as in need of his approval as she was in Paris and Saint-Martin. After all their time apart, it's as if nothing has changed. She covers the painting with a sheet and just as quickly pulls it off. She can't help it. She has to know what he thinks.

When she shows him, he's silent for so long she wants to cover it again. "Let's go," she says, tugging at his sleeve. "It's not done yet anyhow."

"No. It's powerful. The subterranean world is completely Surrealist. It's your own vision. It's brilliant, Nora, but—"

"Yes?" Here it comes. His real opinion.

"For all your running, you're still holding on to England—to some notion that you're not free."

And to you, she thinks.

"Do you feel trapped here?" Max asks. "We could move—to Sedona. The red cliffs and the wide, blue sky. You can feel the earth there."

"Max—"

He takes her face in his warm, fierce hands and turns her to him, slowly. He kisses her. This time she lets him. And she feels the old, wild stirring. It terrifies her.

She pulls away and holds his hands to stop hers from shaking. "I'm famished," she says. "Take me to lunch?"

—⚭—

Weeks pass before she sees him again. She has a cold she says when he calls, or possibly the flu. But now she phones him. She's recovered, she lies, enough to attend the meeting, one of Breton's, to be held at Max and Peggy's new home.

She's been there once before, for the housewarming—a soiree that spun itself into a hot froth toward the wee hours of morning. At some point in the night Max sold a painting to the queen of striptease, Gypsy Rose Lee, and when Peggy protested that he sold it for too little, he gave Gypsy another painting as an anniversary gift. The house seemed like a blank canvas that night, as if the guests, escapees from Europe mixing with eccentrics of New York, if given a shake, could make some new, explosive compound. The war might have brought them all together, but it wasn't going to hurt them here. They could be loud and absurd. They could scream and laugh in the same breath if they wanted to—which was just what Peggy did, while Leonora tucked herself into a corner and played a quiet game of chess with Ozenfant, who'd ended up in New York as well and seemed very glad to see her.

Today, under the heavy sky, the house looks solemn and defiant, its collar raised, its chin up. She knocks on the black, lacquered door. When no one comes, she tries the knob and, since it is unlocked, lets herself in.

She's looking for the living room, but finds herself wandering from one floor to another. Nothing about the house seems to be Max's. No cement figures grow from the walls, and there aren't any murals. The rooms don't seem lived in, exactly. It's like he's still in flight, the way she is. And then she finds his studio. The door is open and she walks inside.

The ceiling is high, the walls white. Huge windows look out on the gray, industrial river. Nothing like the Loire in Ardèche, nothing you'd want to swim in. But the water reflects the meek sunlight, the first of the day, and there's something hopeful about it. Dust motes swirl in the bright, lazy air. Kachinas crowd a shelf. The carved spirit guardians from Arizona. Painted red, black, turquoise, and yellow, the kachinas are geometrical and otherworldly. They remind her of miniatures of Max's sculptures. This studio, she sees, is where he lives, where he dreams. The paints on his palette are fresh. She touches one finger to cerulean blue, another to madder brown. Sky and earth.

The big canvas on the easel has its back to the door, and she walks around it to look. The image takes her breath, it's so like *The Robing of the Bride*. There's that liquid blue sky, like the sky in Saint-Martin. There's the woman in the red cloak of decalcomania, with a breast exposed, a swell of belly. And there's her face. Once again. And then she sees the paintings leaning against the wall. The scenes are different, but in each of them the woman in the red cloak is the same. She shuffles backward until the far wall holds her up. It's unsettling, seeing herself in such a light, multiplied and repurposed. Simplified. No crease between her brows, her forehead smooth, unworried.

If Gala had it right, if it's enough to be the muse of the great man, why is she sucking the paint from the tips of her fingers, as if the bitter, toxic oil might spark some fire of creation inside her? A room with light. A method, a mythology. It's clear. She wants what Max has.

"Are you lost, dear?" Peggy blocks the doorway. She strides toward her, baring her teeth in what must be an attempt at a smile. "Admiring yourself?"

"Oh, no, no, I—" What can she say? She didn't ask him to paint these.

"He won't paint a single picture of me. But it seems he can't stop painting you."

Leonora moves around the easel and Peggy follows her, herding her toward the door. Seeing the painting Max gave her in Saint-Martin, *Leonora in the Morning Light*, she stops. He wanted her to take it when they first got to New York, but she insisted he should keep it, just a bit a longer, this part of them. "He refuses to sell it, you know. Someone was interested, and Lord knows he needs the money. He says it belongs to you." She's more resigned than angry, and for a moment they just stand there, looking at the painting. Leonora notices her hair, how wild it is, a force in itself. Since she's been in New York, she's worn her hair back, curls combed and closer to her head. She's been tamed, she thinks, sadly. The war has tamed her. And if she's being honest, that tiny skeleton caught in the bramble still frightens her a little.

Jimmy rushes in. He's wearing a crumpled brown suit and a red bow tie, and looks, for a moment, like a younger version of Max. He stops short when he sees Leonora. "Duchamp is on the phone for you," he says to Peggy. "He found a space on Fifty-Seventh he thinks will be perfect for the gallery."

"Wonderful," Peggy says, rushing past him. She turns, hand on her hip. "Take her to the living room, will you?" Her tone is curt, dismissive. Good God, how she must hate her.

Jimmy smiles, as if embarrassed. "Feeling better?" he asks when she's gone, and for a moment Leonora isn't sure just what he is referring to. Then she remembers—her fake cold.

"Finally," she says, and coughs to clear her throat. As they leave Max's studio, she recognizes the back of a painting leaning on the wall by the door, the small size and how the edge of the canvas is frayed at the top. The way the sunlight hits it, she can see through the canvas— the blue room, the hyena, the white rocking horse hovering over the girl with her swell of hair, her white riding britches stretched across her thighs. When Max tried to give her painting to her, she refused to take it. It was just too tied to her life with him to keep in her possession. If you're going to look forward, she reasoned, you can't also look back.

She and Jimmy walk down the hall in a silence that's not exactly easy. She has the feeling he'd like her better if his father didn't like her so much. "Any word from your mother?" she asks.

He lights up. "Oh, haven't you heard? The American Consulate is issuing her a visa. All she's waiting on now is an exit visa."

"Oh, Jimmy, I'm so very happy," she says and takes his hand and squeezes it, because it needs squeezing, he needs squeezing, and if she's being honest, she does, too.

They walk into the meeting that way, hand in hand. It's a small group. André, Tanguy and Kay, Max, and Luis Buñuel, the filmmaker. Max looks at them and says nothing. Jimmy sits in a chair at his side, and she takes the sofa, beside Luis.

Max is sitting in what can only be described as a throne. She'd heard of the throne from Breton, but she's not seen it until now. The huge armchair reaches a few feet above his head and makes him look like a very spoiled boy. A prince. He is wearing a white fur coat, and the room, as if to accommodate this whim, is freezing.

Luis nods at her as she sits. He has about him a quiet intensity that reminds her of something she can't quite place. She leans back into the sofa and tries to relax, tries to listen to André, who is saying something about Duchamp's show, the one he's curating to aid the French Relief Societies, but she's looking at Max, who won't look at her now. Outside the sun has come out again, and he's backlit. The white fur could pass for feathers. The way he looks reminds her of the portrait she made of him during their last days in Saint-Martin, when he was part fish, part bird, and part man, in that frozen landscape. He's trying to hang on, she thinks. But then she is, too.

She takes her notebook from her bag, and while André talks, she finds she is drawing two lovers embracing so tightly they seem to share one body. Their hair twists into a single knot. Around their waist, she draws a cord encircling them. Like that ring in the painting Max gave her for their first Christmas together—*Bride of the Wind*. The cord encloses the lovers like a circus hoop, like a magic trick, as if it could make them disappear to some place where they could be alone, where they could make their own world. As if it could all happen again. And then, biting her tongue, she draws a pair of scissors, draws them open, about to cut the cord. She looks up to Max staring at her, dog-eyed, and she feels the tears coming, tears she hasn't allowed until now. Blinking them back, she writes the words, which are the hardest part. *This is past, is past.*

Buñuel must notice her drawing. "This is what André has been going on about," he whispers to her. "Only you've said it better."

"What did I say?" she asks.

"Automatism. Connection with the unconscious," he explains, but she's looking at his eyes. They are the eyes of her doctor. It is Don Luis beside her, and he's filling the room with a charge she recognizes as fear. No one else seems to notice, not Tanguy or his wife, who hang on André's every word, not Max, who stares out the window. And she realizes what she feels is *her* fear, rising up, to her mouth. She's afraid she'll be sick. His eyes are pulling her in, they are swallowing her as they did when she lay strapped to that bed.

She rises slowly, so as not to rile her insides. Finding a bathroom down the hall, she locks the door behind her. She flips on the light, and instead of her reflection in the mirror, she sees only the gray wall behind her. She can feel the blood drain from her face. She reaches for the wall and slowly lowers herself into the tub.

Water, she thinks. The river always made her body come to life. It helped her to see clearly. She plugs the drain and opens the faucet all the way. The warm water fills her loafers first. It soaks her trousers and creeps up her blouse as it rises. She turns down the cold and makes the bath as hot as she can stand. She exhales and feels her body and face go under. In the blackness behind her eyelids she sees the paintings Max made of her. Her exposed breasts and belly, her face smooth as a girl's. If she gives her whole self to him again, how will she possibly be allowed to age? How will she become the woman, the artist, she knows she can be? Her breath bubbles to the surface.

She has nothing left. Only herself.

And that is enough. More than enough.

She bolts up, gasping air. She turns off the hot water, turns on the shower, cold only, and she stands in the hot bath letting the icy water run over her. Stretching her arms out, she looks at her hands, at her fingers, wiggling.

She steps from the shower, shivering, but with heat radiating from her chest. Moving past the foggy mirror, she walks into the living room. They are bickering in French, their voices far away, as though they are speaking at the end of a long tunnel. Breton tells Max to stop buying kachinas; Peggy's worried—he's not saving a thing for taxes. Sitting on his throne, a head above everyone, Max speaks softly. Princes don't have to shout. "If she weren't paying you a monthly allowance, we'd have plenty left over for the taxes."

She sits beside Buñuel. "You are an attractive man. You look just like my doctor," she explains, and she realizes she's speaking Spanish.

The men stare at her, their silence stiff and heavy.

Peggy is screaming. "There's a river down the hall! Jimmy! Max! Help me for Christ's sake!" Jimmy hurries to the bathroom, turns the shower off. Peggy is headed for Max when she sees Leonora. "She's soaking the new sofa," she cries, and grabs hold of her arm. "Get up!" Lifting her, Peggy catches Leonora's hair and she yelps. She's on her feet, water pooling around her.

"Don't touch her," Max growls. Taking hold of Peggy's wrists, he tosses her aside.

She's on the floor, glaring up at him. "You can't treat me this way."

It's a horrible scene, but Leonora can't look away.

"It's over, do you hear?" he says, his body clenched and sprung. She stands, glowers.

Jimmy steps between them. "Stop. Both of you. This isn't the place."

Peggy brushes her hair from her face. "I'm having lunch with Marcel," she announces, as if to everyone, and she leaves, slamming the door behind her. Tanguy and Kay have gone, too, it seems, and Buñuel with them.

Breton is still seated, a hint of a smile on his face. "You must write about your experiences, Leonora."

"Nobody can know the inside of a madhouse," she says. "You have to be there to know."

"Exactly," he says.

She hears a car start up outside. Jimmy wraps a towel around her, and Max covers her shoulders with a blanket. Tears slide down his cheeks. He wraps both arms around her, squeezing her to his chest, and his heart is so even and calm she could sleep standing up, she could hide here, in this tower, this dream of union, for a very long time.

But even as she squeezes him back, she knows this is really the end. She has to heal. To become herself again, she's going to have to find out where he ends and she begins, and to do it, she's going to have to take those shears in hand, and snip.

Max, September 1942, New York

Max holds tight to the reins, squeezes the mare's ribs with his knees to not fall off. He's running her as fast as she'll go, and still Leonora's mare is faster. They are flying through a field. On both sides of them the trees are on fire. Indian red, scarlet lake, chrome yellow, and golden ocher. He hasn't seen colors like these since he was a child wandering the forest outside his home. And here he is, a child again at fifty-one. Beside her he's freshly hatched and the world is new.

And then the field ends, as fields must. Her horse slows to a walk, and he catches up. They are moving through woods, through the pulse of afternoon light.

Leonora's hair is an inky bramble of leaves and twigs. She has never looked more beautiful. It's the first time he's seen her in a month. Ever since her episode in the shower she's been distant, finding excuses not to see him, and he's felt unbearably lonely. A dragon of wind turns through the treetops, raining leaves around them. He wishes he could stay here, with her, until the trees are skeletons, until the carpet of leaves turns to snow.

Her black eyes shine. She pitches her voice over the wind. "I can't do this anymore."

"Do what? Ride horses?"

"I can't keep seeing you. I just can't."

The wind dragon sails off to fly through another wood, another field. He need only whisper for her to hear him, but what is there to say?

He tries to open his throat. "Why?"

She shakes her head, slowly, sunk in that world of hers, intricate and untranslatable. "I need time, alone."

"I'll wait for you."

She looks ahead. Her profile gives nothing away. "Don't," she says.

He hears, in the distance, the call of a great horned owl. "But I need you," he says, quietly, though he'd like to scream at her, at the universe, at the god he's never believed in. He's asked her dozens of times. Why can't she be with him again, as they were before? But she answers him with silence, or with riddles of logic. If he could understand, maybe he could let her go. Her mare stoops to nibble a patch of grass, so he lets his eat, too. "Nora, please, tell me why."

She regards him with such tenderness, he thinks, hopes, she might have changed her mind. Her face breaks into a smile—the same free, wild, open smile she gave him when he stopped her beer from overflowing the first night they met. "There are some rooms you can't enter again, however beautiful they might be," she says.

He's baffled. "How can you not be sad?"

"Because right now you're with me. I'll be sad about it later, when there's time."

The sun has dropped below the far hills, just like that.

In its shadow they turn the horses around, head back to the stables. They face the wind, which has turned cold. He has to say something, anything, or the moment will be over, and he's not ready for that.

"What about Sedona? We could make a life like we had in Saint-Martin. It's wild there. Really wild. So much wilderness, a creek, woods and animals, the big sky. You'd love it. You'd be free there." A gust blows between them. His limbs feel so heavy they seem made of cement, like his sculptures.

"It's too late." Her words are thin, dry as the falling leaves.

What remains of his life seems to stretch before him, an empty ocean of wind, and he's petrified. "But I—I finally found you."

"Yes. You did," she says, and she is beaming again. It's the strangest thing. As if she were happy for all of it—the whole unpredictable, star-crossed, glorious journey.

"You did," she says. "And so did I."

They walk to the clearing in silence, and she takes off again, horse and woman becoming one body, hurtling across the field. His mare lurches forward in an attempt to run, but he tugs on her reins, holding her back. This time he won't try to catch Leonora. This time he sits on his horse at the forest's edge, marveling. He watches her go, watches her vanish into the distance and the failing light. *My God*, he thinks, *she is magnificent.*

At the opening of Peggy's third show, Exhibition by 31 Women, she stands on a step stool at the edge of her gallery before the sea of guests. Normally she wouldn't speak at such an occasion—it's a bit like giving a formal address at one's own party, something she wouldn't dream of doing—but Marcel has insisted.

Marcel clinks his champagne glass with a knife and glances about with a careful impatience, precise, the way he always is. Waiting for the room to quiet, she hears her heart throb so loudly in her ears she's afraid everyone else can hear it, too. They are looking at her, the flock of faces. Breton and Jimmy, Marcel and Max, Gyspy Rose Lee and Kay Sage. Leonora and Max's newest protégé, Dorothea Tanning, a pretty blonde from some tiny town in Illinois. The show was supposed to only be thirty women, but after Max saw Dorothea's paintings, he insisted on its being thirty-one. Even now, in front of Peggy and everyone else, he sidles very close to her. He tucks a pink lock of her hair behind her ear. And is that his arm around her waist? People press in front of them and now Peggy cannot tell.

She knows it's her own fault—giving him the show to curate, making him visit the women's studios, handpick their paintings, and drive them to the gallery himself. But then, she knew what she was doing. She knew she wasn't strong enough to be the one to leave.

She pushes the lovely Miss Tanning from her head, smiles at the expectant crowd, and wipes her wet palms on her skirt. Speaking in front of a group always confounds her—it seems like such a pretense—but as soon as she catches her rhythm, she knows she'll be fine. She has no script, no notes. Speeches, like life, are best impromptu.

"I've spent the last twenty years of my life, it seems, falling in love with artists."

A sprinkling of laughter, thank God. She relaxes, takes a breath, wiggles her toes in her pumps. "And to fall in love with an artist means falling in love with his art.

"I say 'his' because when we think of art, we most always think of men. When you hear the terms Dada and Surrealism, what names come to mind? Dalí? Duchamp? Tanguy? Ernst? Well, I suppose I *would* think of Max," she adds, casting a glance his way. More chuckles. Max smiles weakly, embarrassed.

"There is, however, a group of modern artists that has stayed largely in the shadows, not because they are any less interesting, any less worthy of appreciation than the men, but because they are women, and women, we believe, are supposed to be busy doing other things, namely, having babies, cooking, cleaning, being a muse to the men, whatever that is." She notices Breton has a rather cross look on his face. Though he refuses to learn English, she's sure he understood the part about the dubious *muse* business. No doubt she'll hear about it later. For now, she goes on, feeling inexplicably powerful as she makes her point, surprised by the truth of what she is saying.

"We don't expect women to make art, much less remarkable art. The truth is, for women to accomplish anything of worth in the world, they have more hurtles in their path than men do. More walls they must scale. But this effort, this triumph, all too often goes unappreciated. When it comes to art by women, we're accustomed to hearing such comments as, 'that is really something, *for a woman.*' I hope this show will change that misconception.

"As much as I might have liked to ignore the art of these woman— as they are young and beautiful and so adored by all the *male* artists—" She pauses, letting the ripples of laughter subside. "Alas, I have been unable to." Having hit her stride, she fixes her gaze beyond Leonora, beyond the more troublesome Dorothea. "One look around and you will see why." She gestures to her gallery, The Art of This Century, this space she's made, this shrine to art by *living* artists. Her small contribution.

"This is a show by thirty-one major artists of our time—artists who all happen to be women. And I am proud to host the first showing of its kind in the world. I am very grateful to Marcel Duchamp for giving me the idea, and to Max Ernst for his *hard* work seeing that it came to fruition."

Did she put too much emphasis on *hard*? Why should she give a damn? As the crowd shatters into applause, she sees that Max's arm is, in fact, around Dorothea's tiny waist. Grinning at her, he glows. And Peggy knows their marriage is over. She has lost him.

She looks to Marcel, marvelous Marcel, standing taller even than usual, as if he were truly pleased. He lifts his glass.

"To Peggy," he says, and the flutes of champagne trill.

Leonora, January 1943, New York City

Leonora clinks her glass with Max and Dorothea. "Cheers," she says. "To Peggy!"

Dorothea smiles vaguely, sipping her champagne and not quite meeting her eye. Beside her Max grins, incandescent. She hasn't seen him like this since those weeks they spent at Lambe Creek, and later, at times, in Saint-Martin. When he told her he planned to take Dorothea to Sedona, to live and make a life, she was happy for him. He never *has* been one to waste any time. But now, seeing them hand in hand, brighter by each other's light, she feels queasy. She needed to leave him, needed to rely on herself. She just didn't think it would be this hard.

She excuses herself, kisses Dorothea's and Max's cool cheeks. Walking away, she feels so heavy she thinks she'll sink through the floor. There's a knot in her throat she tries to swallow. She knows she'll never love anyone the way she loves Max.

She wanders from painting to painting, some of them familiar, others delightfully new. There are pieces by Kay Sage, Meret Oppenheim, and even Gypsy Rose Lee. One thing about Peggy, she doesn't hold a grudge. And how wonderfully she's arranged it all. The room itself is a work of art, with its curved walls of cork, its wood ceilings and floors. The paintings suspended on cables so they float in air.

She happens on her own piece, *The Horses of Lord Candlestick*, the painting Peggy bought from her in the winter of '38. Looking at the green mare lodged in a tree, terrified to find herself so far from the ground, Leonora wants to lift her from the tree. To put her on the earth and let her run.

Above her painting hangs Fini's *The Shepherdess of the Sphinxes.*
She's never seen it before, and she can't help but think the black-
haired sphinx looks an awful lot like her. The old her. In the painting,
the sphinx is soft, but sure, with a half-curious, half-mocking, backward glance past her tail at the viewer. A staff in her hand, the shepherdess, unmistakably Fini, stands behind her, protecting. And with
the flock of bare-breasted sphinxes around her, how could Leonora
possibly come to harm? She feels a chill, as if someone opened a door.
All along she had a shepherdess at her back, and here was the proof.

She can hear Breton behind her, speaking with Peggy. "I don't care
if Max loves her. Leonor Fini is beneath you," he says in French. Leonora smiles. Some things never change. Were Fini here rather than in
Monte Carlo, she'd have a thing or two to say.

Breton takes Leonora's arm in his. "Come, I have something to
show you."

"Just a moment," she tells him. She touches Peggy's shoulder.
Peggy turns to her, a little startled and, she thinks, hopeful somehow.
"The show is spectacular," Leonora says.

"Yes," says Peggy. "It's really something, isn't it?" And then she's
talking to someone else, talking up the very painting Breton said was
beneath her.

Leonora finds him at the bar, exchanging his empty Manhattan for
a fresh one. She orders a whiskey on the rocks. "Have you heard," he
says, "Lee is a war correspondent now. She's out with the U.S. Army,
photographing God knows what horrors."

She sips the whiskey, feeling its heat spread through her. "I always
knew she'd do something amazing," she says, aware of just how different they are. The war terrified Leonora, and she came unhinged inside
that fear. And here's Lee, setting off into the thick of it, fearless and
determined, a modern Joan of Arc. She reminds her of another strong
woman, Lou, and she asks André if he's heard anything.

He sighs and shakes his head, looking at the floor. "No one's heard a thing." In November, when Hitler's troops moved into Vichy, Jimmy was wrecked. Any chance of getting his mother out of France was gone. "Let's hope she's well hidden," Breton says.

He walks Leonora to the end of the gallery, where a painting hangs alone, small and potent, like a magnet. At the center sits a woman, a pair of shears in her hand. Her hair is short. She looks like a man, but the suit she wears is three sizes too big. Surrounding her is an empty vista, strewn with the cut locks of her hair. Grief. Accomplishment. A calm determination.

"Frida Kahlo," André says. "*Plus charmante*. I met her in Mexico City with Trotsky and Diego, her husband, ex-husband now. He had an affair with her younger sister, apparently. I can't say this painting is my favorite of hers. I much prefer her self-portraits when she's dressed in her festive Mexican attire and her hair is long. Ah," he says. Hardly taking a breath, he turns to Kay as she passes. "*Mademoiselle* Sage, there's something I must show you." And like that, André whisks her off.

As Leonora looks at the painting, the room, the clatter of voices, of ice in the glasses, fades. She reads the painted words above the portrait, *Mira que si te quise, fué por el pelo, Ahora que estás pelona, ya no te quiero*. "See, if I loved you, it was for your hair, Now you're bald, I don't love you anymore." There are musical notes beneath the lines. It's a verse of a song. She feels that knot in her throat again, feels the tears bubble up from some deep source, a spring that was blocked so long ago she forgot it was there. She wipes her cheeks with the sleeve of her blouse, but the gesture is useless. Beyond containment, her whole body trembles. With each heave of emotion, her shoulders lift up in that ridiculous way she wept when she was a child. This woman, Frida Kahlo, painted her anguish. Raw and plain, without a vestige of disguise it hangs here, for everyone to see. She hides nothing. To become the master, she has killed the muse. It is that simple.

Someone taps her on the shoulder. It's Renato, who said he wouldn't make it here tonight.

"I'm ready to go," she says.

"But *cariño*, I just got here."

"To Mexico," she tells him. "I'm ready to move to Mexico."

Epilogue

Max is up with the birdsong, up a little at a time, as if rising from the floor of an ocean he can breathe inside, rising in slow motion, with all the sea creatures still around him, into the light and the air. He opens his eyes to the girl beside him—moon-faced when she sleeps. Dorothea. American as pie, strong and thrifty, practical. Traits that remind him of Lou, only now, at fifty-two, he is ready, finally, to settle, to ground, to let the world go its own way, or to come to him if it pleases, the way it did that miraculous summer in Saint-Martin, with Lee and Roland, Man and Ady, with Leonor Fini visiting and deciding to stay for a time.

Dorothea and Max are here through the summer, but already they've begun to make plans, and Dorothea's made her lists—the house they'll build, its grounds full of sculptures, and what must be wrapped up before they can pull up their roots and move here. Luckily, their New York roots are shallow. Even divorcing Peggy shouldn't be that hard. Having wasted no time moving on, she seems only too happy to be rid of him.

He kisses the smooth skin of Dorothea's forehead and walks naked from the cabin into the dazzling sunlight. Standing on a slab of stone, he pees onto the rocks and shrubs and the long grasses below him. This cabin is the only building around and below them the creek shines like a snake made of sky winding through the stones and red sand and disappearing around the bend. Sitting on the stone, feeling the sun soak into his skin and feed him, he grows peaceful as a plant.

In the blue distance, the spires of red rock glow, and he has the distinct feeling he's inside one of his paintings, one from the Saint-Martin years, one with Leonora in it. It's still hard to think of her, to think that he may never see her again, but being in Sedona, he has the sense she is near—as if at any moment she might come wandering down the creek, might walk barefoot across the river rocks and offer him a drink of cold, clear water in her cupped hands.

Against the sky the spires huddle, a council of elders. Creased and crumbling, formed of wind and water and time, these spires are wise with the indifference of those who persist, their red sandstone giving way to the palest yellow as they rise into the blue.

He can feel the earth growing hot already, can feel himself sweating in the sun. He breathes the dry air. Maybe this is how one learns to trust the world again, the world which is still here, after all, quiet and pulsing.

Above him, three ravens circle, rising on a thermal updraft. Hopping across a boulder, a canyon wren stops and cocks its head at him. A moth hangs from its mouth, its wings still fluttering. The wren flies into a crevasse, and the cries of its babies soar into the open air.

Leonora, May 1943, Mexico

Their ship hugs the coast. It's just after dawn and Leonora is drinking tea on deck as mist clings to the land like a dream almost remembered, like the breath of a thousand horses dissolving with the sun, which, as it rises, feels as fierce as it did that last summer in Saint-Martin, when she worked in her garden until she became pure and burnished and strong.

Renato is in one of the cabins, having found a game of poker to pass the hours. But she's spent every minute she's not sleeping or eating on the deck. It makes her queasy to be inside too long, and more than that, she wants to experience the distance she's crossing, to know it in her body, to feel herself change with the landscape.

Mexico is a dense, green country, feeding off the very air, a soup so warm and thick she can taste it. Soil and snails, leaves decomposing in a light rain. The hot breath of lizards and the glistening eggs of frogs. Blossoms singing soft vowels with their throats wide open. In this air her hair has come alive, a being all its own, rippling and restless, whisked every which way at the whim of the briny wind. Her skin is so moist she feels as if flowers could sprout from the insides of her elbows, from the backs of her knees, from the thin skin behind her earlobes and from the hollows of her collarbones.

~ॐ

They settle in the old center of Mexico City. Vacant and dilapidated, it is where they can afford rent. Built by the Spaniards in the sixteenth century on top of the ruins of the Aztec capital, Tenochtitlán, it gives one the feeling of being between centuries and cultures. And in a room in their apartment, which is in the deserted Russian Embassy building, she sets up her studio. The grand bones of the building are still intact, and her studio has a high, arched ceiling, and carved doors that lead onto a balcony.

The morning is cloudless, and she opens the wooden doors, welcoming the light and the trickster wind that gusts without warning, stirring the humid air into eddies that carry candy wrappers, bits of paper, leaves, and the pale petals of blossoms high above the buildings. It's spring still, but her studio is warm. She kicks off her shoes. Her skirt sticks to her thighs, and strands of hair cling to her neck. She twists the whole unruly mass into a knot on her head—not smooth or neat, but it holds.

She unpacks her trunk, gathers her brushes and paints. She assembles an easel Renato bought her just yesterday, along with a roll of canvas and boards for her to stretch it on. She's stretched one canvas already, nearly two by three feet, big enough, she figures, to contain intricacies and multitudes, and now she sets it on the easel and screws it tight. She has a little table for her paints, an earthen jug for her brushes, a wooden palette, jars for turpentine. She has all she needs, but the room is too clean, just yet, to actually paint in. If she knew what she wanted to paint, she might feel differently. But she doesn't know. Such ideas must come to you, she thinks. It isn't as if you can just go out and find them.

She takes more things from the trunk—Max's collage novel, and the books she wrote with his illustrations. Inside *La Maison de la Peur* she finds the photo Lee took of them on the stairs of their farmhouse. They sit side by side, their backs to the wall, and yet Max looms, appearing twice her size, his arm around her, protecting. How tiny she looks— happy, but so very small. She closes the photo in the book, puts the books on a shelf. Perhaps one day she'll tack it to the wall, but not now.

There are, however, a few items she means to hang. She pulls *Leonora in the Morning Light* from the trunk and hammers a nail into the wall. She straightens the painting and stands back to look. The jungle is mythic and wildly fertile. It is Mexico, she realizes as she hangs it. As if Max knew she'd end up here.

The morning before she left he came over when Renato was out. They had tea. She gave him the portrait she'd made of him, and the photo album of their time together, the one he'd rescued from Saint-Martin, and he gave her this. "Does it frighten you still?" he asked. "Not anymore," she told him, because it didn't. He curled into her then, pressed his ear to her heart, and she held him one last time.

She takes the framed Morpho butterfly from the trunk and holds it to the light. Under the glass, its wings are still. She hasn't seen them so much as twitch since she was on that train to Lisbon. But now that it's home there is something wrong about the butterfly staying in its frame. And besides, though she's not sure why, she wants to touch it.

She opens her hand and watches it fall. The frame seems to hover for a second before it hits. Shards of glass skate across the title floor. Flying into the air, slivers catch the sunlight before they land. At her bare feet, the Morpho lies on its front, so what shows are the brown-and-white undersides of its wings, like dead, dried leaves. *So it can rest*, the Prince said. When she bends to pick up the butterfly, her bun comes undone. She holds the edge of one wing, turns it over, and cups it in her hand. She tiptoes to the balcony around the fragments of glass.

Lightly, she pets the butterfly's slim, dark body. She traces its branching veins, the scaffolding of its wings from where they attach to its thorax and reach out to the thin, scalloped edges. The blue wings flash in the sun. Below her, the wide courtyard and the street beyond it shine, hot and bleached. The courtyard is empty, save for two cats sleeping in the shade of a dry fountain. Even for this section of town it is deserted, everyone at lunch, or siesta. She looks at the butterfly in her hand, or tries to. Her eyes have a bald spot from the glare, and when she looks at the Morpho, she sees a white hole. She puts her other hand over the butterfly, not touching it, but feeling for life within it—that invisible force that would mean it might still awaken.

Her palms grow warm. And she is thinking of that bird, the robin that hit the window the day she met Max, how it came back to life in her hand, when she feels an expansion of the air between her palms, the slightest push. She swears she can feel tiny feet grip the skin of a finger. She brings the butterfly to eye level, squints to bring it into focus. Its antennae seem to reach out, testing the air. Or is it only the breeze?

In the sun, its wings flex. They close and open.

And then a gust blows her hair into her face. She pulls the long strands back, searching the balcony for the butterfly, but it's gone. She scans the sky and thinks she sees the brown and white of the undersides of its wings as they spread against the blue. Is it falling or soaring? Taken by the wind, it is below her now, a scrap of blue cellophane floating down to the fountain.

Perhaps it's only the wind playing tricks, but she runs down the stairs and out to the courtyard to follow the Prince's butterfly to wherever it might lead her.

Down one street and another, the Morpho sails, lifting and falling, but not once touching the ground. When it crosses a street, she leaps in front of a Ford she didn't see coming. It screeches to a stop and she trails the blue fairy around a corner and onto Gabino Barreda Street.

In the garden of a duplex, overgrown with bougainvillea and morning glory, hibiscus and gardenias, the Morpho finds another of its kind, although Morphos don't seem to be common here, and the two spiral upward in a dance as high as a cloud, until they blend at last with the sky.

"*Hola*," says a woman from the balcony. Her brown hair spills down the side of her white blouse. She wipes her hands on a rag and walks to the railing.

Leonora is standing in the woman's garden, she realizes, with no shoes on her feet, staring up at the sky like a lunatic. The woman shields her eyes with her hand, squinting. "Leonora? Is that you? I heard you'd come to Mexico." Leonora walks closer. The woman is smiling the kind of smile that doesn't ask for anything in return, like the sun. Though she looks familiar, Leonora can't place her. "Come up," the woman says.

Wiggling her toes in the grass, Leonora looks to the sky once more, but the butterflies, having found each other, have vanished into the blue. She climbs the stairs. "The door doesn't work," the woman hollers from inside. "Come in through the window."

Leonora ducks her head in and climbs through. Black cats, five of them, gather on the kitchen table around bowls of food. Pots steam on the stove. Every window ledge, shelf, and counter is a shrine, each stone and shell arranged with meticulous care. She runs a fingertip over the smooth inside of an abalone shell, like the one she still has from her lunch with Max, when he proposed.

"Leonora?" The voice comes from down the hall, from a back room where she finds the woman at work, painting. Using the smallest of strokes, she leans very close to her canvas. Leonora walks around her, to glimpse her profile, and the painting stuns her. She's not sure just what she's seeing. A checkerboard floor twirls upward, forming the checkerboard dress of a woman bent over the machine on which she is sewing the dress, the floor, the fabric of the whole world she is inside. It's extraordinary. The artist looks at her, smiling again.

"Remedios?" Here, in Mexico City, living not more than a few blocks away, is Remedios Varo.

"I had to just—" She touches her brush to the canvas, adding flecks of light to the turrets of a castle in the background. "There. Let's have coffee."

Leonora met her in Paris, at the Surrealist exposition, where their work hung side by side. Remedios took her hand and led her from that dark, crowded room that squeezed the breath from her. And here she is, pouring them each a small cup of her thick, black brew. They sit at the table with the cats, who stop eating to nuzzle them. Leonora takes one onto her lap and strokes its soft fur. "How I've missed them."

"You don't have cats?" Remedios seems shocked.

"I did, years ago, but Renato, my husband, is allergic."

"Renato? Picasso's friend?"

Leonora smiles. "It's a long story."

"Well," says Remedios, "I have nothing but time."

With certain people you know the moment you meet them that you will be friends. Something opens between you, like a clearing in the woods where before there were trees. And in this bright warmth, the two of you talk or dance or cook or paint. You share a space that can only exist for the two of you. If you are very lucky this might happen once, or maybe as much as twice in your lifetime. For Leonora, it happened when she met Max. And it happens again, in Mexico City.

"Oh!" Remedios says, jumping up. The big, black pot is boiling over, and she turns down the heat and gives it a stir. "Frida and Diego are renewing their vows, again, tomorrow night. He's had another affair, it seems. And now that they've reconciled, they're recommitting. I've said I'll bring the food and the flowers. You wouldn't want to help, would you?"

"Tomorrow's the full moon?"

"It is. I was thinking the food and the flowers should be white."

"To magnify the moonlight."

⁓ჵ

They bring dishes of jicama, peeled radishes, and hard-boiled eggs, a tureen of cold potato and leek soup, with the petals of white roses on top, a platter of Mexican wedding cookies, shortbread rolled in powdered sugar, and they set them on tables in the courtyard between Diego and Frida's houses. They float gardenias in bowls of water and arrange long-stemmed lilies in slender vases. Other people are busy, too, hanging strings of electric lights housed in little paper lanterns, dressing the cupola in vines, and setting out rows of chairs.

Frida meets them in the courtyard in her white lace dress, her hair arranged in braids twisted like pretzels and adorned with a single white lily. She looks like she did in her painting, only with hair, and she's so much happier, it almost makes Leonora want to marry, someday, for love. She's tiny, and when she offers Leonora her hand, Leonora holds it in hers, hardly gripping it at all for fear she might crush her. She seems to her like a princess, and before she can stop herself, she bends to kiss her hand.

Diego and Frida recite their vows by moonlight. Leonora dabs the corners of her eyes with a handkerchief Remedios and she pass between them. Renato's at a bullfight, and she sits between Remedios and her husband, Benjamin Péret, who leans over and whispers in her ear, "The moon makes liars of us all."

However much she'd like to believe him, as she watches the tiny woman and the hulking, bulbous man hold each other's hands and look into each other's eyes and say they take each other for as long as they shall walk the Earth—this Earth whirling in a whirling universe made of the music of stars and planets and moons—she knows what she knows. And she thinks of Max, and wonders how the moonlight looks on the red rocks of Sedona, and what he's doing right now under that lit sky.

As Frida and Diego exchange rings, her mind swims with images. Her heart swells with them and will burst if she doesn't let them out. Eggs, enormous eggs, cats, women with the bodies of katydids, women with faces shaped like butterflies, their hair made of branches, a kitchen with a cauldron, a table set for the Sidhe, with a great bowl of golden soup and pomegranates, all of the white, shining people gathered around. Glowing globes of light, moons, and birds, white birds, luminescing in the night sky. A minotaur, a maze, a spiraling snake, and a giantess with the creatures of the Earth flocking around her, geese soaring from her cloak.

Later, after the dancing and the drinking, when the white foods have been eaten, when the candles have burned out and everyone is spent, she goes home, and humming to herself—"*El Barco Velero*," the sailboat song that's somehow made it here, from Spain—she closes the door to her studio and paints until the sun comes up.

And then, she paints a little longer.

Author's Note

What became of them?

In November 1942, when Hitler's troops marched into Vichy, *Louise Straus-Ernst* found refuge with the writer Jean Giano in the Alpes-de-Haute Provence, where she wrote her autobiography. In May 1944, she was taken from his home to the transit camp for Jews in Drancy. She was deported on June 30, on the penultimate train to Auschwitz, where she was murdered.

In 1940, *Marie-Berthe Aurenche* became the lover of the Russian Jewish painter Chaim Soutine, with whom she was involved until 1943, when he died of an unsuccessful operation on a stomach ulcer while hiding from the Nazis in Paris. He was buried in the Aurenche plot in Montparnasse Cemetery. In 1960, Marie-Berthe committed suicide and was buried beside him.

During the Nazi occupation of France, *Nusch Éluard* joined the French Resistance. In 1946, she collapsed in a Paris street of a massive stroke. She was forty years old.

In the wake of his wife's death, *Paul Éluard* devoted himself to the principles of peace and liberty. In 1948, he became a member of the Congress of Intellectuals for Peace, persuading Pablo Neruda to also join, and he was a delegate to the World Peace Council. On the day of his funeral, in November 1952, thousands of people gathered in the streets to accompany his casket to Père Lachaise Cemetery.

Having given up art for chess in the early twenties, *Marcel Duchamp* produced his final work in secret, between 1946 and 1966. A mixed media piece with leaves, twigs, oil paint, velvet, clothespins, electric lights, and other objects, *Étant Donnés* features a landscape with a nude woman (made of parchment) sprawled on her back. Legs spread, face hidden, she holds a lantern in the air with one hand. The piece must be viewed through a peephole in a wooden door and is part of the Philadelphia Museum of Art's permanent collection.

A day after his arrival in Los Angeles in 1940, *Man Ray* met the dancer Juliet Browner. In 1946, they married in Beverly Hills in a double wedding with Max Ernst and Dorothea Tanning. Man Ray returned to Paris in 1951, where he lived with Juliet and made art until his death in 1976.

His writings banned by the Vichy regime as subversive, *André Breton* escaped France in 1941. In 1946, he returned to Paris, where he opposed French colonialism, embraced anarchism, and fostered a new group of Surrealist artists until his death in 1966.

In 1942, *Jimmy Ernst* became the director of Peggy Guggenheim's gallery The Art of This Century, and soon after had his first solo show at Norlyst Gallery. In 1950, he became a member of the Irascible Eighteen—artists protesting the Metropolitan Museum of Art's exhibition American Painting Today and boycotting the accompanying competition, whose judges were openly biased against abstract art. In addition to Ernst, the group included de Kooning, Pollack, Motherwell, and Rothko—all of whom became part of the New York School.

In December 1942, *Lee Miller* was accredited into the U.S. Army as a war correspondent for Condé Nast. She photographed the siege of Saint-Malo, the Liberation of Paris, and the Nazi camps of Buchenwald and Dachau, just after the arrival of the Allied Forces. Her photographs are among the most important artifacts of the war. After

Hitler's suicide, she was one of the first people to arrive at his apartment in Munich, where she bathed in his bathtub and slept in his bed. Returning to Britain after the Armistice, she suffered from depression and PTSD and began to drink heavily. In 1946, discovering she was pregnant by Penrose, she divorced Bey and married him.

Leonor Fini returned to the City of Light after the liberation, where she designed costumes and sets for the theater and ballet, wrote three novels, illustrated the novel *Story of O*, and continued to paint formidable women. She visited with Leonora on many occasions and they exchanged letters, remaining close friends until Leonor's death in 1996.

After her divorce from Max Ernst in 1946, *Peggy Guggenheim* closed The Art of This Century gallery and moved to Venice, Italy. She bought and refurbished a palazzo on the Grand Canal, where she housed her collection—admitting visitors three days a week—and lived with her pack of Lhasa Apsos, who are buried beside her ashes in the garden. She left her collection and palazzo in the care of her uncle Solomon R. Guggenheim's foundation, which runs it as a public museum to this day. She was the last person in Venice to have her own private gondola.

From 1946 to 1953, *Max Ernst* lived with his fourth (and last) wife, Dorothea Tanning, amid the red rocks of Sedona in a cabin he built by hand. In the summer of 1947, celebrating the advent of running water to the house, he crafted his iconic sculpture *Capricorn* out of cement and scrap iron, and compiled his book *Beyond Painting*—which led to a greater recognition of his art as well as to financial success. In 1954, the couple moved to France, where they resided until Ernst's death twenty-two years later, a day before his eighty-fifth birthday.

Soon after their arrival in Mexico City, *Leonora Carrington* and Renato Leduc divorced. In 1946, she married the Hungarian photojournalist Emerico "Chiki" Weisz, with whom she had two sons. Her intense, artistic partnership with the painter Remedios Varo fueled her esoteric interests—experiments with cooking, the creation of talismans, and a passion for tarot—as well as the deep mythic realms she explored in her paintings. In 1973, she became one of the founding members of the Mexican Women's Liberation Movement. Before her death in Mexico City at age ninety-four, she created thousands of extraordinary works of art, and she is considered among the greatest Mexican artists of the twentieth century. After her move to Mexico, she never saw Max Ernst again.

⟿

This is not the story of the Great Man's Woman. This is the story of the Great Woman.

I was drawn to Leonora Carrington before I even knew who she was. Long intrigued by the Surrealist artists, by their playful take on creativity and their celebration of surprise and strangeness, I had set out, in 2013, to write a fictional story placed among them, set between the wars and with a young woman at its center. My heroine would be talented and beautiful, a new addition to the Surrealists' circle. She'd fall in love with an older, established artist who disappeared, leaving her alone and desperate. And then, through her grief and perseverance, she would grow strong, embodying a great inner power. She would turn the notion of the muse on its head. But at the time I had no idea who she was, or if she was even real.

That summer I traveled to Europe to research the Surrealists. As it happened, they weren't difficult to find. Here was a show of Man Ray's photos, there an exhibit centered on the group and their fascination with the occult and witchcraft, and individual works of their art were featured in so many of the major museums. But in all of the exhibitions I saw only the art of the men—as if there had never been any women among them. And then, at the Tate Modern, I found a small piece in their permanent Surrealist section. It was hung high on the wall, and I stood on my toes to see it better. The colors were delicate, the figures quickly sketched. There was something enchanting about it, a sense of one thing becoming something else. I was mesmerized. My husband stood beside me and fell in love with the piece, too. "Leonora Carrington," the placard read. We couldn't believe we hadn't heard of her. In the gift shop my husband pulled a book from the shelf. *Leonora Carrington: Surrealism, Alchemy and Art* by Susan L. Aberth. "*My* book," he said, pointedly, because he already knew I'd steal it from him.

And I did. As I looked at Carrington's art and read about her upper-class, British childhood and how she rebelled against its confines at every turn, about her love for drawing and writing, for horses and Irish myth, about her meeting forty-six-year-old Max Ernst when she was just twenty, and the war intervening in their relationship, I knew that theirs was the story that needed to be told. It was the story I'd write if I were brave enough.

For months I resisted the idea of writing it. I read everything about Leonora I could get my hands on, as well as everything available about Max and Peggy Guggenheim, who was, I realized, an integral part of their story. Still, it didn't feel like enough. I read Max's and Lou's and Jimmy Ernst's autobiographies; Dorothea Tanning's book *Birthday*, which recounts stories Max told her; Peggy Guggenheim's autobiography; and Leonora Carrington's memoir *Down Below*, which describes her time before and in Santander. And then I started hearing sentences—bits of dialogue, scenes—so I jotted them down. My formal training is in poetry, and that is how I came at the writing of this historical novel (my first): through the lens of a poet. I stirred the pot, writing down what came to the surface, and over the course of years the story revealed itself little by little. Based on documented events and real people, its content followed the facts of what had occurred—so far as I could sift them out of the various, differing versions I read—but the characters' conversations and what they might have thought or felt in any given moment were entirely imagined. Leonora was at the center of the novel, but it was Peggy who surprised me with her vulnerability, her humor, and her chutzpah. I fell in love with her independence and her courage. Harder to penetrate, Max riddled and dodged. He quickly changed the subject and did his best to avoid being glimpsed in bright light. But I felt his deep passion for his art. In Lion Feuchtwanger's detailed, firsthand account of Camp des Milles and the Ghost Train, I found the ways Max must have suffered in captivity. And I came to believe Leonora Carrington was the first—perhaps the *only*—woman to break his heart.

As the pages here came together, as I began to truly discover and experience the breadth and depth of Leonora's genius, the voice of doubt inside me grew stronger: How could *I* dare to write about this brilliant woman? But in the end, my desire to know her—to understand her trials and the inner strength that propelled her through them—overpowered my fear of not doing her justice.

Leonora Carrington was one who underwent the individuation process, in the Jungian sense, integrating her conscious and unconscious selves, her masculine and feminine sides, to become her fullest self. During her ninety-four years on this Earth, she created thousands of magical, mystical works of art—drawings, paintings, statues, masks, plays, short stories, and her masterful novel, *The Hearing Trumpet*. She was also an eco-feminist who fervently believed in the innate rights of all individuals—of humans, animals, plants, and the Earth itself. As she wrote in a commentary for her 1976 retrospective in New York City, "A woman should not have to demand Rights. The Rights were there from the beginning; they must be taken back again." And, in closing, "Footprints are face to face with the firmament."

I am deeply grateful for the time I have spent with Leonora, in whose presence I've felt daring, inspired, and expansive. My greatest hope is for this novel to bring more attention to her tremendous and far too little known body of work. Utterly idiosyncratic, immersed in myth and esoteric traditions, her work is an alchemical act of sorcery, of bringing invisible worlds to light. To open yourself to her art is to become an initiate of the mysteries to which she is privy. Truly, there's a touch of the Sidhe in all things Carrington.

Further Reading

For the years it took me to write this book, I lived in the world of these artists. These are the books that made their world come to life.

A Not-So-Still Life by Jimmy Ernst
Art Lover, A Biography of Peggy Guggenheim by Anton Gill
Birthday by Dorothea Tanning
Down Below by Leonora Carrington
Farewell to the Muse by Whitney Chadwick
Ghost Ships Robert McNab
Lee Miller: A Life by Carolyn Burke
Leonora Carrington: Surrealism, Alchemy and Art by Susan L. Aberth
Max Ernst by Werner Spies
Max Ernst: A Retrospective ed. by Werner Spies and Sabine Rewald
Max Ernst: Life and Work by John Russell
Max Ernst: Life and Work by Werner Spies
Out of This Century by Peggy Guggenheim
Sphinx: The Life and Art of Leonor Fini by Peter Webb
The Complete Stories of Leonora Carrington by Leonora Carrington
The Devil in France by Lion Feuchtwanger
The First Wife's Tale by Louise Straus-Ernst
The Hearing Trumpet by Leonora Carrington
The Surreal Life of Leonora Carrington by Joanna Moorhead
Une Semaine de Bonté: A Surrealistic Novel in Collage by Max Ernst
Villa Air-Bel by Rosemary Sullivan

Acknowledgments

Writing a novel is a curious business, requiring one to squirrel oneself away and become something of a hermit for as long as the process takes. To those who continued to love me through the seven years it took me to write this novel—my husband and children and parents and friends—I love you more than I can possibly say, and I am grateful for your unflagging support and encouragement.

Thank you to the readers of various drafts—Melissa Berton; Laraine Herring; Melissa Tapper; my parents, Georgia and Vince Carter; and my husband and best friend, Ty Fitzmorris, who read every single draft and had such incisive suggestions.

Much thanks to the whole Avid Reader team, especially Lauren Wein, Morgan Hoit, Meredith Vilarello, Jordan Rodman, Samantha Hoback, Alison Forner, Grace Han, and my inimitable editor, Julianna Haubner, whose brilliance and love for the work made the publishing process a joy.

Thank you to Three Arts, and my fabulous agent Richard Abate, for standing by me for so many years, and to the wonderful booksellers at the Peregrine Book Company and at the other independent book stores, for your contagious love of books and your dedication to the cause.

And special thanks to my grandmother Nadine Coffin, who reached out from the other side and told me to sit my butt in the chair and write, but to lift my feet off the floor—to work hard and dream big.

This novel stands on the shoulders of giantesses, without whose fascination with, research into, and love for Leonora Carrington, this book would not exist. Thank you to Whitney Chadwick, for her research on Leonor and Leonora's letters, and to Tere Arcq, for her insightful tour of Leonora's 2018 show in Mexico City, which she so masterfully curated. My deepest gratitude to Wendi Norris for her support and insight, and to Susan Aberth, whose book on Leonora and her art sparked the fire that led to this novel.

Additional thanks to everyone else working to elevate Leonora's remarkable legacy—particularly Gabriel Weisz Carrington, Pablo Weisz-Carrington, Patricia Argomedo, Daniel Weisz, and Joanna Moorhead.

And lastly, I am profoundly grateful to all of the female surrealist artists for forging the way with unfailing luster, gumption, and nerve, and especially to Leonora, for her shining example.

About the Author

Michaela Carter is a writer, painter, and award-winning poet. Her novel *Further Out Than You Thought* was an Indie Next List pick, and was the *Arizona Republic* Critics' Pick for Best Debut Author in 2014. Her poetry won the Poetry Society of America Los Angeles New Poets Contest, has been nominated for Pushcart Prizes, and has appeared in numerous anthologies and journals. She is the cofounder of the independent bookstore the Peregrine Book Company in Prescott, Arizona, where she lives with her husband and two dogs.